I0746171

ONLINE NOW

COPPER SHY

Zeta Publishing, Inc
P.O. Box 953
Silver Springs, FL 34489
www.zetapublishing.com

This is a work of fiction. All of the characters, names, incidents, organizations, and dialogue in this novel are either the products of the author's imagination or are used fictitiously.

The views expressed in this work are solely those of the author and do not necessarily reflect the views of the publisher, and the publisher hereby disclaims any responsibility for them.

Ordering Information:
Quantity sales. Special discounts are available on quantity purchases by corporations, associations, and others. For details, contact the publisher at the address above.
Orders by U.S. trade bookstores and wholesalers. Please contact Zeta Publishing: Tel: (352) 694-2553; Fax: (352) 694-1791 or visit www.zetapublishing.com

Edited by Laura Goodner

Rev. Date: 1/24/2019

ISBN: 978-1-950340-00-2 (sc)
ISBN: 978-1-950340-01-9 (e)

Library of Congress: 2019931898
Printed in the United States of America

"The scariest moments in life are when you don't even see what's in front of you."

—Copper Shy

Chapter
ONE

She sits patiently in the living room of her house watching her husband check and reply to business messages from his smart phone.

The maid is there dusting a ceiling fan from a stepladder. Her husband peeks up occasionally observing the swinging of a pulled back, long hair brunette, from a young Latina in her middle twenties. Currently she's working faster than him eliminating each fan blade of dust piled on from last week. While looking at the maid, he is nodding and counting the days he needs to schedule for client showings this week. He sinks his head back into his phone to text something, then lifts it again.

She continues to watch this cat and mouse charade, with hopes their lovely housekeeper doesn't fall off the ladder and hit them with a lawsuit. Suddenly she receives a texting notification. Lowering her head into the phone, she opens the message that reads,

I can't wait to see you in my bed, Monday night.
I want to feel your warm, soft, sexy legs wrapped around me.
-Sent from Kyle -Contact

Taking a huge breath of air, she pulls the phone near her heart, then looks up with a smile. It's almost time to be on the way to her writer's conference in Henderson. She walks over to her husband, where he sits adjacent on the other sofa.

Angela shows off her lingering twenties, runway model figure, as her long blonde hair reaches for her hips, swaying side to side. Her long lashes and gazing green eyes, hooks her husband's attention. He looks up with a smirky smile, snickering out an elongating, "What?"

"There are so many people who are killed by distracted drivers. Do you think my book, can help protect the lives of others, while they're on the way to their destination?" She says.

"Darling, everything you do is a hit by me. It's carved in stone already. You are my beautiful wife, my flickering star… my lustrous sun."

Angela gives him an amorous rub on the shoulders. She admires his poetic words. He pulls her in closer, wrapping his five-foot ten body frame around her.

Briefly, she rests her temple on his chest then pulls away.

"Don't be nervous Angel. Everything you do is amazing, like taking care of the boys. Who makes sure they get to school and game practices on time… Huh? You're their coach and right now I'm cheering you on. Just take care of your endeavor, while I will sell some houses…Okay super woman? The book will fly high."

She looks up to kiss her husband. He meets her. Her level of confidence is just where it needs to be. Pulling away again, she excuses herself to check on her boys one last time, before heading to Henderson.

Tapping her red soled pumps across the Italian travertine in the kitchen, she runs a single hand over their ruby and black marble counter top like a charm.

Collecting no dust, she enters a barrel frame ceiling hallway receiving another text.

When are you leaving?
From Kyle -Text received

She stops at the staircase and types back:

Soon as I find my boys and hug them bye.
From Angela -Text sent

Walking upstairs, Angela hears the pandemonium of Call of Duty. Resonating loud shots and grenades are fired on screen in the theatre. She approaches the double doors, one of them cracked open, and finds both boys intensely playing their game. If she would have been a sniper; they would be dead.

Benjamin, the elder of the two, leads the game. He speaks into the headset to his long-distance friend in the game, who speaks back in a proper British accent.

An unconditional love connection begins to form on this game between two boys who always seems to show up together. On the screen, their men run through warzones blowing heads off enemy soldiers.

Camden, who is seven, bounces in his seat, trying to keep alive in the game with his brother. Neither one notices their mother's presence right beside them. Angela considers this.

"Boys!" She hollers.

Their eyes and ears are devoted to machine gun toting soldiers.

Angela walks and stands directly in front of the ten-foot-wide Draper screen, with her arms stretched out almost as wide, believing that would get their attention.

"Don't shoot… don't kill me boys. Come give me a hug, so I can take off to my conference."

Not pausing the game, they quickly jump out of the front row almost tackling their mother. Angela keeps her balance and holds onto them.

"I love you so much boys." She radiates.

Camden lets go with a fretful exhalation and beats his brother back to the game.

Benjamin hugs a bit longer and kindly replies, "I love you too mom."

Camden needs an extra fifteen seconds to look at the controller, and place his fingers in position of his soldier, before his brother gets back. Benjamin jumps into the game. His game guy has been a sitting duck, fearless and unprotected; twenty-five and half seconds.

Angela directs her steps back into the kitchen, to collect her notes, for the next day's presentation and finds her husband at the coffee bar, pouring his afternoon cup. She walks over to him, one last time, before grabbing her leather-bound edition of *Online Now* and a blue folder full of notes to leave with.

He prepares coffee just the way he likes, as she reaches around him very affectionately and says, "Bye love. I'll see you later."

Embracing the hug, he doesn't want to let go. He follows her over to the doorway with a steaming mug of coffee in one hand, and his cell phone in the other. It's from that door, he releases her natural beauty as she gets ready to depart.

The California sun beams down on Angela's shoulders, April 8, 2016 as she walks on the pebble stone path to her vehicle. Grace of a clear blue sky, on a fresh springy day, she gauges the sturdy palm trees as she handles her purse and notebook. The wind is calming, carrying butterflies from bush to bush. A landscape of shrubs lay still, as she walks past them. Gentle breezes blow across her face and shoulders on the step-up, into her Fuji White Range Rover.

His eyes follow her every move from their grand foyer. He continues to sip coffee. Angela elevates herself in elegance as she steps into her baby. She starts the ignition while simultaneously fluffing the hair from her collar blouse.

After Seven years of marriage, he could see no other woman in his eyes. He plays out in his head both of his sons being born. The tears of labor she cried while pushing Benjamin and Camden into this world. She vanishes beyond the distance. He's left staring at his reflection in the glass door.

A sense of aloneness starts to slither into his soul abnormally, even though she had gone on many writers' conferences before. *Was this the last time I would ever see her again?*

More thoughts start to arise.

Did I tell her I loved her enough? Did I make her smile? Did I do everything in my power to bring her happiness? Was I everything she ever needed? Wait... why am I feeling this way?

He tries to dissipate an unsettled feeling as he walks through the house, taking more breaths then he can release. Uncoordinatedly he sits down his coffee mug on the kitchen counter. Concerned, he texts her to remind her of his love claim.

Both hands are free, as he slides his index finger to the right of the screen, trying to make a connection with Angela. Thoughts about his real estate agency and meeting tomorrow instantly start to seep from the outer surface view of his mind.

He scrolls down a phone list of contacts quickly, to find her name before anything could come in between his love for Angela. He touches her name under contact messages. She is the last person he received a text from. Quickly he begins to type:

Angel, I know you just left the house,
And that's okay.

I don't know what has gotten into me.
Just had the strangest feeling
Something is just not right.
I love you Angela.
-Text sent

He paces back to the living room, standing a little over five feet, Ten inches tall, about one hundred and eighty pounds, dark hair, dark eyes. He begins to type another text to his wife.

My guess is... I just want to hear you say it again.
I Love...

Suddenly, a text goes off and interrupts his message to her. His intuition causes him to check the message.

About to aboard flight now.
See you in 8 hours or so. Terminal B.
-Received from Jeff.

Jolted with energy from his second dose of caffeine, he scrambles his way to the home office, and takes a glance at the list of properties his client Jeff is interested in. Eight properties with exquisite details have neatly been organized inside a folder, the night before. He pulls out the properties to review.

Selling points have been laid out for consideration. Ocean views with breezy terraces in the sun, entertaining escapes, and elegant pools. Each built at different times with a new owner's concept. Showing times on these private beach fronts, began tomorrow at noon. He sends Jeff a text back.

"I will be at LAX at 9 P.M. tonight." –Text sent.

The housekeeper Gabriella has built up a sweat and knocks on the office door in need of payment. He reaches into his pant pocket, and pulls out a white envelope full of cash for her. She kindly collects it from him and tucks it away, in her purse, then leaves swigging a Coke, from the bottle.

After the housekeeper has left the house, he takes a break. In the bathroom he freshens up a little before going to check on his boys. He pumps a couple beads of lemongrass scented soap into his hand and washes the worry off his face.

Inspiring love from sending out that message to his wife, he musters up a great day out with kids.

Sprinting up the stairs to get to the theatre, where he assumes Benjamin and Camden are, he begins to feel his stomach growling. He looks at his wristwatch finding it be lunchtime, and almost trips on the thought of eating cords of lasagna.

After almost falling on the last stair step, he thinks, *a nice deli sandwich sounds fantastic.*

He hears game sounds of machine guns and other artillery, coming from the double doors outside the theatre room. He opens the door and goes inside. "Benji… Cam!" He calls out.

"Make this your last move, and let's go grab lunch. Let's get out for a while… just us boys while your mother is away."

Benjamin and Camden purposefully lose their soldiers life and jump out of an unlit theatre room seat.

Excited to spend the day with their father, the boys run out the front door in competition. Who's riding shotgun?

A proud father, happy to spend the day with his boy's locks up any doubt and trails his kids out the door for some fun.

Benjamin takes the front seat with his dad, giving Camden the whole backseat. The engine to a brand-new black Mercedes convertible is started.

An old DMX – Party Up track is playing loud and fades out any other sounds.

Camden's shaggy brown hair is blowing in the wind as he tries to mirror his older brother. Benjamin has his hat on backwards, wearing dark frame shades trying to be chill to the sun. It's in these moments, Benjamin is cooler than any raccoon hijacking a refrigerator down Beachfront Avenue. Kyle pulls out of the circular driveway and off they go.

Traffic on the way to Santa Monica Pier is heavy. An automobile transporter trailer carrying all sorts of wrecked cars crosses paths with Kyle and his boys at one major intersection. This leaves an unknown indention in Kyle's mind.

Thirty minutes fly by. The boys and Kyle are nearly done cracking and peeling shrimp tails inside of well-known seafood restaurant.

"Dad can I have a refill?" A considerate Camden asks.

"Sure son, but for the rest of the day, its water."

A shorter minute swings around, waiting on little miss thang to stop by their table. They continue to fill up on ocean tails.

She comes back pushing her breasts forth as she asks them if they need anything more.

"Go ahead son, ask the lady politely what you'd like."

"May I have a Coke?" Camden smiles.

"Certainly." The waitress responds, then sinks her eyes into Kyle.

"And I will take my round two, please and thank you." Kyle mimicked.

The waitress runs off.

Kyle looks to Benjamin.

"So, any new girls at school, you are crushing on?" Kyle asks.

"Maybe a little bit." Benjamin smiles

He brushes Benji's dark brown, wavy hair and gives him the all for one, one for all bursting smile.

"That's it boy, keep after it. The erudition from this. Learning what scents, you like… Learning what smiles to go for. You'll see, she will be very similar in the future. And ladies… they want a confident man. Even if you grow a beard and put on fifty pounds… well you know. Tell a girl she's beautiful and she's yours forever."

The waitress stops back by the table. With a seducing batty eyelashes vibe, she sits the drinks down, spellbinding Kyle's attention.

"Would you like me to bring you a dessert menu? I offer a wide variety of sweets."

Awkwardness rattles the unused silverware on the table. Kyle requests the check, right then and there.

They leave the restaurant completely fueled up, and ready to take a fine walk on the ocean shore line. The ocean is a container for many emotions, good or bad. Most of them you can try to find just on the other side of the horizon.

"Pardon me boys, as we walk. I'll be a few steps behind making a phone call."

Benjamin and Camden take off their shoes, rolling up their pant legs, running and splashing cold water, ahead of their father's sight.

"Hello Gaby. Hey, it's Kyle. Hey, I forgot to mention earlier, I need you to come back around 7 P.M. tonight for a couple of hours. I must pick up a client from the airport. Can I count on you to watch the boys? It's twenty-five an hour."

"Thanks doll, see you tonight."

Meanwhile, 4:28 P.M. somewhere else. Angela has been driving on I-15, three and a half hours. Mostly desert and a few cities in-between until Henderson, a suburb, twenty minutes outside of Las Vegas.

Angela alters driving the posted speed, sometimes a little faster, while singing a song from satellite.

Just fourteen years ago, Angela had envisioned herself, singing and dancing in Broadway Musicals. Poise was a muted substitute for her dreams. In high heels she paraded on runways for well-travelled fashion designers. As a walking mannequin, she strutted her long legs amongst hundreds, in fashion wear matching the beat of lyrics that danced around in her head.

She never really had the chance to take singing lessons, therefore she never built up confidence within her God given talent, as she could really sing.

It was unaccompanied time in her Range Rover that gave her a place to conjure up material to write. Driving over twenty-eight hundred miles to her parents' house back in Brooklyn, had given her time to dream up, then emerge words by the thousands, and vend in a bookstore.

Angela had just crossed over the California – Nevada State line, ten miles ago. She is behind an eighteen-wheeler with a full rack of cars in transportation.

Angela belts out lyrics –No, from Meghan Trainor. She is nearly thirty minutes from Henderson. She grabs her phone checking to see if she had missed any new notifications. There are a couple. She puts her phone down.

Angela glances into her rearview mirror. She realizes another eighteen-wheeler is malevolently approaching into her territory. Fearful, she shifts a quick emphasis back to the road, and the transporter trailer in front is losing one of its cars from top of the ramp.

She screams out, *Oh My*...

Firmly, she swerves left, to avoid the lost car, launching at her from the ramp. Colliding with the right side of Angela's Range Rover, it causes her to spin on the highway. There is no red or black on this roulette wheel.

The clock reads 4:44 P.M. from the truck that sideswipes her Range Rover. A smutty, fat bellied, truck driver, takes a gasping breathe of air, and begins to pray out loud. He throws down the cell phone in his hand. It lands in the far-right side of the passenger seat. He pulls the door handle of the truck open and jumps out.

Terrified of what he would see next, he runs to help Angela, screaming from the demolished SUV.

Suddenly a detonation like an atomic bomb ricochets between two eighteen wheelers. The mighty force of flames on earth, ascends two lives beyond time.

A ball of smoke fills the sky. Traffic begins to build up on I-15, both eastbound and westbound. Emergency responders get as close as they can, without drawing attention to the remaining trucks exploding. A small jet flies over the blazing fire and drops a blanket of halon to prompt extinguishing.

The heat of impact starts to simmer down. State police start directing traffic to go, down a narrowed single lane. The rescuing squad search for bodies of both, rear truck and SUV passengers. Zilch to be found.

One policeman turns and looks to the unembellished shoulder of the interstate. He notices a blue object flapping in the wind. He walks over to it and picks it up. It appears to be a notebook with the name of a book title written on the cover. Inside, are pages in reference to distracted motorists who have been killed in car collisions these last two years. Also, inside is a relative date and name of the author who wrote in this blue notebook, Online Now.

CHAPTER
TWO

His hands are clasped and white-knuckled around the steering wheel. He's thumbing emails while million-dollar mansions run through his mind at a standstill on I-405. Traffic's seriously at a dead stop. Any other day he would be flying to LAX, in his black Mercedes Convertible, but today the sun settles down on him, Friday 7:20 P.M.

There's an automobile transporter trailer parked right next to him with a broad band selection of Range Rovers, all with plastic tarps still on them.

Kyle turns on the radio and immediately discovers why the freeway is congested. Presidential campaigning was going on nearby and from the aftermath of it was cars everywhere.

His client Jeff Gandy is set to arrive on the 9 O'clock flight, from LaGuardia. Jeff is in the film industry. Angela introduced Kyle and Jeff when she flew to Manhattan last year, for the eastern writing conference. Jeff had several writing projects in contract, lasting him over five years in business. They all took place in Los Angeles.

Arriving to the airport thirty minutes early, Kyle reaches into the hidden compartment of the Mercedes and grabs a cigarette out of the pack.

He finds an inconspicuous place to park and gets out to smoke. His family doesn't allow him to be a smoker at home.

Rarely, Kyle gets nervous; he likes to smoke to feel a certain tough guy confidence, when meeting successful people living his lifelong dream of acting.

When reading scripts, Kyle didn't sound believable. He could adlib and sell anything he wanted though. Real Estate was just as much an art as acting. Living in L.A. he has gotten to know many major icons and he's even done business with most of them.

Kyle's phone rings. He looks at the screen hoping to hear about the safe arrival from his wife, but sure enough it's Gandy. He answers. "Hawthorne speaking."

"I'm at terminal six… uncertain of the gate yet. I'm making my way off the plane and into the airport. It appears there is a bit of construction going on at

American Airline."

"It's a popular terminal. I will delay driving until you're outside."

"Give me a few… I will call you right back when I'm approaching the exit."

Kyle gets into his Mercedes and reaches back into the compartment for hand sanitizer, riding any smoky smells from his hands. Jeff rings back ten minutes later.

"I'm outside now."

"American Airlines, right?"

"That's the one."

"Driving up now."

Kyle finds Jeff waiting. He pulls up to park, gets out and walks around the car to shake Jeff's hand.

"It's a pleasure to finally meet you." Kyle declares.

"Likewise."

Kyle opens the door to his car, inviting Jeff inside, then walks around and gets in as well. He drives away.

"What time are we driving out to Marisol tomorrow?"

"It's about an hour drive from here. I will pick you up around 10:30 A.M. We will catch lunch, then head out."

"I thought I was going to be a little late getting here. Traffic was backed up on the freeway. Good ol' Trump and Hillary… one of them will probably take Commander in Chief in 2017. Poor Sanders speaks the best for this country but doesn't have much of a chance. What do you think about the politics nowadays?" Kyle directs his focus at Jeff and asks.

"It's a damn clown show. Either way you look at. I can't bear to look at that floppy orange hair, ugly face mask from Trump… you know he is a ruthless actor and the other… well… she would change the whole outlook of what the meaning of chief is. Not sure American's are ready for a woman President." Jeff growled and roared out sitting alongside Kyle, in his tiny car.

"So, Jeff, where does the name Gandy originate from?" Kyle defused the situation.

"It's English… but originates from France in the eleventh century. It comes from the word gante, a derivation of gant, or glove. We were glove makers during the unbearable winter climates known to the longitude."

"Interesting" Kyle noted.

"And what hotel will you be staying at?"

"I'm at the Hollywood Roosevelt."

"They have a nice kitchen restaurant inside that hotel. We can grab lunch there tomorrow. How's that sound?"

Suddenly a tire from his Mercedes blew from the rim. Kyle was driving on the 405 back to Hollywood at speeds of nearly eighty miles per hour. He swerves a hard left, then right, missing every car next to him. He taps the breaks to get the car under control, then pulls the car to a demanding right and onto the shoulder.

"Crap crumbles! I didn't expect this." Kyle blurts out.

The light browned hair, brawny guy sitting next to him is still shaken up and holding onto his seatbelt.

"What happened?"

"We had a flippin blow up? I mean a blow out? Are you okay?"

"Well yeah!"

Kyle reaches into his jacket pocket and pulls out his cell phone. He uses voice command to search for AAA. He finds it quick.

During the call, Kyle peeks on the dashboard for the time. Its 9:27 P.M. The expected arrival on roadside assistance is twenty minutes.

Kyle starts up conversation. "What's it like for you back home?"

"At nearly forty-seven and no kids, it's great. My wife and I don't have to cook and clean all the time, goin to all kinds of kiddie functions on the regular. We go out for wine and food. That's what we do… little bit of bang. Occasionally, we get together with some of the cast and crew, in a penthouse suite of theirs, and bang… have wine and food…total man stuff…we can't seem to get enough."

Jeff takes a glance over at Kyle, then belts out a deep chuckle. He continues, "No. My wife and I are basic. We keep to our self... ambitious writing and directing though. Yeah, she Co-Writes... tries to help me direct... so that's what she thinks she's doing, but yeah, we gotta real good life back home. What about you and your family? What are winters like here? Haven't been here much during November or December time. What should I expect?"

"Real nice man, real nice. You know, in the fall time it's cool breezes and sun. We get some rain, you know, but daytimes are nice. Angela and I like to take the boys to the pier and spend time there. It's always these California nights that come to kill. You know, the arctic blast comes every night no matter what season it is. Summers are fun for that. It can be nearly ninety out during the daytime and if you fall asleep on the beach and wake up at night... well you know, you'd wake up chilly, you know."

Kyle takes in a fresh breath of air and gets a thought of Angela. He is really starting to miss her now. Containing his emotions, he doesn't want to involve Mr. Gandy. He tries to ask another question.

9:44 P.M. The loud muffler of a truck comes flying in on the shoulder behind them and parks. Headlights blind the guys, from the car they're stuck in.

An older man in a denim AAA logo shirt and red ball cap comes up tapping on the driver window. Kyle rolls it down.

"I'm Curtis. From AAA.... You fellas alright? You need some help getting the tire back on I hear?"

"Ye... yes I do." Kyle stammered in fear.

"Do you have a spare tire somewhere?" Curtis asked.

"That's a good question, you know. I've never had a blow-out, so I don't know."

"It must be in the back somewhere. Can you pop the trunk so we can look for it?" said Curtis.

Walking to the back in his business suit, Kyle opens the trunk and lifts a mat. Luckily, there's a spare.

"I'm gonna have to ask your friend to step out of the vehicle while I fix this flat- you know."

Jeff hearing the conversation through the glass, opens the car door and gets out.

The man from AAA, puts the spare tire on and sets them free.

Kyle start the ignition, turns on the radio and continues driving. He makes it through crowded streets of Hollywood, on a Friday night, with no more pitfalls.

Pulling up to the main entrance of the hotel, he lets Jeff out. Both men are exhausted. He watches Jeff teeter inside to check-in, then takes off to go home.

Kyle turns onto his street, and pulls into to the well-lit, newly restored 1920's English Manor Estate, on the six hundred block of June. Perched on one of the best streets in Hancock Park, settling on a lush half acre lot that is surrounded by mature landscaping, complete with a pool and spa, pool house and the most important feature to Kyle and Angela, the tennis court.

Tennis is a hobby the couple perpetually played most nights for an hour, building up a good sweat. They would rinse off in their elegant lap pool and sometimes, soak in the hot tub drinking bubbles to stir in romance.

Kyle glances into windows, where lights are on. He notices Gabriella entering the kitchen. He sees Angela trailing behind her.

Walking through the back of the house, he gradually opens the door, shutting it just as slow, behind him. Tip toeing through a dark room, Kyle is startled by Chips Ahoy, their toy Maltese, running over, ringing its metal dog tag, full of kisses and tail wagging.

Kyle bends down with his briefcase in hand, begins to pat Chips Ahoy.

The lights come on.

"Chips! You gave me away silly boy."

"I thought you said a couple of hours not four. Dónde estabas querida Kyle? I was getting worried hombre."

"I know it… I should have texted you. We had a blowout driving to my client's hotel. I can't get my hands dirty with a film director on board. I had to wait for AAA to get there. Forgive me? It's still twenty-five dollars an hour for you though." They walk into the kitchen. Kyle sits his briefcase down, reaches for his wallet, and grabs a crisp hundred-dollar bill. He hands it to Gabriella.

"Thanks, Gaby, for watching my boys. Was everything okay here?"

"Everything was perfect. I hope you don't mind me using the popcorn machine upstairs. You were out of the microwave popcorn kind and the boys and I wanted popcorn while watching our movie."

"It's never a problem Gaby. You are part of this family. We expect you to make yourself at home when you are here. Hey Gaby, is Angela home? When I was getting out of the car, I could have sworn I saw her right behind you."

"No… I thought you said she was out of town until Monday."

"She is. Nevermind, it's late. I must be seeing things.

The air in the room changes. Gaby looks a bit nervous putting on her sweater and collecting her purse to go home.

"Kyle can you walk me out to my car. It's dark outside."

"I'd be happy to." Kyle takes the lead, protecting her every step out to her car, then opens the door for her. She gets in, smiles through the glass and drives off.

The next morning Kyle feels Angela kiss him on the nose, as he opens his eyes from bed. He reaches for his phone on the nightstand. There is still no call or text from her anywhere. He dials her number. A steady ring is all he gets.

Kyle takes in the morning sun, stretching towards the ceiling for hope, then gets out of bed and grabs his pajama bottoms to wear.

I'll call her again after my shower, He tells himself.

After his shower, he dries off a little, puts on a robe and walks down to the kitchen. He presses the button to make a cup of coffee.

Tasting the dark, earthy, robust of Arabica beans, he carries his cup keeping it close to his mouth. From the other hand, he cradles his laptop and phone as he walks outside to his fine-looking backyard, from which he will fully wake up in.

Kyle opens his laptop and checks emails of the current number of properties he has listed. Right away he concludes six out of the fourteen properties have hits on them. He pens the names and phone numbers to each.

"Good morning Mr. Anderson. This is Kyle with Hawthorne Realty. Is it a good time for you to speak about the condo you inquired about in Santa Monica?" Kyle listens instructively.

"Perfect. It's a two bedroom, two baths, 1250 square feet. Charming condo in a beautiful location. May I ask, how soon are you wanting to take a look at the property?"

Something coils up in Anderson. He lashes out, insecurely, not knowing who Kyle Hawthorne is.

"Mr. Anderson, I assure you the information you provide me is confidential. If we are under fiduciary agreement of some sort, it is so, however this property has an offer on it currently. Is your real estate agent available to negotiate an offer the seller will not refuse?"

Kyle attends Anderson's conversation again, and hears, "… no agent."

"I see, you are without an agent. I would like to meet you at a coffee house. Does that sound okay?"

Kyle awaits Mr. Anderson's response.

"Great! Let's meet tomorrow 9 A.M. at the coffee shop right around the corner from the property. That away we are able to tour the property after meeting." Pausing, Kyle waits for an answer.

Kyle knew the answer would be a yes right away. When people are serious, there will be a push and pull for the demand. Learning not to waste time was a trait he inherited from his father.

Kyle contacts four more people interested in his property listings before Benjamin comes outside with a glass of orange juice.

Benjamin heads over and sits down next to his dad. He's dressed in long green, grey and black plaid bottoms with a black cotton tee-shirt. His wavy, dark brown hair is all over the place. His eyes are still swollen with sand. He looks like a puffed-up duck with the sun shining in his eyes and a broad smile.

"Did you get enough rest son?"

"Yep, I did. Dad, I missed mom at my game last night. I like when she takes me to my football games and I can see her jumping up, when I line drive a winning touchdown."

"And what, you don't miss me at your games?" Kyle coughs in jealousy. "I do, but you are always busy selling houses. I've just accepted when you show up, I'm the luckiest guy out there and we'd automatically win the game."

"I miss her too." Kyle concurs. "Let me wrap up work and go inside. If you'll go wake up your brother, I'll make some breakfast and we can call her on FaceTime."

The laptop clock reads 8:44 A.M. as Kyle shuts it down. He carries it alongside of him with his empty coffee mug, going inside the house.

Benjamin moseys up the stairs and wakes up Camden, then goes to his room, grabbing some clothes and taking a shower.

Camden crawls out of bed after hearing the glass door shut to the shower. The water is running right next to his doorway. He goes downstairs quietly and pulls out a swivel barstool. The back of the stool is larger than him.

Kyle realizes his son is in the room with him as he is putting slices of bread in the oven to toast.

"Good morning my little Cam-eke-dek. Did you sleep well? Want some juice?"

Benjamin comes down in a bubbly cheerful persona, fully dressed, hair combed over to the side with flip flops on.

Kyle pours Camden a glass of orange juice. "You look charming son." He pipes, then dials Angela on FaceTime for Benjamin.

Benjamin takes the phone from his dad and goes over to the island where his brother is. He pulls out a stool, awaiting his mother to answer.

Kyle stands over the stove frying up crispy bacon.

On the cellphone, Benjamin FaceTime's Angela. It rings and rings, then cuts off. Disappointed, he sets the phone on the counter, face up, hoping his mom will call back.

"Dad, do you think mom is still sleeping?"

"I don't know son. I'm anxious myself. She never called yesterday to let me know that she made it there."

"Well maybe she forgot her cell phone charger or something and her phone died." Benjamin speculates.

"You know, that's a possibility I didn't think about yet. I will wait until tonight for her to call. By then, surely we will hear from her."

After a nice breakfast, the boys excuse themselves to go upstairs and play a video game. Kyle stops Benjamin at the stairs, before he goes up.

"Benji, come back for a second?"

"Yes, dad?"

"Son, you're fourteen now. The right age to stay home and look after your brother a few hours, daytime only of course, without the help of Gaby or anyone else. What do you think?"

"You know I can do this dad." He confidently replies.

"Let's try it out, today. I must leave here in about thirty minutes to meet a client. The client and I will be hunting in Malibu and the surrounding areas. I should be home around 4P.M. but I will be calling to check on you and Camden randomly."

Benjamin nods in agreeance just as his father mandates him responsible. Kyle encounters his son for a hug, then releases him to the media room.

It's calm on Highland Avenue. Hardly any traffic pushing on a Saturday morning. Bright as can be outside, Kyle crosses over Sunset, then takes a left onto Hollywood Boulevard. The Roosevelt is on the left.

Kyle calls Jeff from his car, lets him know he's there, then goes inside the Roosevelt and walks to the Public Kitchen and Bar Restaurant.

Inside, Kyle lets the host know, it's dining for two. She places him at a table, for first comings, primarily near the bar.

Kyle spots his client entering in. He goes to the host stand and the same girl directs the client to the table.

"Good morning Mr. Gandy."

"Morning… Man I tell ya, the air sure does feel fragrantly pacifico 'round here. I'm starting to feel like this is home already. Molly will mollify California up, when I bring her back. Totally joking."

Kyle laughs. The waiter stops by and takes their order.

During their meal, Jeff noticed Kyle seemed a little distant. As he spoke to Kyle it was like he was a million miles away.

"Everything okay?" Jeff questions.

Looking a bit more peculiar, Kyle checks his phone notifications. There are no new messages, nothing from her other than the time 10:44 A.M. Heavy worrisome comes over Kyle like a freight train, squealing over rainy tracks.

"You know Jeff, I don't mean to burden you here, but Angela drove to Nevada, yesterday morning for a writer's conference, and I thought surely she would have called me by now, but she hasn't. And every time I try to call her it just rings. Do I sound overly concerned?"

"You kind of sound panicky, yeah. When is she supposed to come back home?"

"Monday." Kyle affirms.

"What else can you do but wait?" Jeff states.

Shortly after, Kyle takes care of the check from lunch. They leave the restaurant, and head off to look at the beach fronts.

Declining through the hills of Malibu with the top pulled back on the Mercedes, Jeff reaches to the sky, while listening to music.

"Hold your hands up high, like a palm tree. This is heaven."

Breathtaking views of the Pacific Ocean blends in with the sky, as they drive, twisting and curving, down the hill of the coastline.

They look at three properties prior to finding "the one". Kyle knew that Jeff had found his home for the next several years or longer, by the way his eyes lit up.

Jeff explored every part of the condo in exhilaration, he could barely contain his excitement inside. Kyle knew to pull coffee and a contract out, when he took Jeff outside to the Oceanside view of his new backyard.

It's 2:33 P.M. Kyle starts discussing the price of the property. Together they come up with the most important details to enclose in the offer. Kyle calls the listing agent up to inquire if anyone else is working on this condo.

Jeff patiently walks around the property, then comes back to Kyle smiling at a contract to be filled out.

"Are you ready to sign a deal Jeff?"

"Let's go!" Jeff eagerly responds.

"Pardon me for a second while I call my boys and check on them, before we get started."

"Not a problem at all Hawthorne."

Kyle dials Benjamin up. His face appears on the screen. He has on his gaming headset.

"Hey dad." Benjamin grumbles.

Benjamin observes the clear blue ocean behind his father. "Is everything okay at home son?

"Yeah, but I'm starving. We haven't eaten since breakfast." Benjamin dreams of eating at the pier.

Kyle laughs at the misconception Benjamin has over strictly watching his brother.

"Son, I guess I forgot to mention that it's okay for you to eat. If you're hungry, go get you and Cam a snack. Also, I need to finish up a contract, then take my client back to his hotel. I will be home shortly after. Just grab a snack fornow. I will be home in no time."

Kyle goes over what he prepares with Jeff Gandy then submits the offer to the listing agent.

Jeff is anxious for an answer before he travels back to Manhattan tomorrow.

Yet he knows some patience is needed, for time is of essence.

Kyle has just dropped Jeff back at the Roosevelt and drives away. It's a very short drive from the hotel to his home in Hancock Park. He looks up at the clock on the dashboard, 4:44 P.M. and feels guilty leaving his boys for too long, as his stomach erodes the lining.

Kyle walks inside to a quiet nest. His intuition of where his boys are is precise to the theatre room.

Chips Ahoy isn't lingering around, as normally he runs and attacks him with kisses.

In the kitchen, Kyle sets his laptop-briefcase, down. He peeps out the window and finds Chips Ahoy delicately sniffing the purple and yellow dwarf irises, alongside the pool house.

Kyle goes upstairs and finds his boys. Sure enough Benjamin and Camden are glued to the big screen.

Kyle stands in their view. "Boys, it's time to turn off the game now.

You've played long enough. I would like your help, while I'm scaling the skin from the salmon tonight. I want you to get the plates down and set them up outside."

The brothers jump out of their seats and walk alongside of their father.

"Has mom called? Did mom call yet?" Camden whines.

"No son, she hasn't. I'm sure she is just busy. Let's call her in a bit. After supper."

The boys help their father cook seafood and potatoes. Kyle pops open a beer, enjoying the serene backyard. Everyone eats, and the boys take off teasing Chips Ahoy with a toy.

Alone at the table, Kyle watches his boys dash around with the dog. His imagination starts building scenarios. He decides to call Angela right away.

The phone rings and rings.

This time fire raises him out of his seat and into the house. He feels that something has happened to her and begins to fear the worse. Suddenly, another option appears. He googles Green Valley Resort from his phone as he walks into the very last memories of where he last saw her.

He takes a seat at the same place he teased Angela from yesterday morning.

Dialing the number, he looks at an empty attendance of where he last saw her gorgeous smile at. Connecting from Google.

"Green Valley Resort and Spa."

"Yes, this is Mr. Hawthorne. My wife was on her way there to a writer's conference yesterday and had booked a stay with you. I know this is a peculiar question, but it's bothered me for a whole day now. Can you please tell me if she ever checked in?"

The receptionist places Kyle on hold. A new person comes on the phone.

"Mr. Hawthorne, this is Craig Legion, the hotel manager on duty. It's against our policy, we can't give out confidential guest information. I'm sorry."

"Listen, Mr. Legion. I understand policies completely, but how about if I give you proof, I am her husband. I need to know if my wife is there or not. My next step is to contact the police." The worried husband declares out loud.

"Okay, okay, hold on. I will see what I can do. I'm gonna look up your last name. Don't tell me her first name, now… It's not important yet."

"Okay I have a Mrs. Hawthorne on file. What's her first name?"

"It's Angela. Angela Hawthorne." Kyle pronounces, with fear in his legs.

'Mr. Hawthorne. Our records show that she never checked in.”

Worry comes sailing in from a far south fissure anchored into Kyle's stomach, flaring up higher than he had ever experienced. At this very moment fear over-ruled everything. He took a deep breath, scared he would live widowed, alone in this world with his boys.

"No, I can't be having these thoughts. She is okay. Something must be wrong with their system. Angela isn't gone. I will call the police, they'll help me." Kyle vents out loud.

"911, what's the nature of your emergency?" Dispatcher asks.

"I would like to report my wife missing." Kyle answers in fear.

"Sir, you will need to call the non-emergency police department to make this report. Would you like me to connect you to them?"

"Could you please?"

"LAPD Non-emergency, how may I help you?"

"Yes, my wife went to Nevada for a business conference and she never checked into her hotel last night. I have tried calling her several times and she hasn't answered. This is very unlike her. Can you tell me what I need to do?"

"Just stay calm for one. Usually we wait a little longer for this kind of stuff. Have you checked your debit statements?" Dispatcher asks.

"Debit statement? I'm not worried about missing money."

"You're not listening to me. Check your bank statements. See where the last purchase from her was at."

"Oh yes! Bank statements." Kyle repeats.

"For now, let me take down yours' and her information. We will do what we can to help you. If we get trace of her, you will hear from us first."

A fuel station near Angelino Heights is the last place to take her debit card.

Chapter

THREE

Alone in the living room, Kyle's mind wreaks havoc. Questioning every possible scenario of Angela's disappearance. Changing the channel on his thoughts, he reflects back to September 10, 2001.

In a flashback, he remembers how he first met his stunning cat walking, long leg, and model wife one evening at a fashion show during New York Fashion Week.

He stands in an event room full of empty chairs focusing on the catwalk in the middle, shaking his hair dry from the pouring rain.

He and Angela had only spoken a few magical sentences before he was ditching his friends for this mesmerizing beauty queen.

Prior to the show starting, he sat in a chair wiping rain water off his pants.

Angela had come in for a dress rehearsal with the International Designer from Mexico.

She comes out from backstage getting Kyle and brings him back to sit with a few of her models' friends, so he isn't alone. They wait for the designer and his assistant to get back from a New York City deli shop.

Kyle sits in a chair as he is the only straight male backstage. Angela grabs his face, kissing it front of all the other models and other fashion designers prepping for the show.

There's a flamboyant male assistant to one of the other designers eyeballing Kyle down like candy on the shelf, as he gets wrinkles out of a silk dresses with a steamer.

An African American photographer with his camera wrapped around his neck pops in the room with his assistant searching for the International Designer from Mexico.

Other female models envy Angela for getting the best dress in the show.

They discuss this International designer she's been working closely with. Tones and volumes speak loud and clear. People envied his education in Florence Italy, at one of the top three most prestigious schools in the world.

The International Designer speaks fluent Italian, Spanish, Chinese, English and American English. A well-travelled, sophisticated designer of wedding dresses with the ability to pursue red carpet designs for the celebrities. His visions of how women carry themselves in high fashion couture is beyond his twenty something years of experience.

Steampunk Styles, the photographer, presents himself calmly in search for this designer, then exits the room checking his lens.

Twenty models wait for their designer to show up while the other half of the room is being shared for fitting on dresses and designs.

The energy changes in the show room. You can hear the sophisticated sound of the International Designer from Mexico making his way into the building. He's giving specific orders to a female assistant. They make their appearance inside the dressing room.

The models face shift from doomed dandelions to hungry fly traps, as they perk up out of their seats adding their best phony smiles pretending to be the highlight of the show. Mad confidence and arousal write on the atmosphere, except Angela's spirit is somewhere next to the man's heart who caught her in rain.

She's been modeling all around the world for way too long. She knows her five foot nine, size zero body works well for all designers. If she's in the building, it doesn't matter what others are doing. She's the star.

On the catwalk she's a diva. In the public eye she has a cocky confidence but wears an angelic smile to go with it.

That doesn't matter to the International Designer of Mexico. He speaks flirty Italian trying to appease Kyle with his dark hair and dancing eyes. The designer gets no reaction from him, but a large laugh from Angela.

Laughing got her in trouble. The International Designer from Mexico flamboyantly pushes Kyle out the door with sword of his mouth.

Angela tells Kyle if he gets out of this chair, she was leaving with him. The designer shifts his expression, then speaks a new storyline in a New York

English this time, "Please… by all means… keep this chair hard against your bouncy back."

Hours pass by. The show room fills up and a DJ plays, Tone Loc –Funky Cold Medina.

Kyle finally leaves Angela from backstage. Smiling he takes a front row seat on the left side of the platform. Her left side was always the best side to look at her from.

He remembers feeling lucky sitting in the middle of her universe the first time he had ever went to New York City.

The only house in Hancock Park feeling lonely, Kyle wipes a tear from his eye. He starts to consider Angela's phone might be broken somehow, or maybe she's broken down on the side of the road somewhere. More bad thoughts axe its way in again.

He blocks it immediately going back to Tone Loc as it quiets down in the venue, dramatic lights pop on and the host of show announces the 2001 Fashion to begin.

Kyle sits back, anticipating Angela to walk out.

Aria by Yanni comes on. Dream for dream beats as each model seductively walks out in Avangard.

Beautiful female models wear the world class International Designer of Mexico seasons best. All designs by him and the assistance of his beautiful couturier helping hand, who travels the world with him designing high end fashionable gowns. The fashion designer of Mexico also travels with his photographer, Steampunk Styles, catching every moment of success on file.

At the end of the stage is the photographer's box. All paparazzi are inside it capturing beautiful dresses walking out in every blueprint model's secret.

Moving along in the desire of grand dream of dreams the last forty-five seconds of Yanni- Aria, is dedicated to Angela, a walking statement of art like New York's finest celebrated coppery-green model, The Statue of Liberty. Wearing the International of Mexico's finest green silk, fitted to her waist and legs, stitched transparent meshing on the top show off Angela's hard nipples as she excites the paparazzi and crowd in what freedom looks like.

She has on jewels around her neck, short dangly sparkling earrings, and a seven-spiked copper crown on her head.

Kyle sheds more tears remembering how stunning his woman was that night and how she shined everywhere she went from that moment on. That was his future wife on the stage as she winks right at him. He knew she was his to have and to hold. She emanated a fiery passion he knew he could build life with.

The last scene Kyle remembers of Angela as she walks back out on encore with the International Designer of Mexico. Their arms are linked together. In the middle of center stage of the catwalk, they stand proud waving to both sides of the crowds in the show room.

The remaining models walk out behind Angela and the designer, clapping with big smiles and his dresses on.

The designer and Angela move to end stage, where the paparazzi box is located. They do a few fun fetching poses for Steampunk Styles, then tease the others and walk backstage.

An after-show party took place at one of Manhattans finest rooftops. The International Designer of Mexico ordered a round of Vodka shots and bottles of Champagne for Steampunk's crew, the models who attended, and even offered Kyle a drink.

Kyle remembers how flirty Champagne made Angela that night as she called him to the dance floor with her seductive eyes and alluring Light Blue scent.

The DJ in the booth plays the hot hits of the 80's and 90's dance music.

The fashion designer of Mexico knew he lost his Brooklyn babe brand ambassador that night to Los Angeles eligible sexy single bachelor, Kyle Hawthorne.

Kyle stops thinking when he gets to the part where Angela took him home to her third level penthouse in Brooklyn and they stayed up

Kyle gets out of his chair tired, then directs his steps to his chamber of the house to get some sleep.

CHAPTER FOUR

Pulsation of a dim light twinkles in a dust ridden sackcloth, hovering at the ceiling of a dark ethereal chamber. An entity inside the bag moves as hollow pipes elongate like the wings of a pterodactyl. Long jaws illuminate the rucksack, opening and closing greater than the mouth of a schnauzer, but less than a crocodile.

Everything inside wrestled together, forming mountains in a snow globe. At the highest peak of it all, a small tear begins to rip open and out falls blonde hair, next an arm. Hanging from the shoulder, her hand extends open, abruptly stiffing before his eyes, muddling beneath the surface.

The headboard and post begin to bang the ramparts.

Suddenly Kyle is awakened from his nightmare.

Instinctively, Kyle is up and out of bed, standing frantically at the frame of his doorway. Flickering at the nightstand, the clock reads 4:44 A.M. Sweaty, his heart pounds hard from the horror he had just escaped. Fearing life for himself and his boys, he calls out to them.

Benjamin had also been rattled out of bed. After acknowledging his father, he goes into his brother's room, pulls the covers back on the bed, and finds Chips Ahoy and Camden scared underneath.

"Come on. Let's go!" Benjamin frightfully quavers.

Together they run downstairs with Chips trailing behind them, barking at the whole episode, and hold onto their daddy. The tremors abruptly stop.

Camden looks up to his father with worried eyes and says, "Is it over?"

"I hope so Cam. Let's wait a little while and see."

The rise of morning comes quick. A nebulous earthquake shook every piece of wall art they owned. What Kyle contemplates most is still missing.

A notification from his phone signals. Quickly he hopes its Angela.

Meeting with Jim Anderson, 9 A.M... The phone reads.

It's 7 A.M. Kyle has not one bit of peace. He takes a hot shower hoping to relax some of his tension. Finally, able to dress, he goes to wake up Benjamin.

A room filled with Oakland Raiders football helmets and jerseys are neatly decorated on the wall and dresser of Benjamin's room. Pirate stuff is everywhere.

"Wake up." Kyle whispers.

Benjamin opens his eyes. "Yes dad?" He questions.

"I need you to watch your brother for me today, while I meet with another client. Can you do that?"

"Okay dad." Sleepy eyed, Benjamin agrees.

Kyle goes into the next room full of Clone Troopers, R2-D2, C-3PO, Yoda, Chewbacca, Darth Vader and Han Solo, figurines among a wall full of stars and galaxies. He gently wakes Camden up with a rub on the head.

"Your brother's going to look after you while I go to a meeting. Come downstairs. I'll pour you a bowl of cereal."

"Is mom home dad? Mom normally wakes us up for school."

"Cam, its Sunday. She isn't home yet."

Kyle ruffles up his youngest, tickling him, then throws him over his shoulders and piggy backs Camden downstairs. Benjamin follows them down. Each of the boys get a bowl of Strawberry Special K.

Kyle rushes around grabbing his laptop, then goes out the back door getting into his Mercedes. He is on Wilshire, near Ocean Avenue. Pulling into park at the coffee shop, he's right on time.

He goes inside and orders the largest latte they have, shaking the sleeve of his suit jacket around to count the time from his Armani. Sweat beads form on Kyle's face. Clinching a notion of her, as his nerves eat him alive.

9:03 A.M. He scans around at every single man inside with juxtaposition, of another coming through double doors. Suspicion of one fella dressed in a silver suit with a blue tie, red hair, deeply buried into his phone, but looks up as they make eye contact. A solid stare down, then the man gawks at his surroundings, and takes a sip of whatever he's holding in cup.

Kyle pulls out his phone and dials Anderson up. Reaching him, Kyle sees a silver fox across from him phontronically conversing. Both men realize they have connected to each other.

"Good morning, Jim Anderson?"

Kyle reaches out to shake his hand. "Please call me Jim."

"Jim, I'm Kyle Hawthorne, from Hawthorne Realty. It's a pleasure meeting you. May I tell you a little bit about my agency before we start on some questions, I have for you?"

Kyle tries his confidence as sweat pebbles off his mid-ear section and sideburns. Humidity makes both men uncomfortable.

Jim surveys Kyle rather sternly, wondering if he hasn't just eaten bad food. Obviously, something is not right.

"Of course, I would like to know about your business first, but is everything okay with you? You seem bothered by something." Jim bamboozles.

"With me…" Kyle smirks and plays it off.

"I'm great, other than this belchy feeling in my stomach. I tried purging something up this morning, yet nothing." Kyle acquiescently pipes with a chirping sigh.

"About me… Back in 2002, I received my real estate license. I worked for a larger agency just starting out. I became a top producing agent in 2004, selling over one hundred million in property sales. Meanwhile, I decided becoming a real estate broker, since I'd established the education and practice hours. Obligations to my family was more important than starting a new agency at that time, however in 2006 my first-born started school, taking a little pressure off my wife. In 2006, I opened Hawthorne Realty with just me and two real estate agents. Donna and Kimberly are still with my company. Currently, we have over fifty agents and multiples of listings we can sell. The one you called about is mine though and was just listed last Tuesday. That's me in a nutshell. Can I ask what draws you to my condo?"

Jim Anderson is flabbergasted by the person he possibly is to do a deal with, spites all that out so profoundly. He drops the chops to his bitter walls. Something tells him to work with Hawthorne.

"I've lived in an apartment for nearly a year, waiting on my divorce to wrap up. I sold my place last year as part of the decree, separated our assets. Now I can finally purchase something on the ocean front, just as I want."

"I see. How soon are you looking to purchase?" Kyle inquires.

"My lease on the apartment is month to month at this point. I'm ready now."

"This particular condo you're interested in has an offer on it. Would you like to submit a higher offer to the seller?"

"Well I haven't seen it yet."

"Right! Let's have a look at it and go from there. Sound good buddy?"

A few blocks west, the men pull into an entrance of the Ocean Avenue. Jim Anderson starts excavating thoughts of the past, remembering how it was, and how it was letting his darling money-grubbing ex-wife go.

Wandering around the property, Jim envisions a new life full of fun, while inhaling crisp strips of ocean air. No longer is he medicated or suffocating to a scent as alluring as one such caramel apple. Alone, he begins to proceed.

Luxurious sun rising views, two-bedroom condo for sale. The only one left in the complex. Kyle unlocks the door and takes Jim Anderson for a walk inside.

"Jim, does this appeal as a fresh escape for you?

"Not exactly. I didn't expect to walk right into the kitchen. This is my entrance? And this! No walkway at all… too small, you know, too small." Jim twists sideways, fitting through the island, following Kyle into living room.

The unsettled sensation in Kyle's stomach stands between the two again.

Sweaty, itchy palms and forehead, thus uncomfortable, he presents this twelve hundred and fifty square foot condo to a larger older coon dog.

That didn't seem to be the problem though. Kyle goes into his thoughts searching for Angela, as he has done on and off the last couple days.

Jim doesn't have a clue of what Kyle is thinking about, but it's apparent he's not doing his job at this condo.

"Kyle! Are you listening to me?"

Kyle snaps out of a panic attack, letting courage be the one to tell this silver suit, of bitterness and sophistication off.

"I normally don't let people whom I've just met into my personal accounts, but since you've asked, let me just say… my wife has been missing since Friday."

Jim punches back with a laugh, "Did she run off with another man kind of missing?"

"You're a real chump. You're bitter still aren't you… letting go of the past is a real struggle for you, isn't it? My wife is missing, as in… Can't be reached fool. I'm done here. You need to leave. Right now."

"Hawthorne hack-shit realty! You're right! This isn't my problem." Jim bends forth out the kitchen, unforgivingly turning around, just to stare Kyle down, slamming the door behind him as he leaves.

Kyle falls into tears pounding the tile. He stays there long enough, realizing his mistake. He didn't like that man, and just lost a business deal.

The phone buzzes in Kyle's jacket. Getting off the ground, Kyle answers it, while walking out the front door. He locks up the condo.

"Hawthorne speaking."

"This is Detective Calc Timmons, I'm in charge of the case for your wife's disappearance. Is it possible I stop by your home… say like in fifteen minutes? I have information regarding her."

"Yes, please do. Make it twenty though. It may take me a little longer getting home."

"See you then." Detective Calc Timmons surmises.

Kyle drives home a little faster hitting yellow lights all the way there. Turning onto his street, he finds an unmarked police car with a detective waiting inside it.

The detective gets out of the car carrying a bag of evidence. Kyle meets him at the front of his home.

"Kyle?"

"Yes sir."

"I'm Detective Calc Timmons. Do you mind if we go inside your house to talk?"

"That's fine, come in."

The two go inside and stand at the kitchen bar. Detective Timmons sets his bag on the countertop and reaches inside, pulling out a blue folder. Right away Kyle recognizes it to be Angela's.

"Kyle, today around 11 A.M. I was handed this folder. I'm sorry to be the one informing you, but on Friday, she was killed in an explosion."

Kyle freezes. Not moving a muscle, hoping he did not just hear that, then breaks into a frenzy, shaking the arm of his suit jacket again and again, like trying to shake off what he just heard. "No, no, no. Wait…What… What explosion? This can't be real."

"I'm sorry man. The license plates and folder are all that remain."

Kyle walks into the living room where he last saw Angela and sits down, burying his head into his knees, and sobs loudly.

Upstairs, Benjamin and Camden hear their father crying and stay at the top of the stairs, afraid to come down as they are hearing everything.

Detective Calc Timmons compassionately follows behind Kyle, waiting for him to pull his emotions together, before proceeding on.

Drowning in a pool of tears, Kyle squeezes a pillow cushion from the sofa, crying against it. The detective tries to console him a bit.

"Be strong. Do you have children?"

Kyle looks up at the detective lost, like he didn't hear the question but then responds. "I have two boys."

"I know this won't be easy for you to tell them. Just take some time to process what's going on. I can recommend a grief counselor."

"Thank you." Kyle sniffles.

"I left the plates and the blue folder in the kitchen area for you to keep.

That is all we have left of her, unfortunately. A Nevada State Trooper expedited these items today around 11A.M. He found it interesting he said, "The notes inside of the blue folder, distracted driving, is what coincidently took her life."

"What do you mean?"

"It was a real tragedy what happened to her. She was wedged in between two semi-trailers. The one in front of her was transporting cars and one came off the ramp somehow. Several eye witnesses say she dodged the single car coming at her. It was the truck behind her not paying attention. He paid for it though. The explosion took his life as well. NCSI pulled phone records. The records show he was texting while driving at the time of the accident."

"What time did it happen?" Kyle sorrowfully questions.

"The truck driver's last text was sent out at 4:44 P.M."

"Omg. The clocks… I have seen the time 4:44 P.M. on my clock, every day since Friday. I was even woken up this morning by the tremors at 4:44 A.M. She's been trying to tell me all along the exact time it happened."

"I don't know what to say, Mr. Hawthorne, other than I'm sorry for your loss. If there is anything I can do, please give me a call."

The six-foot-tall African American, 185lbs solid, stands in black cargo pants and a black polo shirt with a black semi-automatic handgun at his belt.

After Detective Calc Timmons leaves the residence, Kyle tries to gather his thoughts together. His worst fear came to pass. Never did he believe this day would come, not having the chance to say goodbye to his beloved.

Kyle hearkens the footsteps of his boys coming down the stairs. Benjamin and Camden run into the room.

"Daddy, daddy, no daddy, I want my momma back." Camden cries.

Benjamin takes after his dad, standing right in front of everybody, holding it together long enough for cue that he can let it out.

"Come here son." Kyle wept.

Together they hold on to each other sobbing, letting every teardrop wash their shirts like rainfall amongst grey skies. No words could bring the loving mother and wife back.

Kyle holds onto his boys as if nothing else even exists. He doesn't know exactly what to do or where to go next. He can hear the detective's last words, "Be strong." Those words keep him together as he holds on to his boys.

Benjamin's cell phone rings from his jeans pocket. He lets it ring until it cuts off. It wasn't a time to be answering phone calls. Whoever it was, would just have to understand. A shorter minute later, the phone rings again.

"Take your phone out son and let them know you will talk to them later." Kyle advises

Benjamin looks at the ringing phone. The numbers on the phone, Benjamin doesn't recognize. He gives it to his dad. The last four digits are all fours.

Curiously Kyle answers, "Hello."

A young boy with a very distinctive British accent starts speaking on the other end. "Benjamin, is that you? Benjamin?"

"Who is this?" Kyle exclaims.

Waiting for an answer, Kyle says, "Hello?"

The phone disconnects. Kyle dials the number back and it goes straight to a busy signal.

In a still, quiet room, the call is dropped. All three Hawthorne's begin to weep anew about Angela.

Chips Ahoy jumps off the sofa barking out the window. A neighbor walking his dog, stops in front of the house. The dog bends its hind legs in sudden defecation.

Chapter
FIVE

Sunday May 8, 2016

The stars are out, but you can't see them for every light in this city reflects the lenient moonlight crawling amongst a slumbering atmosphere. Double lamps posted at the entrance of the Hawthorne place irradiates a black Honda CR-V pulling into the driveway.

Gabriella gets out of the vehicle with an off the shoulder Pearl Jam t-shirt and skinny jeans. Finding her paper license plate virtually expired at the tail end, she opens the hatch and gets out some groceries.

Two bags in one hand and two in the other, she carries the bags inside. She didn't have to fight after work shoppers, following her down every isle, copy-catting food ideas between the time of five and seven.

She walks past Kyle's office feeling his sorrow. He's downheartedly staring at his laptop screen, appearing to work in real estate. The emotions of loneliness come and go for him.

For being twenty-two, Gabriella kind of understands the pain of what

Kyle's going through, grieving the fate of his wife. She misses Angela too. The last three weeks of Gabriella's stay at the Hawthorne residence, she made sure her care and compassion didn't go without notice.

Gabriella puts away the last bit of groceries. Benjamin comes into the kitchen. He goes into the pantry and grabs the newly bought package of chips, opens them in front of her and starts crunching without saying a word to her. He almost escapes her silence.

"La mitad de una bolsa de patatas fritas…" She speaks in Spanish, then translates to English. "The same flavor was opened already, Benji mijo. The new one was for your brother's birthday party this weekend."

"How was I supposed to know?"

He could have cared less, chomping the salt off the chips thrown into his mouth.

Benjamin adds, "Is that all? Can I leave now?"

Pissed off that she would have to later go back to the supermarket for another bag, she held her tongue from going any farther. A quick glance at the clock reads 8:44 P.M. "Yes, sweet boy, you can go up to your room, but can I get a hug first?"

Benjamin stands in the same spot, looking pouty, while Gabriella walks over and give him some love.

Instead of going upstairs to his room, Benjamin heads to the television room and turns the channel from Sponge Bob to the San Antonio Spurs and Oklahoma City Lightning game.

"Hey, I was watching that." Camden pours.

"I didn't see you sitting here. Go upstairs and watch cartoons." Benjamin laughs loudly.

"You go up!" Camden shouts.

Gabriella observes Benjamin being mean to Camden.

"Benjamin, say you're sorry, and turn the channel back. You wouldn't like it at all, if he came into your room and disrupted your show." She points out.

Unburied emotions of consideration come out of Benjamin's mouth. Camden throws up a bit of confusion when Benjamin changes it back to Nickelodeon.

"Actually, let's watch the game." He approves.

Gabriella shakes her head with a smile and joins the boys on the sofa.

Before long, Kyle puts his work to rest for the night and wanders into the family room. Oklahoma City Lightning's score the next shot in the basket.

The next morning, Kyle wakes up to the annoying sound of his phone at 6 A.M. He gets out of bed sulking all the way to the shower, having a cry and rinsing off bad morning breath.

He's not used to having another woman cooking for him and his children.

His days of being able to cook and serve breakfast half-naked are over.

He smells Gabriella frying up sausage to crumble up into the eggs and tomatoes she has on the other burner. Coffee aroma calls him, swiftly moving through the hallways. Having her stay at his home works great for all on his plate.

"Good morning Kyle." An endearing smile, Gabriella portrays as she spots him coming into the kitchen.

"You're a very, very responsible twenty-two-year-old. Thank you so much Gaby for moving into my home and helping us out. I really appreciate it."

"Your welcome amore. I can't thank you enough for my new SUV."

Kyle smiles in adoration saying, "Having a reliable vehicle is important.

Picking up the boys to and from school programs safe and sound is important…which reminds me. I would like to take the boys to school today. I've been so distant lately in everything I do. Camden's birthday is this Sunday."

"Are there any special errands you need from me today?" She asked.

"Nothing in particular, just get the boys from school and have a nice dinner started for when I get home tonight."

Kyle ambles upstairs, gently waking his boys from bed.

Benjamin advances into a morning shower.

Camden spoons up his breakfast at the table downstairs.

Gabriella loads up dirty dishes into the stainless-steel dishwasher. Kyle loads up the boys into the car.

"Camden your birthday's this weekend. Wouldn't you just love going to Chuck E. Cheese's on Sunday?"

"Yes daddy! Can we?" Excited to hear about it, Camden marvels.

"Sure son." Kyle drives on with pure energy and joy from a little smile.

Kyle notices Benjamin's stone-cold gaze from the rearview mirror. Disconnected, he doesn't seem to care.

Kyle pulls up to Camden's school first. He gives his little tiger a big squeeze and even a kiss on the forehead. The first grader gets out of the car with his bag secured to his back; following the other children inside the campus.

"Benji, aren't you gonna sit in the front with me?"

"Can I just sit back here and think dad?"

Letting him be on his own, Kyle doesn't say anymore to him.

Arriving to Benjamin's school, Kyle opens the door letting Benjamin out of the back seat. Before he walks away, Kyle grabs a hold of him and gives him an unwanted hug.

"Benjamin, I know you are hurting inside… you're missing your mom.

I miss her too. You and your brother are all I have left. We are going to pull through this son."

Benjamin casts out dark energy through dilated pupils, bottled up anger suddenly bursts out. "I am mad! I'm so mad! Why would God take her, dad? And I must deal with this all the time covering up my sadness? I would kill to have my mom back and I mean kill."

"I'm as lost as you are Benji. Somehow… someway we must move forward and try to understand as we go. We're going to make it through this, but we aren't going to kill anyone over this."

Benjamin smirks without saying anything more and urges to leave his father's encouraging tones of optimism. He gets out of the car.

Kyle lets go of him, studying his son's body language all the way up to the Middle School doors.

Disappointment settles across Kyle's fretful eyes. Watching his firstborn having to grieve the loss of his mother brings on pains worse than any sore muscle he's ever from lifting heavy weights.

Kyle heads back home to get his briefcase and shackle key. It's been a solid month since he's been to Hawthorne Realty.

At home he finds Gabriella busy reading a paperback in the backyard. Kyle doesn't want to bother her as he rushes through the house, grabbing what he came in for.

He gets back into his convertible with the cell phone ringing in his suit pant pocket. Pulling out the phone he reads the screen, -Anthony Relako, and then answers.

"Tony, how are you buddy?"

"I'm great, just sitting on my patio in S.D… having some coffee, reading the paper…catching up on some stuff. Listen, I got your invitation about Camden's birthday party, at your place this Sunday. How about I drive up on Friday and spend the weekend with you all, since I didn't get to see you guys at Angela's memorial."

"That'd be fine man… I just need to let you know I have a live-in… kind of a nanny, helping me out right now. I just don't want you to think, I've moved on already, when you see her. I'm having a tough time right now, and Gabriella, well she's doing a great deal of work for me and the boys here."

"Yeah, glad you told me. So, how are the boys taking this?"

"You know, they miss Angela so much. Just before you called, Benji was telling me how mad he is at God. He's really been on mute with me lately, not saying much. Camden is, lost… I'm not sure he fully realizes she's never coming back yet. It's so tough right now. So tough… Aye, Tony why don't you come on down Friday. It'd be great to see you."

Kyle arrives to Hawthorne Realty. He pulls his car into his usual spot on the side of the building.

Quickly cutting his conversation short with Tony who is Angela's older, half-brother, Kyle hops out of the car and goes inside to his office.

Not much passion left in his bones for selling houses, as he just misses Angela, but time presses onward. Kyle takes in some deep breaths trying to work out some faith for selling anything in real estate.

Donna is at the front desk showing another real estate agent how to input active and closed contracts into the system. Kyle carries himself into his office behind the Hawthorne Realty partition.

Approaching Kyle's door is Waylon Warner, setting a cheerful scene with his bubbly smile.

"It's a beautiful day, when I get to see your face back at the office. I'm sorry about what happened to your wife. If you need anything, anything at all, I'm here for you bro." Waylon crosses his arms and legs, leaning into the door frame.

Waylon Warner, an average built guy with natural dark hair, optimistic eyes hidden beneath black frame glasses and a Pinocchio nose that didn't move a wink when his flamboyant smile jumped across the office.

Kyle's eyes spark open as much as Waylon's, both grateful for a friendly face. Waylon Warner is dressed seriously cute though. A single buttoned down, royal blue paisley, sharkskin tuxedo suit takes over his form. His sharp tone and master appearance has Kyle contagiously considering wardrobe shopping all the sudden.

"Thanks Waylon. This is harder than I expected, but I'm putting one foot in front of the other. It's good to see you. You pick up any new listings last month?"

"It's been kind of dead around here. I've got two listed. Felt kind of nice. You know that old liberated house with the lawn of rocks for grass finally sold. You should have seen the seller's faces, when I handed them the offer, after two hundred and forty- four days on the market."

Kyle looks away from Waylon a moment. Out through the window he tunnel visions into his Mercedes, reminiscing a memory.

A Sushi Experience, featuring Angela and Kyle. It was neither of the two's favorite, but getting to laugh at every expression made, as they fed each other with chopsticks, sure made life's ride on the wheel of fortune more exciting.

Kyle turns back, "I'm glad you sold it rockstar!"

Donna from up front chimes in with a call to be transferred to Kyle.

"Hawthorne Realty… Kyle speaking."

Kyle listens instinctively, grabbing a pen to take notes. "It's always a good market to sell. Where abouts are you? I'd need to come by and have a look."

Wisdomactically smiling and taking the address down, "So you're out by Marisol, in Malibu. Is that correct?"

Kyles nods his head, happy to hear from them. "Perfect. How bout I drive out there in a couple of hours? I need to pull up the comps, get the exact activity."

"That's cute Ms. Ramsey, I've not heard anyone call me darling in a while. See you soon."

11:35 A.M. the clock displays, as Kyle enters Malibu.

Beforehand, it took thirty minutes to pull and printout, three properties that sold back in April, one is the Marisol beach condo, along with the one he sold Jeff Gandy. He includes the only other property up for sale.

Kyle finds a drive-thru burger joint and decides to eat, before heading over. Satisfied with a grilled chicken sandwich, it takes out some of Kyle's emptiness.

He gives a knock-on Marla Ramsey's door, waiting patiently for her to invite him inside. He envisions a shorter woman wearing a massive blonde wig of cigar class, behind the door, twisting and turning her face and hair, to the beat of her own song.

"Hello darling Kyle. Please… please, come in." Marla eccentrically verbalizes with her big, puffy wine lips.

Oddly enough, Kyle was right about what he saw on the other side. Never has he been able to guess at anything and get it right. It was as if another set of eyes was already inside, like a fly on the wall, observing her mannerisms.

Feeling of a fashion show, Kyle parades inside dance stepping, on top of the lovely black and white marble, catwalk entry, and to the first thing reaching his eyes, the window wall.

"Kyle Darling. I need to be closer to my only and dearest son Rogan. You see, the beach and driving to glamourous locations to get my nails sharpened and polished, doesn't satisfy me much right now. By the time it takes me walking with a broken hippo hip across my twelve thousand square feet swimming pool reflection… you see out there? Way across the horizon. I need to be where my son is."

"And where is that?" Kyle questions.

"Manhattan, with all my other skyscrapers. I've needed an elevator for some time. The older I have got darling… I thought I could just wish away my age and be the spark of speckle I used to be in my teens, many, many years ago. I just can't see the need to put one of those, airport, walking escalators rambling inside."

"That's wonderful. My last client moved here from Manhattan. I can see the wind crossing ways with the sun. I am starting to see everything under a new moon now."

Ms. Ramsey gently winks over at Kyle like an angel, seeming she has known the beauty of life a long time.

"Let's do a walk through. Enlighten me on important details, such as colors and brands to everything currently on the property. When do you want to have it sold?"

"Darling, I lost fantasy of a lustful, sinning body a long time ago. I need it up and sold, Thursday." Marla purrs out.

Finally, an hour walk around the property was done. They go back into the room where the long window of ocean escape lighting is to work out the listing agreement, presented to Marla.

Kyle wraps up the listing appointment taking three dozen, wide angle photographs of the property. On his way out the door, he finds Marla in her office, filing her nails, putting on an excuse for him to leave already. Kyle recognizes a gesticulation when he sees it.

Driving along the Pacific Coast, Kyle decides to swing by Jeff Gandy's condo unexpectedly, since it was on the way back to Hollywood. It's not often he's in Malibu, unless of course it's for real estate.

It seemed like the right thing to do is speak in person about his wife's death. He would also be checking on them to maintain their friendship.

There is an eighteen-wheeler outside of Jeff's property. The last type of vehicle Kyle wanted to face, appears to be the Gandy's furniture truck, sabotaging his mood as he takes a long look at it. Young, athletic looking guys are carrying what looks to be a California King off the back end.

Kyle gets out of his Mercedes, turns and stares at the massive mouth on that truck. A mouth like that is what shattered his life apart. He walks behind the men carrying another blanketed item appearing to be a sofa and goes through the front door of the condo with them.

"Hey buddy, I didn't expect to see you here so soon. Excuse the mess. This is our second trip of hauling. Does it ever stop?" Jeff mouths, as he looks behind him through the back door.

"Honey, come inside please… I want you to meet Angela's husband, Kyle." Jeff instructs his lovely wife.

Kyle unravels dropping his guard then tumbles out the tragedy. "Angela died last month in a vehicle explosion."

"What the hell happened Kyle?" Astonishment tipped Jeff into a bucket of scorching stew, as his head stayed above the edge. He focuses on Kyle's every emotion emanating from his eyes.

Molly comes inside, wearing a sun visor around her long brown hair, cheerfully excited to meet the guest. She walks into the candor of the conversation, dropping her shoulders down as well, instantly becoming concerned.

Pale as a ghost, Kyle articulates, "There were these two eighteen wheelers… One of them was carrying a freight of cars, and one came unlatched somehow at the same time the truck to Angela rear was on his phone, texting and driving, and slammed Angela right into the other truck. The detective said before she was pulled out of the vehicle, it exploded."

Jeff eyes come back from the top level of shock. "Oh my God! Is this what happened last month when you thought she had disappeared?"

"Yes." Kyle lowers his head.

"I'm so sorry to hear this Kyle." Molly consoles.

"Is there anything we can do for ya, anything?" Jeff echoes.

Kyle shakes his head. "It's already done. I'm left with remembrances of her in a way that I've never considered. I didn't get to bury her, since everything went up in flames, so I'm left with her memory, everywhere I go and all around me."

"I appreciate you coming by to tell me this. You could have called." Jeff replies.

"Actually, I came by because I was in the area. You know, strangely enough, today was my first day back at the office, since the accident. I was offered a listing appointment out here in Malibu, coincidently. I was feeling fully spirited stopping by after the appointment to see if you were home, to see how things are going, until I saw the furniture being unloaded. It was also my first time to be standing next to an eighteen-wheeler. I can't imagine what Angela went through."

Kyle finds the need to sever that part of the conversation. "How has the move been on you? I just wanted to stop by and check on you since I was here in the area."

"Ah, yeah… it's been a hell of time. I tell ya… I'm not moving for a really long time or if we do, I will hire somebody to sell all my things and buy new stuff."

"Would you like some iced tea, Kyle?" Molly thoughtfully considers.

Molly pours everybody a freshly brewed tea, while everybody kind of steers away from the grave thought of Angela.

They take the party out toward the view of the Pacific Ocean, holding tall skinny glasses of iced teas with a lemon wedged on.

Jeff retracts the three parts long, sliding glass door and hides it into the two- story tall, modern style condo walls. The crisp salt water of the Pacific instantly slithers onto their bodies, and into their noses. As they take a short walk, under the second-floor awning, the Gandy's blue plastered infinity salt water pool creates the illusion as being part of the ocean. Which one out of two, rotundas, do they want to take a seat at, experiencing open air, television or the modern style comfort of a warm gentle fireplace brush across their skin as the breeze glides along the terrace?

"Jeff, Molly, I really appreciate you allowing me to stop by and share a glass of tea with you on such are beautiful, sunny day. As I look across the ocean then look over at you two sitting on the sofa, I feel Angela sitting next to me as well. I have been so numb, ever since her death, and I didn't think it was gonna happen this fast, but today, I actually feel a sense of release."

"We are certainly glad to have you here and just know you are not alone. If you ever want to talk or get a night out, call me up." Jeff suggests.

"It's a real honor to know you both." Kyle gulps half of his tea and then continues. "I would like it if you and Molly don't have any plans this Sunday to come out to my youngest son's birthday."

Jeff turns to Molly for a telepathic answer, then turns back to Kyle. "What time on Sunday?"

"1 P.M. Sunday at the Chuck E Cheese on Wilshire Boulevard."

Kyle picks up his glass and takes the last sip of tea with a sense of urgency to urinate before leaving.

"Sure. We'd love to join you and meet your boys. You have two boys, is that right?" Jeff wheezes as Molly takes it all in, listening quite intently.

"Yeah, two boys, really good kids. Hey, do you mind if I use your bathroom? I can't hold the tea much longer." Kyle grits out a smile.

"Yes, that's fine. You know where it's at, correct?" Jeff teases.

Kyle gets out of his seat, "Yes, I remember the property quite well." With a chuckle he goes right under the awning a little way to find the pool restroom door.

After using the facilities, he goes back to his company with a farewell to leave their house. Jeff and Molly walk Kyle to the front door and off he goes in his little black Mercedes.

Just like that, Monday is gone.

Tuesday flies by fast.

Wednesday is like a weeping willow tree full of sappy green branches falling to the ground, waiting for its morning sky to steal the joy.

Thursday's forecast becomes just another day like the others, getting the boys up for school with Gabriella, but on this day, Kyle stays home to upload pictures on the Multiple Listing Service, for Marla Ramsey's, Pacific Ocean Highway Beach House in Malibu.

Uploading some thirty odd photos of her property onto his laptop, he reviews them in order, then selects the best twenty or so to show. Kyle sifts through images noticing on the second one, there is a white glowing orb on the living room sofa. He flips onto the next photo and it's normal.

Just a close up of the corner bar of the living area.

He flips back and still the orb rests on the sofa. Onto the next photos without too much caution, he finds another white orb on the lip of the free-standing garden tub, in the master suite.

Kyle begins to think his camera lens is dirty. He presses the next photo. With confusion, he thinks to himself, *is this Marla in this photo?* Closely, trying to remember everything about the surroundings, when he took the photo, certainly he would have remembered Marla being at the master suite closet door, bent down, holding her ankle, wearing ice skates, and a peppermint stick scarf wrapped around her neck.

What the creepy hell is this! He says aloud.

He seizes into a panic and away from the desk with the vision pressed hard against his foresight from the very next photo. Spitting anger and rage, darts through Marla's eyes as her head shot had been taken. The only thing nice about this was the candy cane scarf, wrapped tightly at her neck.

The chilling sound of a whistling tea kettle startles Kyle even more, but also wakes him up from the façade of pictures. He walks into the kitchen with Benjamin pouring steamy water into his mug.

"Whatcha making?"

"Shit dad, you scared me!"

"Watch your language boy." Kyle demands.

"I'm pouring a hot chocolate."

"This late? You are supposed to be getting ready for bed. You have school in the morning son."

Benjamin isn't really concerned with school now as he stirs in the instant, packet of chocolate. Filching a sip through sticky marshmallows, he peeks over the lip of the mug and finds his dad pondering a response for this snide show.

Frustrated, Kyle walks away from a possible disaster and goes to checks on his other son. Going up the staircase with an indistinct feeling, of why Marla would be in those photos, when he knows she was nowhere around, and she was certainly not wearing ice skates.

Kyle walks past Gabriella's room and finds her with the lights out, and television on. It's like he has the beautiful daughter that he always wanted living there now. He stops by for a visit.

"I'm calling it a night, about to go to sleep, just making my rounds to check on everyone."

"Oh, okay, I'm good. I'm about to sleep as well." Gabriella catches Kyle before he walks away. "Camden should be asleep. I helped him to bed a half an hour ago."

A warmness slithers inside Kyle's chest, sending out a smile that comforts Gabriella, genuinely with thanks, as he's walking over to Camden's bedroom. Sure enough, the lights were out.

A more relaxed man goes back downstairs, uploading the Ramsey's Place into the midnight hour, but it's fully active now ready for the offers to start pouring in.

CHAPTER SIX

Long, feathering, ultraviolet yellow rays awaken Kyle out of bed. He must have slept right through the alarm this morning, trusting Gabriella getting Benjamin and Camden off to school on time. She's done a great job in the past month. She went above and beyond assisting the Hawthorne's.

The house, undisputable calm, no movement or sound, other than a few heartbeats per second of a toy Maltese, Chips Ahoy, which is laying on his bedding, in the living room.

Kyle reaches into the stainless-steel Viking, hydrating his thirst, pouring sugary, pulpy, extract of oranges into a tiny glass. He takes it down in the first gulp, slams the glass to marble, and pours another to take outside with him on quite a lovely day.

Sitting in his favorite chair, he finds clouds in the sky, resembling a dove and a halo. God blows air conditioning on every cherub in mission. The chirping out of the sky allows him to reminisce Angela against his skin.

He holds every fond memory they had together, wrapped in soft pale linen, touching with gentle caresses and steamy down pours of sweat from every kiss she took from the sides of his neck. She would nibble on his ears, working her way under his shirt, diving into his chest. It was kind of his layover for the commander on flight, as they took their roles as captain and flight attendant one night. He remembers locking hands to make sweet love to her, just as she liked.

That image always fueled Kyle more than he could eat up in calories.

Not sweeter than a strawberry. No freshness of bread. No gravy from a roast he took into captivity could be swallowed for his once in a lifetime love affair.

Gabriella opens the door and walks out. "Your door was closed this morning señor, I didn't want to awaken you. I took the boys to school this morning." In her hands, she is carrying a big bag full of stuff, walking it over.

"So much a sweetheart Gaby," once again he shows his appreciation for her kindness, she gives him, verses a life she could be making on her own.

"What's in the bag?" He probes.

"Camden mentioned he wanted a Star Wars, Color Changing Lightsaber and Star Wars Speeder Bike Drone for his birthday. I got them yesterday. I bought it on the account card you gave to me. I hope you don't mind."

"Gaby, I'm not a passive guy by any means. I'm certainly glad you'd take the time to get these things for Camden, but that expense isn't a business write off at the end of the year. Make this the only time you do this. If we need anything other than cleaning supplies, just come to me and ask."

"I understand completely. I'm sorry Kyle."

Gaby takes toys out for Kyle to examine. He holds them like an excited kid, ready to rip open the tops of the boxes.

"Oh, Camden will like these." He raves.

10:17 A.M. Friday, May 13, 2016, Kyle's cell phone rings. A clear shot of who's on the other end is displayed. Gabriella gathers up the Star Wars back into the bag and moves back inside the house.

"Tony – Tony, Hello my man." Kyle kind of shouts as he puts it on speaker and sets the phone down.

An exhalation of breath blows smoke from the mouth of Tony Relako. "Kyle, I'm headed over now. It's a little over three hours, driving over to your place. Will you be home around 2 P.M.?"

"Yeah, I'll be here. It's a nice day outside. Are you in the mood to grill up something?"

Yeah, sounds great… surprise me." Anthony belts out in a deep raspy voice, releasing minuscule amounts of cigarette smoke through his set of lungs.

"See you soon. We'll catch up then."

The phone call drops. Perhaps Anthony hits the end button to get packing.

Staring right at the tennis court, Kyle begins visualizing opportunities. Looking into the clear blue sky, he collects his empty glass and phone, and deciding to go back inside the house to do a little work.

Stepping inside the house, he observes Gabriella dusting baseboards on her knees, acting her role as responsible maid he first hired her as. He walks past her without any further notation into his office, shutting the double doors behind him.

He opens his laptop and signs onto the MLS rechecking the status of Marla Ramsey's property. Dozens of exquisite photos loaded up from last night and still he hasn't the slightest clue of why images of Marla dressed the way she was and those orbs were on them?

His stomach combats disgusting blobs of twisted thoughts echoing about. He's at the point of liquidation hurrying to sends over those bizarre photos. Before exploding his britches, he hits send.

While Kyle is desperately dancing his way to the bathroom, Marla rings him up. She must have had her phone in her hand to call him so quickly.

On the toilet, Kyle lets out a loud rectal cough. Chips Ahoy dashes to the sofa and digs up pillow cushions for shelter. The dog gives a whimpering sigh, buried under the pillow with its tail tucked inside its legs.

This business orbits deftly around two baskets full of eccentricity. Kyle imagines his hands being fully soiled and washes up well, then dries them on a hanging towel. Voicemail notification goes off. He doesn't check it yet, instead he rushes back to his office chair and makes the call on Facetime.

"I was gonna call you shortly after I sent it over to you… anyhow, you saw the photos?" Kyle holds it together.

"Yes! You know, how in the world did those come out that way?" Marla loses false eyelashes over this.

"I don't know, I wanted to ask you the same thing."

Heavily puzzled, Marla glues it together, and remembers something that expresses her thoughts vividly. "You know Kyle, while you were here darling, you must have been taking photos at that time, but those pictures you somehow captured were the memories I'd been having, while doing my nails. I remember now… yes! I remember at the time you were taking photos, I had the intense feeling to be in New York with my son. I remembered this past holiday, I went ice skating. He took me there, but I haven't been in years… years. Oh, it was so much fun. But how in the world did you capture my memories of me holding my ankle, twisted up somehow in those lacey skates. It was freezing that night. It hurt like hell, walking out of central park with my candy cane scarf wrapped around my bent ankle."

Kyle reframes himself as he sat through a winded composition "I don't even know what to think about this Mrs. Ramsey. I'm flabbergasted, really.

I have been experiencing all kinds of weird stuff lately. My stomach isn't used to this. Marla, your property went on the market last night, just as you requested. It's priced to sell. You know, you're going to be in New York in a snappy second."

"The next call I hope to hear from you is the offer." She releases her famous eye wink.

"I will be observing the amount of amount of traffic walking through. Let's get you an offer working this week." Kyle pronounces with a smile, trying to end discussion.

"Darling, I want to move quickly, but you're scaring me now. I didn't think about getting the movers out this week. Darling, it's been good chatting. I'm glad you showed me those pictures, although I don't understand how they came out like that. I'll get everything in order now. Talk soon."

"Talk soon." Kyle ends Facetime.

Freshness of morning captures the ambient show. Kyle takes a big breath of air then releases a gentle gratifying gesture into the simple sun above. Copper rays beam out of clouds, hash-tagging wind for making pennies flow down; but a*t what cost did we lose our hope? God, my life is inside a sea of murky water, and I keep wanting to dive deeper until I reach the floor. A perfect sun rises in morning.*

Chapter
SEVEN

An old rugged burnt orange pickup truck pulls into Hawthorne's place and parks. The truck door opens with a squeal, as a thick furry arm enigmatically, withdraws a man wearing worn out Levi's, not by style, but from protection in every camping trip he's ever taken the last twenty years.

Standing with his back against the world from the door hinges, he reaches inside for his backpack, plows an arm through one strap, then the other.

This is Anthony Relako.

Angela's half-brother.

Everybody calls him Tony for short. He stands six foot- four inches in height and puffs on a cigarette. He latches his old Dodge Ram-Albert Orange shut.

Tony stomps out the cigarette on the pavement with his worn-out brown leather boots. He then picks the butt off the surface, tossing it in the bed of the truck, before treading to the door.

Giving it a big bang, Gabriella opens the door trying to hide lust in her eyes, knowing he would expose her straight up the middle at a given opportunity. Her body goes red real fast making it hard for both to talk.

Love at first sight. She places her hand directly on top of her collar bone, rubbing gently over herself, barely opening her mouth.

"Yes, can I help you?" She quietly asks.

Tony looks around for the physical address on the house.

Not finding it, he looks to Gabriella with a rough bearded smile and dark shade sunglasses on. "This is the Hawthorne house, correct?"

"Yeah..."

"Is Kyle around?"

"You must be Tony... too much kin to Kyle." Shyly utters.

She smiles, letting him in the door, then walks over to Kyle's office. Tony stands firmly like solid protein, topped with a cowboy hat, in the grand foyer.

Kyle enters the scene with excitement. "Tony!"

Kyle bear hugs him, then backs off smelling like thick woodsmen, cigarette smoke and English Leather.

"Come in Tony!" Kyle smacks him on the shoulder.

Tony takes off his backpack, following Kyle through the house. They go across the guest room threshold. Luxury didn't barricade Tony's freeborn spirit though. He tosses his recycled army tent-bag on the bed, on top of elegant pillows.

"Was it a goose neck driving up here?" Kyle asks.

"You know, it was pretty smooth sailing until I hit the city vibe. I started tasting dark clouds rushing around the air, right before Irvine."

"Is it really that bad?" Kyle smirks.

"It's bearable. I never been much of a city kid, hence I went completely opposite longitude and down a ladder, when I left New York, some twenty years ago."

"You know there is plenty of nature in upstate New York, you could have stayed around there." Kyle jokes.

"No, I couldn't. Extreme cold and snowy winters followed by more cold and rainy spring for me to enjoy the green leaves and critters. I couldn't wait to get the hell out of there, once I figured out, what direction."

"Hey, I'm gonna give you some time settle in. Do you need anything?"

"If you don't mind, I would like to take a quick shower, take some of the smog off. Can I get a towel from you?"

"Right this way buddy." Kyle leads.

Showing Tony the bathroom connected to the mother-in-law suite. He opens the linen closet and shows Tony to plenty of fresh towels, then walks over to the shower, opens the glass door, checking for soaps. "There's plenty of shampoo and body washes if you need them."

Tony makes himself at home.

Kyle goes outside and checks the mailbox.

Walking back with stacks of letters and adverts, he opens an envelope from Benjamin's school. Inside, is a progress report that makes him grimace.

It's a Friday afternoon, mid-May. Absolutely gorgeous outside. Gabriella has gone to retrieve the boys from school. No calls have been made on his newest property for sale. Kyle's not ready to dig up any new bones, as he tucks away a point of failure into a stack of office papers, on his desk. He goes out to his backyard, opens the door to the refrigerator, and grabs a cold one.

Later, Tony finds Kyle chilling out back on the patio furniture. He walks up, dressed in a Bob Seger t-shirt, cargo shorts, and classic Van sneakers. His long- ragged hair brushed over to one side, instead of the pony tail and leather hat he hid it under. The beard and mustache have been neatly trimmed down a notch as well.

"Can I get one of those?"

"Help yourself, they're in the cooler behind you." Kyle tells him.

Tony finds the bottle opener pulling the top off a Lagunitas, then turns back to sit with Kyle on the other sofa.

"I see you took some off the beard. Pretty clean man."

"It's been a while, I thought since I'm here for Camden's birthday, I should look a little neater. So that's Gabriella, your live-in nanny? She's gorgeous. What's her story?" Tony converses.

"Gaby is a cutie you know, a nice girl, comes from a pretty good family. She's been a great help around here. Gaby crossed the border with her older brother about ten years ago, started living with some friends of relatives. She came up to us at a restaurant we were eating at back in 2012, and handed Angela a written note, as she was bussing a table, next to us and some asshole was being mean to her. Angela and I both agreed to let her take on some cleaning tasks once a week, as she wanted to earn more money. I'm thankful we did. She has become part of our family now."

Taking down a long swig Tony calls out a time in history, "Ahhh, 2012, that was when I caught the ex-wifey cheating on me. I'm glad that year worked out for you." He takes another sip with stiff bitterness.

Kyle looks around hoping his tears don't fall out of his sockets. He takes a second gulp then escapes the subject. "So… you're interested in Gaby? I believe she's single. Ask her on a date bro. I bet she'd like that."

"Hey now, slow down, I said she is cute. There is nothing wrong with a little flirtation, anything else, I don't see happening yet."

"Well big brother… works for me, but I'll understand if you want anything more." Kyle says chuckling.

Tony deliberates a second. "What exactly happened to my sister? I'm not trying to go sour, but I want to know how the hell anybody could be texting and driving. You know, coming here… twenty years ago we didn't have cell phones clogging up our whole dashboard, and because of instant gratification, I don't get to see my sister anymore."

"I know, we are all still trying to pick up the pieces around here. Her life was cut way too short. The boys are having a tough time and tell you the truth, God do I miss her like crazy. I wake up thinking she is next to me and yet nothing. She's gone. I'm empty. It's painful all around. To wake up one day and the love of your life is just gone." Kyle sobs it out for a couple of minutes.

"So, what the hell happened? Did they lock away the guy who did it?"

"No. The bastard put her through hell, then went in flames with her. I got no kind of apology, other than keep going, you got two sons who need you."

"Damn. This sucks man. I went so distant when I left New York. Got involved with some bimbo, after a payday. Man, I've probably only seen you guys twice, since I came to Cali. I really regret all the times I've missed. Man, I'm only a few hours away too." Anthony downs his beer.

"Yeah, Benji is fourteen and struggling to keep it together. His whole outlook on life has changed, effecting his grades at school. I got his end of school year progress report through the mailbox this time. C's on everything and a sixty- nine in Algebra, his best subject."

Kyle walks over and grabs out two more beers. "Benjamin's gonna hear about it, first thing Monday." He walks back over.

Gabriella opens the backdoor. "Kyle, I just wanted you to know, I'm home."

"Gaby, this is Angela's brother, Tony. Come out and visit with us."

"Can you give me just a second?" She bashfully replies.

Gabriella hurries to the half bath, passing both Benjamin and Camden in the kitchen, who are snatching up snacks.

She plays with her hair in the mirror, putting on special touches, checking out her butt, throwing on a fruity body splash, trying to contain her nerves. A lot more than a second passes by.

She becomes the focal point of the conversation out back.

"Kyle, I'm gonna kill you."

"What man, you like her right? I'm just inviting her to be a sophisticated grown up out here." Kyle makes sure to specify that with total sarcasm.

The door opens, and right away fresh raspberries come out with her.

Except no berries in her bucket falls out, while she's swinging her hips and hair. She sits down, grateful for some adult interaction and a break from working.

Kyle smiles watching the two with chemistry miles away. He remembers his first time with Angela back in New York, one rainy day in September 2001.

"Gaby, tonight I'd like it if you would just take the night off, pretend everything is cooking itself and just hang out with us. Would you do that?"

"Really? I'd love to."

"Would you like a beer?" Kyle bids.

"I don't really like beer."

"How about a Margarita.? I've got top shelf tequila inside and fresh limes. I'll make you one."

Kyle cleverly leaves the two alone, going inside the house to blend up a Margarita with some limes.

Inside he finds Benjamin and Camden in the living room, both on their phones watching videos, while eating chips and cheese. Benjamin feels his father walking over to him. Kyle pulls out one of the earbuds in Benjamin's ear.

"How was school?" Kyle asks.

Benjamin looks around like he is trying to comprehend such a hard question. "It's good."

"It's good? How about you Camden?"

"Daddy, can my friend come to my birthday party this weekend?"

"Who is it?" Kyle asks.

"Finn."

"That's fine. Do you have his number, so I can call his parents?"

Camden opens his small list of contacts on his phone and finds Finn's number. "Here dad."

Kyle inserts his number into his phone, then takes a quick peek at Benjamin for a second, hinting with his eyes that there will be a topic to discuss later. For now, Kyle decides to make the margarita.

Freshly squeezed limes and lemons into water, sugar, tequila and ice, he blends everything to perfection. Spoon tasting it from the blender he decides to add a pinch of cilantro for taste and added color. He pours the tasty mixture into a nice glass, then pours a hefty shot of Cointreau to float.

Walking outside, he notices a set of love birds perched closely, intuitively interacting with one another. Kyle draws near, handing Gabriella her margarita, watching her eyes light up.

"It looks amazing Kyle." She takes a delightful sip through a twisty straw one of the boys had gotten from a carnival souvenir cup. "Yum!"

"We should take our drinks down to the tennis court. What do you say I get some tennis balls and we play two against one?" Kyle throws out.

"I'm up for the challenge." Tony warbles in sarcasm.

Kyle walks down to the cabana and grabs the tennis equipment, meets the two down at the old ivy English court, where he and Angela use to play. Memories come in, but he holds it together, as he is grateful for having a new family portrait being made.

Tony and Gabriella loosen up on court with rackets in their hands, taking swings, as if they're in the game already. Kyle runs to the other side of the net, starts pounding the ball into the concrete. He aims down the court, then fires. Back and forth, the tennis ball crosses the net. Strength in Kyle's upper legs grants him the ability to bounce, side to side, keeping up with the ball.

A vivid bright sun goes down after an hour of playing. The courtside lights come on like a finger snap. Sweat drips from their hairlines onto their ankles, as they'd been chasing the ball back and forth in swift coordination.

Tony and Gabriella are up by two points. Kyle calls last game and swings the ball down the court. Tony strikes it back and Kyle lets it go right past him with no attempt of going after it. He lets them win.

Laughing and out of breath, they all go back to the house to cool down. Kyle walks right past the pool and hot tub, full of endorphin, but lonely thoughts of missing Angela seep in. *Must be part of losing someone. It just comes and goes.*

Tony and Gaby stay outside getting to know each other. It's evident the chemistry between the two would soon bring forth that long lasting first kiss.

Kyle goes inside the house to cook supper.

Benjamin and Camden are busy dipping Oreos in milk with Chips Ahoy watching for crumbs to fall below.

Kyle panics noticing a half the box is gone. "Hey, hey, easy on the cookies. I'm about to fire up the grill."

Disappointment rolls through the boy's eyes as Benjamin puts them away. Out of the refrigerator Kyle pulls out several center cut tenderloins, and equal amounts of sweet corn on the cobs. He salts and peppers the steaks, then rubs Cajun spice on the corn. Putting everything on a platter, he carries it all outside.

Kyle strikes a match, throwing into the charcoal in the grill. Sauntering over to his company, both Tony and Gaby have their mouths locked together. They appear as a wax sculpture in an art museum. Kyle double takes and turns back to the grill, deciding to keep a closer contact on the steaks.

Near the veranda, Kyle clears his throat. "I'm glad to see you've formally met. If you don't mind, I've got a date with Barbie-Q." He grins out.

Not even embarrassed by being caught, the two are completely consumed with infatuation for each other in this moment.

Kyle sees a trimmed down beard and knows the thoughts in Tony's eyes.

The corn crackles and pops on the grill, blackening the layers with lines looking like a bumble bee's taking flight, all through the night. Kyle puts the steaks on, rare to the stare.

"Love birds, how'd you want your steaks?"

"Medium." Tony replies.

Gabriella is smiling, anticipating the thought of eat steak, "No quiero que con sangre roja. No red Kyle."

As the Los Angeles night cools down, the ocean breezes roll in fifteen miles west. Kyle lights up the fireplace, keeping everybody warm outside. The boys eat from a neat ambiance.

Tony could see how lonely Kyle was by the way he overly compensated trying to take care of everything. What kind of person has such a generous heart when they just lost their wife? Tony reframes another thought standing in the way of his own happiness.

Purposely giving out a yawn, Tony calls it a night. He gives Gabriella a hug and says, "See you in the morning." He peeks over at Kyle and gives out a pocket full of appreciation, "Supper was great tonight man, see you in the morning as well." Tony looks around a short second, then back at Kyle. "Thanks for everything."

Everybody rises out of their seats, calling it a night. Tony walks Gaby inside the house with his arms wrapped around her hips. Kyle look around at the mess he is about to clean up. Dirty plates and beer bottles cover the table. He scrapes excess food from plates, trashes empty bottles, and turns off the outside fireplace. His phone starts to vibrate in his pocket.

9:43 P.M. the phone reads, then turns to 9:44 P.M. It's a notification from YouTube. *Since when did I sign up for notifications on this site?* He opens it up and presses play on the video.

A motorcycle causes fatal accident. He drops his jaws at the posted date.

Kyle thinks about this for a second, *that's tomorrow.*

The sound quality of the video was like an old roll strip film documentation. A Police officer suspiciously walks up to an over turned, white, four door sedan at 11:45 A.M. Inside the vehicle, both driver and passenger air bags are blown out. The car seats are empty. A helicopter is landing at the scene. The video abruptly ends. *What the hell was that all about*? He fearfully questions himself.

Chapter
EIGHT

Enormous bedrooms, accompanied by astral size windows letting in natural warm sunlight, which was more than likely the instigator to everybody's wakeup call on this riveting Sunday morning in May 2016.

In pajamas, everybody moseyed around with their thumb on Facebook checking worldly statuses.

The last to open his eyes is Benjamin waking up and of course going straight for Facebook like everybody else did. He checks to see who's online now. Dad got on seven minutes ago. Gaby's been on fifteen. Camden fifteen as well. Uncle Tony two minutes. Everybody seems to be connected but nothing interesting is happening. Benjamin exits off Facebook, then opens Snapchat, while crawling out of bed.

Gabriella signs off and goes to turn on the Keurig machine, making herself a cup. Benjamin walks into the kitchen right as she is pouring cream into her cup.

"Morning Benji, wanna come with me to get the balloons and cake for your brothers' birthday?"

"Nah, I'd rather stay here, pour me some cereal, and then get ready."

Gabriella doesn't say anything more, just leaves him alone. It's not like he's hurting anyone, but she's noticed since Angela's death, he's been troubled. She rushes out the door to gather up all she needs for Camden's special day.

Tony crosses paths with Benjamin exiting the kitchen. "Hey Tomb

Raider, can you show me how to get some coffee around here?"

"Do I look like a girl to you? My names not Tomb Raider." He spat out with flames in his eyes.

"Easy big guy, I'm playing with ya kiddo. All I'm saying you got Raider stuff hanging in your room. Just making conversation. How about that coffee?"

He turns back around, sloshing milk on the travertine. "Yeah, I'll show you how to do it." Benjamin could really care less.

Kyle enters the kitchen, finding Benjamin helping Tony with coffee. "Got enough water in the machine buddy?"

"Morning man, I think so. What time are we leaving, so I'll know how much time I have to get ready?" He chocked in a deep, raspy morning voice.

"The reservation is for noon. We need to leave here…" Kyle looks at his phone in hand. "We need to leave here in an hour and a half. Hungry? Eggs Benedict anybody?"

Tony sips his black coffee, "Sure, that sounds good. Do you have some sort of hot sauce?"

"Spicy kind of guy. Yeah, we have some. Gaby is a spicy girl too." Chuckling like a gutsy little brother.

Gabriella comes walking in the front door after being away for forty-five minutes. She has the cake and balloons in hands. Everyone's been sitting on the living room sofa, waiting for her to get back.

"Does everyone just want to ride with me in my SUV?"

"You know, I didn't even think of that. Good idea." Kyle affirms.

It's gorgeous outside. Kyle and the boys hop in the back of the CR-V, Tony gets in the front with Gabriella. The radio is muted. Everybody feeds off the buzz of a birthday party, in their own conversations, as they cruise along.

"Look at the car in front, swerving all over the road, driving slowly. Pull up to it, I want to see what the driver is doing." Tony snarls out.

A young girl, bopping her brown hair all over the place with her cell phone in hand, not paying attention to the road, the whole ten seconds they were on the side of her.

"I just want you to get in front of her, slow down to the point she sees you, and then bring her to a complete stop." Tony directs.

"I can't do that!" Gabriella panics.

"Do it!" Tony pressures.

Kyle and the boys, in the back of the SUV don't say anything, as

Gabriella takes over the young girl's lane. She sticks her hand out at her, while both vehicles in motion come to a complete stop. The young girl gets out, shouting, "What the… bitch."

Tony hears this and doesn't take it lightly. When the young girl sees Tony's aggravation directed towards her, she hurries back to her white, four door sedan. A motorcycle loudly passes by grabbing Kyle's attention.

Gaby looks at her dash clock. 11:45 A.M. then apologizes to Kyle for stopping and making them late.

Kyle remembers the YouTube video from last night. The one that came on right after cleaning up after everybody's mess. Déjà vu runs through his mind remembering the motorcycle passing by, likes what's happening now. Then there's the cop walking up to the car with discharged airbags. Kyle goes into a temporary stupor in the backseat of Gaby's SUV.

Tony slams huge hands on the hood of her car. The girl is terrified. In fact, everybody is shaken up a bit.

"You just think it's flipping cool to listen to your music, doing your makeup, texting your boyfriend or girlfriend or whatever the hell? You want to die? Do you? Do you want to kill someone for being so stupid on your flipping cell phone?"

Gaby gets out, and runs over to them, "That's enough Tony. You've scared her already. Look at her." Gabriella places her hand on his shoulder. "Come on, let's go. Now!"

He pauses.

She could have driven right over him, but is held captivated under his malevolent gaze. Both of her hands on the wheel, looking at him, planning an escape.

He finally turns away and walks off feeling ten inches taller.

He opens the door with a cigarette hanging out his mouth, still quite frustrated.

"You can't get in here with that." Gabriella spat.

Tony, still mumbling, ignores her advice. "Tony!"

"Oh, you don't want me to smoke in your car? Of course, give me a second." He jeers with a raspy voice.

Tony shuts the door and stares at the young girl taking off from behind them. She doesn't use her blinker, just goes around. A loud car horn comes in from behind and smashes right into her. She is thrown right into the steering wheel. Glass explodes, leaving shards in Tony's face and skin. It appears to be a semi muscular guy with curly blonde hair held back by a dark colored bandana, in an older model Xterra. He takes off.

A thin line of blood drips from Tony's cheek, he knows his influence in this event and runs over to her. She's okay, somewhat shaken up but okay.

"Let's get you out of here."

"Knob-head get away from me. This is your fault."

Tony walks away lost for words, gets into the vehicle he came in and they leave the scene.

"I think we should pull over somewhere and get you cleaned up. You've got blood all over your face." Gabriella mentions.

"Yeah, just take me to the nearest fuel station."

"Uncle Tony, I'm glad you pulled that girl over to talk to her. I'm glad you scared her too. I know my mom didn't have a chance to get her book out and she's dead because of cell phone drivers, but somehow, someway, we have to stop these damned to hell idiots." Benjamin says, infuriated.

Benjamin starts to chuckle hard as he spits out, "It serves her justice, I bet the girl thinks again about using her cell phone, and driving."

"Boy, I hear it in your voice, do you wish something worse would have happened to her?" Kyle defends.

"It wouldn't be in my hands now, would it dad?" Benjamin gives a stone- cold stare at his father.

Kyle turns his head the other way, not wanting to escalate Benjamin's emotions any further, with Camden sitting on the other side of him. He knows there is a lot to deal with, just not now.

Gabriella gets them to Chuck E Cheese albeit a little late.

12:27 P.M. Gabriella pulls into the parking lot. Everyone jumps out of the black CR-V, rushed. She hurries to the back of the vehicle, opens the hatch, swatting the balloons, handing over a big party bag full of presents to Kyle, grabbing a box with a three-layer cake inside, then grabs a string of balloons.

Inside Kyle finds Jeff and Molly, and a few little boys anxiously waiting over at a table. Precipitously walking over, Gabriella sits the box down in the middle, decorating balloons around chairs.

"Hey Gandy, we left early and still got held up in traffic." Kyle pats Jeff upon the back, giving Tony a hulking smirk.

"Jeff, Molly, this is Tony, Angela's brother, and of course you know Gaby already."

"Nice to see you both." Jeff beams. Jeff and his wife have such angelic spirits floating within.

The boys go off on their own, exploring game options in a room full of lights and sounds, with kids everywhere running amongst the place.

Chuck E. the mouse, dances up to the table ready to sing to someone, grabs ahold of Gabriella's hand. She smiles out of embarrassment, but twirls in place too.

"Let me find the boys." Kyle articulates.

Kyle goes deep into the arcade room, and almost bumps into a young girl on her phone, while walking somewhere between games machines. Somewhat annoyed he finally finds his two boys, letting them know it's time. Benjamin and Camden gather up the rest of the party, to come back.

Two large cheese and pepperoni pizzas are sitting at the table. "Can I use your cigarette lighter Tony?" Kyle emits. Kyle lights up the three tier Star Wars cake, spinning around there, instead of serving pizza.

Chuck E. starts the choir.

"Happy Birthday to You…" Everyone circled around the table, singing Camden the birthday song. He blows out the candles. Gabriella takes the plastic lightsabers off the cake, and begins slicing triangles from the top layer. Kyle hands Camden the first slice, then hands out the next piece and so forth.

Everyone eats vanilla cake with blue and green frosting, from the C3PO and R2-D2 layer. The adults eat some of the pizza before having desert. A couple of kids go for the pizza too.

Kyle takes a credit card over to the ticket counter and charges a couple hundred-dollars, getting plenty of coins for the kids to play with.

Gabriella hands Camden a gift to open as everybody has finished eating. She gives him the one he's been eyeballing the whole time. He opens the long- wrapped object, pulled from the table first. His little eyes light up holding his first Star Wars Lightsaber. She gives him another present on the table.

Kyle returns with a bucket full of coins and sets them on the table in front of him. Watching Camden getting plenty of fun gifts and gift cards, Kyle takes pictures on his smart phone. Afterwards, he reaches inside the bucket and counts out some coins to give to the kids. They all run off to play.

Molly, Jeff, Kyle, Tony and Gabriella enjoy conversing with each other while the kids are occupied.

By 3 P.M. The kids come running back to collect more coins, one last time. "The coin machines are broke." Kyle laughs sarcastically.

"We've been here long enough, let's pick up and go. Finn, call your parents, let them know to come pick you up… wait would you like to come over to play with Camden and later we could take you home?"

Finn shakes his little head in excitement, hoping to fly a drone for the first time.

Everyone is packed up and in route to the Hawthorne home. When they get there, birthday boy and his friend hurries and open the car door, running to the back of the SUV, waiting for presents. Gaby opens the hatch and hands Camden his toys.

Tony excited from seeing Gaby's smooth and luscious lips, doesn't waste any time kissing her again.

The boys start *ewwing.*

Kyle takes the leftover cake from Gabriella. Benjamin stands by his dad's side, mesmerized by the girl across the street from them. With long brown hair, extremely short-shorts on nice legs, walking next to a guy similar in size. Benjamin gauges him up and down without shame.

"Easy boy. Your thoughts are written all over your face." Tony instructs.

Kyle sees this too. "A yeah… Benji, later, I need to talk to you about some things. We'll just wait until the house calms down first, so don't get any plans to go out or anything."

Benjamin shakes his head like he's listening, but all senses are fixated on the subjects before him. Kyle slaps him on the shoulders.

Benjamin cocks his eyebrows back at him, "Dad, why'd you just hit me?"

"Boy I will do it again if you keep ignoring me. Tonight, we have some talking to do."

"Dad, I heard you. Why did you have to embarrass me outside like that?"

Kyle looks over at the house across the street, "Son, she isn't paying you any attention. She's already inside. From the looks of it, she has a boyfriend."

Benjamin wasn't concerned about her having a boyfriend. He lusted over them both in different ways.

Tony and Gabriella make their way back to the guest bedroom before he drives back to San Diego.

Kyle, Camden and Finn, convey the drone out of the box, at the kitchen counter space, preparing it for flight. Benjamin mopes upstairs alone.

Kyle takes the boys out back to try out the 74-Z Speeder Bike Drone. The air is gentle with little to no wind blowing. They go through the tennis court gate. Kyle is first to try it out, making sure it works properly.

Slowly hovering at chest range, the drone rider lifts over their heads, carrying out the mission past the enchained fencing of the green top. About to break barrier, Kyle gives it a lateral raise, paralleling the wall, climbing to the top. The Clone Trooper on the bike takes a U-dive aiming for surface, then casts away gently past their knees, soaring off to the other side.

Anthony comes out to the tennis court wanting to fly the drone before heading to San Diego.

"Wanna see how it works?" Kyle asks.

"No daddy, it's my turn." Camden cries.

"Cammy you will get plenty of time with your drone, let's give your uncle a chance at it, he's leaving soon."

Disappointment is written all over Camden's face when Kyle brings the drone back and hands over the controller to someone besides him.

Anthony takes the drone in his hands and gets it up and flying for a short two minutes, before giving over to his little nephew. Watching Camden's eyes light up, is more important than playing with the toy.

From inside the house, Benjamin observes out his bedroom window, the girl with silky long brown hair moving items into the house. He contemplates the day he would meet eye to eye with her.

Also, out the window he sees his uncle Tony walking out to his burnt orange Dodge Ram with his overthrown rugged backpack on. Anthony backs up his truck and goes away.

Kyle's back inside the house now. The young boys are having fun with the drone rider outside still. He's walks up the stairs and goes over to Benjamin's bedroom door knocking.

This startles Benjamin. "Yes?" He panics.

"Can I come in and talk to you?"

"Sure dad."

Kyle opens the door and finds Benjamin at the window. "Son, can we sit and talk a bit?"

Benjamin looks busted for doing something he doesn't even know about yet. Kyle feels the energy shift. Benjamin sits on the corner of his bed, attentively, ready to listen.

"Yeah dad?"

"I'm just gonna jump straight into this." Kyle lays down Benjamin's progress report on the bed for him to see.

Kyle goes on to say, "You went from making all A's to barely C's…. And I mean barely passing. This means you are not trying at all in school. I know this has been very hard ever since your mom has been gone, but I love you and I don't want this to go on too long. I don't want you to suffer anymore."

"How am I suffering dad?"

"You might not see it, but I see it. Your grades… your attitude… Both have dropped. I am going to check into counseling for you, like it or not. I'm getting you help."

Benjamin tries to argue back on this topic but doesn't go very far before Kyle speaks up loud and clear. "You're going."

Benjamin just stares at his father with pupils dilated and nose holes slightly flared, not daring to say anything. Kyle breaks the silence by getting up and walking out the door with his son's progress report in hand. The door shuts behind him. The sky out the window falls grey with a heavy chance of rain.

CHAPTER
NINE

Traffic sucks! Why wasn't I thinking of this last month when I made the appointment?

High schoolers released from their last class, walking out the exit doors, are filling the school yard like lost zombies. Kyle sits in his car, wiggling off sciatic nerve pressure from sitting too long.

Clouds are building up in the sky. A cold front is blowing in from the Hawaiian tropics. The sun is out so there's no pressure putting on the roof of Kyle's convertible. The first possible chance of rain in May could be drizzling away lizard loungers under the marsh of pebbles. He barely feels the rain living in California, but the smell of it coming in brings him to remember the first time he met his wife. His reminiscences locking eyes with Angela, when she fell to her side in the pouring rain, during New York Fashion Week in September of 2001.

Kyle snaps out of his thoughts just as he hears cackles of a woman in a shiny white convertible like his, parked in front of him. She must be in her early forty's and snobbish, sarcastic, soprano charmer that's pissing him off fully deluxe.

Kyle shakes his head with ferocity in his eyes pondering out his breath, *poor woman, it's outrageous she will be indulging spaghetti dinner tonight, and doesn't even know if her husband will be there or not. Hmmm…wonder what take out restaurant she's ordering from?*

He directs his focus on her license plates with starving thoughts and finds a triple set of fours. He doesn't think too much on it as Benjamin walks over getting in the car.

About five to one, convertibles of some sort, are piled up every direction on Highland Avenue and Sunset Boulevard. His little black Mercedes was one of them, zipping in and out of traffic on the way to grievance therapy.

Arriving to an office building, Kyle and his son walk inside, passing a plaque on the wall of staff and floor levels to their offices. Normal Yates, Suite 300. They stand outside the elevators and wait for one to come down and take them up.

Normal Yates, a forensic psychiatrist, referred by a client of Kyle's in real estate. Kyle felt odd taking his law-abiding son to a forensic shrink, but for some reason, he trusted his client's advice on the matter.

Walking out from elegant class in a lift service, they walk down a long hallway, tasting the strongest scent of fresh cut jasmine from the plug-in vaporizers on the wall. Both Kyle and Benjamin fix their eyes on a rectangular sign in the distance. Yates Clinic it orates with a blue florescent light giving it a calming aura.

Inside the glass windows and through the sliding glass door is a very attractive and professional receptionist at her computer station. She gives Kyle an unswerving smile.

"I'm here with my son Benjamin for Dr. Yates, four o clock appointment."

"I will let Dr. Yates know you are here."

"Thanks." Kyle beams.

Kyle and Benjamin have a seat in one of the ten dark leather accent chairs in guest room. The magazines on the table are stacked neatly, collecting dust on them. Kyle and his son both pull out their phones, going straight to social media. They flip around on their screens for two minutes before a woman with black square frame glasses and rich layers of long blonde hair comes traipsing over to them.

First impression of her is middle to late thirties, height maybe a little over five feet tall, probably one hundred and twenty pounds. She's wearing, a black suit paint and jacket with a vibrant blue blouse under it. Her black leather high heels match her skyscraper confidence. She has a real captivating walk.

She reaches out to introduce herself. "I'm Dr. Normal Yates. You can call me Norma for short. Do you mind following me back to my room and we'll start?"

Kyle and Benjamin follow behind her strutting walk. She takes them through a small kitchenette, turns to them and offers up a coffee or soda.

She pulls out the drawer of flavor coffee cups and lets Kyle select a cup, then walks over to the refrigerator, opens it and shows Benjamin the selection. He takes a can of ginger ale. She comes back dynamically and points out an original flavor of coffee creams for Kyle's coffee. Once she has helped them, she decides to make one herself.

"Is your coffee alright?" She asks.

Kyle takes a sip. "Oh, it's delicious."

"Good. You know, you can't go wrong with vanilla. Let's proceed back to my room please."

She takes them into her twelve by twelve session room. Inside is a cream color sofa with end tables on one side of the room. On the other side is the psychiatrist's chair with just a decorative table next to it, all matching of course. On the walls are photos of various places she has travelled among the years, floor to ceiling shelves with books and live plants in a few places.

Dr. Normal Yates turns on a eucalyptus vaporizer that has a sounds of ocean waves, making the room very tranquil.

"So, I see you were referred to me by Dr. Fahrenheit." Dr. Normal conjectures.

"That's correct. How long have you and Dr. Fahrenheit worked together?"

"I've had my practice since 2012. I met Dr. Fahrenheit right after my clinical. He was my professor during my four years residency of psychiatry. He took me all the way to the point I'm making right now. Dr. Fahrenheit is well beyond his time."

"He certainly knew what he wanted when I sold him his house. He's just fabulous." Kyle infers.

Dr. Normal Yates smiles, keeping her thoughts inside her teeth. She gets into the session now.

"Do you go by Ben or Benjamin?"

"It's Benji." He challenges.

"Benji, let's start by me asking you a few questions. When you've answered, I want you to ask me the exact same questions back."

Benjamin seems lost a minute, trying to grasp the concept of this charade.

"What is your name?" Dr. Normal Yates encourages.

"I told you my name already."

"You did." She nods to Benjamin, giving him confidence to speak again.

Like dust on magazines, Benjamin just sits there in idly.

"Can you state your name again?" She requests.

He sighs, rolling his eyes. "It's Benji."

Doctor Normal Yates doesn't say anything, giving Benjamin a chance to parrot back the question. It's silent for nearly ten seconds. Kyle looks over at Benjamin. Dr. Yates keeps calm sitting straight up with pen and paper in her lap.

Benjamin pulls out his phone and gets on social media to break the silence.

"No. That is not what I asked you to do. Can you put the phone away please, and do what I asked you to do?" Dr. Normal Yates summons.

"This is stupid, dad. Why do I have to repeat myself when I already told her my name?"

Kyle raises his voice. "Do what she asks of you, right now."

Benjamin glares back malevolently at the psychiatrist, "its Benjamin."

"It's Normal and can you call me Dr. Norma for short?"

"Can you call me Benji for short?"

Dr. Yates gets him now. She has assessed his every movement, heard his tone, and watched his television show of *Uncomfortable to be here.*

Benjamin is no real threat to harming anybody, or himself.

She pauses dialog, documenting the last five minutes spent, evaluating Benjamin and his father. On her tablet, she jots down their mannerisms.

Kyle turns to his son, calmly speaking to him, "Benji, just follow her instructions so we can get some food soon. I know it's painful. I hope talking about what we've lost will help get our peace back."

Dr. Yates resumes therapy, "Benji, what is your age?"

"I am about to be fourteen next month. What's your age Dr. Norma?"

"I'm about to be forty-five in a few months. Benji, when is your last day of school?"

"It's the same day as my birthday. Dr. Norma, when is your last day of school?" Benjamin kind of chuckles.

Normal Yates chuckles with him, "2012. I'm still learning something new every day though. Benji, can you tell me the month and day of your birthday and tell me what you have learned so far?"

"June twelfth. I know that you and I are about the same. The more we talk, the more we both figure out who we are." Benjamin hints.

Dr. Yates pauses therapy to make a few more documentations. She looks at her wristwatch then starts writing under the previous notes then says, "Yes… that's very correct."

Benjamin Hawthorne   05/13/16

4:35 P.M. - Wearing a blue, grey and white plaid opened button shirt and white undershirt, greyish-blue jeans, red, yellow and white stripe belt, socks showing and checker loafers.

Wants to be called Benji. He appears to be uptight, a bit sarcastic.

4:44 P.M. - Very smart kid. Benji's father Kyle convinces him to act differently. Benji has taken a slightly relaxed composure. Benji's last day of school is on his fourteenth birthday, 06/12/16.

Dr. Yates takes out her phone to see what day that falls under. She notices that June twelfth isn't on a school calendar day. She looks up from her phone calendar, speaking to Benjamin, "You do realize your birthday falls on a Sunday."

Benjamin knew right away, he couldn't pull any greener fabric over her head, as she sits on her phone close and connected.

A rush of emotions starts travelling through his mind, his fingertips, hooking him at the chest. His breathing speeds up. Double tapping, a sounds of a bass drumbeat echoes in his mind space as his heart's pulsates adrenaline, building a wall around a line of abandonment. The room dims. A tunnel forms. Benjamin reaches the end of this long empty passage in his sights, and its Dr. Yates he sees dolling up her hair, self-confiding to herself, really trying to upset him with mean, ugly, and deceiving cackles.

The doctor's cell phone rings from her hand as her other had been writing notes. Benjamin remains in a stupor.

Dr. Yates bends her head down, looking at her phone with her normal set of eyes, squinting at the caller id. The screen reads, *unknown number.* She silences her phone. It rings again with the same unknown number written on the screen. Finding it a bit odd, she excuses herself from the room, answering to the call.

"Dr. Yates speaking."

"Are you feeding him ice cream? Treat my Benny boy. Tell him to wait for his uncle, his mother's hanging her heels up. Write it. Write it now." The unknown caller had raised every bump on Dr. Yates forearm, then dropped the call.

Apprehensively, Dr. Yates queries, "Who is this?"

The call goes dead silent. Dr. Yates looks at the phone trying to gather clues to who that was, and how he got her number. The forensics side of her psychology was coming out.

Dr. Yates jumps back into the session, not apologizing for taking the phone call. She is shaken up a bit, yet jumps straight back into asking questions.

Kyle and Benjamin are somewhat wondering when they are going to finish therapy, so they can go eat.

Finally, a demeanor less than confidant seeps through Dr. Normal Yates structure and tone of voice, "Benji, did anyone ever call you Benny boy?"

Benjamin hesitates to answer but gives away, "Why?"

Dr. Yates is flushed in the face proceeding to speak, "When my phone rang earlier, I thought I had my ringer off like I always do during appointments. Nevertheless, it rang. Something told me to answer. The person on the other end gave me chills. He had a British accent telling me to treat you Benji and to wait for his uncle. I don't know what he was talking about. Could he be talking about you Benji? But wait for his uncle… what uncle? How many uncles do you have?"

"I have two, Uncle Kenny and Kevin."

Kyle blurts out, "those are my brothers, don't forget about your mother's half-brother Uncle Tony."

"Oh yeah, I hardly ever see him, almost forgot."

Kyle's astonishment leads him to admit, "This is totally bizarre. Last month, when we got word of what happened to Angela, we were all standing there sobbing and Benji's phone went crazy ringing. You remember that Benji?"

Benjamin nods his head yes.

Kyle checks his phone for time, 4:50 P.M. He proceeds, "We got that call right after we received the news on my wife's whereabouts, and it was around 4:44 P.M. That's the time she was struck by an eighteen-wheeler. Since her death, every time I see that number, it's like something odd happens. Maybe she is trying to speak to us?"

"That's exactly the time I jotted down these notes. Look."

Kyle looks at the time in sort of disbelief, "do you have another client named Ben?"

"No, I don't actually, that's why this is weird, and it was like she was in the room the whole time we were just getting to know each other. I mean, I'm a psychiatrist. I want you to feel comfortable talking to me, so getting to know each other is how this works."

"Kyle, when you received that call last month, what did your gut tell you?"

He really thinks on his emotions for a second, "You know, I thought he got the wrong number. He put me on edge, I just found out about my wife's death."

"Are you calm now?" Dr. Yates inquires.

"Yeah." Kyle sighs.

"I've taken note of everything needed for today. I would like to see you once a week until further notice. I think in time we can adjust to progress. Will that work for you?"

Kyle and his son look at each other in acceptance.

Dr. Normal Yates opens her calendar book, "What day next week works for you both?"

"You got a Thursday, 5.P.M?"

"Actually, I do. You're my last appointment then."

The three sat in Dr. Normal Yates therapy room, collecting their thoughts before Kyle and Benjamin leave to go home. The sound of ocean waves along with the scent of eucalyptus leave them feeling tranquil.

They exit the office hungry and agree to Italian food at the pier, after having a draining session.

CHAPTER
TEN

Opening his crusty eyes, he scowls at the metal mirror frame hanging on his bedroom wall, as if it was an oven reflecting stinging sunrays directly at his nose. Worn out from all that's happened in one months' time doesn't exactly stir up a Saturday morning cartoon and cereal kind of day. Lifting his heavy hand straight up to the catalyst, he gives himself the finger.

"Why am I up at 7 A. M? Why can't school just be over already?"

He reaches for his cell phone on the night stand.

Of course, it's not where he expected it to be. Vaulting out of bed in solid red boxers, trying to hide himself had put a high alert on his third leg. Grabbing his life line and darting back for bed, he jumps as high as possible landing flat on his back. A plush top memory foam mattress cradles him in support of his efforts.

Taking heaping breaths of air falling from fan blades didn't open his eyes like Facebook is currently doing.

Scrolling around on his phone, he runs across Ethan Rainy's tedious skateboarding maneuvers at Venice Beach Skate Park. Twenty-seven photos and a video, Ethan's remarkable in every one.

Suddenly, Benjamin notices his brother getting online.

Benjamin quickly gets off Facebook, as he doesn't feel like having conversations at the moment.

Thirty minutes of laying on his bed was long enough. His eyes are feeling strains and his feet are starting to itch.

He staggers out of bed anxious to relieve his past due bladder.

Benjamin finds Chips Ahoy laying on his bed pillow at the bottom of the staircase. He walks right past the white ball of fur not saying anything.

This little Maltese doesn't let him get away without following right behind extremely responsive to life.

In the kitchen Benjamin breaks his fast pouring a bowl of cereal at the bar. Chips Ahoy sits beside him begging attention.

At this point Chips would do anything to get some love and attention for from humans.

Camden enters the kitchen with his Star Wars Drone in hand. "Want to go the park and fly with me?"

"I'm not in the mood for the park right now. Let's just take it out front for a while." Benjamin said as milk dribbled out of his mouth.

Camden drags a chair over to get a bowl out of the cupboard. Benjamin drinks his cereal bowl empty, while his little brother struggles to pour the milk.

The task of eating breakfast is over. Camden runs upstairs, throwing on play clothes. Benjamin looking at himself in his mother's long swivel vanity mirror. He's dressed in a short sleeve's plaid, button up shirt along with standard blue shorts.

Outside the front door, excess rain water falls from thick blades of grass onto the earth composure from a fly by night storm. The rising sun causes a dirty face to freckle. All those rain clouds from yesterday are dancing over the Mojave Desert by this point.

Both their feet are wet from slide stepping through untrimmed patches of green and onto the drive. Camden lays his prized possession down, getting ready for launch. The wind is quiet, barely blowing his young shaggy top around.

Benjamin stands by impassively.

Ascending from concrete level, Camden hovers the drone slow and steadily rises it two feet over their heads. The 74-Z drone rider stays put in one place until it fully retrieves a make-believe Star Wars mission.

A beautiful monarch dancing in the distance becomes number one on the hit list. Tilting the controller while pressing the switches, Camden maneuvers the drone trying to catch the butterfly.

Orange and black wings sail the black body of a gorgeous butterfly away in the breeze, following the next scent of lemongrass to light up its way.

A big nasty plastic object taps into the wing of beauty. Taken off course the butterfly gently releases grace amongst propellers of something unreal to its nature.

Like a drunkard, the butterfly zigzags across the sky, while the drone spins out of control and falls, landing almost on the heads of the boy and girl across the way from theirs.

"Crap." Camden stammered.

"Yeah crap. Looks like you need to go over and get your drone." Benjamin spits out in nervousness, in a loud mouth ego.

"Come with me, I don't know them." Camden quarreled.

"I don't either." Benjamin ended.

What's so scary about those two over there? Could it be the girl who has long pulled back brunette hair, holding a football like a Giants Receiver, standing neck and neck to the boy next to her?

There's a mystery radiating polar opposites through their skin and falls at the waistline like their unashamed athletic shorts, yet so matching.

The boy picks the drone flyer up and starts walking over to them. The girl follows his steps.

Benjamin feels the attraction getting closer. Her walk, neither feminine nor masculine has him drawn like a magnet. At one point he thought he caught a glimpse of his mother walking down a catwalk, except his mom wasn't a brunette.

Within ten feet of Benjamin and Camden, and still walking, the boy examines the toy, speaking in complete flamboyance, "This is too sweet, I always wanted to fly one."

Directly in Benjamin's face the boy emits, "Do you mind?" Asked in a fascinating, familiar accent in such assurance.

Taking Benjamin totally off-guard Benjamin asks, "Do you mind what?"

"Your drone silly?" The boy shifts his hips side to side like Shakira.

"Ask my brother… it's his." Benjamin has never felt so vulnerable, given his little brother that much rule over his life.

Camden looks to his brother for cue to talk. Benjamin decides not to act vulnerable and takes back authority.

"First off, is that your house across the street or is it hers… and what are your names?" Benjamin looked so confused demanding all this at once.

"Yeah we just moved in last week. I'm Venom by the way." He sassed.

"I'm Viper, his twin." She crafts out in a militant voice.

Trying to comprehend complete role switches, Benjamin takes away the drone from Venom, then takes a step back.

In disbelief, he tries to gain focus of what his eyesight is trying to report.

"Is this how you'd normally treat someone you've just meet?" Viper quizzed.

Camden finally speaks out, "They're nice people Benji, why are you being mean?" Camden tugged the drone away from his brother.

"Am I being mean Camden?" Benjamin steps into the circle, realizing there is no harm and the confusion he felt was all his.

"Camden... interesting city boy name. We're from Cambridge. Nearby the River Camb, if you know where that is. We were like an hour and fifteen northeast of London. Great to know we still have a Camden a hop, skip, and jump away from our lily pad." Venom chorused.

"What are you like, toads?" Benjamin smirked off.

The four of them finally broke the ice and threw off the snow cold behavior, on this beautiful, almost summer day. The awkwardness was off.

Starting over, "I'm Benji and I didn't mean to be so difficult... So, you wanna try it out." He smiled

"Are you going to show me how to use it?" Venom flirts.

"Are you really not boy enough to figure how the controllers work?" Benjamin teased.

Letting down a couple of walls, Benjamin notices he feels something he never felt before. As he lifts the drone off the ground and into the sky, he can't stop smiling at his new friends, mainly to see if they're taking note of how to fly this drone. But it's Venom's voice he can't seem to rub out of his mind.

Venom seems just as happy watching Benjamin fly something he probably wouldn't even own. His nose is shaded red from the sun.

Inside the house, Gabriella is freshly bathed with her hair and makeup done up perfectly. Rummaging through Angela's cookbooks, she has Anthony on Facetime with her planning to make what sounds the best.

"So... Sloppy Turkey on a Bun or Nadine's Authentic Chicken Enchiladas?" Gabriella quizzed Anthony with effortless, full body and swaying hair.

Anthony laughs, "You mean, you don't have your own chicken enchilada recipe?"

"I'm twenty-two, not fifty-two. You think because I'm Mexican, I got skills with enchiladas mi amore?" She winked out.

"No dear, I thought every woman had her own ways of cooking and just looked through cookbooks for inspiration." He played off ignorant.

They stop a while, slowly taking in breaths of air. She gets a sudden whiff of lavender.

He walks around in his own kitchen showing it off to her.

Gabriella is excited to see his home. She smiles, happy to learn something new about him.

"So, which is it? What do you magically want me to make and send to you?" She teased.

"I'm so starved, make both of them." He said puffing out with a fuzzy face and soul patch.

"Tony?!" Her eyes dances back and forth with his on screen.

"I gotta let you go, I'm getting another call." Anthony stated.

Rolling her eyes, "Really? You're not going to answer which one. –O'Kay call me back." They end the call on Facetime and suddenly the house becomes quiet.

A colorless silence bothers Chips Ahoy off his bed pillow to inspecting the current energy.

Gabriella takes an ice cold, long neck Coke bottle from the refrigerator, sits down at the bar drooling over many recipes. She takes a few swigs, flips a few pages, searching for something very distinctive to chow down on.

Page after page, and not one drop of inspiration she felt, but a sudden urge of urination. She drifts off to the bathroom.

Walking to the closest toilet wasn't far. She has a flashback of Angela on the way there, fixing her eyes to a ceiling fan lightly layered with dust.

It was her last memory of Angela, even though her back was at her while she was cleaning that fan. As soon as the memory came, it left away in a thought, *Monday, I will add ceiling fans to my list of cleaning.*

Drying her hands on a hanging towel, she exits the bathroom walking over to the front of the house and looks out window. She notices the boys are doing great playing with the new kids and flying the Star Wars Drone, she bought Camden.

Facetime rings in her hand. Pulling the screen up to her eyes she answers with a look of bliss.

"Did you miss me?" Asked Tony as he relaxed outside on a lounge chair.

"Isn't a little early to be drinking?" Gaby probes.

"Early? It's a quarter 'til noon. Early for me is like thirty minutes after waking up." He snickers out.

Both are grinning like teenagers in puppy love. Gaby saunters back into the kitchen, pops the socket out on her phone, teasing Tony with a view of her whole body as she sits down on the barstool, legs sprawled and throws back her glass bottle of Coke with masculine energy.

"Does that Coke have some rum inside it?" Tony jokes, as he tries to show off his chugging abilities.

She waves the bottle over the tops of her breasts enticing Tony, then flirts back, "I'm not telling. You can come see for yourself when you get your sexy butt over here and make some chicken enchilada tacos with me."

"What the hell is that? A soft thingy in a shell." Tony mystified.

"Well kinda… I thought about a crunchy chicken enchilada, so really I'm gonna take this recipe I see here, crush up some tortilla chips, layer it down on top of the enchiladas, then right as I pull it out of the oven, top it with shredded lettuce, tomatoes, sour cream and olives."

Tony's mouth is watering with inspiration to get in his truck and go. "Damn that sounds good. Are you making at least two plates for me, and what time are you cooking?"

"Two plates? I'm cooking for a family with growing boys. If you're serious about wanting me to cook extra though, I'll make thirty enchiladas and call it a day."

"What time?" Tony asks.

"I need to run to store and get a few things so most likely around 6pm." She replied.

"Are you driving over here? I don't like surprises." She inquires.

"I don't know… I guess you will have to find out, talk to you soon." Tony makes the O-kay gesture with his hand as he disconnects.

Trudging with his chest puffed out, he enters his three-bedroom, 1975 rustic dynasty with creamy white appliances made perfect for instant oatmeal in the mornings.

He grabs a few outfits and tosses them into his orange duffle bag that's seen better days.

Leaping out of her chair, Gaby goes into her room in search of a new shirt to wear. Pulling her cotton t-shirt over her head, she dances around in a hurry now in her lacey black bra and cut off white jean shorts, showing off her fair mocha skin.

Slipping on her pretty pink top, she fastens up her buttons hurriedly, grabs her purse and is out the door.

Chapter ELEVEN

"We've been out here long enough, let's go inside and see if Gaby will make us something to eat. I'm hungry." Camden whines.

"Gaby isn't home. She rolled out of the driveway forty-five minutes ago."

Benjamin stretches his body, pushing his arms towards the sky almost like he's trying to reach for Heaven.

It's obvious that Venom and Viper want to be invited for lunch by the way they linger around waiting for an invitation.

"You two seem pretty cool… later you guys wanna come over for tennis or swimming?" Benjamin throws out an offer.

"Viper talk to mum, will ya? You know how she is about going over to people's house she hasn't met yet." Venom displays a wiggly hip twist.

"Yeah…Yeah. For Frank's sake, what time shall we turn up?" Viper exaggerated a sneeze, even remnants of pollen and grey skies in England couldn't harbor.

"Turnip?" Benjamin confusedly asked while Camden giggled.

"You know… come back around? What time?" Venom asked. He oozed out pizazz in his pretty petite-boy hips shake.

"Oh like 6:30 P.M. or 7 P.M." Benjamin conveyed back with a smile.

The twins break the circle going to see who can make it home first.

Benjamin and Camden go home anxious to eat lunch.

Inside the house the boys use the bathroom and eventually meet up in the dining area. Benjamin offers a quick easy slap of peanut butter on enriched white whole grain bread. Camden offers to get them both a tall glass of milk.

After eating peanut butter and jelly sandwiches they hustle upstairs to the theatre room to hide away from the wavering afternoon sun.

They surrender their minds to The Call of Duty and comfortably move their controllers around in the dark room.

The sounds of explosions ricochet across room, as the soldier's lives end in gory deaths across the screen.

Benjamin and Camden are so sucked into the game they lose all sense of time. One of the warriors jolts a spear of some sort in the head of Camden's soldier.

Gaby opens the house front door and walks inside carrying groceries of tonight's dinner arrangements. She rushes inside and drops the plastic bags on the countertop getting the pinch off her fingers. Flushing swollen lines and indentions are amongst the bends of her fingers as she shakes out pain from the heaviness of the ingredients. Standing in place, taking out her ponytail and pulling it back tighter, she proceeds on, getting everything ready to make the enchiladas.

Taking out two mixing bowls and three rectangular baking pans, Gaby sets them aside. An eerie calmness exists around her. The tapping and clinging of aluminum bowls hitting the countertops are the only sounds heard.

Gaby wonders the whereabouts of Benjamin and Camden.

Momentarily she steals a break. Thoughts of Tony invade her mind as she walks to the theatre to check on the boys.

Downstairs in the kitchen, she washes her hands before starting to prepare her delightful dish of Mexican food.

Meanwhile in West Covina, nearly forty miles away from home, Kyle is checking out a couple of properties in a subdivision where concrete foundation was poured in the 1970's. Flipping and selling houses is another avenue in real estate, Kyle grabs income from.

Right off I-10 and South Azusa Avenue, Kyle is with his contractor Derick, examining a 4 bedroom, 2 full baths, approximate 1500 square feet property.

They get a glimpse of the shingles on the roof walking up to the front door. Obvious updates are needed straight off the top.

The contractor is what you would call a hippie man in his early fifty's. Construction has been carried deep inside his jean pockets ever since he was old enough to help his father yank out filthy carpet tack strips.

Derick Nelson's face appears much like a scary leprechaun, you'd see in classic horror movies, yet he's harmless.

His height and weight, 5'9 and one hundred and fifty pounds, with long stringy, light auburn hair he wears in man bun.

He always looks like he is got something mischievous going on with his dreamy eyes and carries a vaporized smoking device to smoke when he goes deep into thoughts.

The whites of his eyes become red from the type of smoke he uses and it gives him a peachy smile to perform his carpenter jobs.

Derick does a lot of work for Kyle. His price is great as a contractor. He is also punctual about getting all of Kyle's houses flipped and ready for the market.

Both men walk inside the old garrison style of house.

Kyle rolls up the sleeves to his neatly-pressed, blue button-up shirt, then starts parting the dust particles from the air with his hands.

He utters out, "The electricity has been off way too long. It smells like rotten eggs and cat piss that's saturated into the carpet."

"Yeah, that happens when the electric has been off a while." Derick is wearing a white cotton shirt and jeans with a tool belt around his waist, walking alongside of Kyle.

Kyle examines the living area then says out loud to Derick, "Rip out the carpet and replace it with wood or tile… add that to the list."

Derick moves into the bathroom and sees how rusted the faucet is.

It wasn't one of those pretty, state of art, nickel finishing, and swan neck fixtures. This is the basic water spout. It even fell off the base and into the filthy sink when he touched it.

Kyle walks into the bathroom with him.

Derick laughs out, "These scummy bastards must have been drinking from this fountain… Did the previous owners rush to get out of here or what?"

Both men laugh as they continue walking towards the other bathrooms, checking out the plumbing on everything.

Every bathroom is in need of updating: shower tiles, new toilets, fresh paint and possibly some sort of elegant vanity mirror.

They stand in the hallway looking up at the attic trap. Kyle pulls the string that lowers the legs from the ceiling and is first to climb up into a chilly dark space.

Inside the attic Kyle stands pulling out a flashlight from his pant pocket.

Derick climbs up after him.

A cold breeze brushes across Kyle's shoulders, and slithers down his limbs and into his toes.

Right away he gets a strong notion of Angela that raises every hair on his body. Kyle clasps onto a wooden beam in the attic. A feeling of butterflies escapes the roof fans. Suddenly, the fan blades stop spinning.

Derick crawls into the attic with Kyle saying, "Do you smell that? What is it?" He spits out a bitter taste from the dust in his mouth.

"Yeah, I do. I don't know man… I felt its presence too, whatever it was." Trying not to get grass ridden froggy about it, Kyle swivels his head looking around before jumping over to signs of shredded ventilation tubing.

He taps his hand against the snagged kaput foiled pipe as he aims his flashlight walking across an attic beam trying not to fall through the ceiling.

"Looks like there was a nest of rats once living in these pipes and insulation. Derick, will you add this to the repair list?" Kyle discloses as he holds onto a paper-thin air tubes in the attic.

"This house must be priced dirt cheap?" Derick coughs and wipes around the edges of his light auburn mustache.

The men gather as much information as they can to make a decision on purchasing the house then leave and drive over to the next house for evaluation.

Meanwhile, two hours south of Los Angeles, on Interstate-five, Tony is driving seventy-five miles per hour with a Camel Turkish Blend cigarette hanging from his mouth.

More time passes by on the drive over to Los Angles.

He lights up his third cigarette, holding it out the truck door window, trying not to let smoky grey fumes inside, as if that ever works.

Cigarette smoke attaches itself to everything, and leaves an odor that can take days ridding off. Gaby doesn't like smokers, but knows he already smokes.

He burns down this cigarette like paper on fire, and increases speed on San Diego Freeway.

Tony gets a glimpse of Gaby trying to hug him at the door, before his arrival. Her hands are covered in shredded chicken as he's trying to thrust off her jovial embraces. Escaping, he dashes into the kitchen and to the sink to wash off stale cigarettes from his hands and upper lip area.

Tony shifts his focus back on the road. He's in Los Angeles now and almost to Kyle's house.

At the Hawthorne house, Gaby scrapes all that remains from the enchilada mixture into last flour tortilla and rolls it up. Exactly thirty enchiladas are done. Ten in each pan. She places all three into the convection oven.

Boredom sets in as Gaby awaits. She hangs out on Facebook thumbing around. Straight away she notices Anthony posted a picture of his foot on the gas petal, looking all mysterious in his truck with the caption, "I'm all in."

She bursts into a cackle wondering what century he's from. The silliness she sees in his photo gives her smile. She realizes how cute Tony really is.

The clock on her phone reads, 5:15 P.M. as she walks over to check how the enchiladas are doing. Poking them in the trays, she considers them perfect.

Taking all three pans out of the over, she sits them on pot holders, then goes to get the toppings for the chipy taco part of it.

A loud bang on the door happens a few times then stops.

Gaby puts on a smile and runs to the door excited.

Tony starts sniffing out his hands to see how bad they reek of smoke, then places a mint in his mouth.

Gaby opens the door bashfully.

"Hey…" She hides behind the door showing off her long brown hair and eyes with a huge amorous smile.

It had only been a week since he last caught her eyes blowing red cinnamon hearts at him. Tony bust through the door, and rescues Gaby off her feet. She wraps her legs around him and connected, they twirl in a circle.

Tony stops spinning and kisses her.

She slides off him and her hands run down his prickly unshaven face.

"Smells good in here Gaby!" Tony exclaimed with hungry eyes, and raspy voice.

"Thanks… You drove fast to get here." She starts to walk back into the kitchen as he follows alongside of her.

"Ah… I drove the listed speed limit most of the way. It's only a little over two hours from San Diego." Tony articulates.

Tony's at the kitchen sink lathering up his hands with some pink flowering suds, organic bar in a dish. He shakes most of the water off him and taps his hands dry onto his jeans.

Kyle rolls into his driveway at 5:47 P.M. Walking through the front door, he's pulled straight into the kitchen from the tantalizing smell of tacos. Entering the kitchen, he finds Tony reaching for plates inside the cupboard.

"Tony… Tony, my man. Welcome back." Kyle winks at him as he finds a place on the marble slab to set his briefcase down.

"Yeah, I just couldn't turn down a good woman's cooking, when she offered, you know." Tony popped back.

"Really, is that what it is?" Kyle observed.

The two men use sarcasm as Tony and Gaby's attraction is thick in the air. Gaby continues prepping for dinner, smiling and shaking her head.

Tony carries plates to the table with a smile and pep in his steps.

"So… is it ready? I'm famished… Are the boys upstairs?" Kyle asks.

Gaby nods her head yes to both.

Kyle settles into his house and goes off looking for his boys.

Within twenty minutes everybody is gathered at the table, crunching into every bite taken of taco enchiladas on a fantastic Saturday night in May.

Every time Gaby takes a bite, she digs her fork into another string of cheesy tortilla strips hidden under lettuce.

She watches Tony's expressions at supper tonight. He smacks and licks cheese off his chin and bottom lip. She scans the rest of the room sitting around the wooden round table. Everybody looks satisfied as they fill their bellies.

Camden breaks in with conversation after three bites are taken," Do you think Venom and Viper are on their way over to swim?"

Benjamin opens his mouth to answer but his father pulls the question, "Who are they?"

"They're the new neighbors across the street. The moved in last week." Benjamin smiled.

"Wait, so that was her brother, not her boyfriend and the girl you couldn't take your eyes from."

Tony picks cheese out of his teeth and recalls this incident last weekend when he was down, "Yeah… yeah, I saw that. Boy you couldn't take your eyes off her." He rolls his eyes, smutting up something and over exaggerating a deep barley chuckle.

Benjamin puffs up," I could take my eyes off them if I wanted to, I was just trying to figure out who they were." Benjamin buries his head into the last bite of enchiladas, looking for second helpings.

"There's a whole lot of them left on the stove if you're still hungry." Gaby states.

"So, they're twins. Are they around your age?" Kyle asks as he wipes his mouth with a napkin.

"Ahhhh, I don't think I should eat any more Gaby, we are supposed to swim in a while and dad, I think they are my age. I haven't asked them." Benjamin asks to be excused from the table. He walks off to the upstairs bathroom.

Kyle gets up, walking over to the sink and sets his plate down in it.

Camden leaves the table in awkwardness as he looks back at Gaby and Tony who are fixated on each other.

The clock on the wall reads 6:38 P.M. The doorbell rings. Gaby and Tony get out of their seat and start cleaning up the dishes to put the kitchen back together.

Kyle walks over to the door and opens it.

A boy and a girl who are matched in almost identical athletic attire stands at the door with very friendly faces, waiting on a greeting from Kyle.

"Is Benji and Cam home?" The male child speaks in a British accent.

"You must be Venom and Viper." Kyle glees whiles opening the door wider and inviting them inside.

Camden runs downstairs when he hears the twins at the door. Benjamin chases after his brother excited to hang out with his new friends.

At the bottom of the stairs Benjamin fist bumps Venom and Viper with dad and Camden onlooking.

"Glad you could turn up!" Benjamin exclaims.

Camden and his father just stand there observing Benjamin's interaction with the new kids.

"You alright mate?" Viper questions.

"Yeah, I'm happy you both could come over. We just finished up eating. Dad is it okay we go out back and hang out?" Holding back excitement in his tone but a shout roars through Benjamin's eyes.

"That's fine son." Kyle grins and walks away to his home office.

"So, tennis or swimming? Benjamin asked.

"Both, but first, may we get the grand tour of your cozy castle?" Venom pleads enthusiastically.

"Sure, follow me." Benjamin leads the way.

The four have a look around and end up in the movie theater as their last stop. Jumping into the theatre seats they all recline back just messing around.

Downstairs, Tony and Gaby walk out of the kitchen flipping off the lights on the way to the living room.

Kyle passes Tony and Gaby from his office with a parched mouth ready for a drink.

He re-flips the light switch in the kitchen and walks over to get a polished wine glass hanging on its stem from the under-mount cabinet rack.

The bottle of merlot he pours from only has half a glass. He grabs a new bottle; same brand, uncorks and gently pours giving it time to oxidize.

On the living room sofa, Gaby is laying on Tony's muscular chest.

Tony wraps Gaby in his arms.

Gaby has her feet propped up on the sofa and covered with a quilted blanket which was passed down from a couple generations in Angela's family.

Tony scrolls down a catalogue of Netflix films, giving Gaby a whole list to ponder about watching.

Suddenly, Tony and Gaby hear loud stomps from upstairs. They wait for the commotion to stop before watching a movie.

Meanwhile, all the children from upstairs fox-trot down the steps with racquets. Benjamin is carrying a bag of tennis balls in his hand. They exit the back door and go to the tennis court.

Outside the sun has vanished leaving a full moon in charge. A gentle breath of God caresses the children's faces as they tread down on green to the tennis court.

Inside the court Benjamin and Camden take the left side naturally; Venom and Viper go right taking some practice swings with their racquets.

The play a couple of warm up games, then start keeping score.

The tennis court lights finally come on and the moon umpires their game.

Back and forth the ball swiftly shoots across the net. The four are red faced and exhausted from playing an hours' worth.

Camden takes the last swing and calls the game over. The ball goes flying way out of bounds. "I'm done… I'm too hot to keep going."

Venom looks to his sister, "Yeah, we are exhausted as well."

The twins walk over and give the boys jumping high fives almost body bumping their lights out. Benjamin craving something cold and refreshing, asks the others, "Do you like ice-cream?"

"Who doesn't like ice-cream mate?" Viper adjusted her long brunette ponytail as her long legs carry out walking with the rest of the guys back up to the house.

Benjamin observes her from the back at the rose garden, by the pool.

Before opening the back door to the house Benjamin asks, "Do you like chocolate or vanilla… and I believe we have some kind of strawberry bars?"

"I want a strawberry bar." Camden replied.

"Shock me." Venom says.

"Yeah shock us." Viper pops off sarcastically, grinning at both Benji and Venom.

Benjamin flirts, "Wait out here and I will come back with something that will knock your socks off."

After some time, Benjamin comes back and passes everyone a Neapolitan ice-cream sandwich.

Ripping the wrapper off the bars, they each bite into the sandwiches getting black cookie dough on their fingers, cheeks and noses, totally having fun as kids.

"I need to wash hands before swimming Ben." Viper wipes her hands on the sides of her shorts.

"Yeah let's all go inside and change into bathing suits, wash up if you need." Benjamin says with a sorrowful expression on his face.

"You alright Benji?" Camden sniffles out as the four go inside the house and head towards the staircase.

Benjamin calmly turns around and explains, "Yeah, I'm alright. It's just… nobody's called me Ben since mom passed away."

"Aww Benji, I'm so sorry, I didn't know. What happened? Do you wanna talk about it?" Viper asked.

"Not really, it will only upset me right now, but she was killed a couple of months ago in a traffic accident." Benjamin takes off up the steps.

"Great one asshole." Venom utters.

Camden stands there in silence like he naturally does. He is hardly ever noticed, but at this time, Viper looks over to him and starts trying to communicate with him. She kneels down and gives Camden a hug to begin.

"How are you doing with this?" She sniffles and holds back her own tears.

"Well I miss my mom so much." Camden whimpers as he holds onto the beautifully shaped girl who radiates a sturdy strength like his dads.

Venom stands back watching his twin caress Camden's shoulders in a warm condolence, as he could feel a melting in his heart.

Outside that night, a cold wind came out of the arctic that barrelled through like waves, but that didn't seem to matter to the four playing in a heated pool.

It's like splash-town in the Hawthorne's pool. They each take turns throwing Camden around in the pool.

Meanwhile inside the house, Kyle is at work creating his real estate showings for his cliental tomorrow. At his desk he stands while stacking a list of printed MLS properties for sale and neatly places them on his desk.

On the sofa Gaby is nearly asleep, as her eyes rest heavy somewhere on the television. She lays comfortably against Tony's warm body in the original position she claimed two hours ago. The two are zoned out to a Netflix film they have on.

The doorbell rings.

Kyle stops what he's doing and walks over to the front door for the second time today. He opens the door to a couple of familiar faces.

A highly sophisticated man and woman in their mid-forty's, early fifty's, stand at the frame of the door with faces that look as if they are awkwardly smiling out, *"I know my kids are here and I know I will be staying over a while so open up and let us in."*

"Hello, we are the Gethin's from across the way. Are our children here?" Mr. Gethin articulates in the same posh British accent the twins speak.

Mrs. Gethin seems to be slightly younger than her husband. She has an average body type and is wearing a creamy blouse with airy blue skirt that accentuates her curves. Her medium brown hair falls at the tops of her shoulders. She is oddly off in contrast from the man at her side.

"Greetings to you as well, you've came to the right home. They're out back swimming." Kyle goes half way outside his house and shakes Mrs. Gethin's hand and next, Mr. Gethin's, before offering them inside for a drink.

Kyle pours from a previously opened bottle of red, into the first long-stem glass and offers it up to Mrs. Gethin.

Mr. Gethin says, "This is Darcy Marcy, my perfect little wife."

He grabs ahold of her face and smooches her, then goes on to say, "I'm Rueben. I'm also an anesthesiologist at the hospital. If you ever get a headache, Darcy can hand over the right pills. She is my wife and on my team of techs."

"It's so good to have neighbors nearby, who have kids too. So, you're an anesthesiologist…" Kyle expresses while cuddling the glass of wine next to his heart.

Rueben is six-foot-tall and slender, dressed in a maroon long sleeve button down tucked into his grey trousers, matching dark but short hair from Darcy's, "Yeah, I'm over at Cedars-Sinai Medical Center."

"Fantastic! I can imagine you stay busy being so close to Sunset Strip." Kyle opens a new bottle in front of his guest then pours himself one. He takes them on a walk over to the back door where all the children were outside in the pool.

"I'm on call there, work when needed." Rueben laughs out taking a sip of room temperature wine, as he and his wife follows Kyle out the door.

Crisp Los Angeles air hits their faces as miniscule amounts of pool chlorine seep into their nostrils. The three adults walk out to the pool area where the kids are playing Marco Polo.

Sudden whispering words come out of the twin's mouth as they see their parents. "Mum and dad are here, I guess we are about to get out and go home." Venom sighed.

"Possibly, yet I don't think so. Their glasses are filled to the top. We gotta bit." Viper sounds back under her breath and smirks while waving at them all.

Camden squints his eyes calling out, "Marco" as he walks down the side of the pool trying to catch a Polo.

Benjamin is at the farthest end of the pool, opposite side of Camden with a great exit view. He observes the body language and the intriguing accents of the twins at the sights of their parents. Viper takes a dive under water. The pool lights illuminate her well tone figure and smooth silky brown hair. Benjamin's heart speeds up the second he glances over at Venom, who catches him checking out his sister. That doesn't stop him from passing advances at Benjamin, who has just locked eyes and pleasing Venom back.

Kyle ignites the fireplace as Rueben and Darcy take a seat on the sofa. They smile about their children having found such beautiful company to at, while Kyle walks over and seats himself on lounge chair nearby.

"A quiet cozy arrangement you have here Kyle. I just love it." Darcy looks around breathing in all the fragrant flowers in the background.

Kyle postures up a bit looking around as well, yet he is looking for Angela with half a smile, "We've done a few changes here and there."

"Oh, so you're married… Where is she tonight?" Rueben asked.

"My wife Angela died a couple of months ago my friends. She was killed by injustice driving." Kyle proceeds to sip a little red wine with nothing inspiring to say.

The whole atmosphere shifts.

Aftershock taps on their noses bringing tears to everybody's eyes ducts.

"How'd it happen if I may ask?" Rueben politely questioned.

"Texting and driving did it." Holding back tears from his new friends, Kyle leans back in chair and relaxes.

Rueben gets a little furious then says, "I cannot tell you how many times

I've been on shift, rushing into the emergency room for a patient who was hanging by snippets of veins and limbs, barely mobile and unconscious all because of texting and driving. This is a common plague as it happens more than you think."

Kyle tilts his head down sulking and thinking how to make texting and driving stop. His mind spins from overthinking.

Darcy angers and says, "Even though we hardly see each other at work Rueben, I deal with it too in the operating rooms, on my shifts. Having to scrub up, getting all the instruments laid on the table for the surgeons. There is a wrong focus to be said here… People are risking their lives texting a small sentence like, *I am on my way…* I mean come on, can't those texts wait for Christ sake."

"You know, Angela was a fashion model when I met her. She was stunning. Didn't miss a beat on the New York runways. Softly spoken, she wasn't like those other models, catty for catwalks. I married her because I saw her inner beauty as well as her modeling ways. I knew one day if I had a family with her, she would be there for me and our kids and she was. When she got older and we had the boys she stopped modeling and started living out her true calling which was writing. She was always writing. Everything, you name it. Having a grocery list came handy you know. She wanted to make an impact on our society and better the world. All the new technology we have… she wanted to save lives on the road. She started researching all the cities and states and death tolls from distracted driving, and realized social media was mostly responsible, yet if she could somehow educate people all over the world daily with, Online Now she would forever feel satisfied in her legacy. She was on the way to a writer's conference in Henderson to speak about this when she became the test subject. That was the fate of my beauty queen." Kyle releases all this information feeling much better.

"Would anyone like another glass of wine?" Kyle disengages trying to defuse this conversation any more than it had to go.

Rueben and Darcy agree to a fresh glass of wine as he gets out of his chair and goes into his home and grabs a whole new bottle of red.

Chapter
TWELVE

A lamp post in the front yard flickers to laughter of three newly acquainted adults in the backyard of the Hawthorne property.

Reflections of swimming pool water and lights luster on The Gethin's and Kyle's faces while they tip back the few remaining droplets of wine.

Camden sits next to his father in another lounge chair, in a towel wrapped at the waist like a stubborn bull not moving or saying anything.

Chips Ahoy switches from Kyles chair to Camden's trying to alleviate the tears about to fall down his little face. Camden is cold but finally says, "I've been it fifteen times." He whimpers.

Chips Ahoy shivers and howls a small cry as if he could wipe away Camden's pain with his paws.

Kyle looks over at the Gethin's, smiling and says, "Kids these days."

Kyle stretches over to Camden disrupting anymore splutters, "Is that a reason to give up? Camden you know when I was boy, I solved every problem on my own. I feared my parents would make me go to bed, when instead I really wanted to play with my friends."

Darcy interrupts, "So… You are the one and only, Camden. You know… where I come from there is a Camden, forty-five minutes from my old town of Cambridge. You wouldn't happen to be named after the town of Camden… or would you?" She smiles at him showing him a bit off her nurturing side.

Camden's face starts to glow as he forgets the pity he felt inside. Her fascinating British accent helped too. Darcy quickly became a mother figure to him.

Kyle quickly tells the story of how Camden was conceived. "Summer of 2007, I believe. Angela and I wanted to take our very first overseas trip together. Benji was like six years old, stayed with his grampy in Brooklyn late August. Angela and I wanted to have an adventure alone together. She picked out England of all places. Stayed in London most of the time. On the fifth night of our stay we ventured out to the city of Camden."

Rueben breaks into a short history lesson, "Did you know that Camden is actually a town. It would need to have a cathedral for it to be a city. London has St. Paul's Cathedral, secondary in size to Peterborough Cathedral where King Henry 8th, Katharine of Aragon was buried." Rueben informs.

Parched mouth and lips, Kyle lets Rueben's words seep in a second, "I see now. That's good to know… so on we go into the fifth night of our stay, we end up in Camden town, danced the night away at a nightclub, got belligerently drunk, and like a full-grown bunny, my wife's belly started hopping. Nine months later we had our little Ca-mee-dee."

"Is that how it happened?" Rueben chuckled out.

"Sort of… Kinda, so what's your story back home?" Kyle winks, taking in the merriment.

Rueben and Darcy look at each other in debate of who would tell the story and he goes for it, "Yeah… we met in like 2000, I think it was. Is that right darling?" Rueben hides a guilty face with his hand, covering up his mouth.

Reuben proceeds on, "That was so long ago, it seems like yesterday, but can't be pulled from my memory all the sudden."

Darcy smiles out a fake laugh, "Smooth one butternut squash. The year 2000… Is correct for five hundred dollars, Alex?"

Rueben goes on, "Right… we seemed to be making passes for each other at Addenbrooks. I would laugh inside, watching her pace back in forth right before my very eyes, so I saved her the trouble, approached her, and asked her to tea. She said yes then and yes again, the day I asked her to marry me. We had the twins August 8th, 2002." He pauses to notices Kyle astonished face about to ask something.

"Your twins have great personalities. What possessed you to name them Venom and Viper?" Kyle puzzled.

"What, you don't like the venom of a viper Kyle? We became pregnant quickly… not expectant until October, they came two months earlier. They came quickly. Looking over their long squirmy bodies, we thought Venom and Viper was different and stood out. We also took in consideration the amount of anesthetics Rueben deals with daily." Darcy said sarcastically.

"Those are totally cool names. Really great names you gave them considering the facts and just as good as how Camden came along. Benjamin was named after my father." Kyle said and realizes how late it was getting.

Kyle yawns looking at his wristwatch, Mr. and Mrs. Gethin it's my bedtime… I have a busy day tomorrow, it's been great meeting you and I hope we can all get together another night soon."

"No worries Kyle, it's proper late for us as well. Maybe you would like a roast dinner on a Sunday at our place?" Rueben asked.

"Venom and Vip… come on darlings, let's go home now." Darcy called out.

Kyle answered back, "The kids and I would like that as long as we could bring with us our house mom —housekeeper, Gaby.

Benjamin and the twins get out of the pool grabbing towels to dry off with. Venom and Viper throw on t-shirts and continue on with wet shorts, walking to where their parents are.

Kyle and Camden direct everyone to the front door while saying their farewells.

The next morning Kyle is dressed in a dark blue business suit, carrying a briefcase in hand. He finds Gaby and Tony in the kitchen.

"Good morning." Kyle smiles while grabbing his coffee and a banana for his breakfast to go, escaping two passionate doves whipping something up.

Kyle leaves the house for work at 8:15 A.M.

Gaby pulls waffles off from the iron and sets them on plates. She covers the hot waffles full of strawberries, then carries them over to the table with syrup in her hand like a waitress would.

Tony is sitting at the table, dressed for the day, drinking black coffee.

"Beautiful, these waffles look so good. It's been a while since I've been catered to this way." Tony dared to open up his past history.

"Are you about to tell me about all your ex's now?" Gaby pours syrup over their waffles.

"Amber was her name. My ex-wife. The end." He halts with a smirk as he slides his knife across his fruity wedge of waffle.

"Come on tiger… that's it?" Gaby pressed him diagonally at the table in her sexiest Spanish accent.

"Well there's a lot more… Do you want to know where we met or how we ended?" He asked.

"I want to know all of it mi amore!" Excited she exclaims.

"In 2010, I would ride my bike at Liberty Station Park, near my home normally about ten mile each way, there and back. After my ride, I'd be drenched in sweat, and in need of my refreshing green tea lemonade at Starbucks. Most times, Amber would be inside with a group of girls chatting. We saw each other on several occasions, but I never asked her out until one day I had just finished my ride, and on the way to get my tea, there she was on the outside of this white Dodge Charger throwing her engagement ring at some dude letting her go. Of course, I was next in line for her fun and games. I asked her to marry me a year later."

"Within a year? That's fast." She replies.

"Yeah well as fast as we were married, we got divorced in 2012." He answers.

"What happened?" Gaby quizzes.

"For starters she seemed to be gone for hours, sometimes three or longer it seemed on Sundays, I noticed. I assumed she was just with her girlfriends having brunches and dinners, you know —girl stuff. This one particular Sunday I went to a Chargers football game with a buddy of mine and saw her on a replay screen in the front row kissing a man who could have been like her father's age. I double take at the screen to make sure I wasn't seeing it wrong. I had hoped I was, but unfortunately when I hired a private investigator to follow her on those next few Sundays she went out; she was with him. I wasn't going to wait for her to leave me for an old guy in a football cap, so I asked her how her girl days had been going. She lied of course and when she did, I ended her lies with three weeks' worth of photos of the two of them together." Tony laughs out, then proceeds to tell the rest of the story.

"She was pale as a ghost looking at herself in those photos with him. I filed for a divorce. She tried to come after me saying she was pregnant soon after I filed, but how could it be mine twelve months later. I should have seen the *red flags* when I saw her looking sappy with her previous engagement with the guy in the Dodge Charger." Tony spat out.

"Wow Tony. I'm sorry that happened, but look on the bright side. Now you can have me for everything she wasn't." She wraps her arms around his neck and kisses him.

An early morning Sunday drive along Interstate Ten was peaceful at 8:25 A.M. Kyle is in his Mercedes with the top pulled back letting air flow through his dark brown hair.

In the middle lane of I-10, Kyle notices an eighteen-wheeler fuel truck. He is in the far-right lane, about fifty yards behind the truck. Pulling up fast, on the side of Kyle is a white four door, newer model that catches his attention. He reduces speed.

Now, behind a slow car, he's wedged between all of them. He hits the brakes as a girl on the left side of him is texting and driving and almost hits Kyle's Mercedes.

Kyle swerves all over the freeway with fear of a collision. He takes his frustration out on his steering wheel.

The young girl and the passenger she's carrying still doesn't get it. She is still texting and driving.

Kyle blares on his horn of his Mercedes which doesn't seem to faze the chick. Out of desperation, he picks up the banana peel from the floor of his car and makes a decision to throw it like a grenade at the girl's window.

She prides herself in blowing her car horn causing the person in the eighteen-wheeler to slam on his brakes. She curses Kyle, then speeds around the truck, leaving Kyle critical on the sideline.

Kyle slams his hand on the wheel once more, shaking his head while shouting to the heavens above him, "You took my wife already. Can't we just save a few lives here?"

At 9 A.M, he arrives to the West Covina house for the second time in two days. His contractor's truck is parked in front of the house as he pulls up. They are having the house inspected.

Derick Nelson is out front of the house inspecting the windows while inhaling that wacky smoke from his pipe. Kyle gets out of his little black car.

"The owners should have on the electricity today. Let's get this inspection done so we can close on it in two weeks." Kyle snaps.

Derick spins around, "You okay man? You're a bit jumpy."

"Yes, I'm fine. I am still aggravated by a girl texting and driving on the freeway, not paying any attention whatsoever for others. This seems to be happening more and more I've noticed and I've had —Enough!"

Derick takes a huge puff of smoke in then speaks out with a staring eye, "Makes you want to follow these punk ass kids and pound their head into the pavement, pour out the fresh juice into their cups. See if it's something they'd drink."

"I don't know what you just said but let's just forget about it and get to work." Kyle says.

Meanwhile, back at the Hawthorne place, Gaby and Tony change into their swim suits to spend a nice quiet morning together.

In the pool, Tony lifts Gaby up like a swan, bringing her back for a kiss, romantically setting up his next scene.

Benjamin, who has been up for some time, enters the kitchen area for some orange juice and sees the two in the pool on each other. In one hand he has some juice in a cup and in the other is his cell phone. He slams back his oranges and exits the kitchen with his eyes glued to his phone.

Inside of his room, he sends Venom and Viper a text:

You up? Come find me on Call of Duty.
Username: BenBomber12

Benjamin doesn't wait for anyone to text back. He gets into the game immediately from the dungeon looking theatre room.

The sun bares down on the newly planted flowers the landscapers had done early this morning. Tony has Gaby wrapped in his arms and takes in love that blossoms all around them. He releases her to swim off on her own, so he can watch her equestrian figure soar in the water.

Gaby gets out.

Tony follows her with happiness written all over his face.

He wonders where the red flags are at. The only thing that comes to mind is the two hours it takes to drive to see her, and the fact of no real privacy together at the brother in law's house.

The two take up the lounge chairs next to the pool enjoying the sun. They have on sunglasses enjoying what only their eyes can bring in from the still of quietness.

Outside the theatre room, Camden hears his brother playing The Call of Duty. Sounds of soldiers shooting machine that blaring out bass while he opens the theater doors.

Camden comes inside, grabs a controller and jumps into the game.

Forty minutes later Benjamin sees a user notification from GethinCityVen, then another from GethinCityVip comes in.

Benjamin immediately starts up a conversation in the lobby with them.

"What up Gethin City? Has anybody seen Batman and Robin?" Benjamin interrogated in his best serious tone of voice.

"We're right behind you Ben Bombie." Viper laughs out.

"I know you're not tittering my name off." Benjamin grilled.

An older male in the gaming background comes in over the intercom. "Bombie Ben get back in the game you stuck pig. Quit trying to catch a date brotha."

"Morally! Can you shut up?" Benjamin pounds out.

Midafternoon rolls around. Tony and Gaby are blushful in color while growing a tan from sun exposure.

Gaby pours him and herself the last of lemon water from a pitcher, she made hours ago. Tony's sucks down the water then realizes it's time to drive back to San Diego.

Tony has his rugged orange night-sack over his shoulders, ready to walk out the door. It's 4 P.M.

Benjamin and Camden come down from extensive gamer mode, rubbing their stomachs. They're also in time to give their uncle Tony a hug bye.

"We're hungry Gaby. Where's dinner at?" Benjamin asked.

"I don't know my love. Get a snack and give me a few minutes to say bye to your uncle." Gaby utters.

"Okay Aunt Gaby." Benjamin jokes. They all take in a few good laughs.

Meanwhile, at the West Covina house, Kyle and Derick are wrapping up the inspection. Other than a few shingles in need of replacing on the roof, the ventilation system, some punch hole in the walls, a few cosmetic updates and a few GFCI outlets replacements, the house is in good enough condition to purchase.

The two men call it a night, lock up and drive home.

Tony and Gaby go outside the front door holding hands.

Tony is getting ready to leave. He pulls her in for a kiss.

She feels his heart beating hard against his thin shirt.

He grabs her buttocks thrusting against her, then let go suddenly.

Kyle pulls into the driveway, darts towards the back of the house.

Tony and Kyle make eye contact as Tony walks over to his truck.

Gaby goes back inside trying to get Tony off her mind long enough to figure out what is for supper tonight.

CHAPTER
THIRTEEN

West Covina, a city that grew larger in size after 1960. Some of the largest cities built a ton of buildings after the second war. This city boomed in hospitals, schools, and new home construction to house sum forty-five thousand people who dwelled into city limits.

Monday May 23rd, Kyles walks inside a busy title company with pep in his step at 10 A.M.

He is superbly dressed with his dark hair gelled over to the side. He enters a small room with the title company's senior closing agent awaiting him to sign the deed of trust. She hands him over a small stack of papers to sign with the thought of him wiring nearly a half a million dollars from his bank account to take possession.

Jill the closing agent at the title company hands over the key to Kyle when funding happens. She expressing with gratitude of service, "She is all yours now."

Kyle walks out of the closing agent's office with a pure smile.

Tilting his sunglasses to fit correctly, he dials up his contractor on his phone. "Derick, hey buddy you busy? Perfect… Look, I know I said tomorrow, but let's start today. Why don't you meet me over at the Covina house in an hour?" Kyle hangs up the phone with his contractor, going for a quick lunch in the area.

Meanwhile, inside the Hollywood middle school cafeteria, tables were either packed full of cool kid teenagers, or geniuses still looking for a to sit.

The table's right next to the serving food line, where introverts try to hide, almost always a spot was available for a seat.

Benjamin was seated in his normal place by the serving line all alone, but four others sat at the round table next to him eating from pail lunch boxes and juice pouches. Two slender, tall and dark hair presences approach the table.

Benjamin looks up with a slice of pizza hanging out his mouth.

"Hey Benji, mind if we take a seat next to you and make this the cool kid section?" Venom asked with a pretty convincing smile attached to his twin Viper, who didn't wait for an invitation to sit down.

Viper strums her long hair over to the side which nearly falls right to her waistline. Both twins eat from their cafeteria plated school lunch.

Benjamin's eyes light up from his new friends turning up at his table. He stuffs his pizza wrapper inside an empty chip bag. He is excited to have the twins at his school and say goodbye to lonely 8th grade year.

Viper notices Benjamin admiring them while shifting her long brown hair out of her face to eat chicken nuggets. Venom nibbles gently on his dry and crispy nuggets as he looks around finding a cute little boy in front of him to glaze over.

The three of them finish their lunches in a hurry, to run off for next period, when that buzzing bell rings.

Meanwhile, the new house in West Covina is about to be gutted and remodeled. Both Kyle and Derick are in the house discussing appliance color and brands in the kitchen. A few of the existing ugly white tile are chipped and cracked.

"Derick, call the flooring company now would you…? And for God sake get rid of the horrid carpet in the bathroom… and get us a lighter shade of hardwood throughout the rest of the house." Kyle demands.

The contractor gets on his phone setting up the floor walks. Kyle searches his phone for the roofer he uses and dials them up while getting an idea of the new paint color on the walls from the Cheetos stained hand prints and mechanic oil finger tips rubbed at the seams of the walls.

Derick walks past Kyle giving him the thumbs up on the flooring company.

Kyle struts around in his steamed blue suit with his cell phone tied at his earlobe, but needs another favor, "Derick would you call up the painters, and get them over here, now and pretty please?"

It never seems to amaze Kyle how promptly people in busy-ness can be reached, showing up on time when trust and integrity are involved.

The roofers show up forty-five minutes later, dully tapping their heavy steal toe boots across a semi-angled rooftop. Inside, two men are tape measuring the perimeter of the house for flooring.

A white van with a ladder on top finds an empty parking spot amongst the others out front. Four Hispanic guys in painter pants and t-shirts with a paint speckled degree in their dark hair approach the door to knock.

Kyle opens the door, "Welcome Javier, please come inside."

Showing the painters around the house, Kyle explains all the new colors he envisions from the paint splotches Javier brought with him. Shades of coffee and cream appears to be needed to shake things up with a bit of eggshell white baseboards.

All the contractors in the 1970's, built house —West Covina, works simultaneously together cleaning and fixing the house up to have it on the market next week.

Kyle hands over the keys to Derick, letting him lock up later this evening when he leaves.

Kyle takes off home before the Los Angeles rush hour traffic gets him stuck on a freeway parking lot in the blazing California smoking sunlight. He's driving a steady pace and makes it home.

The next day arrives. Kyle is at the Covina house. New granite countertops and appliances from the local home store are being delivered and installed.

Derick directs the appliance guys into the house and shows them where to set up at. The men from the home store get started on their jobs. Derick goes to the secondary bathroom to take out existing toilet and replaces it without mollycoddles.

The roofers are carrying up boxes of shingles to replaces the whole roof, making it nice and even instead of the patchwork it needed.

Inside the house all appliances have been done up right.

Bathrooms are now upgraded minus the fresh coat of paint.

The old existing carpet throughout the place is being rolled up and taken out, including the pet dander and ground dust. Two people quickly taking out tac- strips along the wall perimeters.

Another set of people are laying tile in one of the bathrooms. Derick is cutting the tiles for the shower in same bathroom where the floor is being set trying not to get in the way of the guys stabilizing the walkway.

By 2 P.M. the house has a new roof of shingles on it, new appliances, hardwood flooring and new tiles in the bathrooms; no more carpet. The painters are the last to show up for a fresh breath of life for the hideous walls.

Once again Derick has the keys to lock up when the house is complete.

Meanwhile, stopped in the hallways at middle school, Benjamin speaks to Venom and Viper at the cream color lockers in between sixth and seventh period.

"So… does Benji wanna take a Lyft rideshare and grab some ice-cream with us after school today? Our treat and well you do live across the way, so you can go home, when we do. No extra cost." Venom asked holding onto his locker.

Viper turns and greets Benjamin while she neatly adjusts her U.S. History book next to her Algebra textbook.

"Really?" Benjamin is thrilled.

"Yeah really Beanie." Venom smarted.

Benjamin pulls out his cell phone from his pant pocket, holding his index finger to his lip, so the twins understand to be quiet.

"Gaby with your permission would it be okay, instead of you picking me up after school that I go with the twins for ice cream? They've just invited me." Benjamin asked while he shakes his head yes, agreeing to whatever Gaby is saying, then gives thanks as he presses end on the cell phone.

"It's on." He said as his energy comes back to earth with the twin's fiery walk down the busy filled hallways of teens hauling buttocks to seventh period.

At 2:24 P.M, Kyle has been flowing in and out of traffic since he entered I-10 access. He goes around an automobile transporter carrying four black cars, same make and model. He finds it a bit strange to see another one of these large vehicles next to him. He fears one could come off and hit him.

Kyle is heavy in thought considering everything that has to be done on the Covina house by Friday night. The house needs to be market ready by Saturday.

A red two door sports car in front of Kyle's black Mercedes slowly swerves right into some sort of black mini bus.

The mini bus is pushed to the side by little miss glossy red lip, right into the next car coming in with no time to spare. The car spins, then flips and rolls four and a half times, leaving the charcoal color car, mirrored to a compact disc.

Everything happens instantaneously. Kyle grips both hands to the steering wheel and slam his brakes, hoping not to become a can of albacore with bent tire rims.

Stuck behind the wreckage, Kyle notifies emergency responders, then courageously gets out of his car in his dark grey business suit to check on all victims involved.

The red two door car is seemingly fine. The woman is scared and not getting out of her car, and anxiously cries as Kyle runs past her to the next vehicle.

Inside the mini bus a man is frantically on the phone with someone placing blame on who's at fault in this situation. He doesn't even see Kyle standing at the driver window checking on him and the passengers.

Kyle slows down his running as he approaches the tiny grey four door hatchback, now in crumpled heap.

Inside, the woman sees Kyle and is barely able to breath out, "My baby. My baby… save my baby."

Blood covers her face running down her cracked skull. She is holding onto her ribcage in pain yet trying to turn to see her if her child is safe.

The baby in the car seat is crushed from the top of the car into its head. Kyle couldn't tell if the child was a boy or girl, other than the child has on boy sneakers on his feet.

Kyle gets nauseous and goes into shock at the thought of what appears to happen now as the woman's head falls to the side. She isn't breathing when he gets closer to her. "Oh God! Hold on… help is coming." He shakes in fear.

Back at middle school, the last period bell rings. Benjamin pulls out his phone and sends Venom and Viper a text.

Meet you at your lockers in ten.

-Text sent

Fifteen feet outside his classroom door, Benjamin finds his locker. He grabs his math book, slides it into his backpack, and runs off in search of the twins.

"It's about time you turned up. BenBomber you said like ten minutes. I've had to cancel like two Lyft drivers already." Viper stands hold her phone trying to request another ride.

"What are you talking about? It's only been about nine… ten minutes max." Benjamin grimaces, positioning his posture toward the twins. "Gotta scat now, there's another Lyft driver right-round the corner. Let's go." Viper stresses.

Out in the driveway where all the other students are being picked up from, the Lyft driver patiently waits by inside his black midsize sports utility vehicle. The three teenagers track him down and go over to open the door.

"Hi, I'm Jake… Are you Viper?" A very confident young man looking like a male model asked.

"I'm Viper, this is my brother and our friend." She confidently cranked back in her British accent.

"Totally cool name and accent. Looks like your destination is set to: 1253 Vine St. Is that correct?"

"That's the one. I heard it's a really good vegan ice cream shop." Viper explains to everyone in the vehicle as they drive away.

Meanwhile, back at the car wreck, Emergency Responders vehicles flash their red and blue lights, protecting the area.

Kyle stands to the side of the freeway with the other passengers whom are alive. Among them stood a twenty-one-year-old who started the domino effect of collision as she was on her way to work. She's crying and repenting her actions out loud. Kyle is extremely quiet, taking it all in, as she spills her guts out. He goes into flashback of what Angela must have went through right before she was killed.

He doesn't dare say anything while she admits to being on her phone while she weaved right into the guy standing next to her, who then drove the bus into the woman and baby's vehicle, causing two death.

Just before Kyle's eyes stands a familiar policeman looping him back into reality. "Kyle… Kyle Hawthorne, your name is Kyle, right?

Kyle tries to recall the last time he saw this man's face, "You're Detective Calc Timmons. You brought my wife's blue notebook, Online Now to me."

"Yes, I thought I recognized you with your dark wavy hair. What happened here? Were you on the scene when it happened?" The detective replies.

"Yeah, I witnessed it, but why don't you ask this young lady what happened while she was on her phone?" Kyle demonstrated holding his phone violently trying to text on it.

"Now calm down Hawthorne. I will need a written statement in my office later today, if you can drive over. I will take it from here now." Detective Calc Timmons turns to question everybody else at the scene of the fatalities.

At a local ice cream shop, Venom, Viper, and Benjamin enjoy double scoops of ice-cream, dipped and sprinkled in a waffle cone. The place is pastel purple and blue with multicolor table and chairs, making it seem old fashion.

Venom sits directly in front of Benjamin. He's reeling his ice cream close to his lips as he imagines loving the flavors of birthday cake way more than he should. The noises he makes just licking his cone severely aggravate his twin.

Venom locks eyes with Benjamin, both share the smiles in the shop.

"Would you stop tonging your dipped birthday balls, before I chloroform you both for being lame" Viper sasses out of a chocolate rimmed mouth, she tries to wipe off after shamelessly delving another bite.

"Are you jealous of my ice cream cake being better than yours sis?" Venom spat out, flirting over Benjamin.

"Not at all." She laughs out.

"Wait… chloroform? What exactly is that?" Benjamin Grimaces.

"Oh Viper, please specify lovely, tell them what mum and dad does keeping the knockers on file?" Venom licks into the barrel of the cone.

"You idiot, they work to doctors' orders they don't put people out cold on purpose like ima' do to you if you don't pack it in."

"Oh, sleeping pills?" Benjamin quizzes.

"Not exactly Benji." Venom winks.

"It's one form of medication anesthesiologists use to sedate their patients having surgeries." Viper explained.

"Right." Benjamin finished up his ice cream cone.

Viper request another Lyft ride this time to June Street —Hancock Park.

Downtown Los Angeles not far from where his son is finishing up from, Kyle is seated in a hardback chair in the police department waiting for Detective Calc Timmons to arrive. Ten- or fifteen-minutes pass by. He is still shaking a bit from earlier as he finally gets the chance to text Gaby, checking on his boys.

Detective Timmons shows up wearing his dark grey slacks and a button up shirt jacket. His shiny black shoes tap against the tile. He immediately eyes down Kyle in the lobby sitting next to a woman with the same dark wavy hair as him. She is on her phone while Kyle's is in his hands.

"Kyle, follow me back to my office, would you?" Detective Timmons requests as he continues walking to his assigned area of space.

Both men take a seat.

"Glad you could make it down so fast." Timmons remarks.

"It's fresh on my conscience. The woman and baby… They made it right?"

Detective Timmons shakes his head in the directions that put Kyle more uncertain about the reality of life as we know it.

"Unfortunately, No. Listen Kyle, I have a verbal statement from all that were involved at the scene. We've taken the girl in account of the fatality, into custody until further notice… but you Hawthorne seem to be on the accounts of what your wife was trying to birth." Detective Calc Timmons conceived.

"What's that supposed to mean?" Kyle grimaces.

"Sorry Kyle if that came out wrong. Forgive me. Kyle, how are you doing since last month? How are your boys holding up?"

"Well it hasn't been easy with my real estate properties, and my boys… Camden gets sad from time to time, but it's Benji, my oldest I'm worried about. His grades and attitude have dropped to almost failing eighth grade this year. We go to counseling now." Kyle released.

"I see, it's been a very rough month of your life. I'm sure you have just relived what your wife's exodus was like." Detective Timmons pries him open.

Kyle takes a moment without trying to sob and sniffles while trying to say, "Yeah, I did. You know it's funny, I feel like I'm being called to get out of real estate and finish my wife's book."

"You mean the blue one I brought to your house last month." Detective Timmons calculates.

"Online Now. Yes, that's the one people keeps driving over. I need to finish her work and save a life instead of writing tragic statement at the station about somebody's last words before death is: *On my way*, from texting and driving.

The detective takes out the affidavit form and hands it to him.

"I'll need you to fill out a statement in your most legible handwriting. In it, include the date, time, what you were doing right before the incident, what happened in the event, what you did immediately when it happened, and what you did after it happened."

Kyle tucks his head into writing the statement.

Detective Timmons gets up from his chair, goes over to other officer about twenty feet over. Loudly, they discuss political issues and opinions of who will win the Election in 2016.

Chapter
FOURTEEN

An iPhone chirps and vibrates on the nightstand next to Benjamin who's been laying in night sweats for almost eight hours. The alarm moves him out of a warm rigid bed, opening his eyes, he hits the snooze button. He wipes his eyes while checking his phone notifications.

He lays in his warm bed pondering how much freedom he felt when the twins called the Lyft company to come pick them up, yet how safe it was being around the two. It was like they were in their unique three-way friendship.

Opening the Lyft in the app-store, he sets up an account using the debit card his father gave him.

During setting it up, he stares at his phone dreaming of Venom's smile when he looks him in the eyes. He thinks about the twins who are probably home sleeping still.

It's like he knows them from somewhere. Like maybe Call of Duty, but who knows.

Venom's agreeable smell protruding his glorious body, opens his senses to his own scent, he's never noticed before. For a first time, Benjamin can hear the twin's jubilant attractive voice speaking volumes in his head while finishing up.

Benjamin grew close to Viper as well. After all, she is the female version of him and would be an easy catch in his subliminal conscious, based off types of females his father and grandfather went for.

Benjamin doesn't understand really what he feels.

Viper has an evident way of staying hard in her masculine strength that puzzles Benjamin, yet her sweet charming long brunette hair that moves with every serious adjustment of her head, makes her attractive as well.

Getting out of bed forces him to use the restroom eliminating last night's liquids and fat components.

After action and before washing up his hands, he sends a text to the twins:

> Hey, you guys, you wanna catch a Lyft with me this morning?

He then turns on Spotify, listening to The Weekend, Can't Feel My Face and hops in the shower, washing up completely for the day to start.

With wet hair and a towel wrapped around his waist, he runs through the hallway into his room to check his phone for missed text notifications. Across the screen Viper's name appears:

> Give us like thirty minutes to get our stuff together...see you then.

Benjamin meets Camden downstairs who's in his pajamas eating cereal at the bar.

Gaby is cleaning the inside of the oven with a blue foaming scrubbing pad.

Benjamin pauses Gaby for a second, while she is in the middle of scrubbing a grid from the metal racks.

"Gaby, I'm going to be catching a Lyft with Venom and Viper this morning, so you won't have to take me to school."

She rises off her knees, walks to the kitchen sink rinses grimy suds from her hands to give Benjamin a reaction.

"Mijo, does your papa know you have been taking these taxis?"

Benjamin shows no emotions and says, "Yeah, he knows. He's the one giving me permission, as of yesterday, to take a Lyft."

He grabs his brown sack lunch out of the stainless-steel refrigerator that Gaby made and rushes out of the kitchen for middle school. Out of sight in the corner of the entryway, he's requesting a Lyft. He follows up texting the twins letting them know they have minutes to catch a ride with him.

A blue four door car shows up outside of Benjamin's address. He sends a text to the twins again, asking where they are, then opens the car door getting inside.

He lets the driver know right away he is waiting for two more to come outside and ride with. The friendly driver mentions he only has three minutes left on the screen for any delays, at the point of either canceling the ride or proceeding on.

A long three minutes pass as the morning sunlight blazes both the driver and Benjamin's face. Benjamin stares anxiously into the phone.

The driver politely says, "Would you like me to drive you to school now or cancel the ride?"

"Can't you just give me like two minutes? I can like, walk over there and get them. They're like seriously right across the street."

"No, I'm very sorry young man, that's not an option here. Do you want me to drive you to the address listed or cancel the ride?"

"I suppose you can drive me to school." Disappointment sets into Benjamin.

Driving into direct sunlight, Benjamin receives a text:

Sorry Benji, Viper is not ready.
See you at school, okay.

The first four hours at school went by awe-so-inspiringly-slow. Benjamin beat his head against every school book in every period, wondering why the twins bailed on him. It was atypical of Benjamin to not give his best performance in his favorite subjects. Death invaded a cord in him since his mother's departure. Hope was cut from his existence until they moved here.

Meeting the twins last week and their parents last weekend had put the glow back into Benjamin's spirit. He could feel something starting to develop, and now this; ditched on the first move he made.

Some of the pain he had this last month was melting away. Dark clouds are casted away as the newly formed relationships offer him comfort, security and friendship.

The lunch bell rings. Benjamin walks nearly sixty seconds blended into every loud teenager roaming the hallways. Standing at his cream color locker he unlocks it, grabs his lunch sack to eat in the cafeteria.

Benjamin lacks confidence as he slouches into his seat deliberating each bite of peanut butter and jelly, hoping purple jam doesn't fall on his light denim jeans.

Venom shows up out of the blue, dressed in a red and light grey plaid button down and light grey fitting shorts. He's carrying a soy burger and crispy fries on a rectangular plastic tray.

He takes a seat next to Benjamin so nobody's alone on his second of day.

"Hey Benji, I hope you aren't too mad at us, not going with you this morning. Just as we were about to turn the knob, Viper spewed her breakfast cereal all over the front door. It was petrifying. Smelt so rank. I felt I needed to stay behind."

"Oh my God is she okay?"

"Yeah, she'll be alright. It's probably one of those day bugs." Venom nibbles some fries.

"I'm not mad by the way. I was worried."

Venom ogles the cutest boy in front of him chewing saturated potatoes with the daintiest movement possible. The tables all around suddenly get quiet. Mockery and whispers fill the cafeteria and echoes become like a striking roll of thunder.

They ignore the empty works of what embodies them, keeping their focus on each other.

Benjamin feels love for Venom.

Looking into Venom's heart shaped eyes at the table made the world around them not matter.

A rage starts to form as the conversations appeared louder and threating.

Benjamin's blood starts to boil a burning sensation flows through his skin.

Benjamin rises up like an eagle and purges, "Does everyone think it's funny, two boys sitting alone at a table eating their lunch, while they talk about their day? Anybody want to laugh out some bullshit to my face?"

Under the breath of the only person who dared to say something was a massive bean stalk. From the mouth of an eighth-grade wrestling team-mate, a single word echoes the cafeteria, "Faggots!"

"Benji… Benji, sit down. Don't worry we are aren't smoking so it's fine, I don't know what the big bubble head is talking about and you don't either… and we aren't in the Call of Duty." Venom winks.

The same boy wrinkles his freckly face smirking and this time stands up with everyone laughing, "What… Little Debbie doesn't protect you?"

"No, you full on idiot." Benjamin yells back, walking over to them.

The boy throws a punch aiming right into Benjamin's skull, but it's intercepted by Coach Becker standing in at six foot-three, two hundred and fifty plus pounds.

Behind the students, the coach demands answers.

"What's going on over here, boys?"

"This fagot called me a flipping idiot."

"Is that so?" Coach Becker glares at Benjamin asking what his name is.

Benjamin doesn't reply to the coach, instead he angers out, "Are-You-Kidding? I was standing up for my friend and myself when you had your whole table laughing at us."

"Okay let's take this to the principal's office." Coach Becker grabs two other teachers nearby to escort the three down to Principal Suzanne Thomas.

Inside a fourteen by twelve, neatly organized room Principal Thomas, in her fifty's, short trimmed dark hair, over average height, little on the weighty side, sits at her desk. Her head is tucked down, pen working hard on whatever she is writing.

Behind her is a wall of books. Hanging on the right side is her Principal of Honor plaque.

Disturbing her quietness, Becker barges in with three boys and a couple of other staff members. "Is everything alright, Coach Becker?"

"Everything is calm right now, earlier, not so much. We need to take disciplinary action against this one attempting to throw a punch at this young man. What's your name sir?"

"Benjamin."

"And your last name?" Coach Becker questions.

"Benjamin Hawthorne."

"And we need repercussions on Mr. Hawthorne instigating and fueling the situation." Coach Becker announces, waiting for reply on Principal Thomas.

Venom swallows a mouthful of apprehensiveness, determined to speak the truth, "Excuse me sir, If I may, Benjamin never started anything. That boy, that blistering nail bed biter, had his whole table whipping out jokes at us? And for what? Being two boys alone at a table? Benji stood silent."

"Is that what happened Coach Becker?"

Standing taller, Coach Becker responds, "I caught sail of Jesse's arm flying into this one here. I didn't hear or see what happened prior."

Principal Suzanne Thomas states, "I believe I know what happened here, but Mr. Strickland, is there anything you want to say before I decide on the appropriate punishments? You've been extremely quiet."

Resting his eyes on the Principal's plaque on the grey wall, Jesse Strickland tries to find comfort on what he would say, how it would come out. He contemplates all consequences of admitting the truth and bending it. That bitter sour side of him washed away looking Benjamin and Venom right into the depths of their souls.

Strife relinquished in the public eye of education. Sudden conscious awakens Jesse and he is ready to assume responsibility.

"I didn't like how it looked." Strickland pleaded.

"How what looked?" Principal Thomas leans forward. "Explain yourself in total honesty, Mr. Strickland."

"They looked gay."

"How so? Were they engaging in any type of sexual conduct?" She ping ponged back to him.

"No, it wasn't that"

"Then describe what gay is to you?" Turning her strings down a notch, she pauses to listen.

"You know… alone at a table, two boys leaning into each other, all smiles, and one of them looked to be slow dancing a french fry for the attention of his counterpart." Flamboyance trundles energy Jesse radiated earlier.

"Mr. Strickland, look here, I'm gonna stop you. Let me explain to you something, if these would have been two females or a boy and girl, would it have looked like something else to you? Benjamin and Venom have human rights. I believe I'm looking into the eyes of a critical spirit, passing judgment here? We will not have bullying in my school. I will not tolerate any form of it. Do I make myself clear? Everyone?"

The room fills in agreeance.

"Thank you, Coach Becker, I will handle it from here, you may be excused from my office.

"Young men take a seat. The secretary will be calling your folks to come pick you up. Two days of suspension starts now." Principal Thomas exits her office looking for a secretary.

Thirty minutes before the last bell rings, Dr. Rueben Gethin is the last parent to show up. Dressed in blue scrubs and neat athletic tennies he walks into the allotted conference room where he finds two other boys and their parents. He takes a seat next to Venom.

"Thank you for all your attendance on such short notice. It's very unfortunate the circumstances have landed each of these students a two-day suspension from this place of education." Principal Thomas calmly speaks at the far end of the table from the door.

She pauses as everyone speaks to their son, questioning under their breaths. In a circle Kyle sits next to Benjamin. Dr. Gethin is next to Venom. Mr. and Mrs. Strickland sit next to Jesse.

Jesse's genetics must have come mostly from Mrs. Strickland side. The color of his eyes, lips, even hair color appears identical to the ginger woman adjacent.

An orthodox knock on the door is given by Coach Becker as he opens it and gently walks inside finding the ninth seat to take at the table. All eyes seem to shift back and forth like confused sheep.

"Everybody this is Coach Becker. Very nice of you to join us. He is here as he was the one who prevented what could have been a massive disturbance of bullying at our school today. Coach Becker, will you please explain what you saw?"

"Of course. During lunch today, your son tried swinging at Benjamin for approaching him, trying to defend his right to sit with your son. Yes, they were alone." The coach pauses while Venom's father speaks in his most sedated tone of voice possible.

"Oh, come on… I get pulled out of medical practice because my son has an attraction to male traits and desires to sit next to a young man who accepts him. I bet this wouldn't have happened if my sons' twin's sister was here balancing it out. This is 2016, but I guess some people still aren't past racism or homophobia. I work side by side to surgeons and when a patient is cut open, it doesn't matter, gay, tan, straight, snow white or male… when people bleed, its beet juice red. Why is my son being punished for this?" Doctor Gethin probes in his transferable English accent.

"I understand your anger and frustration concerning this situation. Our school will not tolerate any bullying and we are going to make an example out of this. We will have order in my school and discipline when it's needed." Mrs. Thomas states.

Kyle speaks next, "So what is my son supposed to do next time... be made into everybody's comic strip, left in humiliation? Made to feel bad sitting with his friend. My son isn't gay." Kyle makes his point directed into the amber eyes of Jesse.

Benjamin tenses up and speaks to dad in embarrassment, "Would it make a difference to you if I'm gay or not?"

"No son." Everybody hears the crackling high pitched tones in his voice.

"I understand everyone's frustration here. I assure you we are not going to make the matter any worse in serving two days, out of school suspension. Hopefully by Monday when everybody has had the opportunity to think, this will be, and I do mean resolved. Now let me cut this short and quick with everybody signing the suspension form. As stated on this form, the next step of action will be one-year full suspension in terms repeating your eighth-grade year. Are we all clear?"

"Yes, Principal Thomas." In unison the three students speak in repentance. No other arguments are made as pens move fast along the lines from all hands supporting the disciplinary action.

The first ones to sign and get out of their seats to leave are Benjamin and his father. Kyle looks for any kind of signs written on his face, as he nods his head at Dr. Gethin and his boy.

Kyle doesn't hold the door for his son when he pushes past it with a *what the hell thought*? A bad week for getting a fixer upper on the market and holding an open house tomorrow.

Flashes of his buyer assistant Waylon Warner appears to his mind as Waylon dances around with fruit trays at the open house tomorrow. Waylon has always brought fruit for home buyers and baked cookies in the oven. Buyers really love to feel at home while considering a property.

Benjamin trails his dad all the way through an empty parking lot with his lips zipped.

Oh, but those thoughts of his son being gay makes Kyle sick to his stomach, running him flush with premature wrinkles in his eye brows.

They managed to skip the busy school yard of traffic.

An awkward silence is broken after ten minutes of driving. Kyle rolls back the top of his convertible, flipping radio channels to fit his mood.

He strolls through Los Angeles to get to the four o'clock appointment with the Psychologist —Doctor Normal Yates.

The whole way there, Benjamin worried what his dad thought if he came out gay. It was something he had never considered before now, so it's a possibility. Benjamin's mind was busy trying to find some clarity.

A Cute British accent. A great person. The special buzz he gets around him. This has never happened with any other male. It's like Venom is his magnet, his imaginary friend from the game he plays and just now realizing it.

Kyle parts the air with his thoughts. He tries not to think so hard about what his son said back at the table around all the other parents.

Was his son gay? How did Kyle not know about it?

Kyle drives a little faster on the settled pavement, surrendering to wavering palm trees into the bright indigo sky.

112

CHAPTER
FIFTEEN

Taking it easy on the back end in a cozy blue waiting room, Kyle and his son are quiet and seated anticipating Dr. Yates to finish up a session to then come out and get them.

The receptionist in front catches Kyle checking her out. They meet eyes, and she plays it off grabbing the phone to make a call. For a few minutes her friendly smile took his mind off his son's bad day. He looks down at his phone letting out a huge breath of air.

"Would you like some coffee or tea?" The receptionist asks with minutes left on the clock to spare.

"Son, are you thirsty?"

Benjamin nods yes.

"Yes, I'd love a coffee and perhaps a cold beverage for my boy.

Kyle and Benjamin follow her back.

"What would you like?" She smiles into Kyle's growing eyes.

"Just a simple coffee and cream guy. Benji, what would you like?"

"Last time I had a ginger ale. Do you have one?"

"Let's check and see." She spins around with her long legs, showcased in black slacks, opening the stainless-steel double door to get a wide view of what's inside.

"Would ya lookie here, one left. That's also my favorite drink too." She winks.

"Do you have a name, so I can thank you?" Kyle politely asks.

She looks down batting her eyelashes bringing out her shyness. "It's Anne."

Her name dives off the apprehending tip of her lips releasing a pheromone only Kyle could breathe in.

Developing a dry coughing spell, he turns away from Anne and Benjamin in order for them not to suspect anything out of ordinary. Her name echoes loud and clear like Angela to him, and suddenly he appears sick.

"Are you okay Mr. Hawthorne?" She asks sincerely worried.

"Please call me Kyle. I don't know what got into me. Possibly dust. I'm okay now, thank you." He smiles and follows her and his son who seems to be extremely thirsty gulping down the contents of the soda can.

He caught himself sizing her up, walking next to her, about four inches less than his wife. Drowning those thoughts immediately, he proceeds to walk on by, and he and his son take their seats back in the lobby.

A woman comes walking in behind them blowing her sniffling nose with a handful of saturated teary-eyed tissues. She sweeps on through the doors.

Next comes Dr. Yates tapping her heels in short-fast strides down the tiled hallway and entering the room where Kyle and his son awaits.

"Sorry I'm running a few minutes behind. Are you ready? Come on back."

In a warm cozy room, the vaporizer blows the same eucalyptus oil from before. Dr. Yates delays the time on the clock as she rushes to put away notes from previous engagement. She takes a seat.

"Benjamin, put away your phone son."

"Sorry dad, Venom sent me a text."

"Turn your phone off. You can talk to him on Monday." Kyle sighs, pushing back his hair.

"So… how are you both doing since we spoke last week?" Dr. Yates sits up with perfect posture and a convincing smile reflecting at them.

"Doctor Yates, this week has been hell on wheels for me, that's for sure." Kyle lets out his worries.

"What's been going on?" Dr. Normal Yates bites the end of her eye glasses frame.

"For starters, I bought a fixer upper to put on the market this week. I have been driving back and forth an hour each way and on the way back home yesterday, I ended up in a fatal car wreck. I drove over to the LAPD still shaken from watching a woman take her last breath, I had to give a statement about it… and then today, this one over here decides to stand up for equal rights during lunch and landed a two-day suspension.”

“I hear your frustration Mr. Hawthorne. Okay, let’s start with the car wreck. What happened?”

“There was a young girl texting and driving, not paying attention. She went flying into a mini bus, who then sailed into a small car with a baby inside, killing both the mother and baby on board.”

“How are you feeling today about it?”

“I’m extremely sad about it and I know they are leaving some poor man sobbing somewhere like I was last month, still am. I had to fill out an affidavit and the same detective that was on my wife’s case is assigned this one. I keep crossing paths with Detective Calc Timmons. You know, Dr. Yates, I gotta tell you, I feel like I should take it upon myself to usher my wife’s book into this world, save some lives, so I don’t keep reliving the nightmare.”

“What’s it called, if you don’t mind me asking?”

“Online Now.” Kyles responds.

“Interesting. What’s it about?”

“Ironically, it’s about distracted drivers and the amount of people they kill each year, including the family and friends that are affected by it. And each year, nobody has really done anything.”

“Oh wow. Yes! Sounds like you are being called to act. Do your wife some justice and go for it Mr. Hawthorne.”

“It’s defiantly brewing hot through my veins.” Kyle breathes.

“Have you found a way to release what happened yesterday with the car wreck? It must be weighing on you.” Dr. Yates propels.

“You know it’s still too soon to tell, but I really do feel called to put a stop to texting and driving. I can’t count how many times I see it in a day and I know it’s against the law these *unawares* do it. I totally get why Angela titled her book, Online Now. It’s everywhere. Before long kids will be playing Marco Polo with it.”

“That sounds like a very productive way to release what has happened yesterday and the pain of losing your wife, and possibly even saving your family from anymore disturbances like yesterday’s nightmare… So Benji, what’s going on at school.” Dr. Yates queries.

“Well, since last week I’ve really been thinking about my thoughts before taking action. Partly because I didn’t know just exactly how my mother’s death was affecting me… affecting my surroundings, and then there are the twins coming out of the blue, totally filling my past week with awesomeness.

I really like them a lot. I haven't felt this way since my mother left. It's like I'm experiencing my mother's love in the 3D and mainly with Venom. He is so cool. To be completely honest, I haven't ever been drawn to someone so much, not for a girl, not for a boy… but for him, I do, and I'm scared." Benjamin looks around the quiet room hoping his dad and the therapist doesn't stone him to death by what he just mentioned.

After two leg adjustments crossing her legs one way and then the other from Dr. Yates and Kyle shaking his wristwatch like he does when he is anxious, Dr. Yates asks, "Benji, what kind of feelings are you talking about? Do you mean you have a crush on one of the twins?"

Dr. Yates has strong intuition of it being the male version of him by the vibes she can feel catching wind. Kyle Hawthorne sits quiet with his hand puzzled together, looking right into his son's skull as he speaks his truth.

"Well yeah, I really like one of them that way and I'm still trying to understand why I'm feeling this way. It would be unnatural, wouldn't' it?" Benjamins fears he said too much now looking right at his father.

Benji, it's okay that you have a crush on the new neighbor. I saw how you first looked at her when they were moving in across the street. But I don't think you have a chance. She's lesbian." Kyle pivots in an uneasy way.

"Dad, I'm not talking about her." Seriously and softly spoken he said bravely connecting into his father's heart from the depths of his eyes.

"What do you mean, you think you're gay son? No chance! You've never showed any signs of playing with dolls or playing with female clothing… or accessories or any of your mothers' stuff."

"Dad this doesn't have anything to do with what I identify with. I felt obligated to stand up for us when others were saying mean things towards our friendship, but also it is more than that. I want to kiss him when I look into his eyes, I see something so familiar to me. I feel like I've known him all my life."

"This is very good. Communication kills assumption." Dr. Yates breaks in.

"I can't believe I'm hearing this from you Benjamin." Kyle covers his faces with his hands mumbling out to his deceased wife in the astral realm, "Oh my Angela, this is not what I imagined. Help us somehow."

"Mr. Hawthorne, everything happens for a reason. Life still goes on even when it seems like everything is being torn down and set ablaze, one scene ends just as another sets up before you. Life happens for a reason yet undefined and none of us can control this game or battle perhaps, however you choose to look at it. Even when we think we can, there will always be a new unseen iceberg ripping out the bottom." Dr. Yates described.

Taking a few moments in silence, she writes down some notes of this session. Kyle and his son keep to themselves. The eucalyptus spritzes go off and put some tranquility in the air.

Dr. Yates checks the clock on the wall giving them a que to end the session. "We have about six minutes before we need to schedule our next appointment."

Kyle and Benjamin's eyes float around the office a few times before Dr. Yates says, "Kyle, how are you doing now on the tragic incident from yesterday?"

"I'm okay and will deal with it in the days to come. I really feel I need to do something with Angela's book."

She smiles and nods, accepting and agreeing then looks over towards Benjamin stating, "You have two days of out-school-suspension. How will you spend your time reflecting on how to handle this type of situation if it rears its spotty face again?"

"I guess I will stay in my room the whole time in fear of everything now." Benjamin surrenders his worth as a person in exchange for his father's beliefs and feelings, even though he knew Venom made him feel better in this cold, long distance world that he couldn't control any more than *life* itself.

"I would like it if when we get home, we talk father to son about what is happening with your sexuality if that is what it is, okay. You're my baby boy and I love you."

"I really like the sound of that Mr. Hawthorne. Okay, shall we set up for same time next Thursday?"

"Thursday, same time is perfect."

She pens down Hawthorne's, four o'clock meeting for next week and follows their footsteps out the door, grabbing her last appointment of the day.

Driving home in silence was like eating unsalted cooked cabbage the next fifteen minutes. Benjamin found freedom in reaching for the radio on the panel to break apart the silence.

His father on the other hand appears to be understanding his job as a parent is not to justify what is right or wrong based off what he would do. His job as a parent is to love his child unconditionally, and now in ways that makes up for Angela being gone.

To love both his boys. To protect them. To teach them what he has learnt in his thirty-eight years of experiences, and to teach them how to be better than him.

CHAPTER
SIXTEEN

Waylon Warner leaps out of a red luxury Jaguar SUV, shutting the door behind him. He takes a Hawthorne Realty metal frame black and yellow sign out of the back, walking it over to a visible site placing it into the ground for every house hunter passing by to notice; it's up for grabs.

Waylon Warner is a handsome mand that's dressed in an impeccable grey suit with polished black dress shoes to match. He looks sharp.

The super approachable human being beaming every color of light, carries it all in one smile. Dark fabulous looking hair, well gelled, not bending from any Q and A follicles, while he steps and jumps onto the metal frame sign, posting it into the yard.

He opens the front door with a silver house key retracted from the shackle Kyle attached to the fancy doorknob, put on the door Wednesday.

He goes back to his red Jaguar with a new owner smile, grabbing a case of water, a pineapple, a watermelon, a container full of raw chocolate chip cookie dough in the process of three trips.

Everything ready to bake and serve to hungry after school shoppers is right on the new granite kitchen countertop.

Back outside, he grabs a big vibrant red balloon full of helium from the back seat and ties it to the mailbox a few feet behind him.

Kyle Hawthorne, at home has just finished uploading pictures with romantic descriptive word in every submission of his listings to the Multiple Listing Service of California. The MLS number is tied to every site that sells houses.

It's a little after 2 P.M.

Kyle kicks back relaxing and taking deep breaths so he might exhale another six more days next week. His hands are folded behind his head but that doesn't last another second without the thought of calling Waylon.

He rings him up.

"Hey buddy, just letting you know, West Covina is on the market. It has your cell phone number listed. Keep it handy, this one is selling quicker than your old fashion oats you like to stir up in the mornings."

"Roger that! Thanks for getting it up so fast. I gotta go now… put out a line of cheese, so I can get people here before school lets out." Waylon bursts out laughing.

Waylon locks up the house.

Driving the perimeter surrounding the property, Waylon Warner sets up open house signs directing chocolate chip cookie crunchers where to go for this priced to sell gem. Selling real estate is just that simple to Waylon.

Inside the Hawthorne residence, Gaby enters the hallway right outside Kyle's office. His feet lay across the desk. "Mi amore, are you not going to your other office?"

"No…ah, I'm beat for a week. My mind is robbed. I'm staying home." He smirks with hands folded behind his head, feet not budging.

"Kyle, I noticed Benjamin's birthday on the chart in a few weeks. Are there any specific plans I can help organize for you?"

"No…ah, oh that's coming up too? I haven't been able to think at all this week. Let me go upstairs and have a talk with him. I need to talk to him about school stuff anyhow. Thanks for the reminder." He smiles at her then sighs and tightens his lips for what's to come.

Gaby exits into freedom of the Hawthorne place.

Kyle struggles out of his chair and heads for the stairs.

Benjamin is in his room staring at social media, but really, he's overthinking about if he was gay, and what that meant.

If being picked out of a lunch crowd at school was odd, what was the real world like? Benjamin wasn't in a place to make any decisions about how to be his own hero in his life. All he could do it think about what he could see. How people treated each other now.

You know the same people who multiply and fill the earth with children — Do these people see when they give birth to a child, how each child can be different? Benjamin has a visual in his mind how even his brother and he are different.

And then Benjamin goes into more thoughts of those having sex before marriage. Those who only go after the most popular ones in school. Then another thought pops his thoughts. What about people who cross the borders and get married? He tries to understand if that is love or a benefit for oneself.

Knocking on the door Kyle opens it finding Benjamin laying down on his bed with his phone screen glowing on his face.

"You know Benji, you can come outside of your room. You don't have to stay hidden." Kyle brings Benjamin into an ego fit.

"What's that supposed to mean father?"

"It means ever since yesterday, I can feel how this is going to separate us if we don't communicate on an understanding here."

"An understanding? Dad, what's there to understand?" Loud and clear Benjamin speaks.

"I don't know how to say this. Are you gay? Kyle asks.

"I don't know yet. I mean I am still trying to figure all this out. I've never felt this way for a girl or boy before now, so I don't know, I don't know dad."

"So, you've never had any girlie crushes? That explains the day we had a walk on the beach, before we found out about your mom's death, you didn't really have much to say about girls." Kyle examines.

"Just because you haven't seen the right girl to grab your attention doesn't mean you're gay."

"But dad I have found plenty of girls to be cute, but I never had the urge to go out with any of them like I do with Venom. I want to kiss him."

"OOOK... OK... OK, I not ready to hear all of that." Kyle is sickened, letting the air sterilize itself. He sits in a daze.

"Do you think it's because Venom is pretty flamboyant and is attracted to you, causing you to feed off of it?"

"Well of course it is, but why am I only experiencing it now and with a boy?"

"Son, you are at the age where you are noticing these kinds of emotions, and it's okay. I get it. You know when I first saw your mother, she was jumpingout of a cab in New York. Something told me to look in her direction. There she was twenty feet in front of me, when that cab door slammed shut in the pouring rain. She tripped and fell but somehow, I was there to catch her. The sweet smell of Light Blue still lingers in my mind. Her eyes danced with mine, every word I spoke to her."

"What did you say to say to her?" Benjamin asked.

Kyle straighten his hair grasping for that youthful pride he had once upon a time. "I said… What's a beautiful young woman like you doing all alone in a big city?"

Benjamin lets down about fifteen walls just to hear his dad speak about his loving mother and how they first met. "And what did she say?"

Kyle laughs a bit, "After she could breathe on her own, she said she was running late to her show, and asked me if I would escort her and watch her from the front row."

"Did you?" Benjamin feels a heart and stomach flutter of excitement.

"Yes! I left my buddies behind and I went. It was fate. That night after the show we went to dinner and she asked me to spend the night. I thought I would sleep on her sofa five steps away. As I was about to fall asleep on the sofa, she said, aren't you going sleep over. I knew right away when I crawled in bed with her and we just held onto each other that she was the one I wanted to marry. The next morning, I was at the airport and on the plane when the pilot came over the intercom saying all flights have been cancelled. That US was under attack as we know it today as September 11th.

"Woah, so then what happened?" Benjamin frets.

"So, then I called her up and asked if I and my buddies could stay at her apartment until we could figure out how to get home nearly twenty-eight hundred miles apart. It was fate that brought us together and kept us together, because if those planes hadn't crashed into the towers, I'm not sure you and Camden would be born."

"Hey dad, so as you are telling me how you and mom met, I feel this small clearing allowing me to see why I feel the way I do about Venom. After mom died, the twins were the first people who I felt myself around. At first, I did notice Viper and her long brown hair, athletic built, but it was her twin brother's voice and smell that pulled me to him like a magnet. Also, it's weird. When I play The Call of Duty, I feel like I've met him inside the game, and he helps save my life every time. He has a British accent in the game and makes me laugh. It's funny because I feel drawn to him. I feel totally connected to him and you know what, maybe mom led his family to us from oceans apart. What if this is fate for me too dad because I can't control how I feel for Venom either."

"I really see how it is for you now after hearing more about your story too. Look, thirty years ago my father wouldn't be seated at my bedside discussing homosexuality like I am with you, and somehow, I see it's just a word now. What is the difference in heterosexual or homosexual? I don't know what it's like to be you. You are still my baby boy, and I will love you no matter who you decide to love. But when it comes to the romantic stuff, I don't have any secrets up my sleeve. You will have to figure out what to do on your own there. Just be safe is all I can say."

Benjamin reaches out to his dad for a hug. Kyle brings him into a strong hold embrace and gives him comfort.

Kyle is about to leave the room when he remembers something else to discuss. "Benji, June 12th is right around the corner. Is there something you would like to do? A party? Something low key, in our backyard, or maybe at the beach you know?"

"I haven't really thought about it dad. Maybe a party… but can I think on it first?"

"Yeah, just let me know soon so Gaby can send out inventions if need be. Hey, how about coming out of your cave and getting some lunch with me. Have you even eaten anything today?"

"No." Benjamin said.

"Well come on, I'll making you something then."

They go downstairs to the kitchen discussing what to make.

Meanwhile, at the West Covina house Waylon Warner has taken off his suit jacket and has rolled up his sleeves, pulling out a hot sheet of chocolate chip cookies. Not far from the front door he hears potential clients walking inside.

Waylon lets his presence known from the kitchen.

It's the first showing since it's been posted onto the MLS. A man in his late twenty's or early thirty's, a woman around the same age, and an infant child wrapped in a satchel around her waist.

"Hello, I'm Waylon Warner, the buyer's agent for this property currently. Would you like a freshly baked chocolate chip cookie, while you look around?"

The young man and woman each take a cookie right off the hot cookie sheet with a napkin.

Waylon hands each of them a bottle of water from the ice chest. "Make yourselves at home, I will be right here if you have any questions."

After the couple walks away to look at the rest of the house, Waylon takes the remaining cookies off the sheet, decorating them on a fancy platter.

Next, he muscles over the watermelon to the kitchen sink, washes off any potential hazards. He cuts into it letting the sweet succulent red juices fall onto the newly done granite countertop. A large spoon allows him to carve out round pieces and he puts them into a long tray.

He cuts open the pineapple and can hear the front door open with a set of feet tapping inside. He waits for whoever it is to find him in the kitchen.

"Hello, I'm Waylon Warner the buyer's agent for the property. Would you like a warm cookie or some fruit to enjoy while you walk around looking at this spectacular home?"

"Oh, these cookies smell wonderful, yes we would love one, thank you." The young woman with a small child clinging to her side said.

The first couple makes it back into the kitchen after searching through the house for signs of their future property. The man asks Waylon, "So what's the details on the house?"

"Please if you don't mind, take one of the flyers from the counter and look it over. Everything you might be curious about is more than likely listed."

The woman takes a flyer off the bar for him, and starts to read it aloud.

"So, are you looking to purchase a home soon or getting ideas for what you are looking for…?" Waylon Warner brings out his charm.

"My wife and I recently had our baby and we live on the other side of L.A. in an apartment. We'd like to raise out family in a quiet neighborhood like this one." The gentleman said.

"Sure, that's understandable. Are you currently working with an agent?"

"No, we just started looking around recently. This is our first house to even walk inside of and look at."

"So, what do you think about this home?" Waylon throws a pitch.

"It looks good. We'd like the backyard to be a little bigger, so we can put up one of those really nice wooden swing-sets for our daughter to play on, not one of those hot metal kinds we used to burn our hands on." The man chuckles.

"I think those were a little before my time." Waylon pitches back.

"No way… You can't be that much younger than me sir."

"You would be surprised." Waylon lets the ball roll off the mound.

The woman steps up to bat, "Waylon, thank you for your time. We need to get going, and start on dinner. Do you have a card or something?"

"Cards are just so ancient like those metal swings are. How about we exchange phone number and I promise not to call you without first sending you a text. I only want to check on you in a week and see how you're doing. This house will probably get an offer by tomorrow morning. This house is listed about twenty- five hundred under the market value."

"Yes, here's my number. My name is Nathan Rhodes."

"One other thing since you don't have an agent, maybe you are unaware of having a pre-qualification for intent to purchase, or do you already have one?"

"No one had told us about that. That's good to know. Thanks." Nathan Rhodes and his family walk out the front door.

Waylon goes the next couple of hours without an offer. Cookie crumbles are the only thing on the plate. All bottles of water have been depleted from the ice chest. He locks up the house thinking about the next day when everybody is out looking around after morning cartoons. This house is too darling not to sell.

Saturday May 28, 2016 starts the open house process all over again for Waylon Warner. He is dressed in an all silky coppery brown suit and pants with a blue shirt underneath it, baking chocolate chip cookies. The home fills an aroma that brings in the first guest buyers.

11 A.M. Waylon notices it's the same couple from yesterday.

"Well hello again, what brings you back?"

"My wife and I was hoping the house didn't sell yesterday. As soon as we drove off, we went to our bank and was able to get a pre-qualification letter for this house."

"You're in luck. No offers yet. So, you like the property?" Waylon smiles feeling the sincerity of his next sale coming from Mr. and Mrs. Rhodes.

"Yeah… we really do and tell you the truth our lease is up on our apartment in like sixty days. We love the neighborhood."

"So, I take it you need representation on writing out an offer on the home?"

"We do."

"You mind if we go into the dining room table and go over everything?"

"Not at all, we're ready."

"Before we get started do you have any questions for me?" Waylon asked.

"So, when we put in our offer, how long will it take before we hear back on an answer?"

"That's a great question. Well —you see this property is listed under my brokerage, Hawthorne Realty. We should get an answer back tonight."

At the table, Waylon Warner takes over as The Rhodes buyer's agent. He goes over his fiduciary duty as their agent first and has them sign on the dotted lines. Next, he listens to his clients for the offer they want to make on the home, then fills out more paperwork.

"Mr. and Mrs. Rhodes, I want to be up front with you. This is an offer. It needs to be accepted by the seller before it changes listing status in the multiple listing service. Which means it is still being viewed by all over the world."

"Does that mean somebody else can put in an offer behind us and steal our property?" Rhodes asked.

"Technically yes. If the seller likes another offer more. Then yes."

Meanwhile at the Hawthorne residence, Gaby is preparing lunch for the two starving boys who woke up late for breakfast.

Kyle is getting dressed for success. He can feel it in his veins, his fixer upper is about to profit eighty thousand plus in cash. No sooner as he's tying his shoes, his cell phone rings.

"Hawthorne here."

Forty-five minutes away east over in West Covina, Waylon Warner speaks up about an offer being presented. The buyers would like an answer by tonight."

Kyle clears his throat, "I will defiantly consider this. Are you going to email me the offer or would you like for me to swing by the property now for the action?"

"Yeah, go ahead and swing on by. We'll be waiting."

"Alright, I'm on my way buddy."

Forty-five past 2 P.M. Kyle parks behind the fourth car back from the property. He gets out of his black Mercedes freshly dressed in a designer silky silvery blue suit wearing dark framed designer sunglasses.

He takes them off right as he is walking up to the door, where an elderly man and woman are walking out. Both look like they slept on the same side of the bed for years as the both walk with a limp, in need of hip surgery.

Letting them by, Kyle soon enters the property finding Waylon in the kitchen with his clients.

"Mr. and Mrs. Rhodes, this is Kyle Hawthorne also the broker, also the seller of the property."

"Hello, I hope I didn't keep you waiting too long. Traffic was a mess." Kyle Hawthorne waits to receive the offer.

"Are we at a disadvantage on buying this house?" Mrs. Rhodes asks Waylon Warner.

"No darling. Not at all. You are serious buyers on this home. You came in yesterday knocking my socks off when you took it upon yourselves to get prequalified when you left here. You're serious, I'm serious. And we are about to walk the rest of these folks out of your new house when we show the seller the offer." Waylon replies to the buyers.

"Are you ready to hand over the offer so I can read over it Mr. Warner?" Kyle Hawthorne asked.

"Absolutely Kyle. I've all the attachments bound with a paperclip." Waylon Warner smiles.

"Waylon… ah, give me a few minutes to take a walk out back here and consider everything on this offer. Excuse me folks." Kyle takes the forms out back to read in privacy.

Within twenty minutes he comes back inside a little dissatisfied, "Waylon everything looks promising except the closing date. The most I can do is forty-five days, not sixty days. Besides, in doing this, it will give your clients time to move without rushing everything and they will get like a free month moving in. You know it takes time getting deed of trust transferred. If everybody can agree to this new term, then we have a deal." Kyle leaves the ball in their court having the strong sense of the West Covina house being sold. He puts on his dark shades and is done for the day.

Chapter
SEVENTEEN

Outside in the pool area, Kyle stretches out, laying on the lawn lounger next to Gaby who is on the phone being cutesy with her boyfriend on the first hot Saturday in June 2016.

He's in a bit of reflection as he stares into air particles floating around in the sunlight's warm penetrating golden rays. A solid week has passed by since Benjamin had gotten his first ever, suspension. He was always the good kid, achieving easy A's, an honors society student, essentially just an excellent person.

A lot is on Kyle's mind. The fatal car accident. Benjamins two-day suspension. Benjamin coming out as gay. Back and forth to the police station and a forensic psychologist. Driving back and forth remodeling a fixer upper then selling it.

After the West Covina house went under contract last weekend, Kyle decided to take a tiny break from life.

To top it all off, Kyle is alone. Sure, he has support at every angle. Waylon Warner and team of processors Kimberly and Donna at his Brokerage.

He has Gaby, bless her heart.

She stepped at twenty-two taking care of the whole Hawthorne house and the boys, including Chips Ahoy. Transporting the boys to and from school and events.

There is Doctor Normal Yates who is doing a fantastic job of talking with and supporting Benjamin and Kyle, giving them both a place to speak and explore their feelings without judgement.

Then there is Tony Relako, a treat for Gaby to have on the weekends. Real fun stuff.

Oh, and then there's the sweet baby angels, Venom and Viper, who arrived just in time to pull Benjamin out from the dark places he was going in his mind. The twins came at such a divine time, crucial in Benjamin's self-love for the first time.

Kyle likes Mr. and Mrs. Gethin as well.

Out of all the sudden changes in his life, Angela was the biggest loss he would never get to wrap his energy into anymore. His safe place was gone.

Kyle has just publicized in his mind all the people he is thankful for. He takes in the nature and glowing sunlight beaming down on his fit body.

He's bit thirsty now, parched at the mouth, sensing the vibes Gaby is having fun with Tony on Skype.

Rising out of his lounger, he questions Gaby if she would like something to drink.

She still has puffy eyes from waking up only twenty minutes ago. She is too busy to respond.

Chips Ahoy follows Kyle inside the house. At the refrigerator he grabs a carton of lemonade, pouring himself and her a tall glass. He even garnishes it with a lemon wedge.

Benjamin walks into the kitchen with his eyes glued to his phone. He opens the pantry grabbing a box of cereal for brunch.

"Morning! Hey, it's a beautiful day outside, why don't you wake your brother, and both of you eat before taking Chips on a walk. The dog seems a little depressed." Kyle directs.

Benjamin doesn't want to disappoint his father and immediately agrees.

"Dad we don't have any more cereal." As he pours the rest into the bowl filling it up with milk.

"We have plenty of eggs. How about eggs, toast and jam? Go get Camden up and I'll start it."

Kyle serves the boys eggs and toast at the table. He sets the jam on the table with a butter knife on top of the lid. The boys dig in.

Kyle carries both glasses of watered-down lemonade outside with him.

He finds Gaby on Skype with Tony discussing coming over. "Why don't you ask him about next weekend?" He coughs.

"Oh yeah." Gaby retorts.

"Ask me what about next weekend?" Tony asks, in his best smoky voice.

"Benji's birthday is this Sunday. I was going to ask you but totally forgot to."

"Yeah, well duh! I will be there. Do you know what he likes?"

"I don't know. He's into music and on his phone a lot. Football stuff maybe, The Raiders."

Tony laughs, "I better not get him anything that reminds him of Tomb Raider. I kind of cracked a joke the last time I was over. He didn't respond well."

"You're bad." She cuts up with him.

"No, I will just go out today and get him something really nice." Tony decides to get off the phone and complete the task.

An hour later Benjamin and his brother finally muster the energy to take their multi-color maltase on a walk.

No other kids are outside enjoying the beautiful smell of flowers and cut grass, next to all the palms.

Only a few older folks are pulling up weeds in their flowerbeds and a lawn service is blowing away the cut grass.

Benjamin's heart starts to flutter fifty feet into walking. He presses his hand to his chest like its heartburn but then something else runs up and down his spine.

He hands the leash over to Camden starts to worry.

Benjamin witnesses the streets around him passing him by in slow motion as his heart pounds harder against his chest. His eyes go numb, but he totally has heightened senses during whatever is happening.

His knees start to burn like fire.

"Benji, are you okay?" Camden marvels a few tears up.

Benjamin snap out of whatever funk he was inside of. "Yeah, I'm okay. I think it's just gas." He ricochets a belching rocket tank of gas from his breath.

Chips Ahoy gets up off his hind legs and belly, as the boys proceed on.

Not long after, they turn the corner and find Venom and Viper at a pause from riding skateboards. Venom appears to be wiping off his knee.

They walk right up to them. "Are you Okay?" They asked.

"Yeah, I'm good. I fell off my board like a complete blooper pooper. I must have caught a rock and slipped. My knees just hurt a bit." He swears off in pain.

Viper just stands there laughing.

"You need a hand?" Benjamin asked.

"I'm good, really. You hungry? We are on the way home for lunch."

They lock eyes and suddenly any pain the both felt on their knees gone away, miraculously healed.

"No, we ate already, we are just out walking the dog. Maybe we will see you later?"

"Yeah maybe." Venom closes and walks away.

Benjamin and Camden continue.

The twins fade off in the other direction.

Camden teases his brother about the eyes Venom has on him and vice versa. Benjamin's not bothered by it and keeps on walking.

The thought of Venom falling and scraping his knee is like what he experienced before he found him the next street over.

Was that a coincidence he questions?

He doesn't think so as he looks at his phone it's 1:11 P.M.

Whatever it is, Benjamin has a warm calming energy over him now full of light and love. The reflecting sun beams the rest of their walk with Chips Ahoy before they walk in a complete one-mile circle and go home.

Meanwhile Tony steps out of his truck at a Best Buy parking lot and stands against his truck door finishing off his cigarette. He smiles and nods his head at the people walking by him coughing out the disgusting smell of smoke.

He doesn't pay any mind to how rudely they ignored him as he finishes up and walks inside the self-retracting glass doors.

Tony aimlessly walks throughout the store looking for a birthday gift.

Three or four rows make a graveyard in the music section. Only one person inside it is searching for some inspiration.

He frowns.

Not at the person, but because of how fast everything changes, how dead it is inside a store he remembers was the place to be fifteen years ago.

The movement on the far-right side of the store has Tony puzzled what could be going on in the laptops section. He looks around rationalizing what a fourteen-year-old boy might like from an uncle who has rarely been in his life.

He fidgets around with the different colors of laptops and its keyboards.

Crossing paths with a pink Mac, he chuckles from the reaction he might if his nephew unwrapped that.

Something calls him over to the cell phones.

Remembering what Gaby said about him being on social media, he thinks a new cell phone might work.

Something else takes Tony's attention as he's walking over.

A young boy, about Benjamin's age is wearing big black goggles on his head. He creeps over curious to see what he's got on.

An employee at the store is giving the young fella a tutorial on what is called: virtual reality head gear.

The logo on the front face of the product is unique with what appears to be, two sevens on both sides and the number eight in middle.

Tony picks one up, trying it on. He finds himself blind folded at the main menu. He tilts his head looking up and down and all-around, pressing buttons on the side.

Lost on YouTube, he searches the box for a live concert captured by an audience member.

He smiles with the goggles on feeling like he is on front row stage next to U2 –Bono as Tony watches a show recorded live.

"Looks like you're really enjoying the Noon Virtual Reality Head Gear. Let me know if you have any questions?" An employee stands right next to him asked.

"This is pretty cool man. We didn't have this kind of stuff growing up." Tony marvels.

"Yeah, it gives Xbox and Netflix a whole new experience." The young man said.

Tony takes the head gear off and asks about the specifications and release date.

He's convincing himself to purchase one for Benjamin and one for himself, and possibly even Gaby one, so they can watch Netflix and chill on the sofa.

He carries two boxes up to the front of the store to check out.

Tony leaves Best Buy and lights up a cigarette to smoke on the way over to his truck.

He decides to Skype up Gaby.

"Hey Hun, I thought I would show you what I bought for Benji's birthday. Do you think he will like this head gear technology?"

"Of course, he will, I can see him getting in a Lyft with his new friends. Maybe they have facemask too." She laughs.

They both laugh together.

Tony finishes up his cigarette flicking it into the shrubs.

"I better get off here now, I need to drive on and get a gift bag for his facemask. I'll see you next weekend."

They blow kisses to each other on Skype and go separate ways.

133

Chapter
EIGHTEEN

The lawn guys are over doing their jobs. Blades are spinning from the high-powered engine lawnmowers spitting grass on the sidewalks.

Another guy blows the grass into the street. The engines of the lawnmowers are loud —one in the front yard —one in the back yard.

Gaby's inside the Hawthorne house and has just taken all the glassware, plates and bowls out of the kitchen cabinets for late spring cleaning.

Its mid-day Thursday. Kyle isn't in the mood rushing around parking lots so close to the end of school year.

From home, Kyle texts Dr. Yates and he decides to cancel the next two remaining sessions.

Benjamin appears to be coping with life better now that he has his new twin buddies to play with. The next text he writes is a payment for lost time.

Kyle does a bit of real estate marketing, but not really planning to act. Not thrilled to keep scrolling through tens of thousands of properties sold or just listed. He stands up with a hurting in his heart and takes a book off his dusty shelf.

No matter what he does, he can't seem to get Angela off his mind. He's lost inside. He knows if he doesn't accept the fact she's gone, he won't move on.

In his heart he feels like he's cheating or something. It's only been three months. Her energy is still on him caressing his arms and legs gently. That's where he feels it most when he thinks of her.

Kyle pictures himself living a third dimensional life with just himself and the boys. Going to eat at five-star restaurants alone. Going on date nights to the movies, a nice walk on the beach, and family trips. It would be him alone with the boys.

Flipping page after page of an old Nicholas Sparks book, he intended to read three years ago, he takes a deep breath, trying to give this book some justice, trying to comprehend it forty minutes later. –Yeah, that didn't work.

The only thing on his mind is the lonely thoughts of missing his wife. He puts down the book, escaping the stale low vibes he sat in for hours.

Getting off his angry tailbone, he's in need of a quick stretching alignment.

He goes into the kitchen hoping to find Gaby in there and to ask her out on a drive. When he sees every dish in the house out on the ruby black marble, he decides not to bother her.

Instead, he goes to the long glass window in the kitchen and just stands.

Vulnerable, he's in need of a woman's support. He says to Gaby, "I don't know what to do with myself anymore. I'm here for a reason, right? I still have the boys, I'm here for my clients in real estate, but to enjoy myself… I've lost it. I can't even pick up a book without thinking about how lonesome it is without my wife here. I miss her so much." He lets out his breath in pain.

"Give it some time handsome. When you are ready for your next move, you will make it. Right now, you are detoxing from everything. You need to heal." Gaby takes a break from polishing each glass to a clean shine.

She walks over to where he stands, next to a gigantic glass wall full of sunlight reaching both of them like angels.

The hug of a woman gives Kyle some feeling of healing and comfort he had missed.

He finds peace from Gaby and goes on about his day. She goes back to polishing dinnerware.

The next day Kyle wakes up full of warrior strength. One hug from a feminine touch could move him into strong colorful rays, while he lifts his children out of bed this morning.

Friday, June 10, 2016. It was last day of school.

An overwhelming perception of freedom gave a chariot a way of vacation.

A break from learning new things, especially lately.

The last day always ends in an early release. Gaby doesn't have to bag up a healthy lunch for the boys. Kyle will be picking them up and taking them to lunch.

A really great thing about California weather is the cars all turn into convertibles when on a drive, nearly all year around.

Kyle gets to blast his hip hoppy and poppy music to be the cool dad. The kids bop their head to the beat on the way to school. Benjamin is on social media.

Camden is the first child to get to school. Benjamin lets him out of the car and slaps the back of his neck. "Have a great day at school son." He laughs.

"Silly. Are you reading my lines again? You do realize I'm the father in charge here."

Benjamin laughs out, "Sorry."

Camden turns around with his backpack on, waving to say goodbye, while he walks into the last day of second grade.

Kyle drives Benjamin away to school.

Arriving, Kyle speaks to his son before he gets out. "I'll pick you up around noon. We'll go to our favorite boardwalk place and eat. Have a great day."

"See you later dad." Benjamin finds the twins getting out of the car behind them. Naturally Benjamin gravitates over to them.

"Hey guys, you look great on the last day of school. You got any plans later when schools out?" Benjamins teases.

"No, our parents get off work late most night, and can't make plans on a sudden impulse." Viper says while walking next to her brother who is collecting Benjamin's energy while staring him up and down.

"What about you?" Viper inquires.

"Later my dad is picking my brother and me up from school and is taking us to the boardwalk to eat. Maybe, I can ask my dad if you can join us." Benjamin replies.

"That sounds fun. We haven't really been many places since we moved here a month ago." Viper murmured.

At the lockers they put away their stuff and each of them go separate ways to their classes.

Hour by hour that passes Benjamin thinks about walking along the shoreline with Venom by his side, full of experiences of England and how he seemed to handle tragedies, his receptions for love, his meanings of friendships and family gatherings.

Benjamin went through three periods with Venom on his mind. The next place they would meet is the last period.

Out of the blue, walking to his locker, Benjamin has a revelation of grabbing Venom's face and kissing it.

Back at the lockers, Benjamin grabs his last textbook, from health class, to turn in.

Venom brushes against Benjamin walking to his locker, five doors down, never breaking eye contact. This sparks fireworks inside of Benjamin. The magnetic pull between the two is obvious.

Normally, Venom has a lot to say, but all day he chose to make it clear with his eyes instead.

Benjamin shuts the locker door and walks towards Venom. "I thought you could use something for your thoughts."

He relives the wildest dream of grabbing his face and kissing him in front of everybody on the last day of school.

He wanted everybody to witness his love for the boy who made him smile. Every second their mouths were locked together, expressed gratitude in a completely freeing way.

In total bliss, Benjamin just wanted to say, "Thank you for making my days better."

They kiss the next ten seconds in public and in bravery.

"I thought you had been trying to tell me something all day long. You get quiet when you need some love. So, this is what you've been trying to communicate since we've met." Benjamin feels fully alive.

"Yeah, I didn't want to scare you away. I didn't know how you would take me as being gay." Venom is being unusually shy, beaming of pink hearts and glowing from head to toe.

There must be twenty students staring at them when Viper walks up all the sudden. Of course, she knows. She has caught the tail end of them pulling their lips apart with a mutual glow completing their present figurines.

She could see a sparkling smile transfer over to Benjamin from Venom.

Surprisingly everyone staring were only trying to process two boys kissing. Everybody's eyes walked off in awe except one boy, who's slamming his locker shut.

The anger is in his own world and hopefully, none of anyone's business.

The two make it official on the last day of eight grade, holding hands as they walked into health, last period.

Mr. Franklin's Health class was the only class Benjamin and Venom had together.

Last period. Last day. The last day in middle school.

They sat on opposite sides of the classroom from each other, but felt like they were connected telepathically, both of them feeling the love radiating between them.

The lights are off.

There is a short film about peer pressure on the projection screen.

How to say no to drugs and sex was the lesson as summer break was rapidly approaching, only thirty minutes left.

The classroom giggles during the film. Some of the students hide their phones in obscure places, reading their phone screens. —Social media surfing.

Benjamin catches Venom checking him out from the corner of his eye.

The bell rings. Everyone rises out of their seats.

Benjamin walks over to Venom grabbing his hand. They take a moment to connect before walking out hand and hand to their lockers.

"I need to text my dad and see if you can come eat with us."

"As long as Viper can come too."

"Of course."

Viper joins them at the locker while Benjamin is texting. Venom explains to her the plan. They walk outside where Kyle is waiting on them.

Tony pulls up to the Hawthorne house. He has a special lunch date with his girl who's inside the house probably touching up her face with makeup.

He smells like a half a pack of smoked Camels as he gives the front door a good solid knock.

Gaby opens it dressed in cut-offs and a tank top, her swim suit on underneath, flirting with her long golden-brown legs. Her hair is down. She flips it to one side while she extenuates her non-curvaceous body.

"Hello beautiful." Tony flirts.

She doesn't say a word. Only kisses him, and gives back a greeting.

"Are you ready to go?" Tony asks.

"Um-hmmm." She smiles, keeping her eyes locked with his.

Together they walk on the grass to get to his truck.

Tony takes Gaby to a pretty casual wing shop right on Hollywood Boulevard. The split two different flavors of wings from the menu. Tony orders a green bottle neck of beer, squeezes a lime into it.

Gaby orders a strawberry margarita.

Both have everything they need right at sight.

They take their sweet time with every bite of hot and sticky, bone in chicken flesh.

Afterwards Tony takes a smoke break outside by his truck while Gaby washes up in the restroom.

He drives her along Venice Beach and then over to the Santa Monica Boardwalk.

Tony circles around the strip forever searching a place to park. It's packed more than normally for today is the last day of the school year. Everybody seems to have the same idea of soak up the water and sun.

The sand is covered with people and seagulls. Tony and Gaby carry their sack ridden folding armchairs, umbrella and ice chest. They find the only place available, next to man and woman wearing swimwear from twenty years ago.

Tony grabs a beer out of the cooler. "Want one?" He offers Gaby.

"No. I still don't like beer. I will help myself to some water and a little bit of pineapple. Want some?" She flirts.

"No thanks, I'm trying to watch my girlie figure."

Tony strips down to only his swim shorts, showing off his hairy chest.

Gaby takes her top off, a little unsure of her body. She unbuttons her jean shorts and lowers them down to her ankles onto the sand. She has her swimsuit on.

He ambles down to the water. She follows him through the crowds of people having total beach fun. They dodge the boogie boarders on the current riptide crashing into the shoreline.

Tony dips himself under the cool water, soothing his hot body. Gaby follows him inside the shallow ocean blue. They swim around in a salt bath, holding onto each other, and kiss.

Soon after they get out of the water, they walk over to their umbrella. Gaby recognizes Viper, who is bending down and collecting seashells.

"Oh hey, you're the new people across the street from us." Gaby stands there twisting out her drenched salty hair.

"Yes, I'm here with my brother and the Hawthorne's. They're right over there." She points out and walks over to them.

"Didn't expect to see you both here." Kyle's excited to see them.

"Yeah, I got here for lunch. We had some wings, then decided to come see what this part of the pacific looks like. I've seen San Diego plenty of times." Tony slurs out words and stumbles in his walk.

Benjamin clutches Venom's hand and takes him away for a while.

They walk over to the pier rides.

The big wheel is slowly turning. The sea dragon boat is gliding back and forth. The lights flash all around in the daylight.

Tony nods his head scratching his sun burnt arms. He waits for the boys to get out of sound distance before asking, "What's going on with those two?"

"Are you asking if they're a couple? Yes, I think they are, but let's not stir up anything right here, right now. Tony, if you want to talk to me later, please do. This is new for all of us including my son… Okay?" Kyle implores.

The sun begins falling into the water way over yonder by Alaska.

One by one, crowd surfers begin to pack up and either run to the boardwalk for grub, or get in their cars to go home.

The Hawthorne's get tired of idling in the sand as their stomachs growl. Gaby starts talking about dinner and what sounds good.

Tony takes the lead and walks away to find a place to urinate. The six pack of beers he drank is about to go right through him.

Kyle helps Gaby pack up and waits for Tony to come back, before Kyle takes the boys and the twin's home.

CHAPTER
NINETEEN

Sunday, early morning, Tony and Gaby are on the sofa swapping the virtual reality head gear he brought for Benjamin's birthday.

They get a kick from new age technology. Gaby gets over the gawkiness of being blind to reality and stuck under goggles.

Kyle joins them in the living room for a minute as he's just waking up.

He has on his long pants and a black cotton sleeve shirt. Greeting them on the sofa, he wonders what the hell kind of concoction she has on her head, covering up her eyes.

Both Gaby and Tony are in their own world, so Kyle doesn't bother them. He wanders onwards into the kitchen puzzled.

Tony's relaxed out with his hands folded in content. Gaby plays a ten- minute tutorial on how to make a lemon pound cake with a fruity iced topping.

After seeing Kyle go into the kitchen, Tony thinks about having his first cup of coffee. He gets up and leaves Gaby behind. Maybe she will conjure up an imaginary cupcake for breakfast as his stomach roars.

She rests on the sofa in amusement this Sunday morning.

Benjamin and Camden come down to join everyone. They see Gaby on the sofa vegged out with googles on her face.

"Gaby what is that? What's on your head?" Camden nudges to get her attention.

She takes it off not knowing what to call it. She looks at the object for a

141

better description. She keeps as quiet as possible. "Noon goggles, I guess."

"They look like virtual head gear everyone is raving about. Can I see them?" Benjamin asks.

He tries them on seeking a thrill. He lets out some words of amazement, wishing he had a pair.

"Oh, by the way, somebody's birthday is today. Happy birthday Benji." Gaby said out loud giving him a rub on the shoulder.

"Well there's birthday boy all awake and ready for a party." Tony blurts from across the room. He's with Kyle, both with steaming mugs of coffee.

Benjamin stretches trying to take the focus off him.

Camden takes over the goggles.

"I didn't expect you to be up so early on your birthday son. It's supposed to be summer break."

"Schools been out like two days. I'm still stuck on the 7 A.M. schedule. I did sleep in a little though, it's ten til' eight." Benjamin giggles.

"Oh Benji, I got you a little something for your birthday. Let me run and get it from the guestroom." Tony darts out of the room.

"Son, have you decided what to do today? Would you like to go out or plan something here?" Kyle asked.

"Yeah I was hoping we could pick up the twins and go back to the boardwalk. Venom mentioned yesterday it was their first time to be there, yet they didn't ride anything. So, I would like to go to the Santa Monica Pier for my birthday. But first, can we get cheese cake at the factory in Marina Del Rey?"

"That's perfect. What time… around noon?" Kyle plans in his day.

"I don't know. That's kind of early. How about 2 P.M?"

"Did I hear someone mention Noon?" Fretting over give away the goggles, Tony enters the room handing Benjamin his gift.

"Yeah 2 P.M. works great dad."

Benjamin takes the gift bag off Tony's hands. He carefully peeks inside knowing how his uncle likes to pack old rugged stuff.

"Camden, will you open the door for Chips Ahoy? He's dancing to go pee." Kyle asked.

Camden waits to see what his brother pulls out of the bag for his birthday, then goes towards the kitchen door, letting him out.

"Thank you so much Uncle Tony. I tried yours on from Gaby's head. These are way cool."

"Enjoy them. They will defiantly give you something to Google about.

You will be looking up at everything."

Kyle puts on Tony's VR head gear checking them out for size.

Tony goes outside for a smoke break. He's jittering from morning coffee and everybody else's excitement.

Outside he lights up, takes a puff like men who smoke do, holding between his index and thumb. Tony's Sunday vibe currently is to blow smoke at the dog.

Chips Ahoy stares at him, then gives a frown turning to meet up with the birds chirping down by the tennis court.

The morning sun quickly settles to mid-day position. Everyone seems to have gotten up early to get ready and go. That's how fast time is flying today.

Benjamin and his family get in Gaby's SUV and Tony's truck to drive to the place they will have brunch and cheesecake near Marina Del Rey.

It was five minutes until 2 P.M. Benjamin and his family sat waiting for the twins to arrive at the restaurant.

The server had already been at their table for a drink order and then brought the drinks out on a big black serving tray. She placed each custom drink in front of their view.

2:07 P.M. The twins come prancing through the door, and with the help of a server, they are assisted over to the table.

Viper is carrying a large gift bag with a balloon tied to it. Venom has in his hand a yellow envelope, a pure hearted smile on his face and a glowing pink aura for his boyfriend.

"Hey guys, thanks for making it out." Benjamin strikes up.

"Happy Birthday buddy." Viper sets down the bag at his side, giving him a hug. She takes a seat two down from Benjamin.

Venom hands him the card and gives Benjamin a smile, his almond eyes twinkling, then takes a seat next to him saying, "Happy birthday gorgeous."

"Thanks guys." Benjamin sparkles.

The waitress comes back over. Kyle orders sharable appetizers for everyone. Fresh bread is picked over at the table.

Tony takes a sip of beer, gobbles his slice of bread and butter in two bites, then takes another gulp.

The waitress sets four different plates of appetizers down in the middle of the table, and takes everyone's request for cheesecake.

As everyone enjoys the food and the company of each other, the cheesecakes arrive on a huge serving tray.

Seven different flavors of cheesecake are placed beautifully in front of everyone's watering mouths.

Kyle places a single candle in Benjamin's chocolate mousse cheesecake.

Tony lights the candle for him.

Everyone at the table, including some of the wait staff, stops what they're doing to wish Benjamin a *happy fourteen years*.

He blows out a single red candle.

Everyone cheers him on, then picks up their forks, and gobbles into a decadent slice of cheesecake.

After eating, Benjamin opens his card Venom brought him.

"Oh, go on Benji, read it out loud. Let the table know what you got." Tony pestered.

Benjamin continues to read, while contemplating if he should stop or not.

Benjamin identifies parts of himself inside this card with symbolic hearts and kisses drawn next to his name. It was shown in the card that right away Venom loved Benjamin more that words could express.

"Ah, that's okay. Some things I would like to keep all to myself." Benjamin deters from sharing Venom's exact admiration.

After reading the card he sticks the crisp Ben Franklin's in his wallet. He leans over to hug Venom.

"Thank you. You're a thoughtful boyfriend. You didn't have to get me anything though. I already have you."

"Normally I like warping up gifts, but today I thought since your name is Benji, I would get you some Benji's."

Reaching for his next gift to open, Benjamin grabs the gift bag Viper brought with her. Inside is a black and white yin-yang decked out skateboard.

It's totally official, the three of them would be skating around all of Hancock Park this summer.

Gaby gets up to use the restroom and freshen up a bit before leaving.

All packed up, in Gaby's SUV and Tony's truck they drive to Santa Monica Boardwalk.

They are at the pier inside of Pacific Park. Kyle gives his son a couple of hundreds to get tickets for all the rides and games they wanted.

"Benjamin, watch over your brother. Call me when you are ready to go or need more money or anything." Kyle pronounces.

"Yeah, yeah."

Tony, Gaby and Kyle walk around on their own leaving the kids to have fun.

"Call me or send me a text when you're ready to meet up or need more money for something. We will be around here and along the shore line I'm sure. Enjoy your birthday son."

After walking around for some time, Benjamin, his brother, and the twins decide to hang out in the Midway Game section for a while. Inside of Pacific Playland Arcades they scope out the games calling their names.

It's nearing 5 P.M. The sunlight falls right on the structure's awning top.

Lights are blinking and flashing everywhere. Mainstream pop music blares on speakers competing with the noises of video games. The place is packed with all age groups and tourists. Benjamin catches sight of a couple of games opening across the room.

"Do you want to play air hockey?" Benjamin asks.

"It's your birthday. If you want to play air hockey, let's play air hockey." Venom dances in place building up energy. He's not holding back like he did in tennis when they first challenge each other across the courts.

Benjamin rushes up to the cashier to change in the hundred-dollar bill and returns with four cards loaded with twenty dollars on each for starters.

He hands each of them a card and is quick to jump on one of the available air hockey tables. Viper and Camden grab the other table, two over from the boys.

Viper swipes her card getting their games going. She grabs the puck, slides it down to Camden. He scores right away.

"You little punk devil. You're already pulling a fast one me." She laughs grabbing the puck, and lays it on the table about to scurry it off the wall.

Venom finally stops twirling the hand piece on the table waiting for Benjamin to get it to work. He had card issues or something. The lights turn on and the air on the table is now blowing.

"Way to go Ace. Thought we would have to wait to take over my sisters table. Ready now?"

"Yeah, I am." He walks to his spot grabbing the puck from the hole.

Intuitively, they ping the puck back and forth not letting the other score. It's a legit game between the two. They both focus hard, each keeping guard of their hole, while keeping direct eye contact with each other, sear starts to roll down the tops of their face. Still, no score on the board.

Benjamin takes a wide-open shot and scores.

Venom let him win.

"Hey, I thought you were bringing your A-Game. You're just gonna let me move in on you?" Benjamin wipes the sweat off his face.

"Happy birthday Benji." Venom blows a winking kiss at him, bending down for the puck.

Benjamin takes what he feels to heart while looking to see what the scoreboard says on Viper and Camden. The score is five to four.

Benjamin gets back into his game.

Venom strikes the puck hard against the right side of the wall with his left hand. Benjamin blocks it. Back and forth they go again. The challenge is on.

Camden and Viper finish their game and walk over to their siblings to cheer them on. The score is six to six. Next one wins.

Benjamin lets Venom take it. The game shuts off immediately without spending more money on electricity.

"I'm thirsty Benji. Can we get shaved ice?" Camden asks while walking alongside the others.

At the shaved ice stand, they look over flavors as the ocean water rolls up calmly. The sun reflects into their eyes.

The twins step up to order. Both reach for red flavored ice in a cup.

Benjamin agrees with Camden on the flavor blue raspberry.

They enjoy eating their flavored ice at a table nearby.

Venom strikes up a conversation with Benjamin. "What was your favorite foods growing up?"

"My mom used to give us blueberry yogurt with fresh bananas, and strawberries on top with like this granola crunch on it too. My dad would pour us a huge bowl of Strawberry Special K… in the evening I remember eating street tacos with my dad. He would bring like fifteen of those suckers' home. You know what street tacos are don'tcha?"

Venom laughs from a red shaved ice mouth, "I've only been to the States like a couple months. The only thing I had on the streets of Cambridge are Jacket Potatoes. I'd be up for trying street tacos one night and…the next night you can try a jacket potato from my mum."

Benjamin looks like a Smurf with his blue mouth, "That sounds lovely. So, what are your favorite foods?"

"Growing up, mum made us buttery crumpets. Occasionally, I would pour a tip of honey on mine. We would make roast dinner on Sunday's. I remember back home how she'd cover my whole plate in brown gravy including the brussels and bread. Now we're still getting used to so many fast food places to eat out."

"I've never had crumpets or roast dinner like you're describing or brown gravy…What the…?" Benjamin licked his lips.

"You've never had the gravy at KFC? The brown gravy drizzled onto the potato mash." Venom asked.

"Oh yeah, I have. Okay and your roast dinner makes a ton of sense now.

Everything covered in juicy brown would deffo be like a steak dinner or roast dinner, whatever you called it."

"So, what are crumpets?"

Venom finishes his cherry ice, "Crumpets are like pancakes with a flat bottom, but not as thick as a pancake. Crumpets are airy, having about a million holes, so when you put a spat of butter it melts into them and gushes from pockets in every squishy bite you take." Venom is now licking his lips.

"So, what about animals? Did you have any in England growing up?"

"No, we never had any. We did go out to our neighbor's field and feed horses from time to time, but no we didn't have any dogs or cats. Allergies… our parents wouldn't let us have any. I've always wanted a pretty little prancing poodle. A black and white one." He smiles.

"Nice! We got Chips Ahoy right before Camden was born. I was five. Wow! My dog is nine years old and still full of playful energy."

Benjamin and Venom take a break from conversing, shifting their focus onto their sibling's conversation about walking next to Harrods during wintery white Christmas's, sipping hot chocolate from Costa's.

Viper notices the boys are ready. "Let's get up and go ride some rides."

The first ride they stand in a line about fifty deep is the Pacific Plunge. Twenty minutes of anticipation goes by fast at nearly ten people at a time riding.

There is a gap in the middle seat since there are only four riding in Benjamin's group.

The Pacific Plunge takes them straight to the top then drops them thirty feet below. People on the ride scream and some lose their stomachs. About six more times until it's over and they get off, pumped to ride another one.

After waiting in line ten minutes they get on the Scrambler. They sit two by two. Benjamin and Venom in one cabin while Viper and Camden are in the one behind them.

As the ride starts, a cool Pacific breeze blows across their faces.

This ride speeds up as their feet dangle five feet from concrete. The ride pushes them forward in their cabins and to a complete stop, as the machine in the middle rotates them and shoots them in a new direction for five minutes.

Getting off the ride they put their faces back into place after being stretched out from wind pressing against them.

The next one is the intimidating looking roller coaster clicking its way all the way to the top then gently gliding them around the park giving them a view of the ocean as well as the other rides and games.

Venom took Benjamin's hand on this ride and it gave Benjamin butterflies.

By dusk the lights are strobing and glowing all around Pacific Park.

All four children enter the short line to the Sea Dragon. They get on the ride pretty fast.

Waiting for the ride to start, Camden wants to ask his brother something.

Camden's brother is sitting behind him and as he turns around to ask, Camden catches Benjamin's mouth latched to Venom's.

In shock, Camden turns back around in his seat fast.

Viper catches wind by the blushing of Camden's face. "Why's your face gone red?"

She turns to see her brother pulling apart from Benjamin. "You're telling your secrets. Now everyone on here knows how smurfity red dragons play around with green sea monsters. Jezzz…"

She faces forward in her seat laughing to herself. The ride takes off to a slow start, aiming towards the ocean. Then gravity pulls the sea monster back, and darts them faster towards the ocean over the course of a few minutes.

As the children are in the air at full speed of the Sea Dragon, Kyle, Tony and Gaby spot them on the ride and stand on the other side of the fence line, waiting for them to get done. They are pooped from a long day and ready to leave the park.

Kyle witnesses how close Benjamin is to Venom.

They are practically leg over legging each other with their hands locked together like they are so happy together.

The ride ends. They get off.

Benjamin spots his dad in the dark waving his lit-up cell phone, calling them over as it is getting dark outside.

"Hey dad, if it's okay with you, can Venom sleep over tonight?" Benjamins stand next to everybody trying not to give away how happy he is around Venom.

Venom looks a bit anxious all the sudden.

"I don't know son. This is too early for me to think. He is your friend, yes, but he is also your boyfriend too. It's my job to protect you."

Tony and Gaby whistle their way out of the intense awkwardness.

"Protect me from what dad? Eww." Benjamin gets a sour face thinking about something he isn't ready for yet.

"Wouldn't his father care to know, he's staying the night?"

Benjamin turns to Venom, "Will you text your folks and see if it's okay?"

"Yeah, sure." Venom nervously begins to type.

Turning completely away from the situation Kyle gives out a loud sigh, pretending to look for Tony and Gaby.

Venom gets back a text, responding out, "Yes, I can sleep over."

"So, can he dad?"

"His parents already believe he is so yes, but one of you is sleeping on the floor or something. That's my rule."

At home Benjamin and Venom shower in separate bathrooms washing off the sand from being at the Santa Monica Pier all evening.

Getting into comfy pajamas after showers, Benjamin entices Venom with a large bowl of cheesy Doritos and some cans of soda.

Laying on the bed, Venom is watching videos of Benjamin's new birthday present that Tony got him.

He bops his head to the beat of a music video while popping into his mouth cheesy tortilla strips.

Benjamin admires the love he feels for him. He likes that Venom can be himself around him. That he is comfortable around him. The loss he felt from losing his mother is being healed by Venom's companionship. His soft gentle touch. His warm sweet embraces. His gorgeous sexy smiling eyes.

Yes, Benjamin found Venom attractive.

They lay together holding hands until the sodas are gone, the music stops, and their eyes fall back into their heads as they were not supposed to do. Welcome to being fourteen years old Benjamin Hawthorne.

Chapter
TWENTY

It's the first day of March 2018,

The Hawthorne family has survived the death of Angela like a prickly thorn bush as the seasons changed. Everything in the last couple of years has settled into place, although Angela went to Heaven, The Hawthorne's must move on.

A significant amount of sorrow has been swept over like withered leaves falling in the wind that came barreling around to carry the dryness away.

Kyle hasn't cared for his grooming standards in the last few weeks. He's let his beard get rough around his face.

He comes out of his room and into the kitchen scratching his scruffy beard and rubbing away hermits of sand that's camped around the slits of his eyes from last night.

Kyle gets himself ready first, before waking up his second grader and sophomore in high school child, so he can get them off to school on time.

Kyle stands at the refrigerator grabbing bite-size blocks of cheese and freshly washed grapes from a plate, prepared by Gaby.

Gaby comes into the kitchen and starts to clean up her mess from earlier. It appears as if she has just gotten off of a call from Tony by the looks of her face.

Not much food is left in the refrigerator, Kyle notices.

Typically, Gaby grocery shops on Thursday mornings for all the meals she plans to prepare for Friday and the weekend. Then she goes again on

Mondays to last them until Thursday rolls back around. She has it down to a science.

Kyle pops a juicy red grape into his mouth and catches Gabriella before she leaves for groceries. "You know, I appreciate everything you do around here. Has Big-T asked you to marry him yet?"

Kyle continues to pop cheese and grapes into his mouth.

Gaby gropes her baby bump on her belly saying, "I'm twenty-four now. You know I can't stay here forever with a spoon in da' bowl, growing over these zippers on my pants. Tony and I are getting married soon, I just know we are."

Both exits the kitchen.

Kyle goes in the direction to his office.

Gaby goes to the front door then stops as she sees Chips Ahoy just lying on the fourth step on the staircase. She grabs Kyle's attention before he sits down in his office seat.

"I think something's the matter with Chips. Look, he's been laying on that one and only step up there at the top for days now. Is he sad or something, maybe sick?"

Kyle comes out of his office to see what she is talking about, then climbs up the staircase.

"Yeah I saw him there the other day as well." Kyle uses the wall and places his hand on it to sit down. Chips Ahoy doesn't seem to care if Kyle is there or not.

Kyle cocks an eyebrow and begins to feels something in his spirit shifting. His hands get sweaty. His palms start to twitch. His heart begins to flutter like the wind is being knocked out of him as he tries to catch his breath.

Gaby walks out the front door.

A gentle breeze blows across her face producing a soft honeysuckle fragrance nearby. She forgets about Kyle and the dog by now.

Kyle rubs the fuzzy part of Chips neck. "What's wrong buddy?"

The dog only budges a little, blinking his eyes, then decided to sniff Kyles hand as if something else was sitting there with them. Chip Ahoy lets out a sigh.

Pressure builds up inside of Kyle's right ear. It feels like something is moving around his equilibrium.

Not hurting, he holds onto his ear until the pressure subsides. It feels like some kind of entity inside him wants to communicate.

His thoughts become palpable and deeply roll inside. He sits in this frantic state of mind a minute or two, then changes the channel, trying to calm down.

All along Kyle could hear a sentence trying to come out, *"Wait for Tony."*

A release of pressure interchanges from his ears unto the crown of his head. He hears this inner voice again, except this time it was trying to say something else.

Kyle shifts his focus all the way to the bottom steps in disbelief.

Again, he hears, *"Wait for Tony"* and it slithers through his mind as if someone else was talking though.

The voice of the person relaying this message sounds like Angela's. This time he's certain she has been with him all along.

Home alone, he speaks to Angela like she is inside him. "Angela, is this you?" He whispers.

The air parts putting off the soft scent, Light Blue —Calvin Klein.

Chips Ahoy jumps out of place and darts down the staircase.

Kyle sits on the step having a conversation with someone he doesn't see physically. Everything about why Chips was sitting on the fourth step gives him a little more clarity.

#1. Angela's presence is here with him.
#2. He is to wait for Tony.

The pressure alleviates from Kyles head. He feels the need to get up and find where Chips Ahoy went to. Walking downstairs he ponders paying attention to Tony, but he didn't know why, or what about.

In a super marker, Gaby pushes a shopping buggy around with a few items in her basket. She makes her way to the produce section carrying a baby the size of a super-sized bag of Jolly Ranchers inside her belly.

Gaby is twisting up a bag of cucumbers in the produce section when she gets a Facetime call from Tony. She answers the call.

"How's my two babies' doing this morning?" He said showing a close up of his lips moving while speaking to her.

"You're silly. We're okay, I guess. I'm thirsty and hot all the time. I think this child is a boy. He is already wiping me out."

Tony gives her an awe out of sympathy then switches subject. "Gaby, what do you think about recycled jewelry pieces? Tony asks, standing behind the counter at his pawn shop.

"What do you mean... jewelry pieces? You mean like a necklace with no charm?"

"No." He laughs out. "I mean like a very rare diamond that I've been keeping my eye on and I could turn into the engagement ring for you."

On a busy isle in the supermarket, Gaby lets out a pleasing yelp of excitement. Suddenly a pinch of pain occurs like her baby's legs kicked her.

She smiles nervously, "I don't have any problems with that."

"What size ring are you?

"I think a six."

Flushed, they take a moment and stare into each other's eyes.

Meanwhile at the Hawthorne place, Kyle decides to go for a run in Hancock Park. Pacing himself, he listens to Breaking Benjamin – Angel's Fall through his headset.

He clears his mind focusing on every breath he takes in, then releases. While this song plays, he remembers what Angela has said, *"Wait for Tony."* The run was supposed to clear his mind but wasn't making any difference. What had happened to him with Angela on the staircase and Chips Ahoy was weird.

Kyle drips in sweat as he arrives back home.

Mr. and Mrs. Gethin are getting out of their Mercedes G-Class series, SUV. The three make eye contact and wave, giving out hellos.

Gaby pulls up behind him. Kyle stays behind helping her carry the groceries inside. He grabs the heavy stuff since she's pregnant.

She's glowing, but waits for the right moment to tell Kyle the great news. She has her sunglasses on still.

Kyle presumes something is up by the way she is walking and hiding under her dark framed sunshades.

"You're overly happy... What's up?" He puzzles, while setting a case of water on the countertop.

Gaby sets her bags down as well, then taps her flip flops against the tile saying, "He's gonna ask me to marry me soon... He's going to ask!"

"Oh really?" Kyle smiles in confidence.

"Yep, he just asked me about ring sizes while I was at the super market."

"Well you see, us men have a special connection. I could sense this within a few hours of him asking you... that's a pretty good guesstimate. I just hope I can find somebody as good as you Gaby when you leave us and move in with him."

"Thanks for saying that. It really means a lot." She continues to retrieve groceries from outside. She picks up the pace as frozen foods start to melt.

Several hours pass by. An Uber driver is pulled up to the twin's house dropping Benjamin, Venom and Viper off.

The three get out and walk up to the twin's front door. All three are a few inches taller now and have longer hair.

Venom clutches Benjamin's hand outside before he goes inside his house. Viper opens the door and goes inside giving the two boys some privacy.

Venom kisses Benjamin on the lips then goes inside with a smile.

Benjamin saunters across the street carrying his back-pack. He has a tablet inside for homework; with his textbooks on the digital library.

In a few months Benjamin will be sixteen. He has been taking driving lessons after school. His biggest hope is to have a blue Range Rover.

He goes inside the house and is in direction up to his bedroom when he finds Chips Ahoy laying on the upper fourth step.

Benjamin trips on the step the dog is sitting. He doesn't pay any mind to it as he continues on to his bedroom.

At suppertime Gaby prepares a plate of fully loaded nachos made with blue corn tortilla chips for everyone.

Sending out a text at 5 P.M, she calls everybody to the kitchen to eat. Everyone hurries into the kitchen like a herd of cattle.

"I cut up fresh cilantro and jalapenos in case you want some… oh and here's some guacamole, I just made it." Gaby wipes the side of the guacamole bowl.

Camden is the first to get a plate. He snacks on rich layers of beans and queso, while finding a seat at the table to sit.

Benjamin goes outside to eat on the veranda. Camden decides to follow his brother outside and eat too.

Gaby stands in the kitchen eating a nacho when Kyle asks, "Could you take Benji to his last driver's education class today and also pick him up afterwards?"

"Of course, I can. That's in an hour, right?"

"Yes, and he'll need to be picked up at 8 P.M."

The two proceed to walk outside where the boys are at. Kyle turns around wondering why Chips Ahoy isn't following anybody out the door like he normally does.

At the fourth step from the top is where he finds the dog again. Kyle tries teasing him down with a blue corn chip. The Maltese lays unhappy. Kyle ignores it for now, and goes to eat with his family.

The outside temperature is around seventy degrees Fahrenheit as the sun begins to fall for the night.

While crunching nacho chips, The Hawthorne's talk about which vehicles Benjamin might be interested in for his birthday.

Wrapping supper up, everybody takes their plates to the kitchen sink.

Gaby takes Benjamin to his final class. Camden rides with them.

After everyone leaves the house Kyle goes to Chips Ahoy on the fourth step. Static electricity flows across his leg hairs as he takes a seat.

Kyle observes Chips Ahoy as tingles build up his leg into his chest and arms. His body temperature rises causing his feet and hands to sweat. His face is hot. His eyes are drying out, causing his face to go numb.

The beat of his heart sends his emotions into the deep end. He can't feel the right side of his face. He can't even feel his right hand hitting his face. He breathes in the best he can, but everything is spinning out of control.

His thoughts begin to race vehemently against something inside of him. Voices echo inside of Kyle's head and it drives him crazy. He holds onto the wall while an earthquake is happening inside his erupting emotions.

Chips Ahoy stands up frightened, watching every move Kyle makes with this entity inside of him. Kyle is locked out of his mind for time being. The dog frantically runs down the steps.

Kyle begins to catch a breath. It's like he can hear Angela's voice calling him through the ringing of his ears that is measured from the amount of times she is calling his name, *"Kyle."*

He comes to a state of peace, yet he's still in some sort of delusion. He remembers from earlier Angela asking him to, *"Wait for Tony."* But now it's like she is back from the future. Kyle's senses are heightened to the max.

Sitting on the forth step with everything magnified up to the sky it seemed, Kyle waits in faith that Angela appears to him in third dimension or something this time.

He's tranquil for just coming out of an anxiety attack. His face is back to normal skin tone. He has the cold chills now that her spirit has left his body.

Angela has finally figured a way to enter his soul from the spirit realms.

In a ruffled white color designer gown, Angela appears next to Kyle, sitting with him on the staircase. Her body becomes full in contrast than when she initiates conversation with her husband, who's eyes fill up in tears from disbelief.

Norah Jones —Come Away with Me, plays in the background.

"Hello, my love, I've been in this house ever since the accident. These cell phones will be the death of us all." She laughs.

Kyle grabs her angelic face sowing tears of joy. He meets her gaze. They take in the moment. He snickers with her.

"You've been here all along?" He smiles holding her angelic hands.

"Yes, I've seen you and the boys heal from my death with every breath of spring like the mornings after a long winter fall… and I've watched Gaby grow into a woman of valor and honor. She's with my brother, right?" The ghost of Angela pauses.

"Yeah, is something wrong with that?"

Kyle can't help but think how crazy this is that the spirit of Angela is right in front of his eyes.

"I don't know how much time I have left here on earth. I was told soon I'd be leaving to go into the promise land, but first I have to…" She pauses again.

Kyle caresses his wife's hands which feels very much like his own hands. He finds it amazing because he's never been so close to another human this way.

"Lovey, what do you have to do?"

"I have to wait for Camden." She chokes on her thoughts and wants to cry.

"What are you talking about?" Kyle shakes in fear.

"Kyle, unless you finish the publication of Online Now and get it into everybody's hands that can drive, there will continue to be more tragic deaths that could end up worse than mine did. Camden will be taken next unless you hurry. You have everything inside of you to proceed, but in case you don't publish soon… then, *Wait for Tony.*" Her eyes and smiling face start to fade away, along with the scent Light Blue.

For the second time, Kyle doesn't get the chance to say his good-byes to his beloved wife. Her body just vanishes like a dust storm.

He sits on the forth step collecting his thoughts, trying puzzle it all together. He considers if he should speak about what he just witnessed.

Even though it was Angela's body that sat with him on a lonely night on the first day of March, everybody will think he's become a paranoid schizophrenic if he says anything about it.

One thing is for certain. He is confident about publishing Online Now before anyone else could be written up as a spectacle in the *Headlines of Breaking News.*

The front door opens. Gaby and Camden are home from taking Benjamin to driver's education class.

CHAPTER
TWENTY-ONE

Angela said it was all inside of him, yet Kyle didn't have the slightest clue on earth who would help him finish Angeles's work, to bring fourth awareness in the world.

In 2017, over two hundred and twenty-two million drivers were listed with a license to drive. The astronomical amount of people who could be touched by Online Now was staggering. Imagine all the people who could be saved by resisting the urge to text and drive.

Outside Kyle's house, he fills a blue bucket full of hot soapy water. It's been a while since he's done a project at home.

He rinses a sponge out good from the water in the bucket. Last time he used this sponge was at least half a year ago.

Hooking up a garden hose, he turns on the water spout and gives his little black Mercedes a good rinsing off. As he washes the car, he's able to just mediate with the repetitiveness of the task. It's around 8:30 A.M. — Saturday, March 3, 2018.

Washing his car makes him think of Mr. Miyagi's Wax on Wax Off from the Karate Kid.

From the front end to the back end, windows and all, Kyle lathers the car full of suds.

Kyle contemplates who his spear of influence is and on how to get Angela's book into this world. He needs it done quickly to spare the lives of many.

Self-publishing was a highly considered option in the short twenty minutes of washing his car, but he questioned himself of how he would market this book to the audience of all who drive automobiles in the world.

The sun starts to peek out of the sky causing a rainbow bridge to form between the water nozzle and his car. It was through those seven magnificent stripes of glory, Kyle sees a flash of Jeff Gandy's face, who is connected to all of Hollywood and NYC as a movie director.

It has been a couple of years since he sold Jeff the mansion in Malibu.

Kyle rinses his car faster than a duck quacks for food, wraps the hose up, and takes all the supplies to the pool house in his backyard.

He pulls his phone out to check the time. 8:45 A.M. He goes back to his car to towel dry it off with fifteen minutes to spare.

Now finished, Kyle wipes sweat from his face and neck with a clean towel, as he rushes to get inside his home.

The house is quiet. Everyone is still asleep.

Kyle finds Chips Ahoy drinking at his dog bowl in the kitchen. *'At least it's not the fourth step this time'*, he thinks. Kyle goes into his office and shuts the door.

Dialing up Jeff, it rings a couple of times then goes to voicemail. Kyle lays the phone down on the desk and starts to pray out loud.

The phone rings and he answers right away. "You must have felt my urgency buddy. I need to ask something from you. What would it take to turn Angela's texting and driving novel into a movie?"

"Do you have a script I can read over...? I must tell you, I'm pretty booked up for the next ten months." Jeff replies.

"Crap man, do you have any recommendations? I need to produce something soon... Like Now! I'm willing to shell out money. I need it to happen ASAP."

"Hold up! Is everything okay?" Jeff pauses, waiting for Kyle to answer.

"Yes and No! Something weird happened to me last night... like an epiphany or something. I have the strangest feeling if I don't get this book published today, then one of my sons will die."

"That sounds more like a revelation? Are you afraid what happened to your wife, will take the rest of your family out? ...relax Kyle. I like the texting and driving concept, but I'll need to look at the script. I could possibly start in eight months. That's the best I can offer with all that I've got going on."

"I hear you." Kyle says a little perturbed, while thinking of who to call next.

"We can't rush into it, Kyle. I've got another appointment calling now. I'll call you in a couple of days, okay buddy? I should have some free time by then. Let's have lunch."

"Yeah that's fine man, call me in a couple."

Ending the call, Kyle frees his desk of all real estate papers. Clearly, he makes the decision to abandon real estate for some time to take on this project.

The desk is now a fresh canvas. He starts to strategically plan how he will save lives on the roadways.

Kyle pulls Angela's blue folder out to see what's inside. He knows everything required to get started. One thing is needed first.

He makes a call to Waylon Warner at the office.

The phone rings. Waylon answers.

"Hey friend, I need something from you. If you don't have any major plans for the next ten months, I'm gonna need you to hold the castle open for me as boss. I need to work on something that requires all of my time. As for my existing contracts that are listed on the market; you can have them all. I will release them over to you under my broker's license. Will you do this for me?"

"Kyle, is everything ok?" Waylon puzzles.

"Everything's fine. I have to get Angela's book published. I promised her a while back." Kyle swallows the white lie to protect his sanity.

"You promised her? What do you mean? I thought she was the author?" Waylon asks.

"Evidently, this one is mine to handle and now is the time. Look over my brokerage for me, will you?" Kyle pleads.

I'd be honored darling." Waylon smiles from the other end of the phone.

The two hang up the call.

Kyle opens the Angela's blue folder and pulls the content from inside.

A manuscript bound together with burlap rope. Kyle unfastens it and see's the back page first. The last page number is *two hundred and twenty-two.*

In admiration of what he reads so far, it sounds like a story Angela had written about their family, except the husband is a famous author and the wife is a multimillion-dollar real estate listing agent. She switched roles on Kyle.

Kyle pauses reading. He decides to grab a cup of coffee. What is written sounds great already. The brilliance of what she wrote has captured his attention.

In the kitchen, he finds his boys with Gaby eating donuts. She must have gotten up and gone to get them within the half hour.

Kyle walks over to his boys giving each a hug. Benjamin and Camden continue to eat their donuts with puffy faces and sleepy eyes. Kyle grabs a glazed twist, then goes to the coffee machine to make a cup.

"Gaby, I'll be home the next ten months working on publishing Angela's book, instead of real estate, Okay?" Kyle pours cream into his coffee mug.

"That was a sudden jump. I thought you would have done this a long time ago Kyle."

"Don't patronize me. I didn't feel it was my call to make, until now."

"What does patronize even mean?" Gaby thinks to herself.

Kyle takes a sip of coffee, then another bite of donut with determined eyes as he gazes over Camden who is enjoying his chocolate donut.

Benjamin drinks chocolate milk from a carton, "Gaby, since I have my paper permit now, would you mind driving with me in your SUV, so I can get some practice in?"

"If it's okay with your father, I'm cool with it."

Kyle's in a daydream nearby finishing his coffee, but hears every word Gaby and Benjamin say. He shakes himself out of the trance then says, "Ah… make sure you wear your seatbelts and don't text and drive."

"Ah dad, that's like rule number one in driver's education class."

"I'm serious son."

Gaby observes Kyle's demeanor then raises her brow saying, "You're extra careful today."

"I'm just being a good dad, that's all."

"Can I come too?" Camden asks.

"Especially you Ca-mee-dee. Gaby, will you make sure Camden wears his seatbelt? And Camden don't let him text and drive." Kyle says to everyone.

Camden feels trusted for once, "I'll be in charge dad."

Kyle goes back to his office to read more of Angela's work.

After lunch, Gaby offers Benjamin an hour worth of drive time before she has to come back home to prepare food for the family later.

In the vehicle everyone buckles up and Benjamin backs out of the driveway. He has a problem straightening out the wheel, but seems to figure it out rather quickly.

He drives to his school, circling the parking lot a few times, pretending he's driving his new Camaro, Jeep or if he is really lucky, a Range Rover. He exits the school campus using proper blinkers. At a four way stop sign he comes to a complete stop instead of a California roll through.

On the freeway, Gaby gets little baby jitters in her stomach. Feeling nauseous, she asks Benjamin to turn around and go back home.

Five blocks away from home, Benjamin spots a huge sign across a building. A Pokémon Comic Book Festival is going on tonight.

Benjamin looks to Gaby then says, "It says it starts at 5 P.M. If it's okay with our dad, would you bring us later?"

"No, I can't. I must stay around the house. I'm expecting a call, plus I will be cooking food around that time." Gaby replies.

"I suppose we can walk or take an Uber or Lyft. Camden, let's ask the twins to go with us." He exclaims.

At home, the boys see Kyle through the glass of his office French doors. They open the doors and go inside.

"Dad, there is a Pokémon Comic Book Festival really close to our house. Do you care if Camden and I go with the twins?

Kyle comes from behind a page of the manuscript and asks, "How will you get there?"

"Either walk or take an Uber or Lyft."

Holding the next page of texting and driving manuscript in hand Kyle says, "It's a nice day outside, why don't you consider walking?"

"Okay, we can do that…Thanks dad… See you later."

Benjamin and Camden exit the room closing the doors behind. They go up to Benjamin's room and call the twins.

Kyle continues to read the manuscript. He's been trying to read it all afternoon, but little distractions have kept him from complete focus. He's on page four.

Later, Venom and Viper meet up with Benjamin and Camden in front of their house. They take off walking to the comic festival.

Fifteen minutes later, inside the building, some of the people are wearing costumes. The Hawthorne's and Gethin's come wearing what they had on already. Moving across the exhibits like turtles, they check out the galleries of art.

Benjamin finds the Eighth Generation Nintendo Gameboy, Ultra Sun Ultra Moon, game and gets excited.

Venom is with Camden looking through Pokémon trading cards.

Viper is looking at the long wall of art a little way over from everybody.

There are food and beverage vending trucks parked outside. They walk over and each get a bottle of soda. Walking home discuss their favorite parts of the Pokémon Comic Festival.

The four walk a short distance then come to a four way stop sign. Camden, thirsty, stops long enough to take a drink. Benjamin and Venom are holding hands while continuing to walking across the street. Viper is next to her brother and leaves Camden behind sucking up his can of soda.

Camden tightens the bottle cap, then runs after his brother and twins feeling left out and far behind.

A driver of a brand-new, white Chevy Suburban flies through a residential stop sign. With an accelerating speed of forty miles per hour, he strikes Camden at crosswalk, flipping his body over the large SUV.

The man in the SUV hears the loud thump and drops his phone into his lap, slamming his brakes and looking around to see what he hit.

Tire screech right past Benjamin, Venom and Viper.

The driver of the Suburban looks into his rearview mirrors and shouts, "Shit! …Why God?" He covers his face in his hands and is frightened. He stays inside the SUV and doesn't dare get out to see the damage.

The man panics in his seat trying to dial the emergency number.

Eight-year-old Camden never felt a thing. Blood empties out his skull, out his nose, out his mouth, even out his ears and eye sockets, saturating his shaggy brown hair into a resting place for mosquitoes and flies. Camden's skull is imprinted into the pavement, with his brain chopped and hanging out uncoiled into pieces on the outside of his head. One of Camden's eyeballs had ruptured out of socket and is found next to his hand, which rests next to his face.

Time is still as he lays cold in the middle of the road. Traffic builds up.

Benjamin, Venom and Viper hear everything happen. Frightened, they turn and see Camden laying in blood, not moving. A bright, glowing energy hovers over him.

"Camden!" Benjamin yells, breaking free from Venom's hand, and runs to him. Everything is in slow motion now.

Viper gets her phone out and dials 911.

Blood continues to gush out of Camden's head. Benjamin and Venom are both in shock. Venom hovers over Camden's body like he can heal him.

Benjamin cries out, "Pick my brother up. Make him breath."

Venom bends down to pick him up. In disbelief, he raises back up and goes deeper into shock.

"Pick him up, I said… make him breathe!" Benjamin hollers again.

An indescribable hue of red, orange, shimmering purple, pink and blue was the smear of colors that puddled up from the fluids of Camden's head.

The driver of the SUV never gets out of his vehicle. He continues to hide.

A backup of vehicles stops the flow of traffic. Some drivers look for alternate routes, while others stay at the accident.

Nobody gets out of their vehicles to check on the surviving children, as they stand alone panicking and crying over Camden's dead body.

Viper stays far enough away from Camden's body out of fear. She knows what his fate is and doesn't want the scars of what she might see up close and personal. She sits on the ground and cries while on the phone with Los Angeles emergency line.

After the ambulance gets there, she hangs up and calls her parents.

It took her five attempts to search out her mums or dads' number on her cell phone. She is so distraught.

Finally, she reaches her mum and father. They panic now. Both Rueben and Darcy are off duty from the hospital, and rush over to Hawthorne's house.

Gaby opens the door.

After getting wind of the fate of Camden, she screams for Kyle.

Kyle runs to the front door in fear. Learning half of what happened to Camden, the Gethin's offer to drive Kyle and Gaby to where the accident is.

The four jump into Rueben's Mercedes-Benz G63, revving the twin turbo 6.0-liter, 12-cylinder engine, and goes to where Viper said they were at.

Blaring sirens from emergency responder are nearby. A helicopter hovers the area at 6:40 P.M, March 3, 2018.

At the scene of the accident, Venom holds Benjamin, as they stand next to the corpse sobbing and chanting to God, "Bring him back to life."

In much guilt and remorse, the boyfriends grieve their loss for letting Camden lag behind, while they continued on walking across the four-way stop.

A firetruck is the first to arrive the scene. The rescue team runs over with medical supplies to see if they can resuscitate the young man on the ground.

Dirty, hot and sweaty, one of the firemen examines Camden's pulse and checks for breathing. The paramedic disregards the blood draining and a half slab of brains pointing to the side of the road where Viper is.

Rueben pulls behind a chockablock of police vehicles, a fire truck, an ambulance, along with every car that has stopped to witness this tragic event.

He throws the Mercedes-Benz G63 into park and the four get out running fifty yards away. They see Camden's body from a distance.

Kyle spots his Benjamin and the twins on the curb sitting and sobbing.

Kyle's pale as a ghost when he sees the image of his little boy laying helpless in a pile of blood. He runs to the body.

Some officers hold him back.

"Get the hell off me. This is my son." He shouts at three officers in charge.

Rueben stands by Kyle's side trying to hold himself together. He gets sick and wants to throw up.

Darcy and Gaby have intuition concerning the fate of Camden and run over to where Benjamin, Venom and Viper are, twenty feet away to be with them instead of Kyle who faces this alone.

"What the bloody hell happened here?" Darcy yells.

Venom and Viper both weep into their mother's embrace. Benjamin sobs for his brother.

"Mum, Camden is dead because of us. He stopped to take a drink or something over there at the stop sign and we kept walking. The lanes were clear, we thought, when we were walking through. I suppose when Camden proceeded… that knob head over there in that big SUV was texting and driving. How else could he have not seen Camden?" Viper rages through her teeth.

At the crime scene, investigators stand by observing Rueben, who is now standing over Kyle, who's kneeling at his son's side.

"I'm so sorry Camden. I'm so sorry baby boy." Kyle cries out to God.

A chaplain intervenes and tries to pulls them away.

"Sir, what is your name?" The chaplain sympathetically asks.

Sorrowful saying, "Kyle Hawthorne." He looks to the chaplain for hope.

"I'm Chaplain Donny Millard. I take it this was your son. What's his name?"

"Camden Hawthorne." Kyle wipes his red face that's soaked from tears, and questions, "How the hell did this happened?" as he darts pain and sorrow into the chaplain's heart.

"Easy Kyle, I know this is hard, but from the looks of it you have another son over there who need his father. Mr. Hawthorne, the owner of the white Suburban appeared to be using his phone while driving and never saw your son crossing the intersection."

"Son of a bitch. Texting and driving." Mad as hell, Kyle stands and walks over to the officers detaining the suspect and putting him into the squad car.

The chaplain and Rueben try to deter Kyle from going over there.

"You murdering bastard. How flipping important was your last text that you sent while you killed my son?" Kyle attempts to strangle the man who is in his late fifty's and has the shape of a five foot-eight body builder.

The officer's shove Kyle off the man, keeping it civil, and stands between them while another officer loads the suspect into the back seat.

The suspect looks at Kyle, full of guilt and remorse. Before the officer shuts the door, the man says with the expression of his lips, "I'm sorry I did this."

The way Kyle see this man and his family sized SUV, is this man was probably sneaking out behind his wife's back, texting some young hottie while in a mid-life crisis, but who knows.

At 7:40 P.M. a paramedic covers Camden's body with a white sheet from a gurney.

Finally, investigator Calc Timmons arrives to the scene. Straight away he sees Kyle Hawthorne.

"Oh, my Lord." Calc hangs his head, trying to find the courage to face Kyle with another death in his family.

"Kyle, I'm lost for words here, really. Twice now." Calc Timmons refrains from crying over this little boy's death, knowing that Kyle had lost his wife the same way a couple years ago. He expresses his condolences and goes over to Camden's covered body and pulls the sheet back. He says a short prayer to God.

Detective Timmons accesses the damage on Camden.

Kyle and Rueben walk over to Benjamin, the twins, their mother, and Gaby who's holding her nauseated stomach in tightly while talking to Tony on the phone.

Tony is in his truck driving as fast as he can from San Diego.

Kyle kneels down to hold and comfort Benjamin.

Rueben and Darcy hold onto each of their kids, crying and thanking God for their lives being spared while in sorrow of Camden's.

The police car hauls the suspect to the station for booking.

All the while, Camden lays on the pavement, as evidence to what happens when somebody texts and drives. The sun fades away.

The Chaplain speaks to the firemen assisting the paramedics with putting the corpse into the body bag.

Detective Calc Timmons goes to work while Camden's spirit lays there in a body bag another hour. People drive by with their phones out and disrespectfully take pictures.

How shallow can others be? How can people not pay attention to people other than to capture the after effects of life? What's happening in our lives today? Why are people caught up in a perfect illusion, instead of keeping their eyes focused on what's directly in front of them, right here and right now?

CHAPTER
TWENTY-TWO

Natural lighting peeks through the Hawthorne's residence, trying to lift everyone up from a long, dark and dreary night. Emotions run dry leaving the atmosphere like beef jerky.

Vomit from Kyle's insane amounts of bourbon he drinking, seep out of the door crack and into the master bathroom.

Alone on the bathroom floor, Kyle open his puffy eyelids from his Jack Daniel's face, as he lays on the cold tile trying to escape the fate of Camden.

Kyle holds his throbbing head.

He crawls on the floor trying to stand up.

His foot slips on a half a bottle of Jack Daniels that's leaked to the floor. It must have fallen over or something.

He props himself against the wall and gives a blank stare while flinging off dried vomit from the side of his face.

Kyle's head spins in a dizzy drunken state. His mouth is parched.

Rueben and Darcy stayed over last night until Tony arrived around nine o'clock. Worn out, at least they had the privilege of going home with both of their children.

Kyle wasn't so lucky. His family was being annihilated by idiotic texting drivers.

The sun shines fully into the house. Kyle is now seated on his bed with a pounding headache. Feeling lost, he tries remembering last night's horror show. Wasted, he brings himself into a dizzy standing position and stumbles back to his bathroom to check himself out in the mirror. He looks hopeless.

Turning on the shower, he strips naked, getting inside. Cold water blasts last night's dinner off his face and dark hairline.

He's cleaned up now, with fresh clothes on for the day. Full of grief, he moves slowly, like it takes everything in his power to press forth and keep going.

The scab on his memory begins to tear open from the death of his little boy. In short term disbelief, Kyle leaves his room and goes to Camden's room.

Kyle sees a full room of guests sleeping in his living room, but no Camden. He finds Benjamin snuggled in between Venom and Viper and clinching Venom tightly.

Shifting his eyes across the teenagers, Kyle spots Tony and Gaby on the sofa wedged together. Tony tries to get comfortable on the make shift bed. He decides to get up instead, when he sees Kyle standing in the distance.

"What time is it? I don't think anybody here got a wink of sleep. Maybe two hours if we're lucky." Tony says, with the sound of cigarette lungs.

"Maybe it's 6:45 A.M. I don't know anything right now." Kyle gives more blank stares then saunters off to Camden's room.

The smell of Camden lingers as he opens the door. An empty unmade bed is all Kyle finds in a Star Wars themed bedroom.

He laughs out saying, "He forgot to make up his bed yesterday."

Kyle pushes out a few more tears and gently lays across his bed, cradling his pillow in his arms. He takes in his little boys' buttery scent then soaks the bed with what tears he has left inside.

In the living room, Viper is disturbed out of her sleep by Venom's moans and Benjamin's kicks. Simultaneously, they appear to be stuck in the same dream, motioning and maneuvering something around.

Shaking the boys awake, Viper asks if they are okay.

Venom jolts up, gasp for air, finding Benjamins eliminating the imaginary tree bark from underneath his fingernails.

Mystified, she tries to envision what type of dream they're in.

Gaby awakens as well. Everybody is exhausted from the sudden death of Camden but can't sleep anymore without waking up every hour feeling sick.

Benjamin starts to describe his dream.

"I had my cell phone in my hand. I was tied up to you, Venom. You were sitting with your legs sprawled out directly behind me. I held onto them on the side of me, that's where they were. We were sitting on the ground somewhere… I couldn't see a thing because I was blind folded. I could hear a man with a familiar voice. The voice was cut-dry-deep and demanding. He said something about payback was his… An evil voice. Then I heard the loud engine of a vehicle coming for us like a train."

Venom listens with ears as big as his eyes then says, "Whoa! We had the same exact dream, except I wasn't blind folded. I saw the man in the car at a distance. He was older, but I couldn't make out who he is since he was covered behind the veil. Wow, this whole thing's creepy. We were tied to a tree in nature… don't know where but somewhere nearby I feel. The man was trying to drive the car right into our heads, but I woke up before the car hit us."

"Oh my God, that's so weird… the both of you having dreams like that. You two are both like telepathically connected for sure." Viper says with her brow knitted.

"That's some dream boys. We are all going to have nightmares for a while. Don't worry, somebody's going to stop this chaos of texting and driving." Tony rasps in his cigarette lungs.

The three teenagers look around at each other creeped out. Benjamin recognized the voice in the dream. He cocks his eye, looking right at Venom, to see if Tony was who he saw.

Gaby puts her hand on Tony's chest comforting him. He pulls her closer into him.

Viper feels a bit disgusted as she checks herself out in the wall mirror. She excuses herself so she can go home and get cleaned up.

"Benji, will you be alright for a couple of hours, if I leave? I'm a bit slimy from last night and in desperate need of a shower."

"Yeah, I will be fine. Thank you, a thousand kisses, to you and your brother for staying with me last night. This is just so surreal without my little brother here."

"You're welcome bro. I'll be over a little later to check on you." Viper leaves the house in a hurry to regain her strength and let out her tears at home.

Venom sits on a pallet of blankets next to Benjamin, with his arm around his back, to comfort him.

Tony sits next to Gaby with his arm around her.

Everyone in the living room just sits there, in a world of depression.

Kyle wakes up from a short nap finding himself on Camden's pillow.

He rises off the bed, not quite as dizzy as before he went searching for his little boy.

Kyle's never buried anyone, including his wife that went up in smoke when she died. He knows what he must do as he saunters downstairs where the rest of his family is stuck like nails.

He does a Google search for the funeral home Camden is at. Procrastinating, not fully ready to dial the number, he sits muted in numbness like everybody else.

Time passes. He knows Camden deserves to have fresh clothes put on him eventually and a final place to rest. He researches the number and calls. Nearing ten O'clock in the morning, Kyle speaks to someone at the funeral home.

Everyone in the room hangs tight listening to Kyle make burial arrangements, except Gaby who gets up and leaves the room.

She knows everybody should try to eat, but really, she doesn't have any appetite. Beyond grief at this moment, from losing Camden, she practically looked after this child from his toddler years on.

Lacking motivation, she grabs the butter and some cheese slices from the refrigerator and grilled cheese sandwiches for everyone. It's the easiest and fastest thing to make that she can think of.

She makes like ten sandwiches, cutting each into triangles, puts on a serving platter, and takes them into the family room.

Everyone eats slowly, allowing the day to fade away.

The second day after Camden's death, everyone awakens in their own bed a little more rested up. The tears have dried up some, but everyone is still heavily grieving in this house.

Afternoon arrives and Tony requests a Lyft to come and take them to a men's suit shop. They need to pick out something for Camden to be buried in.

Kyle and Benjamin look around thirty minutes finding the right one. A solid white three-piece suit. They get him matching shiny dress shoes to go with it.

Leaving, Tony and Gaby stand by the Kyle and Benjamin's side. Tony requests another Lyft to come and get them, taking them to a low-key place to eat at.

After everybody eats, Tony orders another Lyft to take them all back to Hawthorne's place. Kyle has carried his baby boy's suit around long enough.

The night becomes turbulent knowing the very next day would be a farewell to Camden.

Upstairs, Kyle lays Camden's suit on his bed, wishing it was his graduation suit for high school instead of his burial suit.

Benjamin is alone in his room. He misses his brother terribly and begins to type up a poem for Camden.

Around 9 P.M. he finishes the poem. He then texts a small questionnaire to a few family members, including Venom and Viper, asking how Camden had touched their lives.

Benjamin has felt the calling for a while now and since his mother was a writer, he knew he'd be taking in some of her spirit to write Camden's Eulogy and give the speech.

Kyle sits in bed, half-naked watching replays of baseball highlights, while sipping a small dose of scotch. His phone rings.

Picking the phone off his nightstand he notices its Jeff Gandy calling. He answers. "Hey Jeff." Kyle slurs with no energy left inside.

On the other end, Jeff says in condolence, "Kyle my friend, I've just seen on a social media site, a special report about your younger son getting killed by a person texting and driving. Wow, I am so sorry to hear about this and at the same time I remember our conversation about Angela's book and producing a film about it before something happened to one of your boys and… Wow, it happened! I'm blown away over here. I want you to know, I'll help you get this done now and in memory of Angela and Camden. There's a veil covered over millions of eyes, in the world. It's time everybody understands how to stop this madness."

"This is so terrible Jeff. I feel so lost. First my wife, now my little boy. Yes, I am committed into getting her message out and getting it out before half of America experiences this nightmare."

"When and where is Camden's funeral at?"

"Tomorrow at Forest Lawn Hollywood Hills, 11 A.M."

"Molly and I will be there okay, and let's try to find time this week if you are up to it and fully develop the storyline for this motion picture."

"Thanks Jeff. I really appreciate this from you. Okay, I better get some rest. I'll see you in the morning."

They end the call. Kyle shuts off the television and night light, then lays in bed until he falls asleep.

Chapter
TWENTY-THREE

As the long winter ends, the sun naturally protrudes and becomes a pacific coast warming oven, heating up the region. The days becomes longer. Every magnolia and forsythia tree open a new bud.

The final resting place.

Even Camden's body would feel the expanse from earth growing around him as cool air blows from a clear blue sky. Gentle flights from speckling butterflies surround the landscape in the distance, begetting apricots and cherry blossoms to cascade an ironic scent of life.

Forest Lawn Cemetery, 10:30 A.M. March 6, 2018. So far fifty guests have arrived to Camden's funeral ceremony. Everyone stands outside, about ten feet away from a green velvety mat coving the ground for family and closest friends to sit.

Camden's casket is opened for public viewing in hopes people would get an eye opener for when they get behind the wheel to drive.

As remaining guests arrive, everyone else is gathered out on the lawn a distance away from the neatly placed ground covering.

Kyle and Benjamin stand with Kyle's mother Ivy Hawthorne, and fiancée, alongside with Angela's parents Charles and Roxanna who flew in from Brooklyn last night.

Benjamin clings onto Grand Rox, while the rest of the adults are gathered in a circle communicating.

Tony and Gaby walk up to the group. He kisses his mother on the forehead then taps his stepfather Charles on the shoulder.

Camden's second grade teacher and student principal give their condolences to Kyle and his family, paying their respects.

Rueben, Darcy and the twins come walking in the distance. They're in all black attire, except Mrs. Gethin who has on a black and cream lacy blouse over her long skirt. The rest of the Gethin's have on matching long sleeved button up's, black trousers and shiny black shoes.

Jeff and Molly Gandy arrive. They have just enough time to find their way over to The Hawthorne's and family before the service starts.

The funeral conductor announces the ceremony will begin a few minutes before 11 A.M. He stands with the priest at the head of Camden's casket. Everyone proceeds to move in closer to Camden.

Moving down the isle of family and friends, the priest completes a hymn about grace. He walks to the front where Camden is at and stands at the podium where his notes are, then proceeds, "Dearly beloved's, we gather here today to celebrate the short-lived life of Camden Hawthorne, who has now returned home with our Father God, El Shaddai in Heaven."

The priest proceeds to say, "As we praise God in all his glory, we ask for mercy on the fellow who was distracted while driving, and who took the life of Camden. God, we learn more about your love as we forgive those who trespass against us."

Kyle Hawthorne has given the priest a few scriptures to read from the English Standard Version, Holy Bible:

"Ephesians 6:1-4. Children obey your parents in the Lord, for this is right. Honor your father and mother, the first commandment with a promise, that it may go well with you and that you may live long in the land. Fathers, do not provoke your children to anger, but bring them up in the discipline and instruction of the Lord."

The priest pauses letting it sink in. He walks away from the podium and continues to say, "Young Camden was obedient to his father and mother whom was also taken by a distracted driver and the rising road rage on our roadways. This ungodly act is taking our youth, our mothers, our fathers, our grandparents, our family and our friends. You see, Camden never raised his voice at his mother or father, his teacher or principal who are both gathered amongst us showing their support. As Camden's father, Kyle Hawthorne sits here sobbing from the loss of his youngest son, please make sure to embrace him everyone. Losing a child is never easy and it will take God's Strength inside us all to help Kyle proceeding on."

The priest, back at the podium and reads another scripture from the English Standard Version of The Holy Bible:

John 3:16. For God so loved the world, that he gave his only son, Jesus Christ, that whoever believes in him should not perish but have eternal life.

"For God did not send his son into the world to condemn the world, but in order that the world might be saved through He who served us. Today, Kyle understands what it's like to love his son so much that he must give him back to the Creator. Having to sacrifice his youngest son. You see, Kyle had two boys to love and care for when God gave away his only son, so that we might have more. For he knows the plans to prosper us and not harm us. Plans to give us a hope and a future. That if we call on his name, we are saved. What was the purpose of eight-year-old Camden's life when we reflected who he was? He honored and obeyed his elders. He was learning all he could to have a future adulthood and to be mighty in the land. He was made to surely prosper but he was taken too soon in our eyes. Maybe, so that others may see him today at his final resting place and would remember to put your cell phones down while you are driving. Act sober and diligent in all you do for the destroyer seeks to devour you."

The priest takes a break for a moment, going over his notes then says, "I hope if you come see Camden at his final resting place you see all the pieces and cracks, we did our best to put back together. May he rest in peace. Now may I ask each one of you to remember Camden? Remember this could be you or your loved one. Please, do not text and drive. God bless you all. I would like to welcome Benjamin Hawthorne, Camden's only surviving sibling who will present his final story, the Eulogy."

Benjamin thanks the priest at the podium, then tilts the microphone to speak.

"I wrote this for my brother last night, as I was laying down for the night. Not knowing exactly what to say, I mean who really thinks about how to write a Eulogy. I never thought I would ever be writing one for my brother who was only eight. Camden, if you are here with us, I miss you and if I had known three days ago would have been your last day, then I would have spent every waking moment with you. Camden, I wrote this for you, my little brother.

"What Remains"

Camden, I know you are with our mother in heaven, watching over us like the charm you were to all of us, What Remains.

You may have been taken, piece by piece, your soul might have been taking its last sip, quenching your thirst, as you stood back enjoying your last day, three days ago of, What Remains.

From your very first steps in our living room and every step you took getting in and out of cars, our house, kindergarten, first and second grade, you took all you could from what little time you had on this earth of, What Remains.

An angel heart, legs and arms. A brand-new suit on your little man's body. Shiny dress shoes on your size two feet. That will never spout much farther, laying in your new bed, a peril white casket but, What Remains?

You're still my little brother, our father's favorite boy, our mother's new best friend from regions above. You were here for a short time of our new friends the twins, our uncle Tony and soon to be Aunt Gaby which is having a baby boy I think... who will probably grow up to be somewhat like you for, What Remains.

Camden, I will never forget you, even if what took your life continues to take thousands of others. My biggest hopes for everyone who's bold enough to see you for the last time, knows this is what happens when they text and drive. My little brother I am so sorry this had to be you with all that remains. "

Benjamin walks back to his seat wiping the tears he couldn't hold back. His father and Uncle Tony smile and wipe their tears as well. He glances at his boyfriend and reads his lips that say, "That was beautiful."

The priest concludes the ceremony with bringing up all the guests from the back to view the body first. A long line forms, passing Camden by in shocking tears when they see the many stiches holding a prosthetic skull together.

The line dwindles down to the immediate family and friends stand guard to the last memory captured before the conductor seals the casket shut. Kyle, Ivy and Benjamin stand directly in front of Camden's body as they say their goodbyes.

Tony, Gaby and his parents gather behind Kyle's left.

The twins and Mr. and Mrs. Gethin stand next to Benjamin's right.

Kyle sobs loudly.

Jeff and Molly Gandy make their way up to stand with them. Jeff places his hand on Kyle's shoulder with a remorseful heart, regretting not being able to help his friend when he first came to him.

Kyle looks him over in forgiveness as tears stream down his face, falling to the earth. His little boy lays to rest shattered before all.

This public affair has everybody sobbing with Kyle nearly twenty minutes before Tony pulls Kyle and Benjamin away to let Camden fly.

A ton of flowers and plants left for the family to take home. Most will be placed over the mound to cover Camden up.

One by one the families start to get into their vehicles and leave Forrest Lawn Cemetery.

After everyone is gone from Forrest Lawn, Kyle and his whole family including the twins and their parents drive over to have lunch at the nearby, Smoke House, arranged by Jeff and Molly.

Inside the restaurant, the group of thirteen dine in the banquet room with red stackable chairs and tables with white linen tops.

At the side of the room, Rueben and Darcy look over the menus that have possibly touched the hands of many famous celebrities throughout its time.

Even though they didn't need a menu for what the Gandy's had set up, the Gethin's found it fascinating to look it over.

Benjamin is seated next to the twins looking over the menu with them too. It was his actual first time to go where his father had been on several business occasions.

The next table over Kyle and his mother sit with Jeff and Molly.

"I want to thank you Jeff and Molly for booking this place for us during our time of need. It was very generous of you." Kyle said directly to Jeff.

"Of course. It's my pleasure and it was the least I could do for you and your family."

At Tony table, sits Gaby, his mother and stepfather. Every section in the banquet rooms' in their own world speaking as a new season develops in their lives.

Gaby and Tony sit together holding hands in front of Roxanna and Charles.

Gaby has met them before, but it was when they would come visit Angela from Brooklyn on occasions. They were always nice to her as their maid, when they would pass by in the hallways, kitchen and such.

Roxanna and Charles beam with joy looking over their son and soon, mother to be of their third grandchild.

"You look so beautiful Gaby. Never in a million years would I have thought you would be our future daughter in law, bearing us another child in place of what God took from us twice. You are truly a blessing. We are thankful you are in our son's life."

Gaby straightens out her posture and holds back joyful tears with a speech, "With much respect to you, I need to say this in my language for my family back home in my country and I will then translate to you…"

"Estoy muy honrado de venir an America. Tener la oportunidad por Dios. Conozca personas maravillosas que se preocupan por mi como persona, para que pueda hacer el bien a todos los que me rodean. Eres buena gente. Muchas gracias."

"I am much honored to come to America. Have the opportunity by God. Meet wonderful people that cared for me as a person, so that I might do well for everyone around. You are good people. Thank you very much." Gaby expresses in gratitude.

"Life sure is funny how it ends up being. You will make a wonderful addition to our family." Roxanna smiles as Gaby holds her baby bump.

Rueben spots something on the menu as he sips fruit punch in a glass. "Would you look at this Darling, I can eat my name how lovely." He laughs as he points out a Rueben sandwich on the menu.

As Venom and Viper look over the menu, Benjamin lowers his head in sadness then says, "Somethings missing. Like you two are the arms, Ven and Vip, but we are missing our little leg Ca-mee-dee keeping us in balance."

Off the banquet menu, Molly orders nine jumbo shrimp cocktail set up's and world's greatest garlic cheese bread as a starter.

It comes out.

Everyone grabs a tail, rips the bread apart and goes for a dip in cocktail sauce.

A tray of deviled eggs, fried zucchini and cheeseburger sliders come out next, along with another gallon of fruit punch.

Shrimp cocktails and garlic bread have been emptied from the serving plates for some time now. Everyone seems to be picking up the last of cheeseburger sliders.

Jeff sits back, gauging Kyle, wondering if it's a good time to ask a question that moves everyone forward. "Have you had any chance to look over Angela's blue book?"

"You know that's the thing. I read about five sheets of what she had in there, then I got the call about Camden."

"Okay here's the deal. Are you free on Sunday, say about 5 P.M?" Jeff asks.

"Yes, I've completely taken off real estate. I'm ready to do this."

"Count me over around 5 P.M. or how about 6 P.M. after dinner, then we'll go over everything together. We'll start planning it out. Does that work for you?"

"Sounds great. Thank you for this Jeff. I really appreciate your generosity." Kyle thanks him through his sorrow.

"You know my great uncle and aunt lost their only son during a camping trip. Out of nowhere a thunderstorm came. Rain fell out of the sky while lightning crashed, and the thunder rolled. They slept right through it. The next morning, they woke up and a bolt of lightning must have gone through his head. He was burnt to a crisp when they found him the next morning. He was ten. They went through the first two years not understanding the big question, why? Then one day their neighbor's house caught fire. These people were Swedish. They had two children ages eleven and eight, a boy and a girl. The kids somehow made it out, but the burning roof fell right on their parent's bed suffocating and burning them alive. It was a sad time but in the end my uncle and aunt gained two kids from the whole tragedy and the kids ended up taking care of them later in life. It all turned out okay. I know it doesn't seem possible right now but hold on Kyle. The bigger picture is coming for you. Understand?"

"Yeah, I do. It just sucks hard right now." Kyle drops his face.

"I'll be over Sunday and let's write an amazing script to save some lives from these texting drivers."

Kyle smile. His mother Ivy agrees with Jeff and Molly about working on the project.

At Benjamin's table he asks Venom, "Will you catch all my assignment in Biology this week?"

"Of course, I will lovie." Venom gives him a comforting hug.

The food was enjoyed by all that joined the family dinner. Jeff Gandy takes care of the check and everyone says their goodbye. Rest is needed. Everyone goes home.

Chapter
TWENTY-FOUR

Pretending to move through one's life after a death of a loved one can either be an easy transition or buffering state of mind. The decision is yours to make.

One by one, people who stayed over at the Hawthorne house last night, wake up. Rain clouds start to roll in after a roller coaster week of emotions.

Everybody's eyes are opened, yet they are still laying in a presumed resting position in their beds. Benjamin is the first to get up and get moving.

He goes downstairs and pours a bowl of strawberry, Special K.

8:37 A.M. Venom is either Ubering to high school or dialing up a ride. Benjamin texts Venom anyways.

"After school you wanna go for a walk on the beach? Miss you."

Benjamin puts his phone down and dips his spoon deep into the bowl grabbing as many strawberries as he can. Taking a bite, he forgets how much milk might fall off the spoon.

A loud roar of thunders crashes outside.

He receives a text back from Venom that reads, "You okay? I think if we have a walk on the beach, we won't be needing any sunscreen, we'll need umbrellas instead. But yeah, I'm down my little lovie… lol."

He puts down his phone long enough to take another bite. He looks outside finding it dark and gloomy after all. Benjamin drinks the strawberry milk from the rim of the bowl and reconsiders the beach, then texts back, "Ah yeah, I just heard lightning."

Benjamin gets a reply almost immediately, "So you still wanna go? Lol"

"Yeah, let's go anyways. We can grab a taco or something off the pier, then ice cream and get on the sea dragon in the rain." Benjamin texts back, his phone glued to his hand.

"Are you sure you're okay darling?" Venom replies.

"What, are you my father now? You've never called me darling, darling." Benjamin adds a double wink to the text.

"Almost to school now, let me ask my folks, but yeah then." Venom texts back.

Tiny footsteps enter the kitchen. They are too big to be Chips Ahoy's. He starts to have visions of never seeing his brother walk through this house again.

Gaby enters in the kitchen, as quiet as can be, in lacy pajamas Benjamin's never seen before. He blushes.

"Oh, I didn't realize you were in here." She grabs a kitchen towel only able to cover her naked mid-section and grabs two bottles of water, then hurries back to her room where Tony awaits.

Benjamin holds the phone in his hand looking through Facebook and waiting for his boyfriend to call or text back. His connection keeps him moving. He keeps scrolling each picture by hoping something interesting jumps out or that high school ends soon.

Kyle and his mother, Ivy Hawthorne, enter the kitchen finding Benjamin with an empty bowl. Ivy comes in behind her grandson with her long dark hair, earthy gracefulness and tall, slender, youthful body giving him a loving embrace.

"Are you doing okay, my love?" She bends holding him dearly.

"I'm okay. Just planning something out with Venom later."

"Oh… are you and he trying to meet up tonight?" Kyle asks.

"Probably after he gets out of school, if that's okay." Benjamin questions, looking between his dad and grandmother.

"Son, why don't you stay here with the family tonight? Angela's parents are down from Brooklyn tonight." Kyle said.

"Oh yeah, I almost forgot about Grand and Grampi. Then, can Venom eat with us tonight?" Benjamin requests.

"That's fine." Kyle and Ivy peek into the half empty fridge.

"What would you like to eat for breakfast, my son? Let me cook for everyone. Call Roxanna and Charles and see if they want to join us for breakfast. Will ya?" Ivy asks.

"Mom, they are late sleepers, if I'm remembering correctly. We better let them sleep and join us on their own time." Kyle smiles, hugging his mom.

Later in the evening everyone has had a chance to see the rain blow over and dry up. It was just enough to water the palm trees and give the seagulls a bath.

School was out and instead of doing homework, Venom sacrifices his school work to be with Benjamin the day after his brother's funeral.

The night moves along well, considering a child life was taken too soon, and the family is forever affected.

Ivy takes it upon herself to do the cooking. She made a wonderful vegetarian quiche for brunch. Tonight's menu consists of beef stroganoff, salad, and cheddar biscuits.

Gaby walks through the house fifteen minutes before supper is ready. She lights all candles in the house, even the bathroom candles of the wall sconces.

Plates of stroganoff circle the table completely to the top with buttery cheesy biscuits. Everyone works on their salads while the beef smiles back them.

"You know I never do this, but I am feeling it deep in my heart to talk to my son through prayer. Would it be alright if we all would just join hands a moment… say a little prayer for the ones not here tonight?"

Everyone motions in agreeance with Kyle, putting their utensils or long stem wine glasses of cold water down. Everyone joins hands.

"Father God in heaven, I know I'm not one to ever pray at the table, while I am ready to eat and starving, but today I hear you calling me to set aside my food for a moment and give some grace for Camden and my wife, Angela's life. Jesus it appears I needed to be saying grace a long time ago. Thank You Lord for all I've been given… even now with all I have and those who are gathered with me today…"

Kyle opens his eyes scanning about the table. Some keep their eyes closed, Gaby and Benjamin are open, as Kyle does, embracing the grace in openness with him. Kyle continues to pray.

"I guess what I'm trying to say is thank you God for giving me this wonderful family before me tonight and the ones you hold dearly for me. I know they no longer have need for what you've provided us here today. Thank you, God, for what I do have here tonight. I believe you are going to heal our wounded hearts and bring forth a new season. We know you have the plan to give us joy for all who aren't here tonight. I love you Camden. I love you, my loving, Angela. I pray for this healing in all of us in Lord Jesus' name —Amen."

"Amen." Everyone at the table says.

Delighted to have a great meal in front of them, they sink their forks into the creamy beef noodles that steam in the air when pulled from the rest of the plate. They eat in a tranquil covenant of a quiet family who mourn the loss of Camden.

The night falls quick and the next day soon arrives.

Roxanna and Charles stop by after checking out from the hotel in Hollywood before they catch a Lyft to L.A.X.

They pull out their suitcases from the back of a Lyft driver's trunk, and roll them into Kyle's house to visit with everyone before they catch a flight back to New York in a few hours.

Even though the weather is nice in California, it will be a different story when they get off at La Guardia Airport. Roxanna and Charles pull the scarfs from around their necks and push their long-knitted sleeves back.

Tony packs his bag, getting ready to drive back to San Diego, when he hears his mother and stepfather in the house. He exits the bedroom to greet everybody. Tony runs into Gaby who's exiting the kitchen with about six bottles of water in her hands.

"By the way you're dressed, you look like winter in California mother. A very sophisticated mother that I love so much." Tony gives his Roxanna a hug.

"Morning Charles." Tony smiles confidently.

"Good morning." He reciprocates.

"Darling, will you be bringing Gaby and the baby home for the holidays?" Roxanna starts to consider the space she has in their small, twelve hundred square feet two-bedroom apartment they've owned for thirty years.

"That would give you plenty of time to organize your craft room, the same one the kids used to sleep in when they lived at home." Charles lets out a chuckle from his tall, slender frame.

"There's an ideology I hadn't studied yet. Gaby, would you like to see the Big Apple?" Tony observe the answer on her face.

"Of course, I would like to see NYC. I only have been here all this time mi amore." She gives off a pregnant glow holding her belly bump.

"Well darling, text a Lyft driver to take us to L.A.X." Roxanna requests.

Charles pulls out his cell phone to summon a Lyft driver as Roxanna stands up organizing their stuff.

Charles then lays a hand on Kyle's shoulder, "If you need anything at all, be sure to let us know. Even though our daughter isn't here, you're still our son in law."

"Thanks Charles, it means a lot. Maybe for the holidays, I'll bring my family up when Tony and Gaby go to visit. It would be like old times. A big dinner and room filled with gifts to open."

Tony looks at Gaby, "I was thinking if you don't have much to do here, would you like to drive back with me to San Diego and see my home and business at the pawn shop? I've got to take you sometime before the baby comes."

Gaby looks to Kyle for some guidance. "I would love to go." She smiles.

"So, get to packing and let's go." Tony sense new beginnings around the corner.

Outside, everyone hugs before Charles and Roxanna hop in their Lyft ride.

The next day, sunlight hides behind the palm trees at the Hawthorne house. Friday March 9th approximate 3:45P.M.

Kyle and Benjamin are in the black Mercedes pulling into Doctor Normal Yates' parking lot for another bout of grief counselling.

They walk inside the fresh and neat office building, scented of eucalyptus. They press the 4th floor button in the elevator and go up.

Kyle and Benjamin both appear beaten down. What was once a life of luxuries, which would have been like heaven on earth to most people, is now like walking down a road of graveled oppression? They enter Dr. Yates office door.

Dragging their feet inside, the receptionist observes their deep-down emotions in the bends of their back posture.

They take a seat after checking in with the receptionist.

Five minutes until 4 P.M. Dr. Yates hurries into her lobby reaching for Kyle, with tears in her eyes, giving him a hug.

"I am so sorry for what has happened in your life Mr. Hawthorne." She backs off of them assessing Benjamin's low vibrational stare, just the same as his father's.

"Thank you for making room for us on a Friday and so abruptly." Kyle says.

"You're welcome. Come on, let's get back to my room and talk about everything. You want anything to drink?"

"Maybe just a water."

Dr. Normal Yates reaches for some small washable cups and fills two of them full of the water from the reservoir.

In the room they sit together on the sofa and Kyle releases tears in front of his son. Benjamin sobs with him.

"Yes, yes, let it all out. This is a good place to let them run. Take your time. All of this can wait for you. Whatever you are both feeling, let your tears wash the hurt away."

After a few minutes Kyle shifts his uncomfortable gaze back to Dr. Normal Yates and then to his son. "I'm sorry son for not holding up like I'm supposed to."

"Dr. Yates, I'm losing my family one by one. Angela, Camden last weekend and now Gaby is probably leaving soon now that she is pregnant." Kyle lets out his frustration.

"Oh… Who is she again?" Dr. Normal Yates asks.

"She is our maid and she took over all of Angela's duties as a house mom when Angela passed. She's now like my best friend."

"I see. She has been a great deal of help in healing the first round of death and now round two and she might not be there to lean on. How do you feel about that?" Dr. Yates questions.

"Benji is all I have left in the world." Kyle holds a sad expression on his face.

"Mr. Hawthorne, have you considered how this could be effecting Gaby? How old is Gaby, if you don't mind?"

"She's twenty-four. No, I haven't even thought about what it's doing to her. She just stepped right up last time and has been so good to us. She did take a ton of stress off me while I got it together. Now she's pregnant with a whole set of her own battles ahead. This time must be different, I suppose. Yeah, she is with Tony in San Diego, at his house, all of this week, preparing now. I've got to start letting her go soon, I suppose."

"Are you ready for all this?" Dr. Normal Yates probes.

"No." He replies quietly.

"Okay just take your time with your thoughts. Benjamin, you've grown a little taller since I've last seen you. How are you taking all this in?" Dr. Yates smiles with sympathy.

"I miss my brother a whole bunch. I miss my mom the same. I'm hurting. I feel lost. I feel so alone, even though I have a boyfriend who loves me and a dad who loves me and accepts me for who I am. My little brother didn't deserve what happened. He wasn't even nine years old, and I'm mad about this. If the guy who hit him had not had his eyes glued to his phone, texting and driving, he would have not missed the stop sign and surely he would have seen my little brother in his white as day t-shirt." Benjamin lets his anger run wild.

"So, are you ready to accept what happened with Angela, and your little brother Camden, Benji?" Dr. Normal Yates surveys Kyle and Benjamin for answers.

"I have accepted… we have accepted Angela's death… haven't we?" Kyle presses into his boy.

"Yeah, but not having mom around hurts still. Gaby has been like a total mom figure. I haven't even thought about what happens after if she moves to San Diego with Uncle Tony." Benjamin wrinkles his face in consideration.

"It sounds like you accept not having Angela and that the letting go process is over. Now it's going to take the same process for Camden. You will still be able to be in Gaby's life I'm assuming, and she may even be a key role in helping you move on completely when that time comes. For now, you need to communicate with her, as soon as you can, to find out her desires for this new life that's blossoming for her." Dr. Yates takes out a pen and her planner for scheduling.

"I see your point of view Dr. Yates. Wow, what you just said, eases my mind a lot more, right this moment." Kyle inhales a few deep breaths feeling somewhat normal. He shakes his wristwatch to check the time.

"Time flies by on this first visit back to Dr. Yates. "Would you like to keep 4 P.M. on Friday, until further notice or what?" Doctor Normal Yates holds the pen as a ready writer. She writes them in the planner for next week.

For the first time in almost a week, Kyle feels a wall come down like an earthquake. Benjamin seems to mirror the same movements as his father.

At home, it's just the two men, well three if you count Chips Ahoy, who doesn't seem to be missing anything now that his owners are there to let him outside to urinate.

Kyle opens the refrigerator discovering how empty it is. He shouts to Benjamin upstairs, "Let's go out for dinner."

Friday and Saturday passes by.

Sunday arrives with a fully loaded refrigerator. Things seem to be caught up enough for Kyle to spend some time going over Angela's blue folder.

The doorbell rings.

Kyle gets up confused on who it would be showing up unexpectedly. He walks through the house and opens the door.

"Jeff, glad you could make it. Come inside."

Jeff follows Kyle's lead back to his office.

Kyle pulls out a chair. "Have a seat. Hey, I think I've matched the number four to everything Angela has been trying to show me or warn me about since her death."

"Show me what you mean. Did you find a key to the production hall?" Jeff cocks an eyebrow, rubbing his chin thoughtfully.

"A what?... oh, Yes, I didn't see this before, but as I was reading her stuff this time, it popped out bright as day. She was in four different text and drive fatal collision reports. She was a witness to all four." Kyle boasts a confident egoist side face smirk of certainty.

"I don't understand. What does the number four have to do with what happened to her and now your youngest son?" Jeff quizzes him, feeling unsettled.

"The night she died, we had an earthquake and when it woke me up in the middle of the night it was 4:44 P.M. I've been seeing the number four on license plates and grocery tabs, odd places. When I see the number, immediately something about Angela appears. It also happened to Benjamin at our grief counseling two years ago. It was 4:44 P.M. and he gets a call right in front of Normal Yates, from some unknown number screaming frantically on the other end, warning us about something. I believe it has something to do with the number of collisions she witnessed before she died, and she was trying to help people with her book. It's just a hunch." Kyle looks worried that Jeff doesn't believe him.

"Doctor Normal Yates. That's a name you don't hear often. Sounds about right for a psychoanalyst. Well anyhow that's more than an assumption, Kyle that's a master key to the lock here. What else do you have?"

Both men stay up until 4 A.M. reading over the typed and written material, piecing it all together. They examine her work in the blue folder diligently to save some lives on the road.

CHAPTER
TWENTY-FIVE

Over the last several months, Kyle and Jeff had met up to discuss a plan to turn Angela's manuscript into a movie. Taking its audience on a journey from Los Angeles to Brooklyn.

They scope over every detail in the blue folder and illuminate the dangers of texting and driving in Angela's perspective, creating fictional characters in memory of Angela and Camden.

Kyle's spent the last three months rewriting and incorporating their tragic events into the outline of her main purpose.

Through all of Kyle's agony and pain, he pens everything on paper the old fashion way. That is how he knew to write and Jeff would transfer everything later.

In the synopsis of — On the Way to Brooklyn Town.

The Wheeler's have a disruption in their family, sending a fearful mother and her two small children packing two days' worth of clothes, all the cash money she had for gas and food then cabooses when she was supposed to be taking the kids to school. She drives over two thousand miles to Brooklyn, to her parent's condo instead. The last time she had drove to NYC was in 2002 when communication technology wasn't as advanced as it is now.

It was a much different story in 2014 when smart phones were on the rise taking over computers and laptops. Cell phones were like third hands you needed and in moving vehicles, it was like you could be on vacation any day of the week, driving to work or home from school. On the escape, on her get away to her parents place how far does she go before she gets caught?

This is the basis of the storyline.

Throughout the next months, Benjamin is in school most of the time. Gaby ping pongs back and forth to Tony's house in San Diego.

Kyle turned most of his pain into strength by writing and staying home, cleaning his own house, and cooking home cooked meals like roasted chicken from a local deli and boxed stuffing.

Kyle lays down his pen and sips from his mug of coffee that's gone cold. He sits back in his office chair trying to envision his future and if it's still lonely.

He continues handwriting the script. His mind starts to ponder over the last twelve therapy sessions with Dr. Yates. Kyle stops writing for a second to understand why his mind jumped there.

Dr. Normal Yates has become the sounding board to everything happening in his life and he's grateful for someone he can trust and talk to.

Some of the topics Dr. Normal Yates picked for discussion were:

How to handle losing the mother of your children?

How to handle texting drivers on the road?

How to surrender the maid?

How to accept being alone with only one son now?

These were mainly what Kyle and Benjamin spoke about to heal from all that has happened in the past two years, but Kyle needs to focus on his writing.

Kyle no longer needs therapy as both Dr. Yates and he agreed he had opened all areas enough to begin to take responsibility for them. His only priority is Benjamin, taking care of the house and to complete, On the Way to Brooklyn Town.

It was Benjamin who needed more time with Dr. Yates. The only way he seemed to open up was sarcastically. He wasn't really dealing with the pain. He was bitter not having his mom and brother anymore.

Benjamin was quiet and didn't speak unless he was asked a question, otherwise sarcasm is how he expressed everything.

Kyle sits up in his chair. He looks around his gigantic house finding the only living and breathing object is his dog Chips Ahoy. Even the dog is feeling the sudden shift of a barren house.

Kyle picks up his pen and glances over where he left off.

Benjamin tosses and turns in his bed. The sun has heated the room up like an oven. It's had only been a week since Hollywood High School has released for summer.

He tries to sleep a little longer, but his bladder is too full.

Gritty eyed, he drags his feet into the bathroom to open fire into an uncleaned toilet bowl.

It's been several weeks since Gaby has been at the house to clean, and even if she could, her stomach protruded far out and her back hurt. Besides she's trying to make her new home with Tony in San Diego.

Standing at the mirror, Benjamin washes his hands, then takes excess water to slick back his long-worn hair. He tucks it behind his ears.

It falls out into his eyes. He shakes it out a little then re-examines it, remembering the blue bandana he almost got a detention for last month trying to be a cool student.

He goes to his closet pulling the bandana off the shelf it has laid ever since he threw it up there that day.

In the hallway he stares himself down in the mirror pulling his pretty boy hair up in that bandana. He smiles at his reflection a moment, then thinks how cool it would be to fool around with the virtual reality head gear, walking around like a zombie camouflaged to the world.

He starts to blow out kisses in the most sarcastic way to an imaginary Venom in the mirror like he is Marilyn Monroe and his boyfriend tries to jump into head gear with him.

Benjamin pulls off the head band and takes it with him into his bedroom. He falls on his bed and jumps right out to get his virtual reality headgear from his dresser.

He grabs the head gear his uncle Tony got him for his fourteenth birthday. Benjamin eliminates the sun from stealing his eye sight.

Watching Shawn Mendez's music video —In My Blood, Benjamin takes notion of everything he sees.

A dark grey brick wall the boy in the video lays on, as concrete, as bricks fall trying to break the wall. Benjamin relates to the lyrics and emotionalizes this and can see he's not the only one alone in the world for time being.

Benjamin tunnel visions during the video when he sees the green turf, flowers and rain scene.

He lays there and grows tired at the tail end of the video. He escapes the horror of vomiting colors of scarlet red-looking like plasma. A picture that would reflect his brother the last time he saw him.

Benjamin goes into his Junior year of high school barley promoted. He managed to hold onto his boyfriend, but Viper grew distant from both her twin and Benjamin. She was tired of being left out.

The last three months without Camden on the second floor of his house was like living alone for the first time. Benjamin tried to restructure his life but kept falling back to what he knew. His comfort zone of machine guns in the media room.

A simple game of Call of Duty became hard for him to play even. He could barely get into thirty seconds of the game without feeling pain from the empty seat next to him. Camden's seat.

It was car rides that seemed to be the release of pain for him. He focused on his driving ability and the surroundings of nature that helped heal his soul the most. Driving was something fresh for Benjamin and something he had control over.

Benjamin drives like an eagle, who can see distracted driver's miles away. He can spot them driving in and out of lanes or driving extremely slower so they can text while driving. Anyone can see this when driving up from behind.

To a driver who is texting while driving, they think a simple, *"What's up?"* or, *"I'll be there in five minutes."* is more important than their own life, not to forget someone else's.

Maybe they don't know what it's like to lose their mom in a car explosion or a brother who's face gets smeared in the concrete like a new form of plum- mustard jelly, or even better, bodies ejected out of moving vehicles and grated from eyeballs to femur bone on the freeway like shredded cheese.

Benjamin has been seeing a ton of distracted drivers lately. Distracted drivers didn't have discrimination behind it. Anybody with a cell phone, which is just about everybody in the world nowadays, used their cell phone like a third arm.

Benjamin reflects on how his therapy sessions are going and the time spent with his counselor where he can speak about everything. His relationship with Venom, schooling, his grades, death, life and even Camden's birthday that just passed last month. He would have been nine years old this year.

A single rolling tear splats Benjamin's pillow as he shuts his eyes, and another music video plays on his virtual reality head gear.

Mid-afternoon —Tuesday. Tony is driving Gaby home to Los Angeles from San Diego.

Smoke from the Stone Wildfires is dense filling the atmosphere, however the fires are ninety-five percent contained. It had been burning more than a few weeks and has burnt over a thousand acres. So far there had been no confirmed deaths. The air quality is beyond toxic.

Tony and his baby-momma enter the driveway in his old pick-up truck. Gaby gets out with gift bags for Benjamin's sixteenth birthday, today.

Tony fiends to light a cigarette after the two-hour drive with his pregnant girlfriend next to him complaining about fires.

He sticks a Camel between his lips. Tony coughs up cigarette smoke that's been sitting in his lungs over thirty years. He takes a puff inhaling as much as he could, like it was the remedy to relieve the stress from his life, as he tries to relax on the steps.

He sets his back-pack down on the step next to him.

"What? Are you just going to smoke, while I carry everything inside?" Gaby grumbles with a four-pound baby in her womb.

"Hey, I just spent the last two hours driving for a birthday party that will last a week. Give me a break, okay." Tony stretches his back and legs on the step.

Gaby goes inside taking the bag with her.

Inside the house, Kyle comes out of the downstairs bathroom rubbing his hands dry on his pants. "Hey Gaby. You got here fast. Say, how about you and Tony giving me a lift up to the dealership to pick up Benji's birthday surprise?"

"Yeah, let me get everything inside first. My man's out smoking his life away on your front porch." She clears her thoughts walks into the kitchen with the gift bags and a store-bought cake for Benjamin's birthday.

"Oh… is that that where he is? You two seemed like a perfect couple last year, what changed? The baby maybe?" Kyle snickers.

"Nothing's changed. Nothing's going to change either… I love my muscly old man. I only hope he doesn't smoke much longer though. He's already twenty years older than me. This baby needs a father, or you will be next in line." She holds her stomach, smirking at Kyle.

Tony comes inside the house, "Somebody crap talking about me … smoking cigarettes?" He echoes through the house.

"Hey Big-T, take me to pick up Benjamins birthday gift. I was going to request a Lyft, but you got here sooner that I thought." Kyle raises up from his seat.

Inside the truck the three of them sit on the bench seat with Tony driving them to the dealership. An eighteen-wheeler automobile transporter is right in front of them with a full rack of cars. The transporter is making a left turn.

Awkwardly quiet, Tony wants to smoke. Gaby wants to cry. Kyle tries to think of transferring funds over to the dealership, but can't think right now for the tension rubbing off Tony and Gaby is making him extremely agitated.

Inside the Range Rover dealership parking lot, Kyle gets out of Tony's truck, and goes inside to meet with the man to signing the title over for one of those beautiful blue babies for his son.

Tony parks Albert Orange on the side of the building. He and Gaby get out and look at some of the vehicles. Both of them are daydreaming about something like that for their new family.

Kyle shakes the hand of the salesperson inside, as he's handed over the keys to Benjamin's brand-new Baby Blue.

Back at Hawthorne's house, Benjamin hops down the staircase from a long morning catnap. He sees Uncle Tony and Gaby pulling into the driveway. Behind them a blue Range Rover enters the premises.

His eyes open wide. He knows that ride is for him.

Benjamin gets out of bed.

Dressed in his long pajama pants, he pushes his feet into his laced-up sneakers and tracks outside acting all calm, cool and collective.

"You weren't supposed to come out until I put a bow on it." His father hurries to lay it across the nose of the vehicle, in purpose of trying to hide the Rover.

"Happy Birthday." Uncle Tony and Gaby standby observing Benjamin gawk over his first set of wheels.

Benjamin walks completely around the shiny blue Ranger Rover, then returns to the driver's door and gets inside this baby. "Snap!" He exclaims.

Across the way, Darcy passes her front window and notices everybody outside the Hawthorne house standing by an unfamiliar vehicle in the driveway. She witnesses Benjamin getting out of the driver seat exuding happiness.

She alerts the twins. "It seems as if Benjamin has gotten a beautiful blue Range Rover."

The twins and their mum step outside to see what Benjamin has.

"Dad, can I take it for a test drive with Venom and Viper? I see them coming over."

"Sure son, but first get dressed for God's sake."

Darcy walk over and talk with Kyle, running her hand down his arm, "A Range Rover. I didn't know they made such an eloquent SUV like this one."

"Viper, get shoes on if you're going with them my lady." Darcy shifts her focus to her daughter who is climbing in the back seat.

"Okay mum, I will." She walks back to her house at a leisurely pace to find coverage for her toes.

Benjamin and Venom go into the Hawthorne house.

Upstairs, Venom blows steam onto Benjamin's soft warm lips. Venom pushes Benjamin against the wall. Passion heats the room up quickly.

"Happy birthday sexy buttercup supreme."

Benjamin grabs ahold of Venom's shaggy brown hair and pushes it out of his face. The both gaze into each other's eyes.

Venom releases Benjamin.

Benjamin stands in undershorts with a bare back showing off in the glistening sunlight from his window, while looking in his closet for clothes to wear.

He puts on jeans and a button down top.

The two boys jolt down the steps and find the parents outside still communicating. Viper is walking back over with jealousy written on her face.

Both boys get in the front while Viper hops in the back.

Benjamin checks out his mirrors and turns on the sound system.

"Not too loud Benji." Gaby speaks out.

Benjamin hits reverse on the gear shaft.

"Take it your dad's at work?" Benjamin asks Venom while driving away from Hancock Park.

"Yeah, dad is scheduled in back to back surgeries. He has to look over the administering of whatever anesthesia the patients get, otherwise they will become his victims instead his patients." Viper jokes from behind them.

"You mean like put somebody out cold?" Benjamin quizzes back.

"No, that would be like chloroforming someone. They're out for a short nap then back poppin. The mixture my dad uses is injected into their veins and he babysits them until surgery is done. Shortly after, he gets their vitals working again with an antidote shot or something like that." Venom explains.

"Interesting." Wobbly spoken, Benjamin slurs his words as a car veers into his lane almost colliding right into them and his new SUV.

"Asshole." He shouts in anger.

Benjamin takes a pause and his racing heart says, "Can you seriously tell me how or better yet, teach me how to properly chloroform someone and where to get it?"

"You can't be serious bro…?" Viper asks.

"I'm dead serious."

Later at the house everyone is back to normal. The twins are over.

Gaby eyes both Tony and the Bundt cake. Surly by now the red velvet and cream cheese frosting has defrosted. Her mouth salivates for it.

Everybody else is working on the hot chili and lime chicken tacos with corn tortilla.

Benjamin looks around enjoying everyone being over for his sixteenth birthday party even though they weren't really celebrating. It was more like they were hanging out.

Uncle Tony and Gaby flaunt their happiness together with a baby inside.

Kyle seems to be enjoying the daughter he never had, in Viper, as he adjusts notches in an old wrist watch of his that he gave to her.

Venom sits next to Benjamin with a red tipped ball cap and shaggy hair swooping out and over his ears. He sits quietly, sipping a soda out of a birthday party cup, holding his boyfriend's hand.

Chips Ahoy walks around the place looking for fallen chicken crumbs.

The only thing missing is the sweet nectarine of his mother's loving words and touch as well as his brother's inquisitive presence.

Then he feels a rush of joy from having a new Range Rover. Now, he'd be driving his junior year in style.

A hot flash bursts through his thoughts about the car that almost ramsacked him earlier. He caught a glimpse of what killed his mom and brother. The guy had his cell phone in hand earlier, and it was so freaking obvious he wasn't paying any attention.

Chapter
TWENTY-SIX

Monday 6 P.M. June 18, 2018

It has been six nights since Benjamin flipped the script in being chauffeured. He's now sixteen years old and has a super cool Range Rover to show of Los Angeles.

The Hawthorne's didn't have a summer vacation this year, but if all was good and Kyle didn't have to dip too far into his savings, they'd be going to Grandpa Charles and Grandma Roxanna's condo in Brooklyn for Christmas.

Benjamin and the twins hang out on the pier. Of course, they won't be getting a car until August 11th this year, when they turn sixteen. Currently, they're taking driver education class this month and have a few more hours to go. As of now, Benjamin is their driver to and from school.

Kyle spends the whole day glued to writing: On the way to Brooklyn Town movie script. He's never published anything. Fear starts to sink into him, but that doesn't stop his focus, will power or self-discipline in pursuit.

He silences his phone, leaving it outside his office door, as he delves into the script.

Normally he wouldn't be watching the news on television, but he has developed the need for a talking reporter or anyone who can break the silence barrier in his home.

Tony and Gaby spend the whole day in the pool at Hawthorne's house. They decide to go out to eat. Sun glistened, they sit down in a booth at restaurant dressed in casual evening attire at a table for two with an Oceanside view.

A bit of jazz music is playing over the sound system. A votive candle is lit in a jar on the table, shining brighter as the sun falls.

They share a shrimp cocktail from a long stem glass with chips and salsa on the table. Tony has a glass of a chilled Pinot Grigio.

Gaby takes her sparkling water and squirts the lemon wedge into her glass. She swirls it around, then takes a sip, gazing at her man as he relaxes more with every sip he takes.

After a romantic evening out, Tony brings Gabriella back home. She has a six-month baby checkup and sonogram scheduled tomorrow morning.

Tony is the one who will oversee opening the pawn shop tomorrow.

At the Hawthorne place, Gaby folds Tony's washed laundry from the week and folds them neatly into his rugged old backpack.

They gaze into each other's eyes in a pale moonlight. He pulls her into him feeling his unborn fetus across his waistline. Grabbing the roundness of her buttocks, he kisses her and passion arcs back and forth between them, crackling like electricity.

Gaby walks him to the door. On the way there, Tony catches a glimpse of Kyle working on his project through the office door. He opens it, giving him a, "See you later."

Kyle puts his pen down and gets out of his chair, stretching his back from sitting a long while writing, and meets Tony for knuckle bumps.

Benjamin has his headphones on and they stop working in the middle of his video. The sound goes quiet, then totally black. He can hear his father and uncle downstairs talking. He goes down for help with the head set.

Pacing down the steps, "Uncle Tony, oh you are leaving?"

"Yeah… I've gotta open shop in the morning. If I leave now, I'm free from rush hour."

Standing at his uncle's side, "Well, before you go, can you look at these goggles? They just crapped out on me."

"Have you charged them in a while?" Tony asks.

"Yes, I just unplugged them from being on the charger all day, like an hour ago. They should be good on the battery." Benjamin says.

"Let me take them with me to my house and I'll look at them when I get a chance. Deal?"

"Yeah, okay cool man." He meets his uncle for a pat on the back then rushes back upstairs to bug Venom on Facebook.

Tony kisses Gaby once more before he driving away.

On an empty tank, Tony pulls into a fuel station thirty minutes outside of Los Angeles on Highway 5.

Getting out of his truck, he reaches into his back pocket pulling out his wallet. He pulls out his debit car and pays at the pump.

Under a covered car port, he starts to fill up the tank. Heavy rain begins pour down. The wind picks up and blows mist on him. The temperature cools down five degree in three minutes. He's just thankful to be getting gasoline.

The rain calms down when he places the nozzle back on the hook.

Exiting the parking lot, the roads are very clear. His blinker ticks loudly as he gets in the far-left lane at the light. He's the only car on his side of the road.

His windshield wipers glide over beads of God's rain water, sent to put out some dry area where the wildfires have been raging a blaze.

The smell of rain engulfs leftover smoke lingering in the atmosphere.

On the other side of the road, the stoplight is green. A car and motorcyclist are neck to neck, about to pass the intersection.

An older model Ford 500 pulls out of the same fuel station Tony just came from like a bat out of hell.

The car next to the motorcyclist finds himself halting his breaks to a complete stop. The motorcyclist never sees it coming.

Blindsided, the motorcycle T-bones the Ford 500, hitting it like a brick wall then his body flies over, landing in puddling rain and rough concrete.

He summersaults a few times, shredding him up really bad.

The boy blacks out, feeling no pain. In shock, he sees his jeans ripped at the pelvic area, but can't feel his legs or the lower areas that blood is pouring from.

The car that was parallel to him, saw the whole thing happen, but couldn't catch the face of the man in the Ford 500 because it happened so quickly.

Tony has a green arrow at the light, but instead of turning he follows the hit and run suspect in the Ford 500.

Undercover, Tony follows inconspicuously about a quarter mile behind.

Parked at a residence, a young Hispanic male gets out of the Ford 500 staggering drunk. He mumbles some swearing words, as he finds a big black dent in the passenger side and a busted-out window. He doesn't recall how it got there.

Tony's parked down the block a ways and is unnoticed by the young man.

From behind, Tony sticks a knife at the Hispanic's jugular vein. "SH…

Don't say one word." Tony threatens.

The boy freezes, in his blood alcohol content so high, he chokes.

Not moving. Not saying anything, the boy freezes in fear.

"Now I want you to get back in your car peachy like. We are going to have a little conversation about what just happened a little while ago involving the huge dent in the side of your car. You're going to drive and you're going to follow my instructions… Shake your head yes or no." Tony demands in a whispering growl.

The boy agrees to get in his car.

Tony enters the back seat.

"Turn your mirror facing me. I want to see your pathetic face." Tony demands.

"Start your car and drive." Tony hits the back of the boy's headrest with his knife still pulled out on him.

"Where too?" The boy shakes, terrified.

Tony yells inside the car, "I said drive!"

The boy rapidly sobers up.

"Turn on your headlights. Are you scared?" Tony laughs.

"Where are you taking me?"

"Just drive." Tony sarcastically yells out.

Driving the speed limit, afraid of hitting the guy on the motorcycle, afraid of the guy sitting behind him with a knife. The young man doesn't know why yet. It's been twenty minutes and the man with the raspy voice hasn't said much other than, "Drive."

Maybe he was about to get robbed or molested, he fears the worst.

"So, you thought you were gonna get away with attempted murder?" Tony finally said something else.

The boy looks at Tony's stern ears in the back seat. They look serious and vindictive. He knows exactly what the man witnessed.

"You were there?" The boy swallows.

"Yes… Now drive."

"By the way, was what you were texting more important than the guy you hit on the motorcycle?" Tony added.

The boy clinches his teeth, holding his tongue inside his mouth.

Tony laughs, "Not important right now, DRIVE!"

Meanwhile, back at the scene of the hit and run accident, a man who stopped to help the motorcyclist, applies pressure to his pelvic area as the boy lays on the concrete unconscious. The boy appears to be in his early twenty's.

A nun is there hovering over both the man and young boy, praying for healing and strength over them.

The ambulance, police, and fire truck arrive to the scene.

The emergency medical technicians handle the boy, checking his vitals. He finally wakes up but, he's in and out of conscious.

The officer interrogates, "What happened here?

"It was a hit and run. It happened so fast. I was concerned about this boy. He T-boned a car that pulled out in front of him and was thrown over the vehicle. I didn't get a good look at the person who hit him, other than he appeared to be male with a lit-up phone scene at his face." The witnessed answers.

"What kind of vehicle was it?" The officer asks.

"It was a four-door white Ford, but I don't know what type, other than it was midsize." The witnessed replies.

"What did you see?" The officer questions the nun.

"No, my dear officer. I saw hazard lights and the traffic backing up. I knew to get out and pray for everyone, but no I didn't see it happen."

"I'm in so much pain. My leg, my leg. Can you give me something, it hurts?" The boy awakens and moans in agony.

Blood continues to gush out his groin area. The paramedics ignore his request and work fast to get him secured and transferred from the ground and onto the stretcher.

"Can I have something? It's hurting and burning." He complains a level louder in fury. His eyes are swollen shut in hues of purple and blue.

"What's your name? How old are you? Can you tell me your height and weight? Are you allergic to anything?" An African American lead paramedic asks.

"Kyle Kairos, twenty-four, five foot- eight, one hundred and fifty-five pounds. Can I get something now?" He hassles.

"Are you allergic to anything?" The paramedic repeats.

"No, I don't think so."

The medic draws fluid from a vile and administers the remedy.

"Can you give me a contact number?" The medic requests, while the team of medics lift him off the ground onto the stretcher. They climb inside of the ambulance.

"My mom, call my mom Alonza Kairos."

The white sheet turns blood red, and drip continuously on the floor in a steady rhythm.

One of the paramedics quickly dials Kyle's mother on his cell phone and lets her know what hospital they are taking him to.

8 P.M. Only seconds away form an old campground Tony has found on his phone, he knows this is where he wants to take the piss any who decided to hit and run.

The campground is dark and creepy with only the moon and tree bearing witness.

"I like this area. Turn here and park in the empty space. Let's go for a walk and talk." Tony demands.

In a distant view Tony sees a huge tree. On the bottom of the boy's floorboard is a twenty feet tow rope just hanging out. Tony puts the tree and rope together in his mind and leads the boy to fulfill the vision while continuing to hold the knife to his back.

"Sit down with your back against the tree."

"You're not going to tie me and leave me here, are you?"

"No, first you're going to tell me what was going through your mind when you were texting and driving? And then I'm going to leave you here… and then I'm gonna call the cops."

Tony ties the scared, naive boy to the tree. The boy cries pleas not to call the cops.

After tying him to the tree trunk the boy says again, "You can't just leave me here. I don't want to go to jail."

Tony looks him up and down now like the devil in disguise. He grins and even throws him a fake laugh.

"You won't have to worry a thing about going to jail… No, that would be too easy, but there's a hell of a fire waiting for your ass. It's Online Now."

Tony walks away in a hurry, checking to see if anyone is around, as he heads back to the boy's car.

The boy cries out, "Don't leave me here."

Headlights beams in the boy's eyes. Tony revs the car up causing the boys to panic. The rope loosens a little and he's able to pry himself up half way.

Tony punches the acceleration pedal and drives it right into his head.

Blood splatters on the hood and windshield of the car. The tree breaks. Tony turns on the wipers, smearing the evidence away, and laughs as he gets out of the vehicle, not looking for any flames of hell behind him.

Tony exits the campsite and finds civilization after thirty minutes of walking. He dials up an Uber.

His driver gives him a ride back to his car with a nice conversation of a make-believe night.

Chapter
TWENTY-SEVEN

A worried mother and her male friend, who joins her on the sofa in the hospital room, where her son lays in the bed with his head wrapped and his eyes swollen black and blue.

Kyle, the victim of a hit and run motorcycle accident, is hooked up to heart and respiration machines that are helping him to function. Fluids from the IV bag drip. The vital signs monitor beeps checking the rhythm of his heart. He lays in a deep latent state ever since he was brought in yesterday evening. The bleeding at his lower extremities have stopped for the most part.

The sun casts its rays through the tiny cracks of the retractable window covering in the room at nearly 7:45 A.M, Tuesday June 19, 2018.

Both Kyle's mother and Bill, her friend, sit tight awaiting her son to wake up. Their faces are buried into their hands, and they didn't sleep at all last night. It didn't help if they tried shutting their eyes for a nurse would come in to check Kyle's breathing, and then another would swing in thirty minutes later.

Kyle flinches his leg and moans. It's the first sign of communication Alonza Kairos has gotten with her son, was in a semi-coma.

"Darling, I'm here. Bill's in the room too. What happened Kyle?"

"Mom, I'm in so much pain. I need some medicine." He whispers from a dry mouth.

"Bill, will you go get the doctor? Please let them know he's up now and in extreme pain." Alonza asks.

He exits the room in a hurry. Alonza stands by her son's side holding his hand. He can't see her for his eyes are painfully swollen shut.

Kyle's face is pale as a ghost. He lays wrapped from head to toe to stop swelling and bleeding.

"Mom, I'm really dizzy. I'm spinning. I feel like I am going to pass out."

"Okay honey. Hold on. Let me grab someone."

Alonza runs out of the room calling for a doctor or nurse down the hallway.

She and a team of medical staff, rush down to check Kyles vitals. Bill and a doctor enter the room, finding Kyle's hemoglobin level is near death zone.

The doctor places a rush order on five pints of blood for an immediate blood transfusion.

Alonza and Bill are told to hang out in the waiting room until Kyle's condition is stable.

The doctor looks over his chart, finding the sutures in between his legs were completed last night, from an incision on a motorcycle injury.

He removes the sheet and discovers Kyle is laying in a pool of blood. His eyes enlarge, and he swallows a deep breath of air.

"How could this have happened?" He bellows, while looking at the leg letting everyone in the room know.

The doctor administers a small dose of pain medicine to Kyle, who moans in anguish.

A male nurse and the doctor observe between his legs. Kyle has been ripped from scrotum to anus from the motorcycle wreck; flying off a crotch rocket.

The doctor shakes his head in disappointment of the night shift, then immediately starts to clean the bloody wound, that is still slowly oozing.

Kyle is stitched up and given blood to restore his life-force.

Alonza and Bill are allowed back into her son's room on his third pint of blood as he appears to be stable.

Very cranky from worry and lack of sleep, she is now cussing the medical staff from last night. Their negligence almost took her son's life.

Meanwhile, at a clinic in Los Angeles, Gabriella lays back on the sonogram table at her six-month examination, anxiously waiting to find out the gender of baby.

The technician rubs cold jelly on the mountaintop of her stomach.

Waving the wand over her belly they both perceive a three-dimensional image of Gabriella's baby.

A disturbance in the air forces Gaby to cough. The six-month fetus whiplashes inside her uterus as Gaby releases the cough.

"Well I can't find a penis, looks like it's a girl." A German technician articulates.

Gaby smiles in happiness. Thinking about the day she met Kyle and Angela Hawthorne at the restaurant years ago and how they've affected her life for the better, she figures out how to honor Angela.

After the ultrasound she walks out to her SUV. After starting the engine and turning on the air conditioning, Gaby calls Tony on Skype. He answers.

"Are you at the shop?" She smiles.

"Yeah, I'm just opening the door to go inside." He yawns from lack of sleep last night.

"You look tired mi amore. Did you sleep at all last night?"

"I got home pretty late last night and did some laundry for the week."

"I washed everything you brought here before you left last night."

"I know. There was another shirt I needed." Tony fabricates the lie through another quick yawn.

"So, guess what we are having?"

"Tuna sandwiches." Tony answers in another yawn.

"No, guess again. Hint… I just got off the examination table."

"Oh… I wager a baby girl."

"You guessed it right. I was thinking she should be called Angelina Cambrielle."

"I see what you did there… After my sister and Camden. I think they would both feel honored by that."

They blow kisses to each other on Skype and end the call.

Tony flips the switch, turning on the open sign to the pawn shop. Gaby pulls out of the clinic and drives home.

Normally a young Hispanic female helps Tony open the shop up, but her grandpapa passed away and his funeral's in Mexico.

The first customer pulls up to the front door parking spot.

The young man in a ball cap holds his phone up to face level scrolling, all sprawled out like he's on a permanent vacation.

Tony sips coffee from a large blue thermos while observing the boy who's just sitting on his tail.

The continuation of the kid flipping his thumbs on the cell phone pisses

Tony off further from last night. He realizes quite a few more entitled young folks should be bettering their lives instead of wasting it on their phones all day long.

Tony flashes back on how it ended for the boy who hit the motorcyclist and considers how to take out.

He ponders on what could be more important than driving up to a pawn shop and parking directly in front of the door on a Tuesday 10:15 A.M. checking out his phone for twenty minutes.

Another car pulls in and parks next to him. Both people give a long stare at the boy on his phone, then get out of their car to go inside.

It never phases the boy. He doesn't acknowledge the patrons and continues to scroll his life away.

Tony rages, keeping it to himself in front of the people inside the store. He starts to believe in following this boy as he leaves and tying him to a tree. Tony finds a way to educate people on the many distractions that's destroying the population.

The boy enters the shop looking around while texting and responding to texts like it's a video game. The boy gives Tony a quick head wave then continues to look on his phone texting away in a cool air-conditioned environment.

The other customers are over by the televisions shopping for the best deal.

The boy walks the store then comes up to the front and checks out the lady's rings in the cases.

"Is that your soon to be fiancés with all those texts? I wonder how many texts it takes to get the ring size." Tony gives a serious smirk with his coffee container pressed at his lips.

The young kid doesn't really respond other than, "Ah… Yeah, what's the price on this one right here?" The boy sways at the glass top like he's high on dope.

Tony considers the price of another's life if he's caught texting and driving like he has been at the pawn shop all morning. He puts on a savvy smile and locates the ring in question for a price check.

Meanwhile at Laguna Beach — Deer Cove at nearly 1 P.M. a couple of hikers are walking to find the perfect place to set up camp for a few days. They come out of a thicket of trees and tread in a semi clear path.

In the distance, one of the men sees a white, four door car crashed into a tree. He notifies his buddy who's on the lookout for vicious reptiles as they tread on the campground site.

Both guys run over to the car with the passenger door left open to find nobody inside it. At the front end of the car bent into the tree.

Dreading what they witness next, one guy vomits on the earth. The other reaches for his cell phone, speed dialing for some help.

Flies swarm over the rigor mortis body of what appears to be a young male.

Both men back away from the body, full of terror that whomever had done this, is still lurking around.

Orange County Sheriffs arrive within twenty minutes. Crime scene tape goes up and over the older make and model white Ford 500.

The coast guard helicopters over the area, searching for anything out of ordinary, trying to piece together any information they can, from the horror found here.

A local news station drives onto the campgrounds where the police and victim are found. The news reporters plan to do a live broadcast and a Facebook live feed, hoping for any tips from the public.

The driver of the news station gets out and helps the photographer and reporter with equipment. The crew moves in closer to the trapped decaying body.

The photographer gets his camera angled and ready to go live in seconds with Cynthia Alado, the reporter from Los Angeles.

The reporter stands at 5'1, mousy brown hair, pulled back in a ponytail past her shoulders and athletic frame.

"Good afternoon or should I say… It's a tragic ending for an unidentified Hispanic male around the age of twenty-five. The 911 call came from a couple of hikers looking to set up camp today around 1 P.M. local time. The report came as a male tied to a tree with a white Ford 500 car wrapped around him. If anyone has any tips or information on how this could have happened or who done it, please contact Orange County Sheriff's Department.

"Now watch, about a hundred ideas on how this could have happened will appear under the live feed." Cynthia Alado spat out.

The photographer at the scene takes photos of the car crashed into the tree. EMT's carry the victim's body in a body bag on a stretcher to the ambulance and then off to the morgue.

At the Hawthorne house, after Gaby cooked supper for everybody, Kyle leaves the dinner table and goes back to his office to finish up with chapter fifteen.

Kyle shuts the door. He's highly focused but turns on the television for comforting sound in the background.

On one of the nightly news, the reporter, Cynthia Alado comes on air. The television shows the time at the bottom of the screen to be, — 1:11 P.M. this afternoon.

Kyle drops his pen on the notebook, captivated by this special report. He perceives the car upon the tree and a single victim being carried off in a black bag. His heartbeat elevates. Intense emotions rise in flashbacks of what had happened to his wife and son. He tries to figure out how to incorporate this into the story. Somehow this tragedy becomes a connection to Angela's revelation of texting and driving.

How could he write this terrifying event into the work of Angela's? A creepy incident occurring last night, and they find him near the water hanging out on a sunny day.

Capturing all he can in the forty-five second replay, Kyle sits back with his arms folded behind his head and ponders how to write the scene for the first victim in his movie script: On the way to Brooklyn Town.

CHAPTER
TWENTY-EIGHT

Thirty minutes outside of Laguna Beach, and inside a of Los Angeles, Kyle Kairos lays on a hospital bed inside the recovering center. He doesn't have all the bandages around his head and neck like he did before he was transported from the other medical center. The bruising and swelling in his eyes have gone away about thirty percent since the accident two weeks ago.

Still not able to walk, he lays around disappointment and depressed. He can't even watch the television right in front of him, as his eyes are hurt from the swelling.

Re-living the accident over and over, he blames God for another trial in his life. This wasn't something new to him. All his life since he was a few years old and moved to America from Brazil, challenges followed him around like thunderstorms.

Kyle Kairos often thought about taking the life God gave him and ending it on his own, for he could not see the plans God has for him. He didn't want a relationship nobody else couldn't see.

He figured if God placed every obstacle upon him, he was cursed, but that isn't true. If he's still breathing, then he was made to be stronger than anyone around him so he could be the blessing others need. There is a season for everything.

But this time, oppression has him by the legs. Moving any part of his hips or legs without a high dose of medication causes him to scream out in pain. He could not see a way out of this mess.

Alonza Kairos comes waltzing down the hallway of the hospital with a breakfast plate for her and her son. She enters his hospital room number, three seventy-seven with a plate of Brazilian cheese biscuits and honey.

Giving him a hug, she can sense how wretched he is.

"Cheer up nutmeg. You are going to get better in no time. Have some of my faith sweetheart. I need you to keep positive… you are strong and the strength in your body is coming back."

"Mom, its 9 A.M. I have the rest of the day to lay here and do nothing with my life. I mean… my soccer career is over and my days in the army are done as well." Hopelessly, he pops off.

He sits up in bed munching from the tray of biscuits. His mother is on a sleeper sofa, nibbling from a plate of biscuits on her lap.

A man knocks on their hospital door, then enters inside.

"Kyle Kairos… Hello, I'm detective Calc Timmons, LAPD. I've come to ask you a few questions pertaining to your accident two weeks ago…, June 18, 2018 to be exact. May I come in?"

Kyle nods and asks, "What kind of questions?"

Detective Calc Timmons holds a clipboard full of notes. Observing them he verbalizes, "All of my questions have to do with the hit and run on that day."

"Yeah, I can give you what I remember, but everything happened so fast. I don't really remember a whole lot." Kyle responds bitterly from the hospital bed.

"Why don't we start with where you were at before the accident happened and where you were going on that day?" Detective Timmons furrows his brow, waiting for Kyle to talk.

"I was going over to my friend's house. I had come from my house."

"Are you related to Kyle?" Detective Timmons looks over at Alonza.

"Yes, I'm his mother. Kyle lives at my home. On the day of the accident, I told Kyle to take my car because it was raining outside. It was dark, and gloomy, and I could just feel something bad was going to happen. Insisted, Kyle insisted to take his bike."

"So, you live at home and you were going to a friend's house. Can you tell me at the intersection from which you were hit, everything you can remember? In fact, I'm going to give you a blank page. Can you draw me a diagram of everything?

With puffy eyes, Kyle begins to sketch a four-way intersection with vehicles all around his motorcycle. A truck in the turning lane. A sport utility next to that and then Kyle who was riding his Ninja Bike at the time. He darkens the image of the white midsize car pulling out of the fuel station. That was the one which pulled out in front of him causing him to T-bone.

"Tell me all the colors, types, makes, and models of these vehicles and if you can remember all the faces in these vehicles around you that night."

"Yeah… the best I can remember on that rainy night was a man in this reddish colored truck in the left turning lane. I don't know what type of truck it was other than it was an older truck. This one right here was a tan color SUV, but I don't know what kind. The driver who pulled out in front of me was a under twenty, that much I could see with his cell phone that was lighting up his face, as I T-Boned him. Oh, he had dark and bushy hair. That's all I can remember, after that I went tumbling into the pavement, blacking out."

"There's another reason I'm here. On the night of your accident, there was something else that happened in the nearby vicinity. We found a young boy tied to a tree with his car wrapped around him. Now we don't have any leads on who did this, but I think it's tied to what happened to you. I'm going to give you a photo of that crime scene." Calc Timmons hands him the photo image.

"Is this the car that hit you?" He said.

Kyle takes a long-lasting look at the photo then comes to a quick realization.

"Yes, that is the car. And look… there is the black mark and dent from my bike from where we collided."

Timmons hands him another photo.

Kyle intensely looks over the photo seeing the exposure of the boy who hurt him. "Yes, I believe this is him. Wow, what the hell happened?"

"We still don't know the motive, but I will find every fact and bring whoever did this to justice."

"Kyle… Alonza, if I have any more questions, can I call you?"

They give him their cell phone numbers.

Detective Calc Timmons exits room number three-seventy-seven.

Kyle and his mother go back to eating. The cheesy biscuits have grown cold.

Getting into his unmarked car, Detective Calc Timmons starts to perceive all the vehicles at the scene. Not all the witnesses stayed behind after Kyle was hit.

Inside the car, Calc Timmons looks over the report. He looks over the witnesses on the scene. The owner of an SUV and a Nun are the only ones on record of who was there with Kyle that night.

Calc Timmons begins to feel an intuition for what had happened on June 18th. Now he just needs to check the stoplight video cameras and see who the red truck belongs to.

Detective Timmons drives to the station with a bit of ease.

In those same weeks that have passed by, Tony hasn't been able to drive back to Los Angeles to see Gaby and their unborn daughter. Tony decides to go see Gaby, since his employee is back at work now and can open the pawn shop the next few days, while Tony is away.

The afternoon ride into Los Angeles has been smooth until two cars fly past him and almost wipe him off the freeway. Rage begins boiling in Tony's veins.

The two cars obviously know each other. A red Corvette Stingray and a blue Dodge Viper fly in and out of traffic.

The Stingray slows down tremendously, then takes the next exit.

Tony decides to follow behind it at an inconspicuous distance.

On the passenger seat of Tony's truck, he sees Benjamin's head gear he promised to bring back on this visit. The goggles give Tony an idea for these irresponsible drivers he faces each time he is on the road.

The driver of the red corvette pulls up to a stoplight, feeling victorious from escaping the blue viper on the interstate.

Tony pulls up in the left lane, beside the driver to get a better glance.

Peering through the window of the Corvette, Tony sees a young man with sun bleached hair, texting like it's the Fourth of July already. Whoever he's in communication with has put a boasting smile on his face. The driver never notices Tony watching his every move.

The light turns green. Blondie boy doesn't see that either. Whoever is on the other end of the cell phone is way more important.

Tony slowly presses on the accelerator to cross the intersection. He then hears the Corvette press the gas, passing him by.

The driver looks right at Tony with a smirking grin, wanting to race on an empty road. He takes his virile approach and accelerates right on by.

Tony gives the Corvette the lead. The boy inside the car has his eyes glued to his cell phone screen. He follows the young driver with the intent to destroy this antagonist before the foe kills somebody else first. The battle is on, Tony decides.

The guy in the Corvette pulls into a shopping mall parking lot, and parks away from the doors. He gets out and walks inside the place.

Tony parks at a distance but follows him inside the building with his eyes. He surveys what his is wearing, how tall he is, and even how cocky he walks. Tony waits for the guy to come back to his pride and joy.

The blue Viper and a florescent purple Jeep Wrangler, with huge monster wheels, pull up behind the Corvette.

Inside the blue sports coupe, another young male driver appears to be texting on his cell phone. The group of guys finally get out of their vehicles laughing profusely, fist bumping and stuff, then get back into their vehicles after the male in blue Viper tags the Corvette with a sticky note.

The memo reads: *MARCO POLO, YOU'RE IT.*

Meanwhile inside the Hawthorne kitchen, Kyle and Gaby are in serious discussion.

"I've been thinking of selling this house and moving closer to San Diego, that way when you move in with Tony in a matter of months, Benjamin and I will be able to have family nearby." Kyle pronounces.

Gaby looks around at the only home she's known since she's lived in America. With a somber face, "Maybe Tony would move here instead?"

"No, I wouldn't ask him to sell his property and risk his pawn shop. It's just that ever since Angela and now Camden deaths, I feel burdened by all the memories. I've been thinking about this for some time, plus I can put Waylon, Kimberly and Donna all in charge as managers of Hawthorne Realty — Los Angeles and eventually open a brokerage in San Diego."

"I understand. I think if you want to do this then Tony will be excited too." Gaby answers.

"I'll talk to him when he gets here." Kyle shakes his wristwatch then says, "I thought Tony would be here by now."

Gaby walks away muted inside the house full of her memories.

Chips Ahoy follows Kyle inside the home-office door with him. "What boy… What? Let's check to see if you have food and water. Are you hungry?"

Inside the media room, Benjamin plays the Call of Duty alone, sitting in a comfy theatre sofa-seat. Venom and Viper are logged on and playing with him.

It's nearing 1 P.M. They've all been playing since 11:30 A.M.

Benjamin hasn't eaten anything and his stomach starts to growl.

"Ven, Vip… let's get off here and go get burgers and milkshakes somewhere. I'll pick you up after I take a shower… let's say, thirty minutes." The twins easily agree. The log off and go get money from their mum.

After a complete hour passes by, Tony regains composure in his truck seat. He spots the boy with the blonde hair walking out to the Corvette.

The guy peels the note off his driver side window, reads it, and then laughs while crumbling it in his hands.

He speeds off from the parking lot with his cell phone at his eye level, swimming in and out of traffic.

Tony creeps up behind the Corvette.

After twenty minutes, the Corvette and the Purple Jeep meet up on the road weaving back and forth playing each other's game. The two vehicles never notice the burnt orange truck following them.

Tony considers killing both drivers as he watches their careless driving show.

The Corvette abruptly turns onto another street. Tony isn't able to make it in time, and now shifts his eyes to the driver of Purple Jeep.

At the light Tony idles the engine with his foot on the brake next to the Jeep. Automatically, he sees similarity in the spirit of the boys; definitely they know each other.

Buzzed haircuts. Dark roots from the hairline visibly present through the glass of the driver's window.

Tony makes eye contact with the guy.

The boy smirks back at him and slurs through the glass, "What's up?", like he's high on something.

Tony gives him a wanking grin.

The boy grimaces back, raising his nose at Tony.

The light turns greens.

Tony keeps his distance on the Jeep discreetly.

The purple Jeep pulls into a shopping center. The driver of the Jeep jumps out.

Tony is already there and sticks a knife to his throat.

"Crap man, you scared me."

"So, I scared you and not this knife at your neck? Get your ass back inside your Jeep, we are going for a little ride."

The driver from the Jeep tries running. Tony grabs him by the sleeves of his shirt.

"Okay, Okay." The boy panics in confusion.

Tony sits next to the boy in the driver seat and says, "Drive off."

The driver presses the accelerator with blood dripping out of his nose onto his shirt.

"What do you want from me? What did I do to you?"

"Let's say I didn't like how you were looking at me, at the light back there, while you were texting and driving. Are you friends with the red Vette, and blue Viper?"

"What, so you've been following us?"

"You have a great guessing game…What I want to know is, were all of you kids playing some kind of game or something while you were texting and driving?"

"Yeah, it's called Marco Polo. Haven't you ever played it for fun man?"

"How about you drive while I text the police… Marco Polo…" Tony goes quiet for a minute.

"No man! I'm sorry."

"Sorry doesn't cut it. You know my sister and eight-year-old nephew died from a foolish driver who was texting."

"I wasn't texting and driving. I told you man, we were playing Tag, Your It."

"This isn't the pool or ocean water boy. This is the road. You can kill someone when you and your friends drive like that."

The boy's cell phone goes off. He pulls it out of his pocket reading the text highlighted from the notification.

Tony knocks the phone out of his hand.

"You think I'm a retard?" Tony probes with his raspy cigarette breath.

The boy wipes his nose smearing blood on his face.

Meanwhile, at the Los Angeles hospital, Kyle Kairos and his mother Alonza Kairos sit inside the room with the television on, but nobody is really watching the advertisements.

Kyle is still not able to move his legs and is suffering in moderate pain.

Alonza's friend Bill knocks on the door, then enters unexpectedly. He is fully loaded in optimism. It's his natural spirit of fervor.

"How's my monkey boy doing? Are you able to move yet?" Bill queries.

Kyle grimaces, he despises being called monkey.

The power flickers off and on, inside room number three-seventy-seven, then completely shuts off.

The nurses outside of Kyle's room scurry around searching for answers. The power appears to be off all of the third floor.

Bill and Alonza peek outside of the door to see or find out what's going on.

An African American male nurse, with long braids, flies by in the hallway.

Bill stops him. "What's going on? Why is the power off? My friend's son is in this room hooked up to monitors and bags of fluids. Is this going to affect him?"

The nurse, tugging his thin brown braids, and holding a fake confidence, panics and sasses out," I don't know sir. We' tryna find answers as we speak. Be patient sugar. Be a little patient. As soon as I find out, I will personally come back and let you know something —Okay?"

Bill considers this man different, then walks back into the room with Alonza and her son.

Meanwhile, tied to a midsize tree in an unknown location, the buzz cut boy from the purple Jeep stands there. He has on Benjamin's head gear and is watching a short film about texting and driving, and how many deaths occur each year. He's about six minutes into it the film.

The boy's lips are visible through the thick framed goggles and says, "Come on man. I said I'm sorry. Why am I watching some stupid video about texting while driving?" The boy smarts off.

"You still don't get it, do ya?" Tony shouts in an empty field with the sun baring down on them.

"You don't want me to call the cops, yet you're still going to be out there tomorrow getting your game fix of Marco Polo, through all of Los Angeles, if I let you go."

"Come on man." The boy cries.

Tony starts the Jeep engine, revving it up loudly.

The boy hollers, "What are you doing?"

He can hear the Jeep but can only see the film from the goggles on his head, with a cheesy narrator speaking on statistics of tragic deaths every passing year.

Tony floors the Jeep into overdrive and parks it into the boy's skull at the tree. Blood and brains spurt out everywhere, turning a yellow field a dirty rubicund.

Tony gets out of the Jeep finding justice served. The boy's brains spill out of his open skull, turning the rest of the victim's body beet juice red.

"Don't call the police… Okay." Tony sarcastically laughs out.

Tony walks off in a virile stride, for this boy's death isn't causing another texting and driving statistic on the internet.

Tony walks nearly thirty minutes, then finds a shopping strip. He requests an Uber to take him to his Albert Orange.

Detective Calc Timmons is seated at his desk at the station putting together photos of the June 18, 2018 crime scene he's assigned to.

He starts to question why someone would kill in such a manner. If he was going to kill someone, why tie them to a tree and do with their own vehicle? All the pieces of the puzzle are here, but why isn't he understanding it yet?

The detective sits at his desk as the sun begins to fade.

Calc Timmons appears to be furrowing his thick dark eyebrows as he meditates on the motive that killed the young driver of the Ford 500.

An officer enters Timmons unit, handing him a few photos of the camera monitors from the night of the accidents.

He opens a yellow envelope and pulls out the eight by ten photo images. He lays them across the desk. These show step by step how Kyle Kairos accident happened.

The first image shows the truck Kyle discussed earlier, sitting in the left-hand turning lane.

Second photo shows the same truck, an SUV and Kyle on his motorcycle before crossing the intersection. The light is green.

Third shows the light-colored Ford 500 entering the intersection parked in front of Kyle on the motorcycle. At his angle, his light is red. Through his window glass you can see a cell phone, lit up.

Another image shows Kyle colliding with the Ford 500 and being thrown over the car.

The last image is the truck turning right on red, appearing to be following the Ford 500.

Detective Calc Timmons knows he's on to something here. He sits a little longer with his hands at his lips like he's praying, as he lets all the photos sink into order. Rising out of his seat he locates his assisting officer.

"Officer Snowlines, will you pull a close up of the truck's plates? Get me the registration of this owner."

CHAPTER
TWENTY-NINE

Tony drives his Albert Orange, chirping like a cricket into Kyle Hawthorne's driveway, half past seven, nearly four hours later than expected arrival.

Gaby has been sitting in the living room worried as she called his phone over and over. It went straight to voicemail each time.

Out the window she observes light coming up the driveway. Cautiously holding her baby inside her belly, she anxiously travels to the front door.

Tony shuts the engine off. He opens the screeching door, stretching and yawning, in front of his lady's eyes.

"What happened Tony? I tried to call you. Your phone is off. I called several times, hours and hours ago." She climbs his neck for a kiss.

He gently pushing her off him, then pulls out a cigarette from his pack and lights it up.

"Gaby give me a minute to smoke this baby. I'm tired and starving. I had a stinking' blow out on I-5… had to hitch a ride to the nearest tire shop and wheel shop… messed my rim up pretty bad. Then my battery on my phone got too hot or something. It wouldn't turn back on. I had to take it to the shop and that was another two hours. Do you have something left over from supper to heat up for me? I'll be inside in a minute." He sits on the top step watching her out the corners of his eyes as she goes inside.

He puts the cigarette out in the grass with his boot. Inside the house he goes back to Gaby's room and tugs his backpack off his shoulder tossing it onto the floor.

Walking into the kitchen he finds Gaby at the stove. Kyle is at the refrigerator grabbing a couple of long neck bottles of beers to pop open.

"Long day buddy? So, the old flat tire and cell phone ran out of battery excuse. Here, takes this beer and relax for a minute."

"Hell don't remind me… It's been a long day already." Tony laughs with his eyes open wide, then gulps half a lager down.

Meanwhile at the hospital, every patient who was being discharged that day had already left. No new patient was being helped or given a room. All prior patients sat in dark daunting rooms in silence, while technicians work on the power cut off twelve hours.

Alonza comes back from charging her cell phone, and changes into something more comfortable instead of the skirt she wore earlier. She carries a bag of burgers and fries in her hands.

Bill turns on his cell phone flashlight, so he isn't in the dark trying to dip a fry into the ketchup container.

Alonza hands Kyle his charged-up phone from home and they turn their lights on as well.

After eating in the musty hospital room, Bill gets up frustrated, deciding to speak to someone about this.

Only a few people in their rooms can be found. Every nurse and doctor have evacuated the floor. Bill enters back into the room with his phone light on.

"I can't find not one nurse or even a janitor on this floor. I can't believe this… the lights go out and they just pack up and leave everyone here. This pisses me off. Come on, walk with me and add your light with mine, so I can record this dark bacterial rising, boiling arid cemetery. Surly not a hospital." Bill vexes.

Bill and Alonza exit room number three-seventy-seven with their cell phone lights on. They walk down the empty hallway recording everything.

His camera is barely bright enough to see the wall colors.

Alonza opens a patient's door, signaling Bill to capture what's stuck inside.

A scared, feeble, elderly woman with white hair sits in her bed with the sheets pulled back off her legs.

"Are you my nurse?" She whimpers.

"No honey, my son is a few rooms down and we are looking for somebody to explain what is going on."

"Oh good. I need to be changed from out of these wet clothes. I had an accident. Do they think a woman my age can hold it all day and night… and I can't get out of this bed without help? And they haven't fed me all day."

"Wow, this is not good." Alonza signals at Bill to do something.

"I'll get you something to eat. What is your name and what would you like to eat?" Bill asks.

"Judy Baker. I'd like a bowl of chili-mac-noodles, cheese and crackers… oh and a larger cup of water, so I can make it another morning… and some pear pudding if you can find it. I haven't seen it in ages."

"The soup I can find, but I don't know about the pear pudding. I haven't heard of that one myself. Give us an hour and we'll be back with some food."

"Oh, thank you Lord." Little ol' Judy said.

"Let me help you into something else." Alonza said.

Bill holds the cell phone light up for Alonza to see what she's doing. She changes the urinated bed gown out for a new one, found inside the linen cabinet outside the room.

They leave the room finding the emergency staircase, carefully stepping up a flight of steps. The fourth floor is just as dark and empty as the third floor.

The conditions of this floor are the same as the one below. No medical professional or staff members at the stations desk where nurses would be at.

"I can't believe this hospital would lose its lights, then leave everyone hanging out here like this, you know?" Bill records his anger in the video as they walk through empty halls.

Back at the Hawthorne place, Tony finishes up the nice dinner Gaby had spent most of the day preparing. She meets his gaze, her top showing off her accentuated curves but still covering her unhatched chicken.

"Let's go out, rent a movie and snuggle in bed together." She licks her lips.

"Can we do this tomorrow night? This old mans like an anchor tonight." His eyes are heavy as he's speaking.

"You're far from old. Come on… let's go rent something out of the box?"

"Gaby, I'm gonna just pass out half way. Is that what you want?"

"Well so you pass out then… Arriba."

After renting a slow drama film, they come back to the house and get into Gaby's shower. Warm water runs down their soapy bodies, rinsing off the wildfire smog and Tony's nicotine scent. They stand face to face kissing.

Gaby then turns away holding her baby bump.

Tony gently grabs her neck, caressing her slippery mocha skin while moving her long brown hair off her shoulders, building up to a therapeutic massage down to her evenly rolling hills on the backside.

After drying off their flushed red bodies, they retire to the bedroom.

Gaby considers waking the heart of Tony up, but he isn't bothered. He falls out cold with his right hand on the rise of his baby girl.

Gaby sheds a few tears, insecure in this moment.

It's nearly 10 P.M. Kyle is halfway asleep in the dark silent room. His mother and Bill enter room number three-seventy-seven. Kyle startles.

"Just checking on you. We are going to bring this soup to a woman down the way from you and we'll be back afterwards."

"Mom this is creepy with the lights all out and everyone else is gone, don't you think?"

"Yes, I agree, but I won't leave you. Bill is here with us as well."

They exit and find Judy's room in the dark. Opening her door, she sits up happy to see someone came back for her. "Oh, thank Heavens."

"I hope this helps you. Judy, do you have any family in Los Angeles that check on you?" Bill asks.

Judy takes the large plastic bowl of broccoli and cheese soup catered from a local restaurant. She tears the plastic of the spoon and digs into it.

"No, my only living son is in Texas. He's a very busy man in his late 60's. I haven't been able to call him because the power is off. I don't have one of those small rectangles from space signal towers."

"You mean a cell phone?" Bill snickers.

"Judy do you have his phone number? Let's give him a call on one of ours." Alonza gives her hope.

At nearly 10:15 P.M. they wake up Mr. Baker, giving him the news of his mother being alone in a dark, twelve by twelve hospital room.

Mr. Baker perceives the message and books a redeye to Los Angeles. He cancels every meeting he has in the morning by emails on the way there.

"Judy, your son has the next flight out here. Try and rest up, after you eat and until your son gets here, one of us will continue to come and check on you." Alonza gives her a sincere, loving hug.

"Oh, thank you. Will you help me to the restroom before you go?" Judy takes a sip from the water she poured into her hospital jug.

Over the Hawthorne house, the sun beams penetrate a crisp blue coppery morning sky. Temperatures rise with the sun, one notch at a time.

Kyle takes a red, white and blue strawberry cake out of the refrigerator.

Gaby and Tony scare him as they enter the kitchen to make breakfast.

"Kyle, put that back. That's for later." She lectures, with fresh morning breath and messy hair.

"Where's the bagels at?" He pranks.

"Not in there." She throws out.

Tony stretches out a yawn and rubs on his stomach saying, "umm a warm toasty cream cheese bagel, egg, cheese, avocado and a sliced up red juicy tomater."

Benjamin enters the room laughing, "Where are you from… tomater? Hey Tony, did you bring my VR head gear?"

Tony turns and takes a sip of orange juice, uncertain how to respond. Facing the window, he looks deep into transparent pool water and the lie emerges.

"Crap! You caught me. I left without it. I laid it on the nightstand, so I wouldn't forget it and I surly did. I'm sorry buddy."

Benjamin loses interest in the thought of Tony's forgetfulness, and grows hungry.

"Gaby, are you cooking breakfast for everybody, I'm starved."

Tony holds guilt in his shoulders.

At the hospital, the power comes back on.

The television comes on and wakes everybody up in three-seventy-seven.

On television, a news reporter, Cynthia Alado is live at a horse ranch on Sunset Boulevard, asking if anyone has any information on who killed the young man tied to another tree, this time with virtual reality head gear over his eyes.

Kyle focuses in on the screen. His mother and Bill stir around in disbelief that the lights are just now coming back on. They step outside finding every nurse and staff are where they are supposed to be. It was as if the power never was out.

The first nurse they run into, "I see you finally got the power up and going."

"The hospital director had to make a few phone calls, but yes it's all cleared up. We will be into your room to check on your son soon." The female nurse tells them.

Bill looks over at Alonza thinking, Kyle is not his son.

They go back into Kyle's room finding his face disengaging from the nineteen-inch television screen wall mount.

"Mom, this is a second murder done up this way. The police believe there is a serial killer on the loose in our neighborhoods and I remember when that detective came by asking questions, he said another guy was found dead and tied at a tree. This has to be connected."

"You've lost enough blood and sleep over what's happened and what continues to happen here. Let's let the police handle it."

"Alonza, your son is onto something here. Two people are dead… against a tree. Tree being the root word here. People don't tie up to a tree, and hope for their last breath." Bill sparks concern.

"What do I know? I'm only the mother."

"I don't think you or your son can do anything but see how it plays out. Your accident was two Mondays ago. Today is July 4th Independence Day. Only the police can find the killer and let's hope soon. It's really gruesome what this killer is doing." Bill grimaces.

At the crime scene, Detective Calc Timmons examines the stiff body lying on the gurney, alone in the back of the ambulance.

Scoping out every inch of the body, he finds no signs of force, bruises or struggle as the victim was brought to this location, tied to a tree and killed.

The only visible reason was to have an open mind about something and literally to be as large as a brain can be exposed.

Calc Timmons assumes the target as reasoning while he loses his appetite and that could be the only reason a person would go with a tree tie killer.

Getting out of the ambulance, the detective finds Cynthia Alado and her camera crew waiting for him. Two EMT's get into the cabin of the ambulance and the ambulance driver rolls away.

"Detective, off record… can you tell us if you have the know abouts of who is doing this and why? People are beginning to panic. I fear for my life as well. What's setting the killer off?" Cynthia Alado asks standing half the size of the detective with her tiny hands pressing against her business attired hips.

The detective never speaks, only walks straight to his unmarked car.

The news reporter and crew follow his steps with the tension of being unwanted.

"Ms. Alado, I've concluded that there is no conclusion at this time. What I do know is the perpetrator is intimidating, possibly a male suspect, and targeting young teenagers and killing them with their own vehicles… so far males under age twenty-five. I'm not sure how this is connected yet, but if you're scared, I suggest taking a bus to where you need to go or stay home. Now if you'll excuse me, I got a killer to catch." The detective shuts the door and drives away.

2 P.M. at the Hawthorne house, everyone is dressed in red, white and blue. Everybody has on sunglasses and is about to leave and go to Marina Del Rey for the Fourth of July Cruise Celebration —summer fun.

Gaby has her trendy designer bag over her shoulder as she flips flops into the kitchen retrieving the festivity cake.

Kyle is about to turn off the living room television, where everybody else is gathered, and suddenly the Californian news flashes another Tree Tie Death.

This time, Benjamin catches the image shown of the victim, who's wearing the same brand and style head gear he has.

Benjamin's jawline drops.

Venom catches it and says, "Hey, that dead boy has the same goggles as you do Benji."

Tony and Gaby see the news report on television too.

Tony's eyes are locked on the television. His body starts to sweat and his heartbeat causes his legs to twitch.

He tries to balance his emotions, trying not to look suspicious in the murder he committed last night. He didn't expect to ever be watching this with his family in the same room as him.

He tries calming down but can't seem to match the right expression with the rest of the room. Tony's nervousness stinks.

Kyle turns off the television saying, "What kind of animal would do such a malicious crime? I hope they catch the sick bastard."

Chapter Thirty

Kyle locks up his front door. Everyone is outside including his listing agent, Waylon Warner.

"Hey buddy." Kyle appears shocked to see him with the sign in his hand, even though he's right on time.

Waylon is dressed in a silk sky blue silk suit with a flaming red, hot-dog in a bun tie. He's holding a black and yellow Hawthorne Realty sign.

"Lucky dog, I hope the following year you take me with you to this spectacular event I am missing out on." Waylon cracks out a little flirt.

"If you sell my house, you can afford your own sail cruise." Kyle laughs and closes the door. He moves swiftly to his drive vehicle and drives off.

The Hawthorne's back out of the driveway with Benjamin driving his blue Range Rover. Kyle, Gaby, and Tony ride in the backseat.

Rueben and Darcy Gethin pull out in their White G-63, following the leaders and of course their son, who is in Benjamin's front seat.

Viper is dressed in an Independence Day tank top and white cut-off denim jean shorts.

Waylon Warner stakes the Hawthorne Realty sign in the front yard.

He then goes into Kyle Hawthorne's home and finds a secure place to put down his laptop bag. Out of his bag, he takes a very wide-angle camera to capture images for the Multiple Listing Service. He then dances outside to get the tennis courts, pool and pool house.

Waylon had only been to Kyle's house one other time, for a realty party when Angela was alive. He remembers himself and about fifteen other agents with their significant others standing around the pool drinking wine.

He continues on, taking photos of the home, to add on the market today.

Meanwhile, at Marina Del Rey, everybody gets out of their vehicles and walk over to bay.

Jeff and Molly Gandy are standing next to the cruise liner at the pier dock that's scheduled to load up at 3 P.M.

Holding her belly, Gaby glances over to the elegant three decker and cabin yacht in front of her.

A gentle breeze, under a warm sun glow, blows onto sand pebbles and water currents. Gaby reaches for Tony's attention and they kiss.

Kyle and everyone stand by, while waiting to get a wrist band at entry.

A low-key bass composition beats across the airways of the yacht, bringing in a full house, nearly seventy-five participants including ten crew members, the captain and his wife.

Everyone holds a spot on the deck, eventually they will fill up all three levels. Food caterers set up hot items under heated lamps. The D.J. is tending his table releasing songs from the 80's, 90's and todays mix.

Guests on the ship range from elite celebrities such as actors and basketball players from LA Lakers, children between the age of fourteen and eighteen, Donna and Kimberly from Hawthorne realty and few other agents. Most everybody has had some sort of connection with the captain a time or two.

This cruise was sailing off to Malibu, docking for a few hours before the sun drops, and journeying back to Marina Del Rey. Everybody will be able to catch the firework shows across the Los Angles night sky.

On the ship a group of women hold their glasses of the finest red, white and Zen. A few men gathered around with green long necks. Some had the best fruit infused sangria dipped fresh from the bowl.

Benjamin and the twins find a few new friends on the ship's upper level. All of them on their phones, sitting on chaise loungers, and sipping fruit punch.

Meanwhile inside of Calc Timmons office, he sits at his desk with photos and questions of who's preying on and killing victims, while destroying trees.

Officer Snowlines brings a couple close up images of the truck and license plate from the night of first accident and Kyle Kairos's hit and run suspect.

The officer lays them flat across his desk. "You're not going to like what you requested on the license plates."

Detective Timmons has a look at both. "These are blotchy and blurry. Damn the drizzle. Snowlines, did you roll every second of film to find who that truck belongs to?"

"I did Timmons, that's all I could get. You have the best image in your hands." The officer exits the room and goes back to his office.

The detective rises out of his seat to shut the door, then walks back to his desk, hunching over it, and furrowing his face over the new images.

Meanwhile, on the celebration cruise, the contrast between day and night approaches. The one hundred and fifty feet yacht respectfully pulls into the pier and anchor down next to luxury condos at the Malibu Pier docks.

Everybody on the ship begins to gather, anxious to unload off the ship in Malibu.

Kyle has met a lady friend he admires. Together they follow, Jeff and Molly, Tony and Gaby, Rueben and Darcy and all their children.

On the warm sands Benjamin, Venom, and Viper walk over to a sand volleyball game that's looking to build up a team to play against.

After two hours of sailing on a large ship, walking felt so good against their bare feet on the warm sand.

The adults walk over to a restaurant and have a few more drinks, not far from the kids. They grab some appetizers and talk loudly amongst the crowds and grab a handbasket of memorable times.

Benjamin and the twins finally gather up a few people to play the winner of the last game. Some of the players aren't even one's from last game.

After a few hours, the ship's captain blows the horn that sounds as humble as a small wave instead of the massive ones.

People start heading back to the ship. It's 8 P.M. Gathered and looking like lobsters as they high-flip-tail back, sun crisped and all from a gorgeous day outside.

The ship starts to sway as the engines rumble and people trample across it and all the upper decks. They back out of harbor gracefully.

After six hours of food, fun, and sun everyone is very relaxed on chairs with heavy eyes, waiting for the fireworks to be set off.

The first one is launched. You couldn't hear the sizzling sounds as it rose up in the air, but amber lights became a flare and a bang, followed by a few more right behind that one.

Everybody has their eyes on the effects and wait for more fireworks to go off.

Fourth of July Celebration songs are playing at disc jockey's plays table.

A channel of rolling waves carry the yacht across the ocean and a rampart sky of fireworks brighten up the night.

A blazing ball of glory goes up and ricochets off the night, falling on the stars, another fiery ball of flames go up, and then another, ringing a bell of freedom every time a new ball explodes.

If anyone on the one hundred- and fifty-foot yacht was tired, they are not now. It sounds like grenades as The Star Spangle Banner plays on the ship.

The ocean carried them back to Marina Del Rey swiftly, but in the most calming exciting way.

Tony and Gaby sit together in the lounger on the lower deck watching a spectacular show in a dark sky.

In the upper deck, Benjamin is found holding hands with Venom. It's their second Independence Day celebration together.

The party comes to an end and everyone departs the cruise ship to go home.

They pull right into Kyle's home. Tony's in the back seat with Gaby and Kyle. They get out of the Range Rover.

Tony stares over his Orange Albert Dodge knowing it is time for a trade in. He begins to vision the police following him on the highway and can't seem to escape this feeling he has.

"Tony, come on sleepy head. The car is off now. Are you hearing me? Wow, your eyes are heavy and drunk looking." Gaby laughs.

He casts out a blank stare. Crawling out of the door he tries to hide his guilt. He stumbles up to the door with hunger pains or alcohol burning a hole in his stomach, but really, he is thirsting for his next victim, as he thinks it's time again.

The next morning, Kyle receives a text notification.

"Be expecting another text soon. I'm working an offer." Waylon Warner texted.

Chapter
THIRTY-ONE

A team of three sit at a table, discussing the transferring of the Deed of Trust for Kyle Hawthorne's property in Hancock Park.

Waylon hands Kyle a sheet off the brief stack he's already signed. He knows his worth.

Kyle places a sorrowful hand over the sale of his five-million-dollar estate. He starts to sign the first form and goes into a flashback of his wife and him raising their children in that house.

Then he flashes into another memory as he signs the next form from the contract. He remembers the time he and Angela were out near the tennis court at the bottom of his property, one warm night in October; chasing fireflies like they were young kids.

They had drunk a bottle of wine on their balcony a few years back and saw the lights of the insect's blink. It was Angela's dare for Kyle to take the clear glass wine bottle and capture as many possible.

Well he did and when she saw him running in circles having so much fun, she decided to take an empty glass jar on the table and run after him, to be the first to get one in jar and make it shine. He kept slipping on the dew of the lush green grass.

She was twenty-seven, he was just a few years older. Falling for her in the rain September 11th was fate.

This time she fell to the grass drunk and laughing, as she had captured her first, except it wasn't a firefly. It was a dragonfly. A baby dragonfly.

Angela placed her hand over the top of the jar, so it couldn't escape. She watched it for a moment.

Kyle saw how lovely and innocent she looked, and he found it to be a moment in time worth stealing her breath away. He crawls on top of her. She lifts the jar allowing the insect to be set free as they kiss.

He admires her more than some stinking dragonfly, and it sure didn't matter if it had some special power to light up like the fireflies they were originally after. Everything he ever hoped for was already with him and in his arms.

She already sparkled to him and somehow, he knew it was forever.

Kyle hated signing off on the sale of the house they had purchased together, but life fell apart when she died and then a couple of years later, Camden too.

Kyle knew he had to walk away so that God could start a new thing in him.

Money from real estate, selling to the highest class of celebrities or rockstars, wasn't truly what brought him joy.

Parties, drugs or hanging out with his best buddies wasn't it.

Having a successful real estate brokerage wasn't it either.

Everything he had ever worked for, and built with his own hands, wasn't it?

Even building a life with his own family, which he loved the most wasn't it, as it was all crumbling against his will. He realized he was not in charge of the life he thought he had created.

All he has left is Benjamin. In that moment of signing the closing papers, he knew everything under the sun was temporary, and that love is all that matters while he's on this Earth.

He remembers hearing the passage in the Holy Bible, God so loved the world he gave his only begotten son Jesus, and if God could do that, then he could let everything he loved go and find Jesus.

Kyle never saw any of this coming. He knows that he has to call on Jesus so he can be saved. In fact, signing his life off his house, pulled at him more to find this Jesus in this book of Angela's.

Hopefully, it would be the miracle needed to help this world stop texting and driving.

Meanwhile, about midway to Los Angeles from San Diego, Tony has a trailer hitched up to load Gabriella's belonging in her SUV. The plan is to ride back together, so they have more places to store her belongings.

Tony feels the need to exit off at Oceanside, which is a little ways outside of San Diego, alongside of I-5.

Off the Interstate, he turns into a casino with high hopes of walking out richer than he already is with his Pawn Shop money.

A blue eighteen-wheeler with the number ten, in big bold letters, on the side of the cabin door, aims right at him. The fifty-thousand-pound truck is destined to crush him if Tony doesn't pull a hard right, almost taking out a row of parked cars.

Instead of blaring his horn, Tony watches him in his rear-view mirror and replays what his saw, as the scrawny male driver in the truck almost sacked him. He caught him on his cell phone and the driver never noticed Tony.

Tony conjures up an evil idea instead of gambling that very second. His appetite to viciously murder a man in charge of these big wheels was enormous. Angela was murdered by an eighteen-wheeler and this would be serving justice in Tony's eyes.

Tony watches the eighteen-wheeler exit the casino from his rearview mirror. He makes a turnaround right then and there, creeping up on that driver, texting.

In the front seat of his truck, Tony finds the brand new, sealed in the box head gear he bought to repay Benjamin's.

While driving and following the eighteen-wheeler, Tony unwraps the head gear from the box, turning on the power.

Along I-5, the eighteen-wheeler is in route to Los Angeles it appears.

Tony's blood pressure raises profusely, examining the swerving of the large vehicle going side to side. It rides right along the lines in the middle lane, causing vehicles to swerve around the large truck.

After riding behind this eighteen-wheeler for fifteen minutes, Tony finds this man guilty twice, crossing lanes and totally not paying attention.

Twice was more than enough, considering each time he done it, he envisioned the eighteen wheel that killed his sister two years ago.

The truck driver exits the San Diego Freeway. The truck swerves off the road more than it should, almost crashing. The driver pulls the eighteen-wheeler back to the middle lane.

This is obviously another driver with a cell phone in his hand, who needs a lesson.

The truck driver pulls into a fuel station to fill up. Tony follows him inside.

The driver of the eighteen-wheeler jumps out with his cell phone in his hand, and of course his eyes are glued to the phone, as he laughs while walking like he has log in between his legs.

A male truck driver of Middle Eastern descent. Maybe 5'7 in height. Dark skin tone. Small body frame. Baggy jeans and blue t-shirt the guy wears. The driver comes back to the eighteen-wheeler.

Full of pride, he walks outside after letting out two gallons of water in the men's receptacles.

Rounding the corner of the truck to his door, he finds Tony there waiting with head goggles in hand.

Concerned, the driver of the eighteen-wheeler says, "What's up?"

"Hey, I was hoping you could help me out. I need some money for gas. I forgot my wallet back home and all I got is this head gear that makes a perfect hook up for a cell phone… was wondering if you'd give me ten bucks for them and help a brother out?"

"Ten dollars. Do they work?" The truck driver asks.

"Yeah they work. Now that I think about it, these are worth more than ten bucks. Give me twenty after you see it for yourself." Tony stands about seven inches over him and laughs.

"What you want me to try them on out here?"

"No silly. Try them in your truck… Say, I've never been inside a big truck like this. Mind if I get in with you?"

"Hop inside." The truck driver laughs.

It was the first time Tony had ever been in a big rig. It was spotless inside, like it had just come out of the carwash or something.

Tony quickly makes friends with the guy, gaining his trust, but never catching his name.

"Do you mind if I check out the back of your cabin?" Tony hops out of the hydraulic chair and walks a few feet to the bed.

"Sweet, twin bunks. This thing even has a refrigerator and a microwave. Does it have a TV somewhere, and I'm missing it?"

"No, but it's got plenty of plugs to charge my iPad and Phone, so I can watch movies on them."

"Let's take it for a drive. Maybe this is something I could do in a few years. What do you say?"

"First, how does this head gear work?"

"Yeah sure man. Turn your Bluetooth on and pair them up. Should be that simple."

The truck driver sticks them on his head watching some video of how to fix a starter on a 2004 Maxima.

Tony scowls him over, with disgust in his eyes, while the young man focuses on the mechanic work shop video.

"Yeah I'll give you ten for these." The truck driver said.

"I'm sorry, did I say ten? I meant twenty. My truck will eat the gas faster than you finish a video.

The truck driver looks at Tony, with alarms rattling inside him, as he considers the twenty dollars being still good.

"Okay twenty is fine. I'll play sex videos at night, hand free, right where you're sitting, on my new TV." The driver boastfully replies.

"So how many gears does this bad boy have?" Tony inquires.

"It has ten in the gear shaft, one in the reverse. Do you know how to use an air brake and standard clutch?"

Tony nods no.

The truck driver gives him a short lesson then allows him to drive a short way to a campsite at San Clemente. Tony pulls to a covered camp ground.

"Can you show me how to back up on that reverse gear shaft, then we can switch positions and you can take me back to my truck?"

The truck driver walks him through the steps. Tony backs up about fifty feet from the covered campground. He opens the door to get out and switch over.

The driver stops. "What are you doing? We can switch over right here."

"I hope you don't mind too much, I gotta find a tree and take leak."

He laughs, "Nah man, drain the lizard. I'll be right here checking out social media with my new toy."

Tony opens the door, vaulting out of the truck, with sure confidence of finding a tree. He walks off in the distance and tries to hide peeing.

He takes his sweet time, letting all fat drippings from last night fall on the trunk of a western sycamore.

On the way back, Tony finds a twenty-foot, rusty jumper cable missing a positive battery cable, somebody has left behind in the grass like a snake. He carries it back with him to the eighteen-wheeler. The engine still running.

Tony throws the cord down and pulls out a six-inch switchblade.

The truck driver waits for Tony to arrive in the captain seat with head gear on, watching Arabic music videos.

Tony opens the driver's door.

The driver never sees or hears anything, other than the loud music from the video.

Tony glares at him with built up anger. As he remembers his sister's angelic face and a truck driver killing her, he takes the switchblade, jabbing it directly into his left quadricep.

The driver comes out of his seat moaning out curse words and tries to take the head gear off.

Tony presses on the knife and says, "Don't move or I'll take the knife out and shove it down your throat.

"Alright. What the hell man? What gives you this right?" The driver moans letting out painful gasps.

"Now we are going to take a little walk. You are going to do as I ask. You are going to keep the goggles on your eyes, and listen to what I have to say, Comprehendo?" Tony speaks into his ear.

The driver blindly gets out of the truck, limping the whole way out of it.

Tony picks up the jumper cables and leads the man to the covered campsite.

They walk fifty feet with the guy limping the whole way over in tears, with the head gear on.

At the covered port, Tony wraps the man who stands with his back against the left beam post that's concreted to the ground.

The driver of the eighteen-wheeler stands up not moving his injured leg. His arms are behind him. The long battery cable is securely wrapped around him. He fears talking to Tony. An Arabic music video still plays across his face.

Tony rips the goggles off him.

The man tries kicking him, but is off balance with the pain in his leg.

"What do you want from me? I gave you the money."

"Yeah you did, but I didn't like how you spoke to me on you bunk bed. Sex videos… where I sit at. I don't think so buddy."

"Oh, come on man. It was a joke."

"Yeah… How about at the casino, you know when you almost hit me, nearly running me into a row of cars there?"

"What? Casino… I didn't hit anyone at the casino."

"Yeah that's right. I had to pull a sharp right. But you'd never knew that because your cell phone was right at your eyes. In fact, when I followed you to the fuel station, you crossed the San Diego Freeway lanes twice scaring the small cars out of your high and mighty machinery."

"Oh, you were following me? That's against the law."

"So, its texting and driving, and distracted driving. You want me to call the cops buddy?"

"No… No, don't call."

"So, here's what we are going to do about this. You're going to put this head gear back on your grimy face and watch a short video about texting and driving and what happens when you do this on the road while you are driving. Then you will be free to go… deal?"

The man frets but nods his head in agreeance.

Tony finds the right video, then turns the volume up and sticks them back on his face.

The driver quickly takes mental notes of the amount of driver's that text and drive, rarely getting caught unless they kill somebody and or themselves.

As Tony walks back to the truck he remembers how to operate it. The engine is still running.

On an empty campsite, Tony is free to drive as fast as he needs, seeking his revenge.

Tony releases the brake and pounds on the accelerator. It reaches twenty miles per hour. He jumps out of the driver seat, flying to the ground. He watches the truck take out the cover port, stopping the truck in its tracks.

He walks over to find out the fate of the man. The truck crushed him. The VR head gear is surprisingly still intact. He leaves them on him as more evidence, should someone find him and solve the case for drivers who text and drive.

Tony feels no remorse for running a semi-truck through every bone of the man. Speed demons, who are really just demons who want to kill others on the road, have taken over with a deadly force and a sense of entitlement.

The less destructive demons on the road, the less Tony will have to worry about his future wife and unborn child getting killed like his sister and nephew did.

Tony leaves the campsite. He finds a civilized point of interest five miles away, and requests an Uber to come get him and take him back to his truck.

The Uber driver lets him out at his truck.

Tony gives him a hefty tip.

He smokes a cigarette partially before getting into his truck and driving to Los Angeles.

Tony arrives to Kyle Hawthorne's house where two moving trucks are parked out front. He finds a place to park down the street.

Tony gets out of the truck and walks over to the front porch finding

Benjamin and Venom hugging.

"You two should really be doing all that upstairs or in privacy."

"Uncle Tony, if you and Gaby can kiss in my backyard with swim suits on in front of me, then surely I can hug on my guy."

Tony walks by, extinguishing his cigarette at the bottom step. He goes inside, and is immediately in the way of two men carrying a sofa to the front door.

He jumps out of their way, and walks to the back of the house, finding Gaby in her closet folding clothes and putting them into a large storage bag.

By 7 P.M and at the end of rush hour, Tony and Gaby have everything packed and ready to leave. Kyle hires a set of maids to do a full-service cleaning of the house to make it ready for the new owners.

San Diego bound, the Hawthorne's and Relako's go.

Chapter
THIRTY-TWO

August 1, 2018

Mid-morning at the Los Angeles Police Department, Detective Calc Timmons reviews the facts of what he has on the Tree Tie Killer. The series of three tragic horror shows can now be classified a serial man hunt.

What the detective has so far is virtual reality head-gear, date, time, place, victims' decent, age, gender, and the types of vehicle involved.

On a large dry erase board, the detective draws a box graph with these facts for all three killings.

After taking a step back to see it clearly, he sits down in his chair to ponder it a while. He also has the gruesome crime scene photos on his desk in heavy thought of what the motivation could be for killing theses victims, tied to a tree with the same style of head gear each time and with their own vehicles.

What point was the killer trying to make?

It doesn't appear the killer targets one specific race, although it seems the victims, he or she goes for are all males under the age of forty.

Calc Timmons puzzles to put a modus operandi together. He notices the location range is from Los Angeles to forty-five minutes North of San Diego.

The date he observes even more closely.

First killing, June 18, 2018 is on a Monday.

Second killing, two weeks later, July 3, 2018, Tuesday.

Third killing, two weeks after that. July 18, 2018, Wednesday.

The trend appears to be every two weeks, and if the detective calculates right, the killer could strike tomorrow, Thursday, August 2, 2018.

'But where?' He puzzles.

His pulse rises with an urgent drive to find the killer before a new body with head gear is found tied to a tree somewhere.

An image of the head gear comes to his mind. All three victims were found with the same brand and style on their faces. He ponders what they could have been watching before they died.

The detective goes to the evidence lab and pulls out the head gear to see if it's even possible to check out what they were all watching.

Ten days pass by since Kyle and Benjamin Hawthorne moved into their new home in La Jolla, San Diego.

Kyle spends the morning unpacking what few boxes he has left. This new house is much smaller than his eight bedrooms with tennis court cottage garden in Hancock Park.

Selecting this home wasn't hard to do. It's right on the ocean front and the tennis courts are across the street —eight courts.

The walls are barren of decorations. Bachelor pad is an accurate description of how it looks right now with two men and a dog living there.

Kyle takes a break from unpacking, and starts to register Benjamin into his junior year into La Jolla High School, which resumes, August 27, 2018.

Meanwhile, at a seven-month baby check-up appointment, Gaby lays on her back, preparing for a sonogram. It's her first visit with the new OBGYN since she's moved to San Diego.

Angelina Cambrielle Relako is set to be born on November 11, 2018.

This is Tony's very first doctor's visit with Gaby. He stands by his fiancées side, holding her hand while the sonogram technician rubs cold jelly on Gaby's baby bump, raised higher than her elevated knee caps.

A few four-dimensional imagines are captured of baby Angelina Cambrielle. Tony and Gaby are in aww over her and ready for her to come out of the womb.

"Look Tony. She has your nose."

Tony snickers, "She doesn't have my nose. She has big birds' nose. It's too long to be mine."

Gaby pays no attention to his suggestion, as she glows, in love, from her baby's beautiful face.

Meanwhile at the new Hawthorne home, Benjamin wakes up late in the morning to a million-texts vibrating on his night stand. He grabs his cell phone still trying to open up his eyes.

A long haul of texts notifications, all from Venom. He opens the top one and scrolls down, reading each and every one.

Are you awake? ☺
(Text one)

I miss you. ☹
(Text two)

I can't look out my window and see you anymore ☹
(Text three)

The new owners have a girl. I'm guessing twelve.
(Text four)

All she does is sit at the window edge like a cat.
(Text five)

Wake up pretty boy ☺
(Text six)

You're still sleeping, aren't you? ☹
(Text seven)

Benji?
(Text eight)

I want you over here.
(Text nine)

Now
(Text ten)

Like now...now
(Text eleven)

Oh yeah, guess what happens in 10 days?

(Text twelve)

My 16th is coming up.
Do you want to drive back here...?
Spend a week together before junior year?
(Text thirteen)

These texts come in so fast. He can't stop himself from smiling at how much he feels loved and missed from Venom.

Ten days apart. Boy do they miss each other.

—Benjamin texts back.
Give me a few minutes. I need to pee and brush my teeth. I just woke up

He takes his phone into the bathroom and scrolls through social media in one hand as he stands to urinate in the other.

Mid-day Wednesday. It's only been a little over a week since Kyle claimed new ownership on their home in La Jolla.

Kyle looks out his house window. It appears to be another gorgeous summer day. He grabs his keys to take a mini drive around his new suburb, needing a break from unpacking.

He calls out across the house, "Benji, I'll be back in an hour or so. I'm going out for a drive."

"Okay dad. Hey dad, can we go shopping later?" Benjamin yells back while texting Venom.

What more do we need son?" "We need groceries."

"Oh yes, when I get back, we'll go out to eat, then we can go do that."

Kyle locks up the door to his home. He hops in his Mercedes, putting back the top, as the sun is too nice to waste.

On the two-lane streets in La Jolla, he drives the posted speed limits of twenty-five and thirty, when he can. Other times, he is stuck behind a line of cars while they are trying to turn. Palm trees everywhere, like in Los Angeles.

Kyle drives into the business district with upscale bars and restaurants.

Later, he drives by three different beaches. He stops at one with seals camping out everywhere. As he carries his shoes, walking along the warm sands on the shoreline, he overhears how it used to be a kid's cove.

In a daydream, Kyle see his wife's beautiful face and begins to imagine what a new life would have been like for them together in La Jolla. He snaps back to the here and now and immerses himself into the glorious sights and sounds of splashing on the beach, while finding seashells all around.

Angela really loved nature and not just modeling and music. She was great at everything. She even had a green thumb with plants. Writing was her true calling though. Most people don't purse their dreams, too afraid of failing or not feeling adequate enough to achieve them, instead choosing to live with regret at the end of their lives.

People know it and fear it when the only thing you should fear is God. If you faint not, then the harvest is the size of heavens windows opened and pouring into your mouth, overflows for generations to come when you believe in Jesus.

Kyle gets back inside his car driving home and starving. He knows Benjamin must be hungry too.

At Tony and Gaby's house, they sit at his old fashioned 1975 refurbished wooden table. Tony took the whole day off to spend time with his fiancée.

Together they work out a thousand-piece Kinkade puzzle for the first time.

Tony has a serious look in his eyes trying to find the right piece to put into the right place.

Gaby catches him in all his cuteness. She rises out of the old wooden kitchen chair and kisses her man.

"I'm going to cook us something to eat. Which do you want… shrimp tacos or hamburgers?" She runs her hands down his back after kissing him.

Tony takes in her sweet fruity breath replying, "Burgers tonight sound great."

He continues to build the puzzle while she cooks their supper.

"We need to start on Angelina Cambrille's room before I'm too pregnant to help you or if she decides to arrive before November 11th."

"I will give you my credit card. Go and buy all the furniture and clothes you need for her. Okay?" He continues building the puzzle.

Gaby flips the hamburger patties on the stove top feeling disappointed that she would go alone to get everything ready for their baby. She fakes a smile, not to kick the gift horse in the mouth, while she continues to prepare their meal.

At the lab, Calc Timmons looks over all three virtual reality head gear devices. Never operating one before, he tries figure out how to turn it on.

Milton, at the lab walks by Detective Timmons and stops.

"Have you ever worked one of these silly things? I'm looking for the power button to see what the victims were watching before becoming taco meat on trees." Timmons says.

"You would have to get the phone records to see what it was they were watching." Milton eats sweet potato chips from a bag.

"Can you get me all three of these guys' phone records then? We need to see what it was and quickly. I have a strong suspicion he could rise up again tomorrow."

"Yeah sure, no problem boss man." Milton takes down the name of the victims while he continuing to eat chips. He walks over to his desk, to get the records of what they were all watching before their deaths.

After some time on his computers looking at times and dates of these cell phone records, he finds the first one linked to texting and driving.

"Boss, we got something here. Looks like this one is related to texting and driving. A ten-minute educational video of some sort."

Detective Calc Timmons instantly remembers Angela Hawthorne's texting and driving book. A new image of visiting Kyle Hawthorne rings a bell and possibly even Kyle Kairos from the hospital, who was also involved in this connection.

The detective thanks the lab department, then leaves in a new-found confidence, and one more piece of the puzzle found, to catch a serial killer.

Chapter
THIRTY-THIRTY

August 1, 2018 6 P.M.

Detective Calc Timmons sits on his sofa with the possible motive in mind. The tree tie killer is after anyone he, she, or possibly an accomplice can find texting and driving.

On the wall, a large flat screen airs the nightly news.

Detective is shirtless, showing his dark muscly chest and arms, sitting on the sofa with his legs sprawled open in black cargo pants. He holds a red disposable cup with the shells of sunflower seeds, he has been spitting out the last hour.

In a daze, trying to imagine the killer's face who's scoping random people out for justice or some kind of vindication.

He shells a half a cup of seeds with his mouth, before rising off the sofa, getting his boots on, grabbing his keys off the bar, and getting into his unmarked car.

The sun sits patiently, waiting to settle in for the night. In Hancock Park, the detective pulls up to the last place he spoke to Kyle Hawthorne.

Knocking on the front door a very attractive woman opens it.

He looks her up and down, believing Kyle had finally got it back together and found himself a diamond.

"Good evening miss. I'm with L.A.P.D. I need to have a word with Kyle Hawthorne."

"I'm sorry who are you after?" The mystery woman questions.

"Kyle Hawthorne."

"Oh, the famous guy that sold us this house. No, you are about ten days too late. He moved to San Diego last month. We are the new owners." She responds as her husband swoops in like an eagle with concerns written on his face.

"Is everything okay dear?"

She backs up from the door giving her husband the front stand.

"Yes darling. We just have a detective here looking for Kyle Hawthorne, the previous owner."

"Is everything good officer?"

"Everything's great. Just stopping by to see a good friend, but it looks like I didn't catch the memo on Facebook that he was moving... You folks have a good night." Detective Calc Timmons gives out a fake chuckle.

The couple smiles as they shut the door, locking it up.

The detective gets back in his car and goes to his office, heavy thoughts on his mind.

At the station, he looks over everything again, this time with Kyle Hawthorne as the lead suspect of murdering three people.

He notices the first is thirty minutes from Kyle's old house. The second is practically on top of his house looking at the map. The last one is closer to San Diego than Los Angeles.

Detective Timmons knows he must act fast before another person texting and driving dies for their addiction.

He puts everything in a folder, wrapping it up and taking it home with him.

At home he packs a bag for two days. By 9 P.M. he is on the way to San Diego.

On the way there, he radios the police department to find out Kyle Hawthorne's address in San Diego.

Driving on a Wednesday night, traffic is steady on the San Diego Freeway. Several times on the way there, he puts himself in the killer's shoes.

And several times, he came close to flashing his lights on drivers who were obviously texting and driving. He could understand the frustrations of wanting to kill someone for dangerously putting everyone around in danger.

It would take a lot more to have snapped and carry out a vendetta like these victims' deaths. Let's say like someone who lost their wife and son to texting and driving within two years' time.

In a hotel in San Diego, the detective sets up camp for the night.

He looks over photos and pin points of where the killer had struck. Now that Calc Timmons is in La Jolla, he decides to drive over and scope out Kyle Hawthorne's house.

He pulls out his 9mm, removing the magazine and checking the chamber. He snaps it back into the frame, ready for action.

Detective Timmons drives by Kyle's house. The black Mercedes and a blue Range Rover is visible in the drive way. The front porch light is lit and gives it a soothing amber glow.

He drives back to the hotel with a new reference point established.

Inside the hotel room, Calc Timmons empties out his bladder, then strips down to his boxers, and gets some rest for the night.

As a cricket chirps outside, the seconds fly by. Tossing and turning, Calc Timmons wakes up looking at his cell phone. The alarm hasn't even gone off but its 4:44 A.M.

He wakes up to the image of a beautiful woman with a model face, sitting in front of a blue hued background. Calc sits up in the bed, thinking about what she was trembling out her mouth while he was dreaming.

Detective Timmons sits up thinking about who this mystery woman is and tries to putting together what she was saying.

"Wait for Tony." The detective believes she was trying to say.

As Detective Calc Timmons scrolls his emails, he questions who this beautiful mystery woman is and who's Tony? He tries to put a face to every Tony he's ever come across, it's like trying to find a needle in a haystack.

The alarm set for 5 A.M. buzzes.

He still has no clue what the dream is all about.

Rising out of bed he showers and shaves.

He gets in few repetitions of crunches and push-ups, needing to keep his body in tip top shape. He grabs ahold of the bathroom door frame, and does a couple pull-ups before jumping down and leaving out the hotel for the day.

Pulling up to Kyle Hawthorne's house, the detective gets out of his unmarked squad car. He holds onto his gun, in the holster, for confidence while walking to the front door. The Mercedes and Range Rover from last night are both sill in the driveway.

He knocks on the door and waits for someone to answer.

Kyle opens it, dressed in pajamas with a mug of coffee in hand.

"Detective Timmons. What in the world are you doing here?"

"Kyle, I was in the neighborhood. Can I come inside and talk with you?"

"Yeah, come in." Kyle looks puzzled.

"I like your big house back in L.A. How long have you been in San Diego?"

"My son and I moved here last month. It was just too painful back there."

"Is your son driving now? Is that his vehicle in the driveway?"

"Yeah, he turned sixteen this year and wanted a Blue Range Rover, like his mom had.

"What about your real estate business?" Detective Timmons quizzes.

"I have a manager and a couple assistants helping me out while I'm over here in some like… time out trying to finish and edit, Online Now."

"The Blue Book?" The detective wonders.

"It's a manuscript my partner and I are working on, we're making a movie for all the ones who are dead each year from texting and driving." Kyle takes a sip of coffee.

"Yes, I remember the blue folder of notes we found now. It looks like somebody has beat you to real live action show, and as you have been moved to write this. You wouldn't know anything about that, would you?"

"Yeah, when we were moving down here, I caught something on the nightly news about somebody had been tied to a tree and killed. Is that what murder you're talking about?"

"Yes, and there have been two more just like it. On calendar it's happened since June 18, 2018 and every two weeks plus one day after. I'm in charge of these murders and it got me thinking about how Angela and your son was killed by texting and driving. These murders are getting closer to San Diego. I noticed you recently moved here. So here I am to ask… What do you know?" The Detective stares him in the eyes.

"So, you are here because you think I am involved with whatever murders these are? No! I don't know anything about what's going on here." Kyle Hawthorne frets.

"Nothing at all?" Detective Timmons replies.

"No!" Kyle exclaims.

Detective Timmons holds a straight face, looking Kyle in the eyes, trying to find any hint of dishonesty. He takes a sigh of relief.

"All three murder victims had virtual reality head gear on their faces. All were watching the same ten-minute film on You Tube about how texting and driving kills." The detective takes a sip of water.

Kyle finishes his cup of coffee.

"What else is known about this killer?" Kyle inquires.

"I don't know, but my guess is that it could happen again today. I did some calculations on the time and days these grisly murders took place. First one on Monday. Second one on Tuesday. Third one on Wednesday and today is Thursday." The detective articulates.

"So how about next Thursday? Why this Thursday?" Kyle poses.

"Since June eighteenth, every two weeks plus one day would be the pattern of how this serial killer moves. It's like his One Day just shows up, for the same justification of texting and driving."

"What can I do to help, Detective?"

"Keep your eyes open when you drive anywhere. His target is anyone who's texting and driving. Look for any suspicious behavior."

"How do you know if he or she will strike today and even in San Diego?" The doorbell rings.

"Don't discuss this with anyone. I mean anyone. I better get going. Take my card and call me right away if you see or hear anything odd."

Kyle nods his head. Together they walk to the front door. Gaby stands with cleaning supplies in her arms waiting to come inside the house.

Detective Timmons walks out, giving her a smile. She gives him a lusty look and goes into Kyle's house.

Tony stands at the tailgate of his truck smoking a cigarette.

The detective walks as smooth as any human man would if they were protecting and serving this great nation.

Right away, he notices the burnt orange truck outside. It looks like it could be the truck from the first crime scene with Kyle Kairos.

The closer he gets to the truck, the more he's able to investigate through the windows, while he looks at both the man smoking and inside the truck while walking.

He shifts his gaze almost every step closer. Detective Timmons catches a split-second image of something very incriminating on the dashboard of the older model burnt orange truck.

"How's it going fella?" Calc Timmons asks.

Tony releases a puff of smoke.

"It's another nice day out here in La Jolla."

"The sun is blessing us as it usually does here. I might try to get out and play in some of it today while I'm still young… You have a great day man."

Detective Calc Timmons gets into his unmarked car and drives away with heavy suspicion about this tall and quiet character smoking a cigarette, like he's guilty of something.

Tony thinks nothing about the man leaving. Gaby comes outside to get the mop and bucket to clean the floors of Kyle Hawthorne's new house.

Carrying everything inside, while seven months pregnant, Tony never offers to help her. He continues to finish his medication before he enters his newly smoke free truck.

Tony is in route to the pawn shop to open it for business.

Detective Calc Timmons follows behind him unnoticed. When Tony turns in the pawn shop center, the detective keeps rolling by with his eyes hooked in the review mirror taking note of where he parks.

Tony gets out and goes to open his shop.

A half hour passes by. Tony never comes back out. The Dodge Ram sits with the engine cooling off.

The detective drives by, getting his license plate digits. He finds this mystery guy to be Anthony Relako, a resident of San Diego.

CHAPTER
THIRTY-FOUR

A long four hours pass by sitting in one position in the front seat of an unmarked police —Charger. The windows are down in the front.

The guy who went into the pawn shop four hours ago still hasn't come out. Bored out of his mind, the detective receives an image in his thoughts of where he could have seen the man in the pawn shop from.

Detective Calc Timmons scrolls through his phone, searching for Kyle Hawthorne's number, saved a few years back.

He stirs up some faith dialing Kyle up, to get some answers.

"Calc Timmons here. Is this you buddy?"

On the other end of the phone line, Kyle is driving Gaby across San Diego to her home after cleaning his house.

"Hey Calc, can you give me like ten minutes? I've got someone in the car with me. I'll call you right back."

"That's fine. It's urgent, so get back in touch ASAP please."

"Give me like ten."

The detective continues to watch the burnt orange truck and front door of the pawn shop. He puts an action flick on his phone, listening to the background noise that's barely audible, while awaiting movement.

The cell phone rings, interrupting the movie. He answers it.

"This is Timmons."

"Kyle here… calling you back."

"Hey, Kyle, what can you tell me about the folks arriving to your place as I was leaving this morning"

"The woman coming to clean my house is Gaby and the man out smoking a cigarette is her fiancée Tony, also my brother in law, as he was Angela's brother.

What is Tony's last name?"

"Relako."

"Did Tony ever come to visit you in Los Angeles when you lived there?"

"All the time. He and Gaby started dating a couple years ago." Kyle replied.

"How often did Tony come to L.A to visit in the last three months?"

Timmons keeps his eye focused on the truck and pawn shop door while speaking.

"Like every two of three weeks, checking on Gaby who's pregnant with his child. That's one of the reasons I moved here with my son, so Gaby could be closer to Tony and we'd be close to family, while starting over in a new place."

"So, Tony is Angela's brother. She was a model if I remember you telling me right… anything else you want to tell me about Tony?" Timmons queries.

Kyle pulls into his home driveway at 1:28 P.M. He gets out of his Mercedes with Bluetooth in his ears and talking.

"Yes, she was a model in her twenty's then she started writing novels before her accident. Her half-brother Tony has been single for a while until he met my house cleaner. He's a bit introverted. Gaby's working on him." Kyle snickers.

"Okay, thanks for your time." Timmons expresses.

"Hey, don't worry man, I didn't tell anything about the tree tie killer conversation, if that's what this call is about."

"Yeah…? Okay keep your phone handy." Timmons imparts.

"Will do."

As soon as they end the call Tony Relako walks out to his truck.

Detective Timmons starts up his white Dodge Charger with intentions to follow Tony Relako.

Tony backs out of his five-hour long parking spot from work and drives right past Calc Timmons, who's across the street.

They cross paths but he doesn't notice. He's too engrossed, trying to find anyone who's intentionally texting while driving. He has three hours to kill before Gaby expects him home for a dinner of spaghetti.

Forty minutes passes by, as Tony drives on a hunt and the detective keeps an eye on the hunter's moves.

Inside of Tony's truck, he reaches on his dashboard for the head gear. He throws them on the passenger seat, anxiously awaiting the discovery of his new victim.

His spirit changes like he's putting on a Halloween costume. He takes a Camel into his mouth and puffs like a train full of coals in the west to the south. He has no remorse for his next move, as his only thought is as a father wanting to protect his family and give them a future.

2:20 P.M. August 2, 2018, Somewhere in Normal Heights, a suburb in San Diego, around a ton of antique shops and people walking after eating. People are everywhere. In the slowdown of cars, Tony is behind a black Chevy Suburban.

The driver is driving slower than usual. The large SUV break-taps unnecessarily and even drives the vehicle onto the curb a couple different times.

Tony grins evilly. His body temperature rises and his blood pressure skyrockets when he sees this large SUV driving stupidly.

He follows her out of the pedestrian area as she swerves herself onto the highway. Fifteen minutes pass by. She exits the ramp and pulls into a shopping center with a nail salon.

A beautiful young lady, maybe late thirties, of Hispanic decent gets out of the SUV with a large designer bag slipped on her dainty sun kissed mocha shoulder. Her phone is tied to her hand, hiding her attractive face.

Like a coyote about to grab a toy poodle, Tony rushes past her. This woman looks like she could be Gaby's twin.

The beautiful woman never sees this 6'3 man run up against her, as she is still inside the world of her cell phone. She enters the nail salon.

Tony goes for a little walk to hide his emotions and gather his thoughts before he heads back to his truck. Guilt had finally crept in for all the murders he had committed. Gaby's twin, who has just entered the nail salon, was Tony's flash point.

Full of remorse, he turns around to go back to his truck.

"Freeze… Don't move…Put your hands above your head…I need to see them." Declares Calc Timmons, LAPD, with a 9mm.

Tony stands in heavy tracks with his arms a little above his head. He takes off running to the right, trying to escape.

The detective shoots him in the kneecap. Falling to the ground in pain, he spouts at the detective who shot him, while trying to stand up on his legs and run.

He doesn't get far, as his crooked leg lingers behind and blood seeps out, pooling on the ground. The man who normally doesn't speak much is cursing this detective like there's no tomorrow.

"I said to you earlier this morning how beautiful the sun was, and I would be exercising in it. Well this is what I do every day the sun is out, while others are dancing in the rain." The detective presses his hand onto Tony's shoulders and reads him his rights as he tightens the handcuffs nice and tight.

Detective Calc Timmons lifts Tony off the ground, walking him to his unmarked car and right past his old burnt orange truck across the street.

Timmons dials up the San Diego police.

A few hours pass by at the scene of what almost was another tree tie murder. The San Diego Police Department collect time, place, intersection, vehicles involved, and pertinent information.

A local San Diego news station covers this report. Fifteen minutes later Cynthia Alado arrives to scene on a helicopter from L.A Times.

The sun beams into the hot car, almost eliminating the feel of the air conditioning since it's on the lowest setting.

Inside the nail salon, the police are questioning the beautiful young Hispanic woman while her nails are drying.

It looks like another victory for Detective Calc Timmons, as the San Diego crime scene investigators gather up all the facts.

He then drives back to the hotel, needing to check out of it. Before he drives back to Los Angeles there is something that he needs to do.

At the hotel Detective Timmons dials up Kyle Hawthorne.

Kyle doesn't answer the call. He leaves him a detailed message about capturing a tree tie serial killer.

Inside of Gaby's San Diego home, she is scrolling through Facebook and sees her fiancée's face as he's being arrested. She takes a gulp of air, in shock. Her life passes by, with her future husband and children being robbed of their dreams.

Gaby runs to her SUV with the intentions of getting some questions answered by the San Diego Police.

Outside of Kyle Hawthorne's home in La Jolla he checks the soil around his property, it's very dry. It's very dry like a summer's taste. He walks to get the mail from the box then goes inside to continue writing Online Now into

On the way to Brooklyn Town.

Gaby cries in her Honda CRV. Both hands attached to steering wheel driving. Her stomach rumbles, it's almost supper time, yet food is long gone from her mind. She's going crazy with worry about Tony and tries to focus on the road.

Baby Angelina kicks in her belly.

She dials up Kyle on her cell phone.

"Kyle, I don't know what's happening with Tony, but I saw a picture of him on Facebook being arrested. The headline said the suspected tree tie killer."

"What? Are you serious? Where are you?"

"I'm driving to the police station… will you meet me there?"

"I'm on my way." Kyle ends the call.

"Benjamin, there's been some kind of accident, I'm going to the police station." He stands at his son's bedroom door.

"What kind of accident." Benjamin frets.

"I don't know the details… Do you want to stay here or come with me?"

"I'm coming with." Benjamin hurries to tie his shoes.

At the police department Kyle and Benjamin find Gaby with the officer. They bombard him with questions.

"What happened to Tony?"

"He's been incarcerated under the suspicion of The Tree Tie Serial Killer." The officer declares.

"What? That's bizarre." Kyle tries to shake off the news.

"When can I see my fiancée?"

The officer peeks around a pile of papers he's holding up in pity of her but no repentance for Tony. "I'm afraid no visitors until after booking and further notice."

"What are we supposed to do right now?" Kyle questions.

"You can put your names and phone numbers right here on this pad and I will give it to the booking officer, for Tony's records."

After jotting down a little note, the three leave the police department disappointed.

Outside Kyle asks, "Do you want to stay over at our house until we calm down and figure something out?"

She nods her head yes. They each get into their vehicles and drive back to Kyle's home.

Thursday night August 2, 2018. 6 P.M, not much to eat in the refrigerator nor pantry as Kyle has not found the time to grocery shop.

He makes a call to order a couple medium pizzas. They end the night in more disbelief that another part of their family had been taken away.

They wipe stringy cheese from the pizza off their faces. Chips Ahoy begs for more toppings.

The doorbell rings.

Kyle gets up to answer it.

Opening the door, he finds Detective Calc Timmons waiting.

"Detective."

"Kyle, I called you earlier. You must have not got my message. Can I come inside?"

Inside the living area, they start talking. Gaby and Benjamin overhear the conversation and leave the kitchen to find out what the detective has to say.

"Kyle, when I left your home this morning, the man out front who was smoking while she came back inside for something, he had a one of those head goggles on his dashboard. My intuition screamed to follow him. He went to a pawn shop for four hours and left around 1pm. I then followed him Northeast to Normal Heights where I caught him in the act of selecting his next victim. His target was a Hispanic woman, who now that I think about it, she resembles you Gaby. He followed her suburban fifteen minutes to a nail salon and headed right for her. I don't know what stopped him but when I questioned him, he tried running. I had to act and bring him into custody under strong suspicion. He's needs a real good lawyer now." Detective Calc Timmons explains as he cuts the night short.

CHAPTER
THIRTY-FIVE

Wednesday 8th day of August 2018,

Peace is settled on the sands of a San Diego beach, as Kyle and Gaby stroll at a pregnant woman's pace, barefoot in the morning. Not many people are out as the coppery sun rises.

"You know Gaby, if it's true about Tony, then he will have to sell his home. If that's the case, then I'm sure he will give you the funds for you and your baby girl." Kyle walks next to her with a container of orange juice in his hand.

"I haven't even thought about it like that. I keep thinking how alone I'm going to be. Tony is the first man I've known and loved."

"I know how you are feeling. It's happened to me twice now." Kyle wraps his arm around Gaby's neck as they walk the coastline together.

Kyle's phone rings in the pocket of his shorts.

"Hello."

"Kyle, its Tony. Hey man, I get to have a visitor today at 5 P.M. Could you and Gaby come up? I'd really like to speak to you about everything in person."

This is Tony's first phone call he's made since confinement six days ago.

"Tony brother, is everything okay? Do you need us to bring you anything? What the hell happened?" Kyle pushes Gaby off him as she panics, reaching to take the phone out of his hand.

"No, I don't need anything, just come up around 4:30 P.M. so you can both get signed in."

"Okay. Hey Gaby, is right here with me and wants to talk now." He hands over the phone.

"Tony is it true?" Gaby frets.

"Hi beautiful. I've instructed Kyle to bring you here at 5 P.M. I'll explain everything then." Tony is commanded to get off the phone as his five minutes is up.

After ending the call, they leave the beach and drive back to Kyle's house.

Benjamin is playing Call of Duty on the Xbox with Venom and Viper.

"Hey Ven-Vip… are you ready for me to drive up now? I don't have to worry about the tree tie killer anymore. No wonder I never got my VR goggles back from him."

"Yeah we heard about it on social media. God, I still can't believe it was your uncle doing it all along. I reckon that you never fully know anyone." Venom states as his soldier on screen runs next to Benjamin's guy online.

Viper breaks in, "Venom hush now, so I can speak, rude boy. Benji… hurry up and come over. We miss you so freaking much."

"Aww lovelies. I know just what to get you for your birthdays. I miss you both so much too."

They continue to play the game as the day goes on.

Later that night Kyle and Gaby get ready to visit Tony at the jailhouse. They drive through and grab a bit to eat on the way.

Inside the San Diego Detention Facility, Kyle and Gaby check in.

Right on time, they go into a room with a bullet proof window, where Tony is seated behind, waiting to speak to Kyle and Gaby.

Tears build up in Gaby's eye as she sits down in front of her fiancée whom she hasn't seen in a week.

"Babe, are you okay?" Gaby cries.

"Yeah I'm good. I want to tell you I'm sorry for the man I've become and what I need to tell you… both of you." A scruffy faced Tony expresses.

The anguish that both Kyle and Gaby must write off their faces as they see the cold brutal murderer right in front of them. It's written in his eyes.

Gaby has thoughts of hugging him one last time, to say goodbye. She knows now that she will be raising this child alone.

Tony starts to spill out words.

"Gaby, Kyle, yes I am the man responsible known as the tree tie killer. I did it and I regret each one, but each of the murders I committed were needed. As I would see these people texting and driving on the streets, the only thing I could think is; this could be Gaby and my baby killed next, like my sister and my nephew."

"Oh God. Do you know what this means Tony?" A disappointed Kyle asks.

"Yes, I know. After I killed the first person, I couldn't stop. It was like I hungered for the next person I found texting and driving. I couldn't stop until the very last one. The woman texting and driving, when I went after her she appeared to be your twin and I woke up. That is when your detective friend put a hole in my leg. I knew it was over. Listen, I haven't made any confessions about this. You two are the first to know. I owe it to the world to make a real change. That is after I review it with my lawyers and it's approved."

"What is it?" Gaby inquires.

"I'm not saying anymore right now. Just know I love you and I never meant to harm our family. I'm sure I will be seeing you both very soon with legal work on my property and stuff."

A moment of silence is taken. The three-take time processing what lies ahead.

A deep emotional wound starts to bleed as Gaby fully pictures her new life as a single mom, uncertain to where she would live.

Kyle senses Gaby's fears as he visualizes moving back to Los Angeles and taking Gaby with him to help her raise baby Angelina. What other options does he have? Gaby has been good to his family and he won't leave her alone.

Bitterness creeps into the door of where Kyle and Gaby stand, both of them to go.

Tony's time of fifteen minutes has concluded, as the guard is pressuring Tony to get up, to be escorted back to his cell block.

Kyle and Gaby walk out of the prison with a kaleidoscope of emotions running rampart through both of their bodies.

They drive home, each completely in their own little worlds.

Three days later, August 11, 2018, Kyle and Gaby make a trip to Los Angeles. Benjamin's in his Range Rover behind his father's car.

Arriving to the Gethin's house Saturday afternoon for lunch, they pull up and see two Jeeps sitting in front of their place, a neon green one with large black wheels and a white Jeep with red seats inside.

The twin's birthdays look like Santa surely showed up in swim shorts and sandals in the heat of summer.

Inside the Gethin's house, everyone visits a while, eating cake and ice cream.

Venom kisses Benjamin on the lips after unwrapping his small box. The present is a silver break apart key chain for his white and red Jeep.

On the heart pendant it reads: You are the missing piece to my puzzle. Benjamin and Venom.

Viper opens her identical birthday box, which has a silver heart key chain engraved: Vipercon Forever.

Later at the Santa Monica Pier, the twins and Benjamin get on the roller coaster for a beautiful night at the ocean.

It's their spot to go and hangout.

They reminisce over the first time when Camden was alive, and they all had a cup of shaved ice. He looked like a smurf with a blue mouth eating a snow.

They enjoy watching the sun go down. Ready to leave, they each take their own personal vehicles to drive.

Kyle and Gaby had left Rueben and Darcy's when the kids did. Exciting the driveway, they catch a glimpse of their old place across the street. Ready to start the search for a new home and a fresh start back in Los Angeles, they head to Hawthorne Realty.

Meanwhile, inside of the San Diego Police Department, the arresting officer, Detective Calc Timmons holds a cell phone, ready to record Tony's full confession. He gives Tony the que to start talking.

In an orange suit sitting in front of a cell phone camera Tony says,

"Good afternoon everyone watching or catching the replay of this feed. Today's date is August 18, 2018. It is 3 P.M on a Saturday. This is my public confession. I am Tony Relako, also known as the Tree Tie Killer. I am responsible for killing three people and was found when I had targeted my fourth one. I would like to share with you why I have committed these acts. In April of 2016, my sister was on the way to Henderson, for a writer's conference. She was hit by and killed by a man in an eighteen-wheeler who was texting and driving. This didn't just affect me as her brother, but she left behind a husband and two sons under the age of fourteen. Then in March of this year the younger of my nephews was hit and killed by a driver who was texting. My nephew was two months away from his ninth birthday." Tony Relako takes a moment and bows his head to bury his emotions.

Meanwhile at Gaby's new home in San Diego, Kyle and Benjamin are over. They are gathered at the kitchen table where the puzzle Tony and she was working on remains untouched.

Kyle has his laptop opened on table for them to watch. They sit quietly, scrutinizing every word coming out Tony's mouth. There are approximately two hundred thousand people live streaming this serial killers' confession. Tony continues Facebook Live.

"The snapping point is when I was visiting my brother in law and my fiancée in Los Angeles. I was driving home and stopped for gas. After fueling up I was stuck at the light. It was drizzling rain. I watched a young kid who was texting and driving run a red light. The other side was green and a motorcycle t-boned right into him. I witnessed the boy on the crotch rocket get thrown clear across the street and the boy in the car continued to text while driving away from the scene. I've had enough of the texting and driving nonsense. I followed the hit and run driver to his house. When I question him, he couldn't even stand straight. He was not only texting and driving, but he was drunk as well. I took matters into my own hands. You know, one of the scariest moments are when you can't even see what is right in front of you. This kid was highly distracted. I took the first action. The second person I killed was driving fast all over the streets. When I caught him, he said his friends and he were playing Marco Polo. They were also texting and driving while playing tag, you're it. I almost got hit. They didn't even notice me, so I acted again. When I caught him, I tied him to the tree, and stuck VR goggles on his face. The last thing I wanted the irresponsible parties to see was how many deaths are happening because of texting and driving. The third killing was a man in eighteen-wheeler at a casino who almost hit me, while he was also texting and driving. With each life that I took, I wanted their own vehicle to be the one to crush them, taking their life-force. I wanted to make sure they were tied tight to the tree. Do I regret what I've done? Well my last target coincidently looked like my fiancées' doppelgänger. Her twin. Suddenly I woke up and had realized what I had done. I did what I had to do to protect my own family but then realized my family would now be missing me. As I close this live feed, I want you to all know that there is always somebody out there watching you. Also, Benjamin if you are watching this, I'm sorry I never returned the original goggles you gave me to fix. Now that you are aware of the circumstances, I want you to know in my garage, inside of a locked-up tool box, there are about fifty, brand new in the box that you can have."

At Gabriella's inherited house, the three of them go out to the garage.

Kyle pries the lock off the toolbox and opens the lid. It's full of brand-new virtual reality head gear in boxes, stacked up and looking right back at them.

Benjamin takes a pair out of the box and tries it on.

There is always somebody on the road watching you.